the tourniquet reprisal

the tourniquet reprisal

ellen curtis
matthew ledrew

Published in Canada by Engen Books, St. John's, NL.

Library and Archives Canada Cataloguing in Publication
LeDrew, Matthew, 1984-
      The tourniquet reprisal / Matthew LeDrew, Ellen Curtis.
ISBN 978-1-926903-15-6
      I. Curtis, Ellen, 1993- II. Title.
PS8623.E424T69 2012   C813'.6   C2012-906261-8

Second Edition ISBN: 978-1-989473-44-3

Distributed by:
Engen Books
www.engenbooks.com
submissions@engenbooks.com

First mass market paperback printing: October 2012

Cover Image: Ellen Curtis

For our friend
Erin Vance
and for Lily Reilly.

PROLOGUE

Atlanta, Georgia

Kelly Saunders picked up an apple out of the large pile in front of her and studied it for a long moment, then placed it in the green plastic basket she held in the crook of her arm. She grabbed three more then stepped away from the pile, paused, then went back for a fifth.

The market was wonderful and alive and open this time of day, crowded with people and smells and colours that she loved. Before her was a long aisle of freshly harvested fruits and vegetables, all of them beaming brightly at her with magnificent reds and yellows and deep, deep purples.

There were no walls here, just posts every ten feet or so that held up the green tile and copper bearing of the ceiling. It let in the fresh air of the Square that could only happen during a Georgia late October, that clean, crisp freshness that clung to everything and made her smile from ear to ear every time she took a deep breath. All around her the buildings of the Square surrounded the market yet somehow cast no shadow upon it, each of them bathed in the warm sun the shone down from al-most directly above.

The building in the center of town had a large clock tower in it that rose above the rest of the box-cut build-ings with its fine old Victorian architecture, but she didn't need it to tell her it was noon and that she should get on her way. She smiled warmly at the old man behind the apple cart and continued down the aisle toward the dairy section.

A year ago when she'd left his house, her father had told her that she'd never find anywhere 'out there' that felt like home. He had said this with a face that was flushed and red as he sat across from the kitchen table from her, annunciating each word with a jab of his fork. He'd dipped into the brandy a few hours before supper and his eyes were bloodshot. It sent cold shivers up her spine even now just thinking about it.

"Nobody that left home at your age ever amounted to nothing or nobody," he'd said with that gruff Bible Belt drawl as he turned his fork back toward his dinner. He took a big shovelful of chicken and cabbage and pushed it past his lips. Bits of greens stuck to the corners of his mouth and looked like the film left over after a severely drunk person woke up in their own vomit. The associa-tion made her want to throw up. "You'll never find any-thing to make you feel as good and as warm as this house and this town and this family. I hope you're hearing me."

Now, when she felt the garden air fill her until she felt like she was flying and the smooth, level concrete be-neath her feet, she knew that he'd been wrong. This was her home now, and the more she looked back on her time before this, the more she felt that this had *always* been her home, even though she'd never lived here.

There was something about this city... it was like a small town that had simply redoubled itself over and over until it was massive and unruly, against the odds keeping that small town soul. That indomitable Southern style. She'd never seen any other place like it on Earth.

She almost bumped into a gray-haired old woman wearing a dark navy blazer and pressed, clean pants. She looked as though she were on her way to stand up in church rather than perusing the farmer's market for fresh produce. There was a slim golden cross hanging between her breasts and a cancer ribbon pinned to her collar. The letters WWJD had been sewn into her sleeve with gold thread, as if to remind her the same way some people tied string around their finger to remind them.

"I'm so sorry!" Kelly said, laughing in that embarrassed why people did after returning from an excursion to cloud nine. "I swear I'm just a space cadet today!"

"That's all right, dear," the women said sweetly, laying one of those small, worn hands on her bare arm. It sent happy shivers shooting up Kelly's shoulder and into the base of her skull where they rested for a moment, the simple human contact causing intense and profound pleasure. "No harm done."

"Thanks."

"Thank *you*," she smiled warmly, stepping around Kelly and walking to greet the man behind the apple cart. He looked at her as though he'd known her for years, tipping his hat politely. "You have yourself a blessed day."

That sent the shivers going again, this time starting in

her back and working their way through her completely. Have a blessed day. She loved that. There was a feeling she got when someone said that to her and *meant* it... a spirituality that was everywhere here, even for someone who didn't believe in it.

Kelly watched her for a moment, pushing her long blonde hair back behind her ear absently as she did. Her eyes glistened the same bright perfect blue of the sky behind her and her face, while slightly sallow, was sweetly soft. Her thin lips rarely ever saw lipstick and were almost invisible until she smiled, as she was now, watching as the woman clasped an apple in her long, bony fingers. She smiled so big that it almost reached her ears.

Filled with that good, tingly feeling; she turned back to the hall and picked up a bright yellow bunch of bananas that caught her eye. She added them to the ever growing assortment of food in her basket and reminded herself that she was going to have to walk home carrying this, then forced herself to go to the dairy section. There was an old wooden display there shaped like a staircase filled with cheese, each block about the size of a paperback novel and hand wrapped in cellophane. Despite their plastic coating they still stood out like orange and white stars in a dismal brown sky, the orange so pure it looked to have been painted on.

She picked up a rather hefty block of cheddar and brought it to her face, convinced she could actually smell it it was so fresh. After taking a moment with it, she held it up to the merchant behind the shelf. "How much for this?"

"Everything you see here is two dollars," he replied,

stretching his arms in both directions as if to encompass the entirety of his stock.

Her eyebrows shot up as she looked at the cheese again with renewed interest, then placed it in the basket at her hip before bending over to pick up two more blocks.

She felt her eyes flutter over him and caught a wry, mischievous smile on his lips. He was an older man, like most of the farmers and merchants that came to the market, but was more wiry than most and appeared to be in good health. His skin was tight to his frame but wrinkled heavily, and in truth didn't look much like skin at all. Instead it looked like long strips of muscle and tendons dyed the pale peach of flesh. His whole face seemed to move and shift when he smiled even a little, and right now he was smiling so big that she could see he still had all his original teeth. She smiled back.

"Thank you," she said warmly. He nodded curtly in response, then leaned forward to watch her as she stepped toward the checkout.

The line wasn't long. It never was, not even with just the one register. Kelly placed all the goods she'd accumulated on the small desk that was used as a counter top, the rubber sheet that covered it doing little to hide its tattered character or the repugnant scent of varnish. It had been a school teacher's desk, she'd decided on one of her previous trips. Lifted from one of those old dilapidated one-room school houses with the potbelly stove and the individual blackboards. Sometimes when she stepped past it, she could swear that she could smell the distinct aroma of chalkdust still clinging to it.

The woman behind the counter was short and portly,

with a tiny bow of a mouth and an unnaturally brunette beehive. When she spoke it was with that kind sincerity that Kelly was convinced only pudgy women in their forties were capable of. She reminded her of Conchata Ferrell.

"Did you find everything you were looking for?" Conchata asked with a twang in her voice that sounded like it had been tuned with a banjo as she carefully placed Kelly's food into a brown paper bag.

"Mostly," Kelly smiled, sticking her thumb and forefinger into the narrow space of her front pocket and coming back with her wallet. She unclasped it and started to flick through an odd arrangement of bills. Most were the faded green hue of American currency, but there were a few blue Canadian fives and red fifties. An euro stuck out near the front, poking out its nose just enough for the cashier to see.

"We can't take foreign bills here," Conchata said crisply, looking suspiciously from the wallet to Kelly and then back again. "I got enough problems getting my head around the numbers already without figuring in the transfer rates."

"Oh, I know," Kelly chuckled, pushing her hair out of her face again as she started pulling out cash. "Just haven't made it to the bank with these just yet."

Conchata nodded, making a little pile of the bills Kelly had already placed on the desk, counting them as they came.

"And sixty," she said, dumping some coins out into her palm and then handing them over. "Hey, do you know where the blueberry guy is? I haven't seen him in weeks."

"Carl," Conchata agreed. She did not look up as she spoke, focussing as much as she could on putting the cash into the correct register slots. "He broke his hip a month or so back. Fell over an embankment while he was out picking stock."

"Ooooh," Kelly hummed, a concerned look coming over her. She bounced a little when she made the sound, like a child deprived of something they desired badly. "Well if you see him tell him I hope he gets better soon, okay?"

"I surely will."

"And if he has any of that jam at his place pick me up a few jars and hide them under the counter for me, okay? I'll pay you back the next time I'm up."

"I'll do just that," she beamed, handing the bag over the register to her. "You come back soon now, y'hear?"

Kelly smiled, suppressing the urge to laugh, and walked out into the daylight. That was one thing she'd never gotten used to about this part of the world: the way some people could succumb to their regional stereotypes so completely and not even realize it. Even more surprising was that she found it was catching on. She'd caught herself referring to the computer as a pooter the other day and had laughed at herself until her sides had ached. Her friends had looked at her as though she'd had eight heads.

The walk home from the market was a long one, but she found that she didn't mind, especially on days like today. Leaves were falling all around her and crunching beneath her feet, kicking and dancing about and making her feel like she was a child again. Pausing by a bus station she stopped and laid down her bag on the sidewalk, then picked up an armful that had freshly fallen. She stared at them for a long moment, the oranges and reds and pale, pale greens melding together until they seemed to be coming out at her, like one of those Magic Eye pictures that you stare at until the image pops out at you.

She buried her head in them and took a deep breath, then let them fall back to the ground.

A tall girl with a purple bookbag stared at her from the safety of the glass bus shelter, her lip curled and one eyebrow raised.

"Try it," Kelly smiled, hoisting up her bag again. "It'll do you wonders."

The girl rolled her eyes and looked away, but craned her head to watch Kelly as she skipped merrily down the soft incline of Barron Road.

The street was long and winding, turning sometimes at nearly a hundred and eighty degree angles as it made its way through the heart of midtown west and out into the residential section of the neighbourhood.

Atlanta was a weird city, she found, weirder almost than any other place she'd visited or lived in. The city itself had a population of just a little over half a million, but it felt like less. Felt like a *lot* less. The city was so spread out that the different suburbs and burrows almost became little towns onto themselves, with the massive towers of downtown and Buckhead looming over in the distance from either side. Within the dip between the two the winter was warm and the summer was unbearable, and there was no mingling of the classes. Everywhere else there was a smorgasbord of the rich and the poor and everything in between, with the Ritz only a half block from the slums. Here they didn't even touch. There were large forested parks separating the burrows or often even within burrows. Grassy patches where not even the bravest tread after sundown that belonged to flashers and muggers. It furthered the perceived division between them and caused rivalries that lasted for decades.

In places where there were no parks or fields, the middle class was used to partition the very rich from the very poor. This was the case here in Midtown West, a fact that became clearer with every house she walked past on her way down the street.

Kelly nodded as she walked by two college students (at least she presumed they were. They looked the right age and dressed the same way all the boys on campus did) leaning on either side of a balcony and sharing a cigarette. One had wavy hair and looked like one of those teen heartthrob types from the eighties, the other a crew cut with ears that stuck off in either direction and black, vacant eyes. The house was a simple bungalow with what appeared to be a very spacious basement. The front door was high off the ground and had a long steep staircase leading up to it. The were Jack-O-Lantern decals on the windows, and they reminded her that she would have to make another run to the store soon to get candy for Halloween. Although she didn't expect many trick-or-treaters, she'd rather have it and not need it than need it and not have it. The next five houses were identical except in colour, as though someone had made them with different shades of play-dough and a cookie cutter.

The boys watched her as she walked past, the one with the black eyes paying particular attention, standing up to look over his friend's shoulder as she disappeared from sight.

Barron Road gave way to Gallant Ave, which lead to Canary Street and quickly became New Gower Road. The houses were further apart here and were much smaller, for the most part. Several had been torn down even since she'd moved here, and one had burnt down just before she'd arrived. It still smelled like ash sometimes, if the day was dry enough and the wind blew just the right way. There was an abandoned lot grown over with alders and thorns held in by a tattered white picket fence. Several incinerated car frames were inside, picked clean by backyard mechanics and vultures long ago. Across the street from it was a low-income housing unit, with four buildings of different pale pinks and aquas facing each other to form a rudimentary square. In the center was a rusted and seldom used playground with broken swings and a slide with a hole in the middle.

There was a nameless dirt road off of New Gower that stretched into a gravelly clearing sparsely littered with evergreen trees. She'd seen pictures of it from years back that showed it all covered in smooth, flowing grass of the type that made you want to roll around and forget your age. Now the only grass was a few stubborn weeds and patches of crabgrass and poison oak. She steered clear of them as much as possible.

Near the end of the road it splintered into two directions, one continuing down to meet the street again on Enterprise Avenue and the other the driveway to a large, magnificent house. It was massive, three stories tall with a basement besides. It had once been a bed and breakfast, back when this had been the good part of town, and was one of the only buildings around that looked like it still belonged in that time... for the most part. The paint was white and was peeling in most places, dried from the sun and ready to flake off like dandruff the moment it was touched by a human hand. The shutters and trim were the same deep green that her childhood home had been before her father had gotten a better job, and it made her nostalgic in ways she'd never expected and couldn't quite fathom. There was a veranda of concrete and hardwood out front that she sat on on warm days, letting the sun beat down on her until she thought she would bake.

There was grass here. The driveway was dirt like the rest of the street, but on either side there was luscious grass like there had been on the picture. It was magical, as though the house and the grounds were contained in a little snow globe bubble that protected it from the rest of the world.

Hoisting up the bag (which had, as feared, gotten quite heavy over the course of her trip) onto her shoulder, she walked up the driveway.

Someone peeked through the white silk curtains at her. There was laughter from inside that was infectious even from out here.

She walked up the steps, listening to the way they creaked in their familiar way, then paused at the door and took a deep breath before going in.

A stale, undefinable smell hit her as soon as she walked in and she sighed sullenly to herself. She wasn't through the door an instant when someone ran past the mouth of the hallway, with such speed that all she could make of them was a red and blue blur. A cacophony of tireless giggles followed the runner, and it brought her smile back to her cheeks.

She brought the bag of groceries through the dining room (named for the large, round dining table off to one side, though it had no chairs) and into the kitchen. It was large and lit from the west with a wall and ceiling made entirely of glass. The sun, just venturing past its noon mark, shone its rays in through them and onto the tiny green tiles that made up the floor. All of the appliances were gathered around the edges of the room, and a large wooden island sprung up from the center.

Charlotte stood behind it, her dark red hair falling down on either side of her face in wet clumps. She was putting the finishing touches on a peanut butter sandwich, and there was a pile of fresh carrots beside her dripping dew onto the countertop.

"How were they?" Kelly asked, hoisted up the shopping bag and bringing it down onto the counter with a loud clump.

Charlotte responded with a glare, shot from her jade eyes from behind tattered bangs.

"That good, huh?"

"Judy and Dennis got in a screaming match over the couch again, only they said it wasn't about the couch. People never fight about what they're really fighting about."

"What did they say they were fighting about?"

"The title to that Marky Mark song everyone knows."

"Good Vibrations?"

"Where were you twenty minutes ago?"

Kelly started unloading the contents of the bag, taking out two large cans of chic peas and laying them on the counter next to the carrots. Next came a loaf of fresh bread and two bottles of jam, one raspberry and one a wildberry mix.

Charlotte watched her as she unloaded item after item. She had moved on to chopping the carrots into circles of near uniform thickness, her trained hand slicing expertly without her having to pay them any attention at all.

Kelly had unloaded a small jar of peanut butter and a head of lettuce before she noticed Charlotte's gaze. "What?"

"Did you remember the sugar?"

"Fuck!" she hissed, letting her hands fall against the table in exasperation.

"How could you forget the sugar?"

"I know."

"That was the last thing I said to you before you left. Don't forget the sugar."

"I know!" she huffed, then went on taking the groceries out of the bag.

Jason came into the kitchen. He was a straggly man in his late twenties with red-rimmed eyes and a plump Irish nose. He scanned the vegetables on the counter, frowned, then stood on his tip-toes to see down into Kelly's bag. He licked his lips, then reached into it and came back with a bright yellow banana.

Kelly considered slapping his hand, but there was a small sore blistering on it near the wrist and she reconsidered.

He nodded at them without a word, then left the kitchen again.

Her gaze followed him, then continued past him and up the stairs. She stared at some unknown spot on the ceiling for several seconds. "Is he still up there?"

Charlotte did not answer, cutting the sandwich she'd made in half.

Kelly turned back to Charlotte, who was scratching at the crooks of her exposed arms for a moment before piling carrots and tiny triangular sandwiches alike onto a glass plate.

Charlotte looked down at it wearily, then back at Kelly. After a moment she picked up the plate and held it out to her like an offering.

"Thanks," Kelly smiled. She gave Charlotte a peck on the cheek, then took the plate and started back out toward the dining room. She got three steps, then turned around and grabbed a bright red apple from her bag and laid it down in the center of the display.

Thomas was sitting on the floor with his back against the wall, almost hidden in the shadow of the dining room table. He was tall when he stood, well over six feet, and had a face so smooth that Kelly often wondered if he were even capable of growing hair. He wore glasses with thick black rims and almost always had a checkered cardigan on. At the moment he was reading from a battered copy of *Catch Me If You Can*. The weathered edge of it was resting against his knee.

Kelly lowered the tray of sandwiches until they were at eye-level with him, but even then it took him a second to notice it. When he did he smiled, reached up and carefully plucked one of the quartered sections between his fingers and removed it from its nest, then raised it to her thankfully.

"Cheers," he said, before taking a bite.

"You're welcome."

He didn't hear her, already re-engrossed into chapter seven.

She walked past the front entrance and out into the living room. There was an old off-white couch creating the illusion of a wall in front of her with flower prints on it and weird little half-cylindrical shalls over each of the arms. There were two people making out on it. One was Theresa, a twenty-five year old stewardess who stayed over mostly on weekends and bank holidays. The other was a boy of about the same age with brownish-red hair that Kelly didn't know.

Across from them, Kirby was sat on the windowsill staring out at the street. He couldn't have been there long because she hadn't seen him as she'd come in, but he looked as though he'd been there long enough to sink into the rotted wood of the sill. There was a waxen look to his face, the scruff on his cheeks coming in in rough patches. His elbow was resting on an old black-and-white television with wiry rabbit ears and a glass tube that bulged out like a pregnant belly. Kelly didn't know how old he was. She'd asked once, and he'd responded: "Perpetually seventeen." She didn't think he'd really understood what it meant.

She stepped out around Theresa and sauntered over to Kirby, who turned and smiled as she approached. "How was the market?" he asked, taking one of the sandwiches and biting into it heartily.

"It was lovely. You should have come."

"Maybe next time."

"Could always use an extra set of hands!" she chirped, dancing back around the couch and making her way up the stairs.

A Robert Frost poem had been hand written on the wall halfway up the stairs. An empty picture frame had been hung over it, the black edges making it seem less like graffiti and more like art. They'd decided to keep it when doing their weekly cleaning.

Richie was sitting on the stairs. He was a blonde seventeen year old that was missing most of his teeth. He didn't seem to register her even though she was standing right in front of him, and when she offered him a sandwich he gagged and turned away. There were dry bruises in the crook of his arm, each with a tiny swell in the middle that was capped by a small hole.

She continued up the stairs and started down the hall. Most of the doors were shut. Steven was sitting on the edge of his bed with his shirt off. There was a tattoo of a spider on his left breast. He was jerking a game controller left and right and yelling at an unseen screen. Megan was laying behind him on the bed, her hand around his waist. She turned and narrowed her eyes at Kelly, who continued past without asking if they wanted anything.

There was a soda can on the floor that had a large gouge carved into the body of it, the edges of which had been charred to a deep black. She did not touch it, but made a mental note to pick it up on her way back down. She picked up the last sandwich and knocked on Mitch's door. A moment later he opened it and smiled graciously, his eyes bulging like balloons stuffed with too much air.

At the end of the hall was a second stairwell. It was dark, an oily black square on the otherwise white walls. The stairs seemed to go up for forever, steep steps seen only in antique homes and Tim Burton films. They swayed this way and that under her weight as she stepped on them, as though she were climbing into some high belltower on a rope bridge instead of the third floor of her home.

The walls were always wet with condensation. They seemed to breathe, the light from the top flickering and making them expand and contract. A heater hidden in the darkness hissed every few seconds, adding to the illusion. No matter how often she came here, she found herself swallowing back hard. And every time, like now, her throat was bone dry.

There was no door at the top of the stairs, nor were there any rooms. The third floor was one large, open-concept space. There was no furniture or even plaster on the walls, all of the house's beams and girders showing. It seemed pornographic and obscene to her. There were light fixtures, but she'd never seen them on. The room was lit by candles of varying lengths. They stood near the far wall across from the stairs, bathing their light upon the blank canvas that had been tacked up on the wall behind it.

There was a sheet on the floor, draped over an old sleeping bag.

Between the candles and the bed was Gavin.

His back was to her. He was staring at the candles, watching the way they danced. Watch a candle with music on and the flame will appear to move to the sound. Through the quiet, the candles were composing a symphony for him, and he was lost in it. He took in a deep breath, the smoke entering his nostrils and tickling them happily. He held the breath for a moment, then let it out. In and out. In and out.

In.

Out.

His legs were crossed. He was wearing a long, tailored black jacket that created a whirlpool of fabric around him. His hair was shoulderlength and curled against the nape of his pale neck like the night sea washing against luminescent sand. His features were clean and smooth and angular, his nose and chin pointing at the fire as if to accuse it. Even his ears had presence, dominating his halo of hair with their angular shape as if they were horns.

Kelly walked around him in a wide berth, never once taking her eyes off of him. He didn't blink, at least not that she could see. The fire shone off his eyes and made them look like marbles. It made his face glow a deep orange.

She looked down at her tray. The sandwiches were gone now, leaving only the bright red apple standing in the center of it.

She cleared her throat.

He didn't move or acknowledge that she was there in any way.

"I – I brought this up for you," she said finally, looking from the apple to Gavin and then back again.

He took another deep breath, but otherwise did not move.

"I thought you might be hungry. It's just I've been

around the house a lot and I haven't seen you eat any-thing, so I figured you might need something. Unless you ate while I was out at the market picking up food. Which you could have, but I didn't think you did. Charlotte said you hadn't eaten."

His right nostril twitched, just a little, and he remained speechless.

Kelly swallowed solemnly, then bowed her head and turned to walk away.

She stopped suddenly as long, slender fingers grasped the bare flesh of her arm. She gasped as he pulled her to the floor, sending both tray and apple scattering into the darkness with a whirling clang.

He stared at her. The fire was at his back now and yet still reflected in his eyes. His hand cupped her cheek, then ran along her jaw until it was behind her ear and he pulled her into a kiss. Her features were soft and gauzy in the candlelight. She opened her mouth.

Across the room, the apple lay bruised on its side against the wall. There was a large chunk out of it from where an errant nail had pierced the skin and torn the flesh from it.

CHAPTER 01

New York City, Then

The hall was empty.

McElheny Square was an expensive block of shops in center city. It had been built nearly sixty years ago and still had its original plumbing. The commercial spaces that lined either the east or west walls were dominated by dentists, travel agencies, and take-out pizzerias. There was one jeweller on the east side that never kept any real gems on hand, only replicas. Every so often some teenage pup would come in looking for something for his girlfriend and not read the display, and then David Bubble, the owner, would have to make a decision about whether or not to let him know before walking out the door with a five-hundred dollar piece of plastic.

More than once that decision had come up negative.

There was a long parking lot separating the east and west walls, and at the far north was a long mall. It had four floors and three restaurants (two fast food joints that the board had fought from keeping in and one fine-dining establishment that had been there in some way shape or form since the Square opened.) It had a drug store, a hair salon, an art gallery (owned by and consisting entirely of one local artist, an expressionist named Peter Frank,) a museum of ancient texts, three travel agencies, a small-press newspaper office, a bank, and an independent video store. The majority of the space was simply taken up by the hallways, though. McElheny Square's board had fought against the overt commercialism of most malls in the area, allowing for open hallways and seating arrangements that made it a pleasurable place to spend time even if one wasn't shopping. It passed these costs on to the property owners, with even the smallest space commanding a rent of nearly a twenty-five thousand dollars a month.

At night when the halls were empty, the moonlight shone in from the skylights and bounced off the smooth slate floor, illuminating the halls in a beautifully eerie glow. It was as though the halls and everything inside it were suspended in time until the owners returned the next day to turn on the lights.

-TISSSH!- The bottom panel of the glass door knocked inward, staying mostly whole for a moment before hitting the floor and shattering back into sand, spreading out in a large arc and making a letter V that pointed back at the door accusingly.

Victor stepped though the open pane and straightened up, squinting his taut face even further as he scanned the line of store windows and waited for his eyes to adjust. He was a tall man, broad across the shoulders, with a full head of blonde hair that travelled down past the scruff of his chin. His shirt was woven black cotton, and it caught tiny flecks of glass it its grooves. He ignored them.

Tash ducked under the pane behind him, stepping up next to Victor and letting glass break beneath her feet. She was tall and thin, with the sort of wiry athleticism typically associated with gymnasts. There were freckles lining her face and her short black hair was pulled tight against her scalp. She wished, briefly, that she hadn't worn her wedges. Frowning, she brushed roofing dust off of her jean jacket and watched as it ballooned out into the atmosphere before dissipating. "That was subtle."

Victor turned to watch her over his shoulder, a small smirk arching up one side of his mouth. "We're in, aren't we?"

She bobbed her head back and forth, then stepped past him into the main foyer. There was a chain coffee restaurant on her right. It had cameras that she knew should have been pointed in toward the cashiers, but right now they seemed to be pointed out at her. In front of her were two wide stairwells, each leading down to the same place on the lower floor. She started down them and made it ten full steps before she turned around and realized that Victor hadn't moved. He was watching the darkness, staring up at the hair salon on the floor above them with wrinkles under his eyes.

"What?" she asked, craning her head to try and see what he saw.

He winced, then shook his head. "Nothing."

"Come on then. We don't have time to be dicking around."

He nodded, then followed her down the stairs.

The bottom floor was darker, with no moonlight to provide the glow that the main floor had. It was black here, with one storefront bleeding into the next and only the occasional glow of a cash machine screen the help them navigate by. Had the halls not been so wide, Tash was sure she might have ended up with a broken nose.

They passed by Prewer Discount Travel, giving it only marginal attention, and continued down the hall. After a few feet Tash took out her cell phone and turned it on, holding the screen out in front of them to light their way.

Victor shot her a wry look, smirking again. "A cell phone?"

"Q forgot to give me my pen light and shoe-phone, okay?"

He held up his hands and stepped a pace away from her, widening the distance between them until he was out of striking range.

She frowned at him, then brought the light up to examine the store logos. "This is it."

They stopped, Victor stepping back a pace so that he could see the lot in its entirety. It was the New York Jezrick Foundation Book Repository, and below it was a large sign that said, in bold black letters, BY APPOINTMENT ONLY.

He tisked. "Did you make an appointment?"

She rolled her eyes and stepped forward, leaning down in front of the lock.

"I didn't make the appointment. I was supposed to get dinner and pick up the car from the shop, and you were supposed to make the appointment. I'm quite certain."

"Shut up," she said, pulling a small black case out of her waistband. "You're not funny."

He snorted, then turned away from her and back the way they'd come. The hallway seemed longer than the distance they'd travelled, the light from the stairwell now only a tiny square at the end of it. It was small enough that it looked as though he could pluck up the light and put it in his pocket.

His smile faded as he let his gaze shift to the dark windows surrounding them. Each had their own logos and slogans painted on them that hid what was happening inside, disguising the chairs and fans and human shapes within. There could have been someone staring back at him from behind the O of Trombly Real Estate, and he wouldn't have been able to tell.

Tash opened the case and took out two thin metal shafts,

each one six inches long with swirling pointed tips, the points on either slightly different. They looked a little like dentists tools from a child's nightmare, robbed of all their natural functionality and left only with their fearsome qualities.

She stuck the longer of the two all the way into the lock and pushed up, then slid the second in and began to tap methodically against the hammers within. "No, it's okay. I don't need a hand."

He did not respond, staring out into the sterile cold.

He took out his own phone and held it out toward the hall at a high angle, then clicked the camera button on its side. The flash illuminated the hall for a brief moment, and then was gone again. He turned the screen toward him and pressed several keys before the picture showed back up on his screen.

She looked over her shoulder at him, still feeling her way through the last of the lock's tumblers. "Everything okay?"

"Yes," he said, flipping his phone shut and putting it away.

She nodded, then turned back to the door. Something inside the lock clicked and she smiled, twisting both her tools to the right and then pulling down on the handle.

The door swung open smoothly.

Victor stepped in past her as she put her tools away, making his way past the aisles of books and to a thin column that made its way from the floor to the ceiling. There was a fire extinguisher on one side. On the other there was a smooth white security panel with a timer on it counting down from thirty.

"It's okay, it was nothing," Tash said, tucking the case back next to the small of her spine. "I didn't just Google that last night or anything."

"Shh," Victor hissed, staring at the timer as it reached

twenty-five. He held up his phone to the keypad at an angle. There was a gloss against three of the numbers: one, eight, and nine. He turned back toward the room.

There were several single pages in glass frames along the wall, each looking to be from a different document. One was a list of names in calligraphy, and seemed to be a reproduction of a Civil War document.

He flicked his fingers against the scruff of his upper lip for a moment, then moved on. There was a small toy panda by the cash register, its head poised and ready to bob if brushed. There was a rack of fake celebrity driver's licences, one showing a prominent celebrity from each state. New Mexico's was an extraterrestrial named A. Leon whose eyes glowed in the dark, he could see the row of them from where he stood.

"Victor?" she asked, stepping up to the stack closest to him.

He raised a hand for silence as the timer counted down past fourteen. He paused, then walked to the other side of the column. He picked up the tag on the fire extinguisher, examined it, then walked back to the keypad and punched in four digits.

The light on it flickered red for a moment, then turned green.

Tash raised an eyebrow.

He smiled, picking up the tag again. "First yearly inspection, August 1988."

"Lucky."

He raised an eyebrow. "No memorabilia or remembrances around, safe bet the code was something to do with the shop and not friends or family."

She shook her head then turned to the stack next to her, holding up her cell phone along the spines presented as though it were a flashlight again. The blue light made the watermarks on them stand out, each one a tiny circle with an upper case J in its middle. "What are we looking for?"

"It'd be under poetry, I think," Victor said, moving over to a series of glass display cases that lined the back wall. "I can't be sure, but it sounds right."

She smiled and took a book from its place. "Any chance it was by John Donne?"

He shot her a look.

She put the book back and continued down the line.

He leaned to one side. "You're probably not far off on the time period. I imagine it would be marked as pre-1800. Maybe not very far before, but definitely before."

She scrunched her face and turned to him, shining the light at him. "Is it pre-1800?"

"Fuck no," he whispered, running his finger along the glass as he read down through a presented page. "I'd be shocked if it was a hundred years old."

She paused, then went back to her work.

He moved on to another display case, pausing to examine the print in the frame above him.

"Why is it here then?"

"An old text hidden among old texts isn't really hidden at all. A new text said to be an old text, placed amongst actual old texts... now that's a disguise."

Tash stopped searching the stacks and marched to the other row of display cases. When she got within five feet of it she stopped, letting out the tiniest breath of air.

Victor turned, manoeuvring the shelves until he was next to her.

In front of her, more broken glass sparkled along the floor

just as the door pane had upstairs. The display case in front of them was open, and the only thing inside was a small paper card: Untitled Poem - Pre-1800.

"Damn," Victor said, glowering down at the ruined case.

CHAPTER 02

Atlanta, Georgia

Nicolas Carry sat on the third-to-last step of the concrete stairway that bridged Commodore Park with one of the busiest overpasses in the city, which led out into the suburbs and beyond out into I-85. His feet were planted firmly on the stair two steps down from him, mud dripping off his battered old white Reeboks in large, chunky clumps. He leaned back until the base of his skull was resting on another stair, the sharp edge of it digging into the skin beneath his freshly cut brown hair. He took a deep breath, closed his eyes, then let it out as slowly as he could. There was a tension in his neck that it helped relieve, replacing it with a calm tingly feeling that stayed in that one area, circling around as though it was trapped there.

He opened his eyes.

The moon looked down at him from the navy sky that surrounded it. There were no stars out tonight, but they weren't hiding because of the street lights as they had in any other city Nick had been to. Here they were outshone by the moon, so big and bright that it seemed to be falling right toward him. The moon had never been like that where he was from, and was one of the few things about Georgia that made him happy that he'd decided to come. The nights here were simply amazing.

"One large regular coffee, as requested," Quinn said, sitting down next to Nick one stair back so that they were at eye level with one another. She put the disposable coffee cup down by his feet and then rummaged through her own bag before emerging with a can of Sprite.

She was a small girl. At five feet she only came up to his chest, which made sitting at the same level like this a rarity for them. She had brown hair that fell down and bobbed around either of her ears like a shield. Her face was round with chubby cheeks that almost hid a tiny mouth with thin lips, and there was a small rhombus of darkened discoloured skin between her nose and mouth that she had tried desperately to conceal before coming out tonight. Her eyes were a dark olive shade of green that seemed to match the grass in the field behind her as it appeared in the night, making them sink into the background.

"Thank you," he said, picking up the cup and taking a sip through the tiny sliver of a hole in its lid. There was no paper holder as there usually was, and it was so hot that it hurt his hands. Still, he took another long gulp right after the first sip, not caring about the way it scorched his tongue and throat.

"Thank you for going to get it," Quinn smiled, opening the tab of her pop and letting it fizz over the top before sucking it off. "Chivalry is not dead."

He stoped drinking and looked at her. "That was the deal. I get movie and dinner, you get me a coffee afterward. That was the deal."

"Okay, by 'get' I didn't realize you meant 'actually, physically go retrieve.' I thought it was more of a way of saying that I'd *buy* the coffee."

"How could you have bought it if you hadn't gone to the station yourself?" he asked, poking his thumb in the direction of the gas station just beyond the overpass.

"I guess I could have just given you my bank card and you could have gotten it for me. Or we could have gone together."

He smiled at her, then took another sip of his coffee. "Well then I'm sorry."

"Better be," she said, rolling her eyes and looking up at the moon. "You sure know how to treat a girl, Nick."

He paused at that, looking at her side-on and holding the cup in front of his face. After a moment he took another drink, but the silence continued for several minutes after.

"Did you like the movie?" he asked finally, having finished off the last of his coffee. He was playing with the cup between his hands, tossing it back and forth between them.

"Yeah, it was okay. I was a little stupid, but it works if you don't think about it too much."

He pursed his lips and nodded.

"What about you?"

"It was alright. I could see kids enjoying it."

She smiled at him, tilting her head down and letting her hair tumble over her shoulders. She held that position for almost an entire minute waiting for him to turn and notice her. When he finally did she locked eyes with him, and he found it impossible not to smile.

"Hi," she said, so softly that she was almost just mouthing it.

"Hi."

"Are you okay? You don't seem like you're having a very good time."

"I'm fine. Really. I'm just... thinking."

"Well, we've got to stop that," she hummed, running her fingers through his hair. "Never good to over-think things."

He actually laughed at that, and when he did she could hear the drawl at the end of every chuckle that identified him as firmly from the Northeast.

She leaned in a little while his eyes were closed. She could smell the cologne he was wearing even with the breeze that was pushing past them at a steady clip, and found it intoxicating.

"So, do you have any moves I should watch out for?" she asked, her eyes fluttering from his lips to his eyes and then back again.

"Moves?"

"Yeah, you know. Moves. Tricks. As in, things you'll do to put the moves on me."

"I don't have any moves."

She smirked, raising an eyebrow at him.

"Okay, I have three moves. But I told myself I wasn't going to use any of them."

"Oh really?"

"Really. Just wouldn't be fair. To you, I mean. Because,

let me tell you, they're good moves."

She laughed. It was a full, throaty laugh that she stifled by bringing her hand to her mouth.

"What about you?" he said, noticing now how close she'd gotten to him. She was leaning forward and the neck of her blouse was hanging open, exposing her smooth neckline and collar. He tried not to notice. "Do you have any moves I should watch out for?"

"Oh, yes."

"Really?"

"Really."

"Name one."

She smiled. "Usually at the end of a first date, I'll let a guy walk me to my door. I'll make plans to see him again, and while we're talking I'll slowly move so that he has to move between me and the door to keep looking at me."

"Between you and the door?"

"Mm. Then when I go to open the door I have to brush right up against him and get in close, and I'll lean my head to one side and my hair will fall away from my neck."

Nick swallowed hard.

"Usually about then they kiss me, but if not: hey, I was just reaching for the door." She winked at him.

"You're devious."

"I try."

She inched closer to him again. Their legs were touching now, and she moved her hand seamlessly from her knee to his so quickly and smoothly that he didn't even notice it happening. Their noses were almost touching.

"So, what are you going to do now?" Nick asked, smiling a little to himself. "We live in the same place."

"Well Mr. Carry, you've forced me to improvise a little bit."

She leaned her head the rest of the way forward and their lips met. His were still warm from the coffee and hers were cold and smooth like velvet. Her hand wrapped around him and her nails danced along the short hairs on the back of his neck, bringing back those shivers that melted the tension there away like they had before. He brought his hand up to the side of her face and pushed her hair back behind her ear with his rough thumb and then traced the edges of the lobe.

She moved to get in closer, knocking over her Sprite can and sending it toppling over the stairs and onto the gravel walkway below, spewing out fizzy clear liquid as it went.

He pulled away, leaning forward on the stairs until his chest was almost touching his knees. "Guh."

"What's wrong?" she asked, her voice high and concerned. "Was that not okay?"

"No. No, that was fine," he sighed, pressing the heel of his hand against his eye. He turned to her then and saw the disappointment on her face. "That was *great*. Just, ah, just not quite there yet."

She nodded, let out a long breath, then laid back on the steps much in the way she'd found him.

Faint laughter rose up over the grassy knoll on either side of them, sounding far away and faded. It was more like the ghost of a laugh than a real laugh, he kind that echoed through the halls of abandoned mansions in old horror movies. They both sat up and looked around, but neither of them could see anything.

"What the hell is that?" Quinn asked, rubbing her hands over her exposed arms even though it was a warm night.

"People, more than likely," Nick smirked, still running his eyes over the landscape. His eyes were a pale steel blue that almost shimmered in the moonlight. "Hyenas are a possibility too, but it's far less likely."

She kicked him playfully in the back. "Jerk."

He turned and grinned at her over his shoulder, then glanced up toward the street above. Cars were passing by and seemed almost silent. He'd gotten so used to the sound of traffic here that he had to concentrate to hear it. When he'd first moved to the city, he'd have called anyone who told him that crazy. He hadn't slept at all for the first four days, and had almost moved out twice.

She watched his eyes as they passed over the street. They seemed to get lighter for a moment, then suddenly darker again, playing with the light the way she used to play with the dimmer switch in the dining room in her childhood home.

Something caught his eye where the street curved up and joined the overpass. It was just for a moment, a flash of white and a shimmer of metal, but he was sure he had seen it.

The laughter started again, much clearer and louder this time. It ended abruptly, but was followed by the muffled sound of conversation.

"There," he said, cocking his head toward the overpass.

She turned in that direction and saw nothing, but didn't stop looking and didn't doubt once what he had seen.

There were more laughs, one of them clearly a girls, followed by clapping.

Quinn squinted. "Let's go check it out."

"What? No," Nick replied, scrunching up his nose at her.

"Why not?" she chimed, already standing and brushing some dust off her jeans. "It sounds like they're having fun."

"Yeah, but maybe they're having fun being drunken assholes. Or even *regular* assholes."

"We won't know unless we go and see!" she giggled, skipping her way over the dark grass toward the overpass.

Nick sighed and followed her.

"Hahaha-Ha!" Billy Oakes laughed as he threw his soda can at the concrete for the third time. It finally burst open, spraying he and Valerie with fizz spewing from the pinhole on its side. He dodged to get away from the shower as if it had been aimed directly at him, ducking his head under his arm and running to the other side of the alcove.

"That was three tries, man," Thomas said from where he sat, motioning at Billy with the neck of his beer before taking a sip. "You said you could do it in two. Five bucks."

"Fuck you!" Billy laughed, patting some of the soda out of his hair. "That was bullshit anyway."

The underside of the overpass was made up of two

slopes facing one another at an angle that made it diffi-
cult to walk up but easy to sit on, with just the slight tug
of gravity pulling you down toward earth and the grip
of your sneakers keeping you in place. Between the two
slopes was a small flat area where three large concrete pillars stood, carrying the load of the street and cars overhead that travelled across it on a low arch. It made the
small tunnel diamond shaped, and it carried the echo of
their laughs very well.

The slopes and the pillars were both covered in graffiti,
some of it intricate and beautiful and some of it scrawled
names and gang signs. There were a few declarations of
affection, one of which had been crossed out by someone
with black paint and replaced with a single word: fucker!

Billy, still laughing, was shaking a can of purple spray
paint even now.

Quinn came over the hill and down the grassy slope
toward them, almost slipping twice on the wet blades.

Billy jolted back upright and shot the canister back
behind his back. He eyed Quinn with some suspicious-
ness, which only intensified when Nick came over the hill
behind her.

"No, it's okay," Quinn laughed, forcing herself to
come to a halt three feet in front of him and kicking up
dust when she did. "We were just wondering what all the
fuss was about."

"Sorry to bother you," Nick said, nodding respectfully
to Billy and then taking Quinn by the crook of her arm. He
tried to walk back the way they'd come with her, but she
shrugged him off.

Billy looked from Nick's hand on her arm to Nick, and

smirked. He was thin and built with a tan that made him look like he'd spent most of his life outdoors. His hair was black and came down in short sideburns on either side of his baseball cap and he wore a white wife-beater that was stained with purple paint and soda. When he smiled the skin on his cheeks started to peel. "It's no bother," he said after a moment, addressing only Quinn.

She smiled. "You sure?"

"Oh yeah," he grinned, taking a hand-rolled cigarette out from behind his ear and clasping it between his lips. When he lit it his face was bathed in soft orange, all save for his eyes. His eyes were sunken and hollow. He took a drag and then offered it to her. She stared at it for a moment, the took it between her thumb and forefinger and brought it to her lips. "You guys local?"

"He's not," she said, turning around to look at Nick. "I am."

Nick had his hands buried in his pockets and was shifting from foot to foot.

"Yea, we got a tourist huh?" Billy said, taking a step past Quinn toward Nick, swaggering from side to side. "I'm from the East Coast myself. Where you from Corn Stalk?"

"Maine."

"Ah-Haha," he sniggered, bringing his nail to his teeth and scraping at them. "Got us some Yankee blood up in here, should'a smelled it. I'm from New York myself."

Nick shifted uncomfortably again as Quinn finished taking her puff of the cigarette and handed it back to Billy. When she exhaled it was light and blue.

Billy took a quick puff and then handed it over to Nick.

"What about you Corn Stalk?"

Nick eyed it for a moment. It had burned unevenly, and the ember was like a jagged little scar running all the way down its base. "No thanks," he said finally. "I'm good."

Again, Billy sniggered that little laugh of his as though he thought Nick were the funniest thing he'd ever seen in his life. He turned to Quinn again, stepping up closer to her. "Where did you get this guy, the Quaker farm?"

Nick frowned.

"Don't mind him," Thomas said, finally getting up. He'd been watching all this from his perch sitting near the top of the concrete slope but now let gravity bring him back down to earth, the treads of his shoes skipping against the concrete the whole way down. "He's under the impression that acting better than everyone makes it true."

He had a battered paperback novel clasped tightly in one hand and a beer bottle in the other. When he reached the bottom of the slope he downed the bottom of his drink and placed the empty bottle back in the case, withdrawing his hand with two new ones. There was dew on them and they looked so cold. He held them both out toward Nick, one further than the other.

Nick eyed the brown bottle for a moment, then reached out and took it by the base. "Thanks."

"No problem," he opened his own beer and took a long swig. "What brings you to Atlanta?"

"School, mostly."

"Oh yeah? You going to U of A?"

"Figured you'd be another Smart Ass," Billy said, rolling his eyes.

"No," Quinn said, laughing. "We're --"

"Yes," Nick said, nodding to Thomas as he popped the top off his own beer and took a small sip that was mostly head. "I'm from U of A."

"That's cool. They've actually got a hell of a English Lit program."

"So I've heard."

Valerie huffed and finally stepped up from behind them, bending over into the case of beer and wobbling on her feet as she did so.

Billy stroked his upper lip as he watched her, then turned his thick-lipped smile back to Quinn.

Valerie huffed, standing up and throwing an angry glare at Thomas. "We're out."

Thomas looked down at the beer in his hand and then back at Nick, who was taking his second sip. He did not respond.

"God dammit May, you said there would be beer."

"And there was beer," he said, motioning with the one in his hand to the empties all around. "The thing is, if you drink them, there tend not to be anymore."

"Yeah there was beer but you didn't bring enough."

"Oh, I think you've had enough."

Valerie shot him an unamused look.

"We'll head back to the house and get some on the way," Billy said to Valerie without even turning to look at her. He kept his gaze fixated on Quinn. "You want to come back with us?"

Quinn smiled.

"Um, thanks," Nick said, forcing a smile and taking Quinn by the arm again. "For the beer. But we really should be going."

"Oh, come on," she smiled, looking back at Billy but stepping back a pace out of earshot with Nick. "It'll be fun."

He frowned. "What about our date?"

She shot him a coy look. "Jealous much? Want me now that there's another boy in the sandbox?"

"I never said I didn't want to be out with you. I'm here, aren't I?" he tisked, bringing his face in close and whispering. "I don't feel good about this, Quinn."

"Then don't come!" she said, loudly, a goofy smile on her face as she broke off from him and walked backward toward Billy and Thomas. "You will be missed."

The four of them started to walk away toward the other end of the tunnel.

Nick watched them for a moment, then uttered a curse.

"Hold up," he said, taking a swig of his drink and then jogging to catch up.

CHAPTER 03

Atlanta, Georgia

Nick finished his beer sitting on a couch in a large house on an unmarked street off of New Gower Road. There was bass music pumping from a stereo located somewhere on the floor above him that played so loud that every thump of the beat shook the glass on the table in front of him. He watched it, the clear liquid he knew wasn't water producing small, circular waves along with the song. The music had no lyrics, just a steady base that cut through his skull surrounded by noises that sounded like his first computer booting up. Every so often there would be a bridge to a song he'd heard before, some oldie that came on the classic rock station, but it always very quickly segued back into the techno jumble and before he knew it there was another, completely different song playing.

He sighed and got up, the cushions on the couch squealing happily as he did. His bottle slid through his fingertips and came to a rest dangling loosely between his index and middle finger. The tiniest bit of beer still swilled around in its bottom.

There was a large mirror on the wall to his right with swirling trim that gave it the appearance of something cobbled together for the set of a high school play. There was an Asian woman next to it with hair that had been dyed dark blue. She was thirty but looked seventeen and acted twelve, and was currently laughing hysterically at something the man next to her had mumbled. He was tall, with blonde hair that peeked out from under the brim of a brown baseball cap. His eyes seemed friendly, but his chest puffed out a little when he noticed Nick.

"Anyone know where I can find a garbage?" Nick asked, holding his beer bottle in front of him by way of explanation.

The woman laughed even harder at this, water coming from her eyes as she held herself up on the man's arm. After a moment he started to laugh too, and it came from him in a series of short snickering eruptions. Nick turned away from them without saying anything.

The room adjacent to the living room was filled with people and smoke now, both of which hung around the room aimlessly and never dissipated. There were a few hands in the air and the constant sound of glasses clinking against one another as drinks were passed assembly-line style out from the kitchen.

Someone bumped shoulders with him hard enough to knock him back, but when he turned there was nobody there.

He started to make his way through the crowd, ducking and swerving around people that seemed to be moving in slow motion. The beat continued from upstairs and people kept moving, shaking the floor as they stomped and danced and jumped. Smoke hung in the air like soup, even when it was being blown from the mouths of the smokers who seemed to be coming out of the woodwork by the dozens. Most were smoking cigarettes, but he knew from the familiar but putrid smell of wet socks that clung in the air that there was at least one joint being passed around amidst the chaos. He cut through the fog it made like a knife, dispersing it in swirls that spiraled out from him in all directions.

Valerie was next to him all of a sudden, her hair wet and in front of her face now, shrouding it in shadow. She looked like one of those little-girl ghosts from a horror movie, and he recoiled a bit when he saw her. She clutched onto his arm and hugged into him tightly, her teeth grazing his shoulder as she pulled him close.

"Jesus!" he hissed, pulling his arm away from her.

She laughed, along with a few other people that had noticed. It was small at first, but then she threw her head back in a full-fledged roar, her hair flicking back behind her shoulders again and revealing that her lipstick was smeared and her eyes were bloodshot. She was wearing a polyester jacket that was two sizes too big for her and nothing else from the waist up, and when she laughed the coat parted and revealed tiny, teacup-sized breasts with large pink nipples.

He backed off from her another pace, bumping into a boy with dark skin and eyes that bulged so much he thought they might come out of their sockets. The veins in them stood out like someone had gone over them with a red sharpie, each one fat with blood too thick to make it through properly.

"Sorry," Nick said.

He laughed.

Valerie still stood before him, her chest again obscured by her jacket. Her laugher had quieted and, although she still faced Nick, her eyes were scanning the crowd as if she were hunting for someone else now. Standing by the window beyond her, two people crouched facing one another. One had a needle held up to the crook of his arm, while the other watched intently.

Nick shuddered, finally pushing his way past the crowd and making his way out into the kitchen. It was large and dark and didn't seem to have any light fixtures of its own, lit solely by the moonlight that came in from the ceiling and west wall made entirely of glass. The room was pitch black at first, but slowly the glow of the moon began to bathe everything in a soft blue outline. The floor was made up of a series of small tiles with edges so pronounced that he could feel them through the soles of his feet. They were the type of tiles that were typically only used in swimming pool bathrooms, and he almost expected to see old unused showerheads poking out from the walls between the cupboards. There weren't though, just appliances of varying ages all gathered around a wooden island in the center as though they were having a secret meeting to overthrow their human slave-masters.

He stepped up to the island and examined it, holding his arms out before him as though he could actually turn it around to study it. He reached over and opened one of the cupboards and revealed only a fresh sack of potatoes, their stale starchy smell wafting out at him and making him wish for the fries he used to have in the hangout back home. He closed it and frowned, as though it were some puzzle he had failed to figure out, then opened the one next to it. There was a small plastic garbage bin within, propped up against the wall of the island with a black plastic bag spewing out of it like lava from a volcano and clinging to his sides. He smiled, let the bottle dangle over its mouth for a moment, then dropped it in.

There was laughter from the darkness around him, but not the wild and frightening kind that Valerie had produced. It was softer, and more honest. He turned past the stove and found two girls sitting next to each other in the darkness, each of them holding a vodka fruit cooler between their legs while the rest of them remained huddled in a case between them. One was a blonde with long, straight hair that caressed her back and blue eyes that looked even bluer in the moonlight, the other had dark red hair that fell down on either side of her face in wet clumps. The former had started the laughing but now the latter had picked up on it. She had been in mid-sip of her strawberry daiquiri cooler when she had and had almost squirted it out through her nose.

The blonde laughed in short bursts of heaven, her cheeks pushing up cutely and making her squint. Her face was soft and round and perfect, and what few lines were on it looked as though they'd been made with laughter. Her shirt was striped across the breast and she wore faded jeans with the knees worn out of them, her legs spread out in a V-shape from her torso to hold her drink. Her eyes seemed to have the moon in them.

"Sorry to interrupt," he said after a moment, realizing that he'd been staring. He forced himself to smile and ignore the fact that he'd stammered on the word Sorry, closing the cupboard door again. "I couldn't find the garbage."

The redhead started to laugh again, her head falling onto her friend's shoulder. The blonde took a sip of her drink and stared at him.

"Most people just use the floor," she said finally, casting a glance in the direction of the doorway.

"Most people weren't raised right I guess," he countered, taking a small step toward them. "I'd have been shot growing up if I'd just left my glass around anywhere."

The redhead laughed again, so hard that spittle came out of her mouth. She brought her knees up to her chest and held them there, her drink balancing precariously in her lap.

"I'm Nick, by the way."

"Kelly," the blonde said, then turned to the redhead and smiled that big, toothy smile of hers again. "That's Charlotte."

Charlotte laughed.

He watched them sit there in the darkness, just the slight caress of the moonlight showing their subtle forms. The flesh of Kelly's face and midriff looked flawless in the darkness. They locked eyes for a instant as Charlotte continued to laugh almost soundlessly, her head bobbing back and forth as her hair attacked her from both sides, whipping into her eyes again and again.

Kelly's fingernails were painted a muted orange that matched the colour of the drink she was sipping on, each tip frosted bright white and forming accent points that stood out in the shadows like spotlights. Eyes. Teeth.

Nails. Her fingers danced along the neck of the bottle aimlessly, the blur of their motion making it hard to focus on any one digit. They moved so quick that the light from the window seemed to catch on the rings she wore on both hands, reflecting the blue until it looked like tiny sparks were webbing each finger.

"You want a cooler?" she asked finally, reaching into the case between the two of them and producing a random flavour.

He tilted his head, nodded respectfully, then smiled. He reached out and took the bottle from her, and when he did their fingers touched briefly. A tingle went up his arm, and he felt the hairs on the back of his neck stand on end. It was marvelous even though it only lasted a second, and he found himself wishing that the feeling would linger. He opened the bottle against the edge of the island and took a sip without looking at the label, discovering it to be the same orange pineapple amalgamation that she had been drinking.

"Who's this?" came a soft, smooth voice from behind him.

Nick nearly dropped his drink, jumping enough to make his shoes squeak against the floor as he turned to the doorway.

Charlotte laughed again.

Gavin stood in the doorway, taking up the majority of it even with his slender form. Even in the darkness of the room and with his back to the light of the dining room the features of his narrow face were clear and visible. His skin was pale and toneless, his eyes and lips dark slits across them. The smoke from the other room wafted in around him in haunting twirls as it must have done for Nick as well, catching in the light and seeming to come from him.

"Jesus, you scared the piss out of me."

Gavin smiled and laughed a little, clapping a hand heartily against Nick's back. His face and hands seemed to float in the darkness as though they weren't even connected to one another, the black of his silk shirt and crisply ironed pants blending in with the darkness and seeming immune even to the light of the moon. Only his belt buckle caught it, and seemed to contain the entire sky. "Sorry about that."

He stepped past Nick and tossed a bottle cap onto the island, then took a sip of his drink. It smelled sharp, cutting the air with a distinct bite. From the smell alone, Nick could tell it was expensive. From their surroundings, he assumed the drink had probably been stolen to impress someone.

"Should be scared," Charlotte snorted, her head lolling back and forth on her shoulders. "Motherfucker was dead once."

Kelly laughed at that, and the both of them wiggled their fingers at each other.

Nick smiled again.

Gavin made his way over to the girls, keeping close to the wall and never letting his drink stray too far from his lips. He bent down and kissed Kelly on the lips, quickly at first and then sinking into a deeper, longer one. He slid down behind her and wrapped his arm around her. Even though he was a slender man, she seemed tiny compared to him. Her engulfed her.

Nick took another sip of his drink and forced himself to look at Charlotte, who was alternating between making eyes at him and bobbing her head back and forth between sleep. She seemed too tired to laugh all of a sudden.

"Is this a new face?" Gavin asked, that tiny slit of a mouth curving up in a smile.

"This is Nick," Kelly said, spreading her hands around the area Nick occupied in her vision as though she were displaying him on a game show. "He's a very polite little clean-freak. Nick, this is Gavin."

Gavin raised his drink to him.

Nick nodded.

"Are you staying long?" Gavin asked, even as Kelly snuggled in closer to him. "We've got a few empty rooms if you need a place to stay the night."

"Just passing through," Nick replied. He looked back out into the light of the smoke-filled room. It was still packed with people, but somehow he felt more claustrophobic in here. There was a tightness in his chest he couldn't quantify, and he had to fight the urge not the scratch at it. "In fact, I think I should be passing along."

"Fair enough," Gavin said, using the mouth of his bottle to salute him. "Don't be a stranger. I'll try not to be quite so scary next time."

"Mmm," he hummed, then took another sip of his cooler and locked eyes with Kelly. "Thanks for the drink."

Their eyes stayed on each other, hers big and wet in the blue glow around her. She blinked twice, slowly, her long eyelashes batting against her cheeks. Gavin pulled her close and she turned to him and smiled. "Anytime."

Nick walked back through the crowded dining room and back out into the living room. Quinn was laying on the stairs that led up to the second floor, her head rested on Billy's shoulder. Her eyes were hazy, and every few moments she would come to enough to run her lips over the nape of his neck and his eyes would close with pleasure.

Nick reached out and caressed her arm. She hummed and smiled dumbly as she lifted her head off of Billy's shoulder to look at him with tired eyes.

"I think we should go," Nick said, loud enough to be heard above the music without shouting. "I need to go."

"NmaGo?" Quinn replied, then laughed humorlessly.

Billy was burning holes into Nick's head. Nick could almost see the rage sweat start to bead across his brow as his breath quickened.

"Quinn," Nick hissed, taking her by the arm and pulling her back up to face him again. "I really think we should go."

"You go then," she huffed, shoving away from him. She was awake now, and was sneering at both him and her newfound alertness.

"No, you don't understand --"

"No, I think it's you that don't understand," Billy spat, his accent even thicker now that he was angry. "The lady told you to piss off, Homes."

Nick shut his mouth, afraid to look away from Billy for a moment, then tore his gaze away and looked back to her. "Quinn?"

She looked at him for a moment, then snorted and laid her head back down into the cradle of Billy's shoulder.

Nick stared for an instant longer, then turned and walked away.

CHAPTER 04

Payson, Arizona

A thin strand of weaning sunshine filtered in through the bookshelves of the library, highlighting the dust motes floating in the air. People bowed their heads over books silently, pens scratching on notepads, momentarily pausing to think between each one. Library assistants pushed trolleys of returned books, placing them in their correct place on the shelves and tuttering to themselves when they came across books shoved haphazardly in the incorrect section. A couple near the back shared one book, gently nudging each other's cheek with their nose and lips, as if the world had fallen away and left only them in a public but solitary place.

A tall woman leaned against a bookshelf near one of the large windows. She sucked on the butt of a pen, staring at the notebook in her hands contemplatively. Her head cocked to one side suddenly and she extracted the pen from her pursed lips, then placed it to paper and made wide motions across the page.

Across the library, a young girl sat with a hardcover

book propped rigidly in front of her, its spine reading *The Myth of Sisyphus*. Her gently curled brunette locks hung just past her shoulders, and her bangs fell over one of her eyes neatly. The other eye trailed away from her page lazily, resting on a blonde boy sitting at a table a few rows away from her. He had surrounded himself with newspapers, pens and pads of paper. A phone book sat next to him, and every so often he would leaf through it, picking out what he needed and jotting it down.

The girl studied him, watching how his brow continued to furrow after each time he entered something into his computer. He had nice a brow, she decided. A little bit moody looking, but there was something about him that she liked. She chalked it up to his surfer look and tan. She reached into her purse and took out a cell phone. Carefully, she edged it over the top of her book, scrolling through the menu until she came to the camera option, when a sharp voice interrupted her.

"No phones in the library," a middle-aged man said, tapping her firmly on the shoulder. "Strict rules, young lady. I'd suggest putting it away before you disturb any of the other people here trying to work."

He glowered at her, and she shrunk back from him, returning his sour expression.

"I was just leaving," she hissed, getting up and shoving her book and psych notes into her purse. She threw her phone in with everything else, careless now that she hadn't gotten a picture of the pretty boy. She turned from the older man, frustrated, and stalked towards the exit.

The warm silence of the library was stifling for Theo Flaherty as he bent over his laptop, his lengthening hair curling onto his forehead. He sucked in his lower lip against his teeth and bit it gently as he hit the enter key and stared at the screen in front of him expectantly. He had been sitting in the same spot for so long that he barely registered his surroundings, and he found the urge to breathe fresh air almost overwhelming.

He let out his breath as the screen loaded, a familiar feeling sinking in.

No results.

He cursed himself silently, wondering why he had thought this search would turn out differently. Giving up, he closed the search engine and started the shut down process. He glanced up as he waited for the screen to go black, eyes flicking toward the large clock above the exit. He had just enough time to get back, and with his luck, they wouldn't even know he was gone.

Glancing back down at the screen, he realized it had finished shutting down, and with a sigh he closed the laptop and slid it into his bag. He zipped the bag closed and slung it over his shoulder, then tightened the strap of the watch on his wrist. He set off toward the exit, breathing slowly and fighting back his frustration.

Ohmigod. How the hell am I getting this paper in by tomorrow? It's just like him to assign something this big for overnight.

What does this even mean? It's so far out there from what we did today.

The one thing Theo hated about leaving the house to get privacy from the rest of Victor's gang was that it meant being vulnerable to the thoughts of every person where he went, including the mindless drivel so common with the young people attending university. Their biggest problems were making rent and writing papers; they could ignore the larger problems of the world around them. Theo couldn't.

He raised his hand and drove it sharply against the door, opening the Pandora's Box of the outside world and releasing it into the library. Stepping across the threshold and onto the steps, he hiked his backpack further up onto his back and headed toward Victor's precious El Dorado.

"Anything useful?" Victor grunted through the window, as Theo laced his fingers under the handle of the door.

"Nothing. I tried everything I could think of. No records of her on any directories that I can find and she's not listed in the public Shane employee file," Theo said, slumping into the passenger's seat and donning his seatbelt.

"It was to be expected," Victor sighed, turning the key in the ignition.

The El Dorado rumbled to life, and Theo drew back in his seat. As Victor spun out of the parking lot, Theo rested his head on the door frame. He stared out the window at the blur of October Arizona, the heat rolling in through the car window. "You don't think I'll find her again, do you?"

"I don't think you'll find her in a search engine. She's not that kind of girl." Victor's voice was terse.

"You don't know her."

"I've seen how she makes you feel. That's enough for me to know her."

Theo turned from the window to look at him, eyes

narrowing, though he did not reply. He turned back almost instantly, and silently.

He remained that way for a while before speaking. "Thank you for taking me."

Victor glanced up from the road. "No problem. It beats hitchhiking," Victor said flatly.

They rounded a rocky bend and suddenly entered forested country. The road wound past old properties owned by older money and broken properties worked by calloused hands. Victor ran a hand through his hair, pushing it back from his face.

He turned his signal light on as they approached a dirt road leading away from the highway. The sun hung low in the sky and he instinctively moved to bring down his visor before the rays even hit his eyes as he changed directions.

The moment they left the main road, the ride went from smooth to bumpy. Theo braced himself against the doorframe, sharply sucking in air. "I will never understand why you choose this car over four wheel drive when you live so far out of the city."

Victor chuckled, accelerating over the uneven road. He barreled toward a thin gap where the trees became dense, bringing them through with inches to spare on either side. Branches whipped at the top of the car, sending splintered wood onto the forest floor. Theo's seatbelt went taught across his chest as they flew over a bump, and he felt his heart rise in his throat.

"Nervous?" Victor smirked, sending Theo a sideways glance.

"Rhetorical question?" Theo rolled his eyes.

Outside Payson, Arizona

Abby stared absentmindedly out the window at Chad. He dribbled a faded basketball around the court-yard, weaving it between his legs in a figure eight. Lining up with the net, he raised the ball to shoulder height and shot. Abby smiled, watching the ball soar through the net for the ninth time in a row.

She turned back to the dishes in the sink, and to Jaycee. He was working feverishly over the stove, pots boil-ing. The sight was almost comical, his bare chest covered by a printed apron and his hands covered with pink oven-mitts that dashed back and forth between different spoons in different pots. His eyes had taken on a look that Abby had come to recognize as serious determination, and he stared intently at the largest bubbling pot.

"If they don't get here soon, the noodles will be over-cooked," he said solemnly, stirring the pot and lifting a long strand to examine.

"Stop your worrying. They'll be back any minute. Be-sides, Theo's been really off since he left Poet Haven. It's nice of Victor to be taking him out for a little while. He really needs it."

The crackle of gravel under the El Dorado startled Chad as he squared his shoulders and prepared for a three-pointer. He spun around to see the orange mass, lowering the ball in his hands and tucking it under his right arm.

The car came to a standstill, and he walked toward it.

Theo opened the door of the car and slid out the passenger's side, straightening himself and giving Chad a quick, wordless nod. Victor emerged from the opposite side, running his fingers through his hair and regarding Chad.

"Good day?" Chad asked, Victor and Theo approaching him.

"Uneventful. This one is a bit particular about his supplies. Small town art store wasn't good enough for him. Needs his brand name paints and brushes," Victor said gruffly, thumping Theo on the back. Theo shot him a look.

"Well, that's all you can do, I guess." Chad muttered, running his hand through his hair.

"You boys ready for dinner?" Abby hollered, sticking her head out the kitchen window.

The trio spun to face her and Victor raised his hand to her. "We'll be in shortly. You can start taking it up," he shouted. More quietly, he turned back to Theo and Chad. "You boys thank your lucky stars that woman doesn't mind cooking you dinner. She's a hell of a lady and could be doing much better things with her time."

Washington, DC

"That'll be five dollars, Miss," the store clerk said as she finished punching the numbers into the old gray cash register she stood behind.

Kat Smith stared at the wall of cigarettes behind her, her eyes focussing in on a pack of Marlboros, blurring everything else until even the red top half started to bleed fuzzily into the white lower half of the package.

A man in a sport coat stepped up behind her in line and watched her, then cleared his throat loudly.

"Five dollars," the woman repeated, the musk on her breath puffing out toward Kat with each syllable.

Kat snapped back to reality, meeting the store clerk's eye with a fake smile. She looked down at the apples and carrots in front of her, then laughed a little and turned back to the clerk. When she spoke, her accent made both the clerk and the man behind her roll their eyes impatiently. "Yes of course." She took out her purse and started to rummage through it, picking out dollar bills and coins and arranging them in the palm of the opposite hand. When she was getting close to five dollars she stopped, staring at the wall of tobacco products behind her again. She swallowed hard, then added, "And a pack of smokes."

The clerk frowned, then took a step back. "Which kind?"

"Whatever's cheapest."

She took down a pack of Classics and laid them down on the counter in front of her. "Seven eighty-five."

Kat nodded then added the extra money to her palm before handing it all to the clerk and stepping out into the street.

She liked Washington. She'd stayed in a few places since coming to this side of the pond, but none of them compared to this one. There was an ethnicity to the place that she hadn't found anywhere else, the people so diverse that there was no one dominant race or language or religion. Her accent, although still bringing scorn from some, was one of the least-obvious 'abnormal' things she could see and hear even on her walk from her job to her flat.

She was an accountant. It had seemed positively pedestrian and boring when she'd thought it up upon choosing her major, and she hadn't been let down once since. She was the only white person in the firm where she worked, and one of only three women. Most of the rest were Asian and couldn't tell the difference between her British accent and an American one (a horrible stereotype, but in this case a true one). One of her coworkers was a black man who was about forty-five and spoke as though he had three tongues whenever he was around her, but always had a large smile and a belly that shook when he laughed, which was often. Another was a Cree woman whose mother insisted on making fresh bannock with blueberries for her once a week.

She'd made a conscious effort to stay away from the White House ever since she'd arrived. A few times while she'd been out for her morning jog she'd found herself venturing toward it unconsciously and had to correct her trajectory to take her through the park or down Pennsylvania Avenue. She always started to sweat more the closer she got to it, and that tight, anxious feeling in the centre of her chest seemed to get worse as well.

She lived only a twenty-minute run from the office, with the corner store and the foul-smelling old clerk and the cheap cigarettes smack dab in between. Usually she'd change out of her work clothes and into some sweats and jog home, stopping in for a Gatorade once she reached the store. Today she arrived home without having broken a sweat. Every house she passed by was decorated with pillowy white ghosts made of toilet paper tissue and witches that looked as though they'd been impaled on tree limbs while flying their brooms at night. Orange and black streamers hung from the eaves of houses and businesses, and there was a pumpkin on every stoop with a smiling, grinning jack-o-lantern face leering at her. There had been one particularly mean looking one by the Warner Theatre whose eyes met in the middle, looking more like a figure-eight turned on its side than a pair of eyes. Although the lantern wasn't lit it still stared at her, some light spot left in the pumpkin's innards acting as an iris that watched Kat as she marched down the street toward home.

When she got in she already had a cigarette lit, taking a long drag from it. She'd been quit for two weeks, but today she'd needed one. Today that tight, pulling, rending feeling between her breasts that threatened to rip her in two had become too much and she had just *needed* a smoke the same way that a man left underwater for too long *needed* air. She lit it and left it dangling from her lips after the first three drags, then put the carrots and apples in the fridge and took out a can of beer. She opened it in her chair and put up her feet on either side of her television, turning it on with her big toe. The news was on, and she quickly changed it. She passed through the channels quickly, pausing at a rerun of *Orange County Choppers*, then continuing until she found a cooking show where a man with large hands was slicing some celery into hundreds of tiny green half-moons. She paused for a moment with her foot over the button and then left it there, turning down the sound until she couldn't hear anything at all.

After one beer she got something to eat, the carrots

and apples cut into slices and dipped into ranch dressing.

After two beers she changed the channel over to an action movie starring Bruce Willis, but left the sound off.

After three beers she was sobbing uncontrollably, but wasn't crying. She never cried anymore.

During her fourth beer she called her mother.

Half way through her fifth beer she fell asleep.

Outside Payson, Arizona

Victor sat in his study behind a large oak desk. It was clean and neat without much on it, just a lamp on an adjustable metal neck and a cordless phone propped up on its base in the far corner. The latter was covered in a thin layer of dust and hadn't been used in many months. The former had traces of paper stuck to it where stickers had once been but had long since been removed.

He was writing in a small notebook that looked as though it could have fit neatly into his breast pocket without even making so much as a bulge there. His handwriting alternated between cursive and jumbled, as fine as Victorian calligraphy for one paragraph and the mad scribbling of a methadone patient the next.

There was an large hardcover book open in front of him. There was a small paragraph in the bottom right of the page for ectrodactyly deficiency that he was copying text from.

Jaycee stood in the doorframe and watched him, his arms folded across his broad chest. He waited a full minute for Victor to notice him, then finally spoke. "Why am

I here?"

Victor finished his sentence, laid down his pen, then folded his fingers in front of him and met Jaycee's eyes. "That's a fairly loaded question."

He frowned as he took another step into the room. "You know what I mean. I'm not trying to be smart or anything... I just can't figure out why I'm here, in this house."

Victor eyed him for a long moment. Jaycee looked from side to side, only meeting Victor's gaze every few seconds and than averting it again immediately. He was picking at the nails of one hand with the other, producing and loud clicking noise and bits came off in sharp segments. "You're nervous about your place here."

"I'm curious."

"Anxious."

"Fine. It's just... I look around the room and I see people so much more powerful than me. There's a guy downstairs who can alter reality, whether he believes it or not. There's a girl that can blow herself up without being blown up. Theo can read minds... I can't really *do* anything."

Victor pursed his lips, then turned back to his book and started to write again.

Jaycee watched him for a moment and waited for an answer, then stood up to leave.

"If ability determined usefulness, we'd live in a different world," Victor said finally, without looking up from his page.

"A better world?"

"Maybe. I'm not here to make that distinction."

Jaycee frowned, still looking defeated.

Victor watched him out of the corner of his eye for a moment, then laid down his pen again. "You are here because I think in terms of columns, not in terms of rows."

Jaycee raised an eyebrow at him.

"It's a line of thought where, when faced with a situation that has multiple outcomes, you think of it in terms of their most extreme possible consequences and then graph them." He turned to a blank page in his notebook and made a simple four-line grid. "If I take you and you prove useful, lives could be saved. If you're not needed, than nothing really bad happens. If I don't take you and you weren't needed, nothing bad happens. But if I don't take you and you *were* needed..." he drew a frown face in the top right-hand corner of the diagram. "If you're here, nothing bad happens one hundred per cent of the time. If I'd left you in Idaho, there was a fifty-fifty chance of something bad happening."

Jaycee looked at the diagram and slowly nodded.

"It's all in the math of it."

CHAPTER 05

Outside Payson, Arizona

Theo stood at the window, staring down at the driveway below. His eyes were bloodshot and rimmed with dark bags, and from the way his lids drooped and his body swayed it seemed a miracle that he was still standing up. The only sound in the room was the ticking of his wall clock as the hands crawled along, keeping time to the thoughts in his head.

There was a knock at the door. Theo's head shot up and he turned away from the window, waiting to see if the knocking would stop. For a brief moment it did, and the tension that had crept into his shoulders dissipated. He had half turned back to the window when another knock broke the silence and Abby's voice drifted in from the other side of the door. "Theo? Are you okay? I'm coming in."

He sighed, striding toward the door to meet her. He shouldn't have been surprised to see her, but he was. They had been so close just a few months before, but she had become reliant on him, and in turn he had become reliant on her. Then it was over. Since leaving the Port Haven Institute they had become distant. She had tried reaching out to him on occasion, but there was only so much prying he would tolerate, and she had given up trying. This was almost acceptable when Victor was around due to the rapport they had seemed have formed, but at times like this Theo had seemingly shut himself off completely from the others. He had seen the worry in Abby's face during the few times he had left his room, but it hadn't moved him.

She opened the door slowly, peeking her head in and frowning at the sight of him. He was so much thinner than the beach body boy with sun-kissed skin that she had first met. His face had lost the warmth it once had.

She walked over to him, getting a better look at the damage he seemed to be doing to himself. He was scruffy, and black smudges on his fingertips and forehead from the stack of newsprint laid out over the floor made him look even more disheveled. Abby felt a knot of guilt form in her stomach. She avoided eye contact with him.

"We're going into town tonight, Theo. There's a little diner in there where we'll all get dinner. You need to get ready now so we can get there before it's too busy."

Theo raised an eyebrow at her. "What makes you think I'm coming?"

Her eyes flicked up. "You need to get out of the house. I'm not asking you to come. I'm telling you we all decided you needed some time out of here."

"We? I'm a grown man. If I want to go into town, I will."

"Well start wanting it, because we leave in a half hour. You've moped long enough."

Payson, Arizona

Theo's hair blew with the air coming in through the window of the El Dorado. He sat shotgun as Abby drove, Jaycee and Chad lounging in the back of the car. The late-afternoon sun shone in through the windows, making the drive dangerously blinding. Theo watched Abby squint against the bright light, watched the way the sun turned her hair to fire. Once upon a time, she had mystified him. Now she was just a danger.

Abby pulled the car into the diner parking lot, shifting into park and turning the car off. Theo's presence had made the car ride silent and awkward, but already she could see his shoulders relaxing and the deep furrow in his brow smoothing out. Still, he seemed distracted.

Chad and Jaycee bolted out of the car, heading for the diner door. Theo stared after them, and next to him Abby unclicked her seatbelt. "Are you coming in, or are you just going to sit in the car and watch us eat through the window?"

Theo seemed to snap out of his trance when she spoke. "Yah, I guess. What is this place anyway?"

Abby opened the door and got out, leaning on the door as she replied. "Ma n' Pa's Diner. Guaranteed to make you sick one out of every five times you come, but worth it anyway," she chuckled. "Come on."

Theo unbuckled his seatbelt and followed her in, though her description of the place did little to entice him. It was a warm day, but the steam coming out of the kitchen area made the diner exceptionally warmer than outside, and the large overhead fans did little to make the dining room less stifling. Chad motioned for them to join him and Jaycee at a booth toward the back of the diner, so with Abby leading the way, Theo picked his way through the cramped and bustling room.

Almost immediately after they slid into the booth, a plump middle-aged woman with curly brown hair and the smell of stale cigarette smoke clinging to her uniform appeared with menus. "What'll you folks all be having this evening? Can I get anyone drinks to start?"

"Shepherd's pie and a cola, Tracey. Just the usual I think for the three of us. Not sure what Theo here wants though, so maybe give us a few minutes to decide?" Abby said smiling.

"Actually, shepherd's pie and a cola sounds great for me as well." Theo handed his menu to the smiling waitress.

"Well, Hun, your wish is my command." Tracey winked at him as she poked her pen into her curly mass of hair and slipped her pad of paper into her breast pocket, then turned to go to the kitchen.

Theo's eyes followed the waitress to behind the diner counter as she passed in their ticket. He glanced over the cluttered coffee makers and stacks of mugs she started to fill and his eyes drifted to the TV screen a few of the other waitresses were crowded around. They had the closed captioning on so not to disturb patrons, and from a distance the scene looked familiar.

A man in a brown suit stood in front of a large "COMING SOON – RENOVATIONS" sign, and a reporter seemed to be asking him questions. Theo watched, transfixed as the captions scrolled across the bottom of the screen.

"As you can see," the man in the suit seemed to be saying, "we're working very hard to get things up and running for next week's launch of the Los Angeles Science Centre Business Technologies Exhibit. We're expecting a fairly nice turnout tonight for Shane's founder's gala, clearly, and we are hoping the residents of Los Angeles are as kind in supporting us as they have in these past months. Without their work, and the work of Shane International, this exhibit would not have been possible."

"Theo?" Abby said, nudging him. "What's so interesting?"

Theo looked at her and glanced back to the TV, but it had already switched to another story. "Nothing really. I was at that museum once. When I lived in L.A."

"Well, next time we're in L.A. getting shot at, we'll have to take a detour to go see it," Abby said, rolling her eyes. "I don't understand your connection with it anyway. LA's brought us nothing but bad."

"I guess it's true what they say then. There's no place like home."

Los Angeles, California.

All around Shane Enterprises West 33rd Street offices, skyscrapers jutted up toward the sky, creating what appeared from a bird's eye view to be a checkerboard of greens and silvers. The city's recent efforts to beautify the West 33rd Street area had included parks and gardens to entice upper-middleclass buyers and businesses, though most efforts were for naught. Despite millions of taxpayer dollars, the parks and gardens wilted in the shadows of office buildings and concrete. Every day it seemed another big name company would move in and the smaller businesses would move out.

Leigh Blackheart looked out from the third floor stairwell as a tired looking security guard pulled open the personnel access door at the side of the building. He was fat and had sideburns that would have put Elvis himself to shame. The rest of his face was raggedly unkempt, with stubble of varying lengths making him look like a truck driver from an eighties B-Movie instead of a security guard. He crushed his cigarette against the wall, embers arching past his calloused fingertips as he did, then went in through the door and disappeared from sight.

She turned and continued up the stairwell, taking them three at a time. The stairs were granite on a black metal frame that rocked and roared every time anyone else went up it, shaking the foundation and amplifying the sound of each step so much so that even the lightest, more careful person sounded like an elephant stamping up the floors.

Leigh didn't make a sound.

Her legs were like black rubber, stretching further than a casual observer would have thought possible and snagging the next stair before snapping back into place and taking her with them. Her lips were a small bow at the bottom of her mouth, and she kept them closed tight, breathing through her nose and taking short, deep breaths. Like a pearl diver, slowly filling her body with oxygen and storing as much of it as she could.

Each floor was almost identical, and the act of climbing the stairs very quickly became one that let her mind wander. She thought back to Theo, and the brief time they'd spent together before he'd left L.A. She thought of how sick she'd gotten afterward, sicker than she'd ever gotten before in her life... that she could remember, anyway.

She was holding her breath now without realizing it. When her lungs ached for air she obliged, cursed herself, then started her breathing exercises over again.

The doctors had told her that her situation was getting worse, and that they didn't really know what to do about it. Her doctors had told her much different, but they didn't come cheap. Less than a day after she'd gotten out of the hospital, she'd been back to work.

She stopped at the next door and carefully slid her face up to the window. Though the halls were dark, the digits on each door and lab were clearly visible: 1601, 1602, 1603, and so on. 1608 was a large boardroom with glass walls and a large projection screen at the end. There was a poster of a pie chart next to it, and she wondered (for some reason) if it had been left over from a meeting earlier that day or if it was there in preparation for a meeting the next day.

Lately her life had been made of far too many leftovers and not nearly enough preparation.

Frowning, she placed her hand on the latch for the door and let it sit there for a moment. At first nothing happened, then after a moment her fingers seemed to seep around the metal. It was hard to tell in the shadows exactly what was happening, and that was the way she liked it. She watched it as though it were a badly-rendered scene from a movie, biting her lower lip as bits of sweat started to form on her ashen brow.

After a moment the door pushed open soundlessly, as though there had never been a latch in it at all. She took a deep breath as though she hadn't been able to in some time, then stepped out into the sixteenth floor.

She stopped and looked at a large, dinner-plate style clock on the wall. It looked out of place here, something homey in a place otherwise smooth and sterile and cold. The hands on it were not moving, and she wondered how long it had been stopped for. Part of her wanted to say months, though another part of her suspected it had only been minutes.

She reached room 1606 and placed her hand on the latch. There was a panel above her head that identified it as Dr. McGregor's lab, though she didn't know or care who he was. She had no more interest in his work than she did the squashed cigarette laying limp on the floor of the building's arboretum. She applied first pressure to the knob and found it to be unlocked, and smile gracing her lips for the first time since the entire event had started.

There was a sound behind her, like the slow whir of gears.

She turned slowly and looked over her shoulder. In the back corner of the hall was a security camera, its lens slowly panning its way across the room in her direction.

She mouthed a curse and then opened the door, much faster than she would have liked to, and slid inside. She closed it slowly, grinding her teeth as she watched the camera swerve toward her just as the latch clicked into place.

She turned and surveyed the room quickly. There was a desk on the far side with a large lamp up against a window that overlooked another boardroom. There were bookshelves and filing cabinets next to it that seemed to be packed so tight that once they were in nobody would ever be able to get them out again.

There was an island in the middle of the room with a sink in it and five nozzles instead of the normal two. One was purple, and she thought it was for gas. There was an egg timer next to it all that stared at her, its one hand stuck at zero.

She turned her attention to a small fridge-like box in the far corner that came up to her waist. Wasting no time she stepped up to it and pulled it out, then leaned over it and pulled all of the wires out of its back. Something inside the box whirred down and finally died, and she pulled it out even further to reveal a small round ventilation shaft sticking out of the wall behind it.

She stared at it for a long moment, then took a deep breath and hoisted herself up onto the box and sat on it.

She inched her tiny foot closer and closer to the shaft until it was plugging it, even her tiny appendage plugging the hole completely. The air and dust inside it tickled her soles, but she did not laugh. She watched it for a moment, wiggling her toes but unable to see them, then pressed forward.

Her foot continued into the hole in the wall, swallowing her arch and then her entire heel. She didn't want to watch but couldn't look away, feeling frozen as one did during a bad dream. Her leg continued down into the shaft until her calf was gone, and she brought her other slender leg up and poked its toe into a gap. Suddenly it started to disappear as well.

Her heart rate doubled and sweat began to pour down her face. She tried to force herself to keep breathing, her lungs and her head wanting to do two very different things. All of her wanted to throw up.

She slid in past her waist and looked like the veterans that lined the sidewalk in West Hollywood begging for change. She winced and braced herself against the wall and the box, lowering herself to the floor and then pulling herself forward into the hole.

When she was up to her chest it became hard to breathe. Her heart was pounding in her chest so hard that she didn't know how the guard couldn't hear it sixteen floors down. How he couldn't feel its rhythm through the pipes like submarines listening for the tap-tap-tap of enemy subs.

As her chin started in she closed her eyes and took one last, big gulp of air.

It was dark for what felt like forever. There was no sound except the beating of her heart, no feeling except the icy cold of the shaft surrounding her. There was air all around her but she could not breathe it, couldn't do anything except feel the pressure build and build and threaten to explode.

Somewhere near her an air vent ruffled, and she wished desperately that she knew where.

Her chest started to ache and there was an itch in the back of her throat that she wanted desperately to quell but couldn't. Her knees screamed and every bone in her body felt as though it were about to explode.

She felt her leg reach open air and wanted to scream but couldn't open her mouth. Her body spilled out into the hallway of the twelfth floor. When she was finally whole again she held her neck as though it were a precious thing and gasped for air eight times, each time feeling as though she could have gotten more. Sweat and tears fell from her onto the floor.

A Shane employee had to be either security, a senior manager or have special clearance to gain access to level twelve. It was their research and development department, and it was full of files, prototypes and schematics for everything that the company planned to release onto the market for the next three years. She'd been there four times before. The last time had been at the annual Christmas party, when one of the higher-ups had had a few too many drinks and tried to impress her with a look around. He had failed to do so in more ways than one. It was different now, lit only by the light green glow of the emergency bulbs. All she could hear was the dull buzz those lights made whenever they snapped on.

When she had her breath, she looked up and saw the security cameras again. There were eight of them in this one section, and she slid across the floor like liquid to get out of their view. Stretching as far as she could, she knocked the wires out of the back of the camera closest to her. She did the same for the next, making her way down the line until all eight feeds were dark.

She spun back around to the door at the end of the hall and waited. When nothing happened she nodded to herself quickly, then made her way to room 1212. It was locked like all the others, and once again she laid her hand on the knob and took a deep, purposeful breath. She could see it now in the puke-green light of the hallway, her hand turning into something like tar and her fingers slithering their way into the lock. A moment later she felt the tumblers within it slip and she opened the door even as her fingers returned to her.

The lab wasn't very big, about the size of her own bedroom. There were three computers, each parked in its own little cubicle adorned with pictures and memorabilia from the user's life. There was a large table in the middle with a few glass beakers on it, one of them very dirty, and a sink in the middle. It only had one extra faucet, again marked in purple to indicate the gas valve. On the far left side of the wall was another desk, this one filled with computer parts and circuit boards of various shapes and sizes ranging from two millimeters to two feet in length. Tools lay about and there was a stench like burning metal in the air. On the right side of the room there were two safes, one mounted on the other.

She stepped forward and pressed her palm flat against the lower safe, feeling her fingers twitch as if they were going to sleep and then screaming out pins and needles as they found their way into the gears and wheels of the combination lock. There were several small clicks and then a large, conclusive clack that made her smile despite the pain, opening the safe even as she withdrew her hand.

Laying on the shelf of the safe was a rectangular piece of metal about the size of a deck of cards. There were wires and ports coming out of its back end, but other than that it was smooth. It was a hard drive, and she picked it up tenderly and looked at it for a moment, her face a dark reflection in its metal sheen.

There were footsteps behind her and she turned around to see shadows cutting through the green light that came from under the door.

She fought the urge to curse and backed up from the safe, bringing the hard drive around and tucking it away next to the small of her back. She heard keys tickling and clenched her fists, her elbow knocking against a glass beaker and rocking it back and forth on its base. She almost turned and hissed at it, then stopped herself.

She heard a key in the lock, the old tumblers making the same sound they had for her.

She stopped, held her breath, and concentrated.

The door opened.

"Jeez," the security guard huffed, taking a step forward to examine into the room.His name was Wendell Voters, and he as was as fat as she'd seen before, but up close it was much more than that. He had a beer gut, one that seemed to be outgrowing the rest of him in terms of girth, making him look pregnant.

He took a slow pan of the empty room, until finally resting his eyes on the opened safe. He cursed softly to himself and took a step forward. His foot splashed into something.

He looked down he saw that most of the floor was covered in a black, gelatinous liquid. He stepped back from it, finding himself in the doorway again.

The black tar ran toward him, slowly making its way toward the door as he stepped around it and aimed his light toward the safe. After examining it for a moment without getting any closer, he turned to leave and closed the door behind him, registering a snap as it locked itself automatically.

He paused outside the door for a moment, listening for more sounds inside, like someone stepping out from behind the door of a closet. There was a small splash, similar to the one he had made when he stepped into the liquid. When he backed away from the door a little more he saw that the tar had made its way to the door and was now spreading out into the hallway.

Wendell turned and ran for the stairwell, his footfalls echoing off the white walls as he did. He slammed into the locked door and began to desperately fumble for his key ring. When he found the correct one he glanced back at the eerie green glow of the hallway. The blackness was still seeping from under the doorway. He opened the door frantically and started down the stairs, taking them two at a time as he tried to make his way to the security desk as quickly as possible.

Leigh pushed her head up through the puddle of tar, her lips turning blue and becoming the only color on her face. She choked back several gasps before her chest came into view and she could properly keep the air, her hair wet and clammy against the side of her head. She took two more long breaths and then stood up and made her way to the stairwell.

She slammed into it just as Wendell had.

"Fuck," she cursed, then laid her hand on the knob. This time instead of just her hand melting, her whole body seemed to. Before she knew it she was pouring herself underneath the door, barely getting the time to take a breath before the ability to do so was robbed of her. She seeped out into the stairwell and tumbled down through the gaps in the metal frame, feeling that energetic push as gravity took hold of her and flung her wherever it wanted.

Half of her splashed down just shy of the entrance to the eighth floor, the other half near the entrance to the seventh.

Her head emerged from the half on the eighth floor and she tried to scream but couldn't, ripples running through her feverishly as her pale skin turned red and purple and blue and every color in between. Wincing in pain but unable to express it, her shoulders and arms crawled their way out of the puddle and pulled their way over to the edge of the stairwell.

Down below, Wendell Voters stood in front of a large puddle of her matter that lay between him and the exit to the seventh floor.

He stared at it for a long moment, and it was like staring into a muddy coffee cup. Even though he knew it was crazy, Wendell could not shake the feeling that the dark puddle was somehow examining him as much as he was examining it, and the thought sent shivers down his spine.

Leigh writhed, her eyes bulging out of her air and her face becoming something inhuman as it longed for air and freedom from the agony, stretching to horrific proportions until it looked like an Edvard Munch painting. Trying to take one last breath and failing, she threw herself over the edge of the eighth floor stairwell.

There was a small pit against Wendell's shoulder, and when he looked at it there was black goop running down his shirt and onto his chest.

He looked up and saw a great wave coming down toward him, and the last thing he heard was the sound water made... when it screamed.

CHAPTER 06

Atlanta, Georgia

Tash took the box of Cranberry Walnut Crunch down out of the cupboard and laid it on the countertop in front of her. One of the three fresh quarts of milk that they had delivered to their door every day sat there as well, along with two clean white bowls with silver spoons placed a quarter of an inch to the left of the base of each bowl. She leaned back and examined it, then turned back toward the kitchen and made sure that the two tall glasses of orange juice she'd prepared were still there. Satisfied, she opened the box of cereal and poured equal amounts in each bowl until they were full, then topped them off with milk and dunked the spoons into each, finally bringing them both over to the table.

The coffee maker clicked and she clicked back with the roof of her mouth, smiling as she took each mug off the table and brought them back over.

The kitchen was small but manageable. There were only four of them so they rarely needed more, and when they did the dining room was right there. The walls were bright and homey, with flower patterns around the trim and dozens of small shelves filled with herbs and spices, as well as antique honeypots and vases.

She poured up both cups of coffee and left them black, taking a long slurp out of one and holding the other out in front of her as she walked back toward the table.

"Morning Tash, I - -" Nick started as he came around the corner from the living room, stopping in mid sentence as he almost collided with the coffee she was holding out to him. He smiled, then took it from her. "Thanks. How'd you --"

She shot him a wry smile.

"Right. Thanks."

She sat down at the table and motioned for him to do the same, then started mixing her cereal around so that it all got wet.

He stared at his, watching as a dark red cranberry bobbed up and down in the white like a life preserver, then eventually sank below the surface with a tiny plop and disappeared.

Tash took one mouthful of cereal, then another, and smiled at him. She had a great smile. It was small in the center of her strong, angular face. Her raven hair was cut close to her head and combed forward into a neat bang and her cheeks were dotted in freckles. Her eyes were the sort of dark blue that Nick hadn't seen since he'd lived near the ocean. "How was your date with Quinn last night?"

Nick's eyes rose up. "How did you…?"

Again, she shot him an amused look.

"Right. Sorry."

"I stayed up pretty late, but I didn't hear either of you

come in," she grinned. "Checked her bedroom before I came downstairs, too. Didn't look like her bed had been slept in. I didn't check *yours* though, should - -"

She stopped, finally noticing how pale and hollow Nick's face had become. His eyes were glossy and his mouth was dry.

"What?" she asked, the playfulness of her tone gone now as she touched her hand to his. "What is it?"

Atlanta, Georgia

Kelly woke up next to Gavin.

His loft was warm this hour of the morning, when the light came in from the window at the eastern end of the attic and filled it with its soft glow, catching all the swirling particles of dust in the air and becoming almost solid. The heat from the rest of the house rose up to here and stayed, hovering in the air so that he rarely needed the soft caress of the sleeping bag he slept in.

She was naked except for the elastic wrapped around her wrist, and she held the comforter close against her breasts as she got up. She felt uncomfortable with sweat, each bead of it catching the morning sun and glinting against her pasty white skin. Her hair still came down in two straight lines on either side of her face.

After a moment she took a deep breath of the humid, dusty air, just to prove to herself that she could.

Gavin was still asleep next to her, his hairless white chest exposed. His ribs on one side were lined with a series of small parallel scars, but other than that his flesh was without a mole or blemish.

She shuddered even though she was warm. She got up but kept her blanket wrapped around her until she found her clothes, then put them on and made her way downstairs.

The house seemed empty at this hour of the morning, but it never was. In fact there were just as many people here as there had been the night before, maybe even more. They had a habit of finding places to stay even if there wasn't a bed that was specifically 'theirs' per se. She knew that Mitch at the very least slept on the floor of a different bedroom every night of the week. There was never anyone asleep in the halls themselves, though. Even if one of them got too drunk and passed out on the stairwell there were always two or three people to help them to their bed and lay them on their side to make sure they didn't choke on their own vomit.

She stepped into the living room and smirked when she saw Valerie asleep on one couch with several people's coats piled around her. Billy and Quinn were on the other, sprawled out on top of one another and sharing body heat. Despite the heat in the loft it was freezing down here, so much that she could see her breath. She adjusted the thermostat slightly when she passed it, not wanting to turn it up too much until Gavin came down.

The kitchen was bright with morning light again now, not like it had been the night before. The case that the coolers had been in was still on the floor in one corner, and she smiled as she walked over and picked it up. There was a weight to it, and she reached in and withdrew the last, unopened bottle. It was Orange Pineapple.

She stared at it for a moment and debated opening it,

then put it in the fridge.

"Maybe later," she said to herself, then made her way to the fruit basket. She picked a bruised apple out of its top and bit into it, piercing its soft flesh easily. There was a waxy quality to it that she ignored, sucking back the juice with each bite as she grabbed two slices of bread from the breadbox and slid them into the toaster, pushing down on the worn lever in its front.

Nothing happened.

"Oh, fuck you," she cursed, the words muffled through her mouthful of red flesh. She pressed down on the lever again. It popped back up harmlessly. She huffed and yanked the plug out from its socket then shoved it back in. There was a short, stunted hiss as the metal prongs connected into place inside the old socket.

When she pressed down on the lever again, it shocked her so powerfully that a blue spark jumped between the metal and her finger.

She yelped and jumped back a pace.

"Oh, it's too early for you to be making sounds that loud," Charlotte said.

Kelly turned to see her propped up in the doorway wearing the same clothes she had had on the night before. Her hair was frazzled all around her. "I'm sorry. Didn't expect to see you up so early."

Charlotte twisted uncomfortably, popping something in her left shoulder. "Thomas kicks in his sleep."

Kelly raised an eyebrow.

"Ha. No. Judy and Dennis were passed out in my bed."

"Ah," she nodded, then turned back to the toaster.

She stared at it for a moment as through she were Clint Eastwood in an old Western, waiting to see which of them would draw first. Biting her lip and wincing, she reached out and pushed down on the lever. It went down without incident, and the wires inside immediately began to glow red with heat.

She hummed triumphantly.

Charlotte made her way from the door to the island in two big steps, almost falling onto it. "My stomach is killing me."

"Well that's what you get."

"Spare me. I need something in me."

Kelly moved the fruit basket over between them with one finger. "We've got apples."

"Ugh. I'll never understand how you can eat something that hard on an empty stomach. I'd be in knots."

"Toast?"

"Yuck."

Kelly lowered her eyes and tried to keep a straight face, then cocked her head in the direction of the fridge. "There's one cooler left."

"Thank you!" she said. She took the Orange Pineapple cooler out from where Kelly had just placed it and used the bottle opener on the fridge to pop the cap. She guzzled down the entire neck standing with the fridge door open and leaking cold air out onto the floor.

Kelly watched her and shook her head, looking past her and out into the living room. She could just barely see the top of Quinn's head from this vantage point, poking out over the couch cushions.

Quinn twisted uncomfortably, then settled back into

place.

Charlotte stopped drinking and gasped, following Kelly's gaze. "You think the new girl's staying?"

Kelly did not respond. Upstairs the familiar sounds of the rest of the house waking up began to fill the walls, like the groan of floorboards as people stepped off of their beds and the old pipes shooting out water after a night of remaining stagnant.

Her toast popped.

Outside Payson, Arizona

The sun beat down through the trees, warming the yard in spite of the fall wind. A large wood pile was propped against a small barn at the far end of the yard, the axe used to chop the logs lodged firmly in a sawed off tree-trunk. Overall, save for the wildlife and some grumbling, the yard was quiet.

The hood of the burnt orange El Dorado was propped up, giving the car the appearance that it had opened its maw to eat Abby has she peered inside. Her tiny frame was almost fully consumed as she leaned in, her coveralls covered with grease. "What exactly am I supposed to be looking for again?"

"Signs of rust or anything that looks like it's wearing down," Victor grunted, standing with his arms crossed a short ways behind her. "I need to know that she's in ship-shape before we need to take off anywhere, and I shouldn't exactly be the only one who knows how to figure that out."

"So you decided to pawn this off on me, did you?"

Abby said, rolling her eyes and emerging from the El Dorado's hood. She stood firmly to face Victor, her hands on her hips.

"I decided teaching you would be easiest based on your scientific knowledge. The boys all like their art and their sports, which is fine and dandy, but you've got the smarts and common sense it takes to fix things up and put things together."

Abby's indignant look dropped from her face as a pale shade of pink crept into her cheeks. "Oh." She turned back to the exposed workings of the car and her face molded into a frown. "Shouldn't the carburetor be in better shape than this?"

Victor smiled. "I would imagine."

Abby groaned. "You mean to tell me you've known the carburetor hasn't been functioning properly and you didn't do anything about it while you were in town? Do you realize how much that's impacting the performance level of this beast? You shouldn't be allowed to own nice things!"

"I take it that means you'll fix her up for me?" Victor said, a smirk creeping onto his face.

Abby brought her palm to her forehead and let out a sigh, leaving a smear of engine grime on her skin as she did so. "Fine," she groaned "but you better promise to make this up to me."

"Deal."

Payson, Arizona

"And a pound of thin sliced pepperoni," Chad said,

motioning to the slicer behind the counter.

The butcher looked at the pile of meat and vegetables that lay between them on the counter. There was ham, chicken, turkey and bologna as well as carrots, turnip, cheese (mozzarella and marble), and two heads of lettuce. He turned and looked at Chad with one eye closed and his face scrunching in on itself, as if he were trying to figure out some complex equation.

"It's for a friend," Chad said to clarify, smiling awkwardly.

The butcher shrugged, then turned around and slapped a loaf of pepperoni onto the whirling blade of the meat slicer.

Williams's Convenience was one of those jack-of-all-trades places that Chad had liked best growing up because it was the type of place that he could go to no matter what he needed. Each aisle was almost its own genre of store, with all of them climaxing at the cash register. The aisle that faced the window was lined with DVDs and old sun-faded VHS tapes that could be rented. The newest release there was over three years old, and appeared to have been replaced by a NetFlix terminal that stood next to the ATM at the end of the row. There were chairs a tables set up across from them under the window, for the few people that ate the items they bought on the premises.

The aisle opposite it was candy and confectionary, and Chad considered it to still be a part of the movie-renting theme. There was popcorn and large bags of potato chips that were perpetually on sale and dips of various flavours all lined up in a row. At the end, and very out of place, was a small cooler packed with cheese and vegetables that needed to be cooled and the sandwiches that the owner made and wrapped by hand.

Other items included all the standard things one would find at a large chain grocery store, but without the variety present in one. For example, there were always cookies, but there was only the one type and rarely was there the same type two weeks in a row. Sometimes they'd be Oreo, another time they'd be Pirate. Sometimes Fudgeo, another Chips Ahoy. Wafer Crisp, Vanilla Crunch. It all depended on what brand the warehouse supplier had on sale that week. If they bought a brand that nobody liked, that brand could stay on the shelves for weeks at a time. It was the same with flavours of cereal and soft drinks.

The truly amusing features of the store came from the back and front walls. The front was simply a deli and bakery, with long glass cases on either side of the cash that displayed the various meats and pastries on either side. The front brought joy because of its staples, its eclairs and cream-filled treats. The back brought joy because of its constant state of flux. It was always selling whatever the owner or his wife was interested in that month, a) so that they could write their own items off as tax deductibles, and b) because they thought that everyone liked what they liked. Because these items often were a long time selling (if they ever sold at all), the back wall served as a hodge-podge graveyard of human interest, with items ranging from cake decorating kits to model planes, Chinese Geisha dolls to wood carvings. There were several superhero toys back there that Chad assumed was more to do with their grandchildren's interests than their own.

The butcher turned back around to face Chad and

plopped the freshly cut pepperoni, cradled in its nest of wax paper, down in front of him. "Anything else?" he asked, almost daring Chad to ask for more.

"No," Chad laughed. "No, I think that's it for today."

The man nodded and wrapped the meat in cellophane, then added it to his total. The neon green lights of the register rang up a startling thirty-four eighty-two.

"Yikes," Chad groaned, his mouth bending comically.

"You got it, right?"

"Oh, yeah," he soothed, reaching for his wallet and taking out two twenties for the man. "Just more than I thought it would be."

The butcher looked down at the pile of meat as if in explanation of the price, but Chad didn't notice. He was looking at the empty folds of his wallet, flipping from one compartment to the next and finding nothing but vacant leather and old receipts. He sighed.

The butcher handed him back a five and some change and began to arrange his purchases into two bags.

Chad put the money back in his wallet but left it out, his gaze falling from it to the glass counter-top of the cash register.

Beneath a plate of glass and plastic was a long, colourful line of scratch tickets.

Bingo, Crossword, Jumble, Lotto-Win and a dozen others, all screaming out at him in vibrant reds and purples and yellows with balloon text and large bold font. Win ten thousand dollars. Win one hundred thousand dollars. Win win win! Win.

His mouth was suddenly dry as he moved the five

spot back and forth between his thumb and forefinger, feeling the warm fabric of the aged bill.

The butcher finished packing his things and pushed the bags forward.

"Hey," Chad started, still staring at the lotto display.

"Yeah?" the butcher snapped, bringing Chad's attention back to him. He finally noticed the growing line of customers behind him.

"Nothing," he said, then took his bags and walked out of the store.

Callahan Street was one of the hubs of Payson, especially in the fall. While fall in Arizona wasn't that different weather-wise from most other times of year, the city itself went through an odd sort of transformation instead. Though it was his first fall here, it was a phenomenon he'd noticed in other places of similar climates. It was like something in you *wanted* to see change this time of year, so the city got to work hanging up orange and black streamers and banners for Spirit Week and Halloween and October-Fest and anything else they could think to celebrate within the thirty-one days the month provided. Callahan Street got the best of it. It was a part of a strip that was equal parts taverns and small-scale shops, catering both to tourists and more homegrown patrons. There were heritage shops selling small statues and snow-globes of Cactus Wren and Saguaros and sports outlets that sold Cardinals jerseys and autographed footballs. There were local businesses that sold everything from quilts to hand-crafted furniture and art. It was a place Chad had spent many hours since coming here, and every time he found something new and wonderful when he stepped into one of the small boutiques and stores. Typically something he didn't expect to find there.

But then, he was lucky that way.

The sun was always hot here, and now it weighed down on his cheeks and shoulders happily. The heat was constant and undescribable, always warm and bright and happy (as long as you had enough water with you). On days like today, when the temperature was just right, the sweat seemed to evaporate off your forehead the second you made it, keeping you just the right temperature for a nice, leisurely stroll. He loved days like this, and tried to make it out for every one there was. As a result he'd grown three shades darker since coming here, and his hair (which had already been a very light shade of blonde) had been sun-bleached in areas.

He grunted. The bags were beginning to cut long, red dents in his fingers under the weight of all the meat and food in them. They were the reusable kind that were supposed to be better for the environment, but the rope handles were murder on his palms and typically by the time he was through walking they were almost bloody. That wasn't what he was thinking about right now though, even as he shifted the handles from one joint to the other to try and relieve some of the tension. He was thinking about those tickets.

Ten thousand. One hundred thousand. One million.

Any one of those tickets held within them the ability to change his life forever, and with even that one five in his pocket he could have bought any two of them. Hell, he could have been real greedy and bought two of the million-dollar winners.

He was getting toward the end of Callahan now, to where it intersected with Baker and could either move up into town or out beyond the city, where the house was. He'd parked his bike next to an old law firm made of brick and concrete on the corner that didn't have parking metres at it and walked the rest of the way. There was an area cut off from him with a wire-mesh fence and then a used bookstore and then the law firm.

"Hey, get out of there!" came a loud voice, followed by another laughing. There was a sound of a scuffle, worn soles scratching against the pavement, and finally a heavy thud and a slow throbbing noise like a ruler snapped off a desk.

Chad stopped, his face going white.

"Oh, fuck you!"

Scuffle. Scuffle.

"All right!"

"That's how we do it!"

"Shut up."

His brow creased, he inched his way forward until he could see into the fenced-over area of the street. Wedged in between the brick walls of two shops and the back of an old apartment building was a small square of pavement. It looked like it might have once been used as an entrance or perhaps even for garbage collection, but had since been blocked off (likely to do with the shelter such areas provided delinquents, as often happened in such places on Callahan). There were lines painted on the pavement with white house paint and chalk, and a hoop hung from a patricianly-open window about seven feet up the side of the used bookstore.

It was a basketball court.

He smiled and found himself laying his bags down on either side of him and lacing his fingers through the mesh of the fence to watch.

There were four of them; two black, one white and one that he guessed was Hispanic, based on the accent of the curses he was letting out every time the larger of the two black men stole the ball from him. The Hispanic man and the shorter black man both wore white wife-beaters while the other two were bare-chested, their lack of tan-lines showing that this shirts-versus-skins team division was the norm among them instead of the aberration. Despite what it had sounded like at first, they were having fun. The four of them all probably lived in the apartment complex that loomed in the background and had decided to just *have fun*. It was a concept he'd forgotten so long ago that it almost seemed foreign to him.

The Hispanic teen, Fabian, seemed adept at getting the ball despite his small stature. He would dribble as close to the ground as possible and not give the others any chance to smack it away, but at some point he'd always have to come up to take a shot and that was when either Sammy (the white man) or Wedu (the larger black man) would bat the ball away from them. The shorter of the two black men (Charles) didn't seem to be doing much in the way of defense.

"Two sharpshooters on a team with no defense against two offensive players," Chad mumbled to himself as he shook his head.

Fabian faked left and then zipped right, all the while keeping the ball at just a little over a foot away from the ground. It was incredible to watch him dribble, the ball moving from his palm to the ground and back again so quickly that it formed a solid orange blur between the two.

He spun around on his heels and came up to make his shot, the ball arching from the swerve of his wrist and soaring in a straight line for the basket.

Wedu reached up and caught it in the palm of one great, gargantuan hand and then pushed it forward again with a simple squeeze of his fingers, the ball moving up and then coming back down through the net.

Swish.

"Ha ha!" Sammy laughed, twisting his baseball cap around and holding up his hand to Wedu, who connected it with a high-five. His hand dwarfed Sammy's as though it was a child's hand.

"Good shot," Fabian nodded, sweat pouring down off him. "Nineteen-fifteen?"

"Twenty-fifteen," Wedu corrected.

"We're counting the other?"

"We're counting the other."

"Alright."

Sammy took the ball and stood under the basket, then tossed it out to Charles, who quickly shot it back over to Fabian. Fabian turned immediately, tossing the ball back toward Charles but actually bouncing it off the wall of the building and sending it right back to himself, an act that seemed to fool both his opponents. Ball back in hand, he dribbled around to get a better shot at the net.

When he turned and looked over his shoulder, Wedu was behind him again.

He stayed there, dribbling for what seemed like an eternity, then finally spun and stepped back quickly to try and get as much space between he and Wedu as he could, bringing his arms up to make the shot.

Wedu pulled his hand up from underneath the ball and scooped it away from him, his elbow connecting with Fabian's upper lip and nose as he did. He turned without noticing, bending his arms back and bouncing the ball off the backboard and into the net.

Fabian hit the ground and skidded a foot, pulling his shirt tight. When he turned around there was no blood, but his lip already appeared fat and swollen.

"Twenty-one!" Sammy yelled, holding both thumbs and forefingers high in the air in two victorious letter Vs.

"Oh, what the fuck," Chad cursed to himself, shaking his head.

Sammy turned to face him, noticing their spectator for the first time. "I'm sorry, you have something to say?"

"That was bullshit. Foul game, man. That was dirty pool."

Wedu looked down at Fabian, as if only now realizing what he had done. "You okay, bro?"

"Yea, I'm fine," Fabian said, rising to his feet but still pressing his hand against his lip gingerly. "Not the worst I've had."

"See?" Sammy smiled. "He's fine. We won. It's no big deal."

"If you say so," Chad frowned, gathering his bags.

"What? What's that all about? You think you could do better?"

The other three laughed.

Chad smiled, then stood back up straight and facing him through the fence. "I know I could do better.

"Is that so?"

"Yeah, actually. That's so."

Sammy grinned, backing away from the fence with his arms open. "Well why don't you come over here and give it a try?"

Chad smiled, reaching into his back pocket and fishing out his wallet again. He produced his five dollar bill, clasping it out in front of him as though it were all important. "How about we make it... just a little interesting?"

Sammy laughed, then nodded and reached for his own wallet. The other three did the same. "Looks like we got ourselves a game."

Chad picked up his bags and tossed them over the fence, then clasped the mesh and climbed over himself. The thin metal hurt his already calloused fingers, and when he landed on the other side he felt the reverberations of the concrete all through his legs and up into his torso. It was cooler over here, in the shade of the three buildings, but there was still plenty of heat. Enough to make even the pavement sweat.

He smiled and handed his five over to Sammy, who took off his cap and rested all five bills in it and set it to one side. The other three were already moving to sit along the steps of the apartment building, passing around a bottle of coke and each of them taking a swig of it in turn.

"First to five?" Chad asked, pushing his hair back.

Sammy nodded, then tossed him the ball.

Chad coiled and shot, hopping a little as the ball sprung from his fingers and travelled through the air and into the basket.

Swish.

"Ooh!" Charles and Fabian bellowed in unison, as the ball fell from the net and bounced at Sammy's feet. Wedu just smiled and sipped his soda.

Sammy grabbed the ball, nodding to himself and sniffing as he ran his fingers over his scalp. He bounced the ball to Chad as they passed, Chad taking his position under the net.

"That's one-oh, right?" Chad smirked, pointing between them. "Just making sure. In the last game, it didn't seem like you were sure."

Chad threw Sammy the ball and immediately moved to the left, giving himself some room at the side of the net. Sammy turned and started that same fast, close-to-the-ground dribble he'd done before, the ball becoming an electric smear between his hand and the pavement. His back was to the basket and he kept one eye trained over his shoulder, watching as Chad kept his distance. He turned suddenly, his hands coming up into a longer dribble as he ran around to the net, jumping a good two feet from the ground and the arc carrying both he and the ball toward the net.

Chad ran forward to try and block him, but it was far too late. The ball slammed into the orange metal rim and dove through the basket with enough force to send it bouncing to the other side of the court.

"One-One," Sammy sneered, fetching the ball. There was sweat lining his eyebrows in a glistening line that made him seem much grayer than he was. He'd been playing for some hours before Chad had shown up.

"We keep going tit-for-tat, I wonder which one of us will reach five first?"

Sammy's lip twitched. He threw Chad the ball again, but this time moved up close to him immediately. Chad turned his back to his to protect the ball, but he could feel the heat off the man's chest against him. He'd never been claustrophobic before, but with the walls looming all around and this angry man hovering above him, there was a tightness in his chest that he thought might very well be it. He tried to turn, but Sammy's hand came around quickly to try and swipe the ball away. He tried to turn the other way, only to be met with the same result.

"Fuck this," he growled, then drew back the ball and hurled it toward the ground in front of him.

It bounced off the ground, then off the wall opposite the net, then travelled up and over the court in a high arc above either of their heads toward the basket.

Swish.

The ball hung in the net for a moment as though it were in suspended animation. As though not even the net could quite believe what had just happened.

"What the hell was that?" Fabian whispered.

Chad smiled, standing up slowly as Sammy backed off from him and took his position at the three-point line. "Two-One."

Sammy smiled, catching the ball when it was tossed to him and again turning his back to the basket, dribbling the ball close to the ground. This time Chad moved in close right away, his hair falling around him in all directions as he spread his arms out to encompass Sammy.

Sammy turned quickly and jumped, releasing the ball

with one arm and catching Chad in the face with the other.

Chad fell to his knees and scraped them against the pavement as the basketball ricocheted off the backboard and sunk into the net.

"It's like that, is it?" Chad asked, getting up and dabbing a small hint of moisture from his eye.

"Yeah, it's like that."

"Very good then," Chad snorted, catching the ball as Sammy passed it to him from behind his back. He slammed it to the ground immediately. It bounced high, even higher than the fence, and seemed to hang at its acme forever before finally coming back down. Swish. "As long as I know."

"Oh, you should see the look on your face," Wedu laughed from his spot on the stairs, slapping his hand against his knee.

"Shut up," Sammy barked, handing the ball to Chad as they passed each other. Chad threw it back to Sammy again, who started forward toward the basket with that same down-low dribble again.

Chad stepped forward and swooped down, and in one fluent motion took the ball from him and arced it up and tossed it over his back.

Swish.

Sammy kept walking for a few steps, as though not completely aware he'd lost the ball until he saw it bounding toward him. He stopped and took a few deep breaths while resting against his knees, then glared over his shoulder at Chad standing at the three point line.

"Lucky shot," he spat finally, between breaths.

"No doubt."

Sammy tossed him the ball and Chad started to dribble, moving back as Sammy came in close.

"Where'd you learn to play like that, anyway?" he asked, bobbing this way and that, trying to cover all avenues that Chad could go on.

Chad fumbled the ball twice and then got it back, unable to get the rhythm of dribbling down correctly.

Sammy tilted his head, watching as the man continued to fail at the simplest part of the game right before him.

"Let's just say I'm learning as I go," Chad smiled, then leaned back and rolled onto his heels and let the ball go. It flew through the air as though it was weightless, finally bouncing off the rim and falling into the net. It made a soft, silky sound as the rubber caught in the mesh for a moment, swinging out to its fullest before passing harmlessly through.

Sammy watched it happen, no longer surprised but more in a state of respectful awe.

Chad leaned over and grabbed Sammy's hat off the ground, clutching the bills in his hand and pushing them down into his pocket. He loved the way they felt, warm and smooth, the ink almost worn off some of them. He'd missed it. He handed Sammy back his hat. "Good game."

"Yeah, def was," Sammy laughed, smiling as he snatched his hat back and replaced it on his head. "You should drop by for a rematch sometime."

"Yeah?"

"Yeah," he smiled. "Just not for cash next time."

Chad smiled, then worked his way back over the fence and into the light of Callahan Street. He could feel the bills rubbing against each other through the thin fabric of his pockets, and smiled.

CHAPTER 07

Outside Payson, Arizona

Victor sat at the kitchen table in a beam of sunlight that came in from the window next to him. There was a hot cup of coffee on the table that barrelled steam out into the morning air, getting caught in the light from the window and almost appearing solid before wafting up to the ceiling and dissipating. He had a newspaper open in front of him and moved from page to page tentatively, scanning up and down the articles before moving on to the next page and taking small sips from his coffee between each. The house was quiet and still, and the more he became aware of it the more relaxed he became. There was a tingling sensation spreading slowly from the base of his neck down his shoulders as knots he wasn't even aware of in his musculature began to unravel and ease.

"Bullshit," Abby said, walking into the kitchen. She held out the side of her shirt awkwardly and glared at the large grease stain that ran along its cuff.

He watched her as she walked past him and made a bee-line for the fridge. She opened it and shoved her head in as dramatically as she could. He turned back to his paper.

"Do we have any baking soda?" she asked, fumbling about the assorted contents of the door and displacing packets of ketchup and other condiments that had been saved from fast food deliveries. "Dear Lord, did you ever cook before I moved in?"

"Once," he replied, taking a sip out of his coffee. "It ended badly. The town issued a citation."

"Cute," she sneered, then pulled out a large bottle of orange liquid. "Can I have the Strawberry-Banana?"

"If it's there, you can have it."

"Yeah but I don't want to take it if it was for somebody. Jaycee loves his fruit drinks. You'd think the boy had never had a mango before."

"I doubt he did."

She paused, then shrugged. "Maybe we should get a Sharpie and put it on the door or something, and if you want something saved you just write your name on it."

"If we're out of something, we'll go to the store. It will be fine." He turned the page of his paper.

She hummed, then unscrewed the top of the bottle and brought it to her lips.

Victor turned the page of his paper again. He grabbed his cup by the rim and took a loud slurp. The cup was large and round at the top, but his massive hands palmed it as though it were one of the paper dwarf cups found in highway rest stops. There was a picture of Wile E. Coyote on one side, holding up a sign that said 'help' as he stood over the open mouth of a cliff.

She watched him as she drank, even as the bottle began to blur and obscure her vision of him. When she took the bottle down there was an orange ring around her upper lip.

"Is that a tabloid?" she asked, motioning with the mostly-emptied bottle.

Victor glanced at her a moment, but said nothing.

She laughed, so hard that orange-tinted spittle came out of her mouth.

He did not respond.

"I'm sorry, I really am, but that's just too surreal for me. You with the coffee and the paper and everything else, and you're reading about Elvis being impregnated by space aliens or some other ridiculous shit. Did you have to fight with some blue-haired biddy to get it?"

"Port Haven Institute, or PHI for short, seems on the surface to be a long-standing finishing school; the last in a long tradition once held in this country," he began to read aloud. "But beneath its polished exterior lies a foundation of murder and bloodshed dating back to 1883, when one of the foremen working on the project was killed while working on the southeast tower. Last month, according to inside sources, the southeast tower was the site of another grisly murder, which may have been linked to allegations that the school cultivates individuals with a penchant for the supernatural. Using a school in this manner is ludicrous and they were just asking for trouble."

He closed the paper and put it down on the table, then turned in his chair to look at her.

She swallowed.

"It doesn't actually say that last part, but I thought I might punch it up for effect."

"It wasn't that bad, you know. I learned a lot there."

"Mm," he nodded, his eyebrows bobbing. "Fencing is a forgotten skill. I mean, imagine if someone tries to rob us with a foil. You'll be set to strut your stuff."

He got up and walked over to the counter next to her, taking the head off a ceramic chef behind her and revealing a small stash of assorted cookies. He took out two, a chocolate chip and a knock-off Oreo, and dunked one into his coffee before biting into it.

She stared at him a moment, then laughed again. It was smaller this time, and sweeter, a smile slowly spreading across her face. He tilted the chef toward her and she reached in and produced a rainbow chocolate chunk cookie.

A dull tone pierced the calm stillness of the kitchen and he frowned, though it was hidden behind the scruff of his beard. He pushed his thumb and forefinger into his jeans pocket and produced his cell phone, holding it out in front of his face and squinting to read the display screen.

"I have to take this," he said, stepping away from the counter and grabbing his coffee. He left the room without another word, leaving the half-eaten chip cookie and Oreo behind.

Abby stared at them for a moment, then drank the rest of her juice.

"Talk," Victor said, bringing the phone to his ear. It was almost hidden by the bulk of his hand and the hair that came down long on either side of his head.

"That's real nice," Tash said, sitting on the dining room

table with her phone to her face. Hers was much larger and much more sophisticated, a touch screen smart-phone that she kept with her at all times and had begun to use in place of her computer. There was even an application for it that allowed her to keep track of her daily events, but she tried to limit herself when using that one, or else it had a tendency to get out of hand. "Some people would have gone with: hello."

"I assumed it was urgent," he replied, taking a sip of his coffee. He'd made his way to his study and did not bother to turn on the light, the glow from the hallway casting a bright halo over his head and chest. "You never call."

She turned back toward the kitchen. Nick had gone upstairs to wake Iseult. She could hear the shallow beat of his footfalls even from here, but she still had to check. "Quinn didn't come home last night."

Victor was silent for a moment. His mouth went dry, and he tried one last sip of his drink to quench it. When it didn't work he poured it into the garbage pail next to his desk and laid the cup down. He turned, eyeing the crack in the door to see if there was anyone listening out in the hallway, much as she had a moment ago. When he spoke again, his voice was lower. "Is she safe?"

"I think so. She's staying at some local teen hangout place. I've heard the place mentioned a few times on the police scanner. Just minor disturbance stuff, nothing that would make the papers... seems like whenever a kid goes missing around town that's a spot the police always check first."

"Who owns the place?"

"No one. I think they're squatting. But the last few months it's been different. I mean, usually kids go there and party for a few days and then get sick of a diet of beer and ice cream and go back home to Mommy and Daddy."

"But now they're staying."

"Yeah," she frowned. "I've been meaning to check it out, but it's a little outside our purview."

"It's way outside our purview."

"*Anyway,*" she stressed, running her nails through her hair. "I wouldn't even be calling but... well, Nick was there with her. He's back, don't worry. I think he was a little freaked out by the whole experience. It was their first date."

"Your group dates within each other?"

"You think yours won't?"

"There's only one female, as of yet."

"That'll make it interesting then. Nick was telling me about the place, and it's pretty much what you'd expect from that sort of teen-dive crack-den sort of place... at least for Atlanta. But there's this new guy there, and they all seem to follow him. I think he's the reason they all stay there now."

"Drunken teens have found their Mecca," he snorted, rubbing the bridge of his nose. "Will wonders never cease."

Tash was silent on the other end of the phone for a long moment. He couldn't even hear her breath.

"Tasha?"

"The guy's name is Gavin. I haven't been able to find anything on him, but one of the girls said something about him to Nick... She said he'd been dead once."

Victor turned and checked the door again, the line of light coming through it bisecting his face down the middle. He was silent but for the clicking of his tongue against the roof of his mouth, which had suddenly gone very, very dry.

"Victor?"

"I'll be there as quick as I can," he said hoarsely, then hung up the phone and slid it back into his pocket.

She took the phone away from her ear and watched as the screen went dark. There was a picture of him driving in the background, a small smirk working its way into the corner of his mouth as he looked at her side-on in the passenger seat, one eye still trained on the road. She sighed, listening as Iseult and Nick started their way down the stairs.

Victor sat in the chair in front of his desk. It was small with comfortable cushions patterned to look like leaves and a bamboo back. He rested his elbows on his knees and clutched at his hair with both his fingers, the light from outside still slicing him right down the middle.

CHAPTER 08

Los Angeles, California

Leigh sat on the floor, leaned against her bed, crying. She coughed in between sobs, clutching at her chest. The anxiety of going to work last night had already been enough to kill her, never mind what was actually making her sick.

She pulled herself up from the floor using the edge of the bed, still shaking profusely. Her hair was skewed and mussed from running her fingers through it. Now, more than ever, she felt like a monster.

Stealing from her own boss was bad enough. It wasn't that she felt remorse over the fact that she had stolen important files, but that she was terrified what would happen to her if he found out. She wasn't screwed in a warm and fuzzy, federal prison kind of way. She was screwed in a might-as-well-be-dead kind of way.

What she had had to do was worse than stealing though.

She had a rule: no injuring the people around you, and she had done just that. And that she had injured Wendell, of all people, put the cherry on top of her guilt sundae. He had three kids and a wife. She just hoped that Shane would pay for his medical expenses. It wasn't exactly like the group health plan had been much help to her.

She pulled a tissue from the box on her dresser and wiped away the mascara running down her face.

Washington, DC

Kat sat with her back aligned perfectly on her chair and her wrists resting comfortably on their own individual foam divots on either side of her keyboard. It was an ergonomic setup that she'd looked up with her doctor after multiple visits regarding a nagging, constant pain that started in the middle of her back and shot up to the base of her skull sometimes after working for only a few hours.

In truth she'd suffered from the pain for almost a full year before finally going to her doctor. The real reason she'd gone had been Suzy Weir.

Though there were no assigned seats at McMillan Accounting, there were more seats than people. As a result, everyone ended up sitting in the same seat everyday... except Susy Weir. Susy Weir was a floater and a self-proclaimed "social butterfly" that flitted back and forth between desks, sometimes even changing seats in the middle of a shift as the mood struck her. She was also an incurable morning person, often arriving before everyone else and claiming her spot.

Three times she's chosen Kat's seat.

The first time Kat ignored it. The second she asked her not to do it again. The third time she'd gone to her doctor and gotten the seat ergonomically assigned to her. She was now the only accountant-level employee at McMillan Accounting with an assigned seat, and that was just how she liked it. She could auto-pilot to and from her chair and back home again without ever really paying attention to anything or anyone.

But the pain had been real.

It had started years ago as a sudden pull toward her centre of mass. It was like her shoulder-blades had been trying to dive into the small of her back and turn her inside out. The spasm had lasted almost a full ten minutes and left her a wreck on her bedroom floor for nearly an hour afterward.

It had never been that bad again, but it had happened again. At first it was infrequent, then slowly becoming a biweekly if not weekly event - then one day she woke up with it after a long sleep and had gone to work like it, suffering through it the entire day... and then the next... and the next... until the pain had become something that she just lived with.

No one at work thought it was real; just a way of protecting herself against Switch-Seat Susy.

Even her doctor had thought it was a ploy with an eventual endgame of disability, finding no medical justification for the pain she described.

But it was real, and even now it throbbed up her spine and arched out along her shoulders, making them burn with agony.

She switched to the third page of accounts payable for the file she was working on, and for a moment all the numbers on it started to blend together into a whirlpool of digital mush that made no sense at all. She sighed and leaned forward, rubbing her fingers against the bridge of her nose.

When she opened her eyes she was staring past the screen at a framed picture on her desk. The girl in the photo was twenty and looked the typical Irish, her heritage obvious the second someone saw her red hair and bright green eyes.

The picture smiled at her with all its teeth, its cheeks beaming with sun-kissed freckles.

Kat turned away from it and started adding up the long row of numbers along the right hand side of the screen.

This isn't what you want to do, the picture said. The leaves behind the girl in it were so clear and defined that they looked like they should have been turning with the rest this time of year.

Kat stared forward and continued adding the numbers together. She was fairly certain that the final total did not make mathematical sense, but moved on to the next page anyway.

From across the hall, Suzy Weir looked at her and smiled.

Outside Payson, Arizona

Abby slowed her decent down the stairs as she neared the bottom of them, her hand running along the rust-coloured wall for support. She stopped at the fifth from the bottom, her mouth open slightly and waiting for her brain to wake up and provide her with something to say.

Victor stood in the hall clasping a rugged bookbag across his chest. It was old and worn and the faded green colour of army fatigues, and he went about the process of clasping them together with the methodical exactness of someone who had done the same task millions of times. His face was drawn down and expressionless, devoid of all emotion and metallic.

"You're leaving?" Abby asked.

He looked up as though only now noticing her, his eyes sallow and dark beneath his bangs. He nodded.

She closed her mouth, stood and watched him for a moment, then folded her arms across her chest.

When he finished tightening the strap he looked up at her again. "I'm coming back."

She nodded. "Why are you going?"

"I have to look after some things. Things that need looking after."

She stopped, then nodded again.

He turned and opened the door, then looked back at her. His face was half-covered by the door and she couldn't see his eye through the mess of his hair. "I am coming back."

She nodded again, and he left.

Atlanta, Georgia

Kirby Romerez had been living in the house off New Gower Road for almost six months.

He was from Texas and had lived there all his life. His father had been an investment banker until a sudden heart-attack had killed him when he was forty and Kirby had been only eight, and his mother sold real estate.

Five years ago Kirby had come into the ownership of a property in Fort Worth. It was an office building that had been built in the sixties and served as storage space for the government for nearly a decade before being passed on to Kirby. It was purchased in nearly-condemnable condition and soon after was declared condemned. But that had been fine, it hadn't been the building itself that Kirby had been interested in, it had been the large parking lot out front. Businessmen and workers in the area used the parking lot frequently, and Kirby had wasted no time in charging drivers for that service.

He also rented the vacant space on the far end of the parking lot.

For the past five years every February 14th a flower company called *Jessica's Roses* had setup in that vacant area and sold flowers out of the back of their company van, paying close to a thousand dollars for that right each and every year. Every year Kirby received his check without trouble or complaint and was happy to get it.

This year, however, had been different.

This year had brought into Kirby's life a man named Roland Montgomery.

Roland was a stay-at-home Dad to his two children, Clea and Denise. His wife was a nurse for the local children's hospital and often helped with local church events. This Valentine's Day, to make some extra cash, Roland had ordered flowers online and arranged them into bouquets of roses, irises, and posies to sell to the patrons of the office park. He'd brought his daughters and wife along to help. They set up shop no more than ten feet from *Jes-*

sica's Roses and sold their own bouquets, of which they had only twenty, for ten dollars apiece.

Jessica called Kirby, furious that Roland would be taking some measure of her business.

Kirby called the police.

The police came, examined the situation, and informed Roland that once he'd finished selling his bouquets he would have to leave.

Jessica called Kirby.

Kirby called the police.

The police did not respond.

Jessica called Kirby.

Kirby called the police.

The police did not respond.

Jessica called Kirby.

Kirby got in his car and drove down to the lot. There had been an elderly man at Roland's car buying a bouquet of roses for his wife, who was smiling happily just to one side. It was the type of smile only an elderly woman can have, after a lifetime of marriage to a man that still bought her roses on a whim.

"You can't be here," Kirby said, stepping up to Roland's car.

"Yes I can," Roland smiled, shrugging his shoulders and arranging a posy that had fallen from its place.

"This is private property. Leave."

"No."

"If you do not leave, I will call the police."

"Go ahead."

Kirby called the police.

The police did not respond.

Kirby walked up to Roland's van again. Roland was standing in front of it, handing an assortment of flowers to a teenage boy who paid his fee in nickels and dimes. "Get off of my property, now."

Roland smiled and turned to get another basket. "The police said I can stay until I finish selling my flowers."

Kirby drew his gun and fired it.

The bullet narrowly passed over Roland's head.

Roland's wife screamed.

Roland ducked to the ground.

Kirby lowered the gun until it was aimed directly at Roland's chest. "Get off my property."

Roland left the property and immediately called the police.

The police responded.

Kirby was arrested, and after sixty days of trials and legal battling, was released on time served with a fine of five thousand dollars.

He'd left Fort Worth the next day, and a week later had ended up in Atlanta. Three days after that he found himself on New Gower Road, and he'd rarely been off it since.

Now he puffed on a cigarette while a cold beer rested between his legs. He wore only his briefs from the waist down, and the condensation from the bottle felt good against his bare skin.

A girl named Janice sat next to him. One half of her hair was strawberry blonde and the other half was deep black. There were bits of cocaine clinging to the hairs on her upper lip, and he leaned forward and kissed her just so that he could sniff some of them off her as he did.

Gavin stepped up to the bedroom door and pressed his hands to either side of it, bracing himself on it as he leaned forward into the room. He was shirtless, and his skin was pale. It looked like new bristle-board, like the type Roland had made his sign out of with his children. The sign had read *Montflowery*. Kirby remembered it suddenly, as though it had come from nowhere.

There was a scar on Gavin's chest. It was small and circular and right in between his breasts. There was something dark in its middle, as though whatever had made the wound was still hidden, just below the surface.

"The girls want more eggs. Can you run to the market and get some?" Gavin asked, cocking his head at Kirby and smiling.

Kirby stuck out his lower lip and nodded.

Gavin took a large wad of cash out of his back pocket and counted out thirty dollars, handed it to him, then turned and smiled at Janice.

Janice blushed.

"Anything else you wanted?" Kirby asked, feeling the soft warmth of the money between his fingers.

Gavin squinted. "There's a store that sells ammunition down by the market, right?"

Kirby nodded.

Gavin clucked his tongue against the roof of his mouth. "Yes, just the eggs."

He left.

Kirby and Janice did three more lines each before they left for the market.

Outside Payson, Arizona

Abby massaged a pat of butter into the black grease spots on her hands, her skin becoming covered in an inky film that shone prettily in the light coming from the vanity. She took a sheet of paper towel and rubbed away the blackness, her skin smooth and pale underneath. She dropped the soiled paper towel in the trashcan beside her, then placed a hand under the soap pump. Two squirts. She turned the water on and lathered up the sweet scented soap.

The steam from the water rose up and coated the mirror, Abby's naked reflection becoming hazy in the glass. The soap swirled in the washbasin, slinking off like smoke in the water. She flicked the water droplets off her hands into the basin, deft fingers moving to end the flow from the tap.

She brought her hands to a plush cream towel, gently patting them dry. Her grease-filled clothes were in a small bundle on the floor, which she scooped up and deposited in a laundry bag. She slid her arms into a turquoise silk dressing gown, cinching it around her waist and accentuating her hourglass figure. The hair she had pinned up to avoid getting in her face while working on the car now fell around her shoulders in grand auburn curls.

She tiptoed out of the bathroom and toward Victor's study. Crammed from floor to ceiling with books and carvings and artifacts, it was Abby's favorite room in the house. She pushed open the solid oak door and slipped inside, her warm bare feet leaving their ghostly impressions on the floor.

Her fingers traced the spines of books, gently grazing over the gold embossing on the hardcovers. She had walked halfway around the room before she stopped at a book that caught her attention. No name graced the worn brown spine that she gently coaxed from where it was wedged in between *The Ancient Mediterranean World* and a book about Afro-Brazilian Art. The book lay flat in her hands as she made her way to the plush window seat Victor had constructed to overlook the ravine outside.

She sat down gingerly, her robe riding up and revealing her long legs. She crossed them and opened the leather bound tome. She felt a jolt as she recognized Victor's scratchy script scrawled across the page. He had written, as far as she could decipher, "Details of Nguni Tribal Life" along the middle of the first page. Eyebrow cocked, she flipped through the pages. Every so often, sketches and pressed flowers caught her eye, but toward the middle, a photograph was wedged into the binding of the book, and it stopped her casual flicking through.

A younger Victor was pictured leaning over a small wooden crate along with a thin, pretty woman with strong cheekbones and tanned skin. Her short blue-black hair was held back with a dirty-looking yellow bandana. They were both smiling up at the photographer, eyes twinkling. Victor had a mischievous look to him that Abby was not used to seeing, as if the years had built a shell of seriousness. She flipped the photograph over. In an unfamiliar pen, someone had written "Tash and Victor at a Nguni village".

Abby's brow drew together, and she flipped the book back to the beginning.

CHAPTER 09

Outside Payson, Arizona

Chad sat on the pavement of the basketball court with his back and head rested against the pole. The ground was damp and soaked into the bottom of his jeans, making his flesh clammy and moist. His mouth was open and he was working of blade of grass around its rim with his tongue, leaning back and looking up at Victor's house.

There were shutters along the upper windows that were barely noticeable unless you focussed on them for some time, stained the same redbrick colour that the rest of the house was. The three windows that lined the top floor all had them, two open and one shut. The sunlight glinted off the half-rusted heads of nails that had been used to keep the shutter held to; each one of them shone like stars in a crimson night sky.

Abby was standing just within his peripheral vision. She was wearing the grey tank top he'd seen her wear a few mornings on lazy days... days when she didn't do much except watch Comedy Central and stay in her pajama bottoms all day. She wasn't wearing pajamas with them now though, she was wearing tight jeans with metal clasps going up each side with little bits of leather hanging stringily from each one. She was holding her arms as though she was cold. He didn't know how long she had been standing there.

He looked at her straight on for a moment, that one strand of her auburn hair that always seemed out of place billowing in the slight fall breeze. He remembered the first time he'd ever seen her. He'd been crying alone in his house for hours and had thrown up, but she'd run right to him... her fingers had been light and fluttering over his hair and had sent tingling jolts through his scalp.

She folded her arms and frowned, turning her head and looking up at the shutters that lined the top floor of the house.

"The place looks different when he's gone," he said finally, shifting his focus back toward the house.

"He's coming back you know," she said, walking over to him until their feet almost touched. She was blocking his view of the house now and he had to crane his head up to see her. She looked as though she could have taken the whole world in her hands, sunk her nails in, and crushed it. The sun was behind her and caught her hair, making a picture of her that looked like the one's he'd found in his mother's photo album while cleaning out the attic.

"Yeah, I know," he said, getting up with a grunt. The gravel over the pavement slid under his jeans and made that horrible crunching noise that made his teeth grind.

She looked at him with her eyebrows raised.

"I know," he said again, with emphasis.

"He said he had to go take care of some things."

"Probably off looking for another..." he trailed off.

"Another what?"

"Another of us. Whatever we are, whatever you want to call us. Another one of us."

He made his way over to the other side of the court and propped his foot up on the picnic table, leaning forward on his knee. He was staring at the house again, at the emptiness of it. All the windows were dark and the less-than-perfect aspects of it seemed to dominate now... he could see all the nails that stuck out and the foundation that wasn't quite right and the spot where the gutters were so clogged that they were overflowing.

She stepped up close to him again until she was just behind him, like they were doing some strange interpretive dance. She moved close, he moved away. She moved close, he moved away. Close, away. Close, away.

She looked past him at the house, the way the sun caught off the metal fasteners that went all the way across the roof and gave it a heavenly glow. The window in the back door was sectioned off into four quadrants and looked just like the window that had been on her grandmother's door, the type you could usually only have in close-knit communities. Anywhere else it would be an invitation to simply smash through the pane and unlock the deadbolt. It spoke miles to the comfort of the place, and she was convinced that even in harder places it still wouldn't get assaulted. Nobody would want to break into a place that looked like their grandmother's house.

"What're we doing here, Abby?" he asked without turning around.

She opened her mouth to answer, let it hang for a moment, then shut it again.

He turned around to face her, and his eyes were a strange mix of anger and sorrow and nothing. "He brought us all out here, and for what? To build motorcycles? To bake cookies? I had a life, and it won't just wait for me. If I fuck off too long, it'll just be gone. No second chances. And he just packs up and leaves."

"You miss Koy," she said softly.

His shoulders dropped a little, as though the air had been let out of him. "I do."

She nodded, then reached up and touched her palm to the side of his face.

"Don't you wonder?"

"I do," she smiled, so big her cheeks popped. "I really do. But I get the feeling that this is important, and important things can't be rushed."

He snorted. "That something you learned in finishing school?"

"That's something I learned dating a server."

He smiled at her, and the tension slowly began to seep out of his shoulders. When he met her eyes again she was looking past him. He turned to see Theo and Jaycee navigating the winding pathway of flat stone steps that led from the back porch to the basketball court. Jaycee was barefoot again, the thick toes on either of his feet clasping at the stones like fingers as he tried to land on each one along the way. He looked like a small child skipping down a trail, and it made Chad smile.

"The hermits return," Chad said, slapping Theo's hand when he came close enough. He tried it with Jaycee too, but missed and ended up bumping his pinky against the rough skin of Jaycee's pointer finger. "I didn't think you guys ever came outside."

"Hardy har," Theo said, waving his head mockingly.

"Saw you in the window," Jaycee said, motioning back up toward the house. "Looked like maybe you could use some time away from the grounds."

Chad shot Theo a look. "You been poking around?"

Theo raised his hands defensively, then panto-mimed an x over his left breast. "Cross my heart."

Chad looked from he to Jaycee and then back again. "What'd you have in mind?"

"There's a movie marathon over at the Odeon today," Jaycee offered enthusiastically.

"No thanks," Chad smirked. "Not in the mood for that level of escapism. At least not yet. Talk to me if I stay like this for more than a week."

"Drinks?" Theo offered. "It's early, but I found this great little place right on the edge of town... this guy in the mall had no bad thoughts about it at all. You can get any mix drink for a fin, no matter how many shots are in it."

"Not really in a drinking mood either."

"Well what do you want to do then?" Abby asked, giving him a little shove.

Chad smiled.

CHAPTER 10

New York City, Then

Jona knelt down on the floor of The Pasta Palace, *a restaurant that had been a part of McElheny Square for nearly six decades. Booths protected him from all sides but he skill shook, a thin gloss of sweat covering his hairless lead.*

Jona was a oculocutaneous albino, his skin a tattered grey colour that always made him look tired and worn around the edges. His knuckles and elbows were especially dark and arid, always looking dirty and unkempt. His lips were large and his brow sloped downward, bathing the eyes beneath them in a veil of constant shadow.

He wore a necklace around his neck with prayer beads on it, capped with a charm that had two pieces of curved metal encapsulating a round metal marble.

His hands shook as he slid the parchment paper out of the manilla folder he'd carried under the crook of his arm and let it fall down onto the tiled floor gracefully.

The pages were worn around the edges and cracked in the corners, bending it toward the centre after only a few minutes in the open air. His eyes fluttered over them, reading the poem line by line over and over again.

> *Who but we two, e'er dear*
> *would arise the latter ladder*
> *ne'r pause, ne'r eating words*
> *'till the morning after?*

> *Two such sweet in prim and folly*
> *dance until the days end*
> *ne'r dreaming, n'er worry*
> *what the crime of youth may lend?*

> *Two bloods one, together linger*
> *till escaping from thine womb*
> *ne'r rising heaven's ladder*
> *mortal man, you've gone so soon?*

He clicked his tongue against the roof of his mouth for a moment, feeling the metal ball that pierced it scrape along the edge of his teeth. He reached deep into the pocket of his blazer and pulled out a pocket knife. He extended the blade and the plunged it into the meat of his left thumb, turning it clockwise and then counter clockwise until there was a small circular hole in the pad of it.

Licking his lips, he brought it forward and smeared it along the margin of the parchment.

At first nothing happened.

After a moment a slow smile spread across his face, so wide that it showed off his canines all the way up to their gums.

The letters changed, moving slowly from one position to another as though animated by some unseen force until finally neither was in the position they started in.

"Yes," he smiled, holding up the parchment again. He

cleared his throat and started to read:

> omo rit ir ne'l bommy dos
> pri n'er tw blo ne yolf caned
> pin noose nam ven hea's thaw houty
> geher ase ne'r ords orning

> Ok'Tid weet may'd ream
> der g've sing lad crme yorr
> ne'r ri das end til unthe thew morf fo
> e'er dea owo ewtub how tow

> reddal rettal het douwl illtheer
> ne'r weause pating 'taft
> illtheer ner ding till escag os eno uyo romtal
> enith regnil landsin hows tuc

He waited, closing his eyes and tilting his head up toward the black, black ceiling.

After a moment he frowned, then looked back down at the page. The letters remained in their confused, nonsense state as he scanned down over them again, making sure there was nothing he had missed.

"Hey!" came a voice from behind him.

Jona turned quickly and stood, rising to his full height of over six feet.

The security guard pointed at him accusingly. "You're not supposed to be in here!"

Jona smiled.

CHAPTER 11

Payson, Arizona

"Cover him!" Wedu screamed, dancing back and forth in front of Theo and Sammy with his arms spread wide. The ball was caught between their feet with both of their hands on it, hovering between them an inch off the ground. Their hands had it almost completely enveloped, so that the ribbed orange surface was only clearly visible through their fingers and scuffling legs. "Cover him!"

"You fucking cover him!" Sammy bellowed back, his cheeks shaking as he tried to get a better grip on the ball.

Wedu turned and saw Chad coming up behind him. He pushed him against the chest with an open palm, sending his back a full foot into the chain link fence and then pointed at him as if to say *keep your distance*.

Chad glared at him ruefully. He was wearing a grin he couldn't suppress, the type of thin line that cut across his jaw from one ear to the other. There was blood on it that had smattered down from his nose after Sammy had elbowed him. Some of it had dried and turned black.

Jaycee kept his large feet firmly planted on the pavement across from Wedu, making the same back and forth motion with the upper half of his body. He looked like a cobra swaying back and forth and waiting for an opportunity to strike, those yellow tinted eyes examining the shuffle of hands and feet as they jostled around the basketball. When he moved down he moved further than Wedu thought he should have been able to, as though there were ball joints in his ankles. It was hypnotic, and he found it hard to look away.

"Get it out!" Chad yelled, clapping his hands in encouragement. "Come on, you can do it!"

Theo shot him a look, sweat pouring down his face and dripping off his nose as Sammy's husky form loomed over him. He was sweating too, and every few seconds Theo felt what he was sure was a large glob of the man's perspiration drip from his hairy armpit and splash onto the back of his neck.

Jaycee reached in quickly, rolling the ball forward with the arch of his massive palm and then pushing down. It released from both men's grasp and bounded off the ground toward him where he caught it continued it into a frantic dribble around the other side of them.

Wedu stepped into his path, the large man looming like an eclipse.

Jaycee bounced back a pace, the ball bouncing with him. "Sunrise Nevermind!" he yelled, leaning back on the balls of his bare feet and hopping as high as he could before letting the ball go. It arched across the air over Wedu's head and slammed into the brick wall above the net before falling through it.

Wedu watched it, then turned and raised an eyebrow

at Jaycee. "The fuck was that?"

"I dunno," he shrugged, wiping the sweat from his brow.

Wedu smiled, giving him a friendly punch to the shoulder.

"That was awesome," Fabian said between pants, leaning forward onto his knees as Theo and Sammy passed the ball back and forth again. "Little freak's got game."

Chad shoved him hard, then grabbed him by the collar of his wifebeater and pulled him back again. "Don't ever call him a freak," he said through his teeth so that Jaycee couldn't hear. He shoved him again, letting him go. "I'm sure you wouldn't appreciate it if we started calling you Air Spic."

Fabian rubbed his chest for a moment, then nodded. "Alright. Point."

They both turned back to the game.

Theo threw the ball to Jaycee again but it was caught by Sammy and passed back to Fabian. Fabian laughed, palming it for a moment before making his way to the opposite side of the court. He was trying to dribble but was carrying it most of the time, not that any one of them would have pointed it out. With every minute that passed the rules seemed to matter less and less, until the only rule that mattered was getting the ball into the basket.

Chad ran up behind Fabian and checked him into the brick wall, digging his elbow deep into his ribs. Fabian barked, bringing both his hands back to push him away but catching his nose with his biceps again and bringing fresh blood.

Chad laughed loudly.

Theo grabbed the ball and turned around swiftly, then jumped quickly to the right as though he'd known that Wedu was about to step in front of him and block him. He pulled back, lined his eye up with the ball, and threw it.

It bounded off the rim and made it vibrate, then fell to the ground.

"Damn it!" he yelled, punching the air.

"Free ball!" Sammy snickered, grabbing it while it was still bouncing from Theo's botched shot. He turned and fired it almost without looking and it went in, forcing the net to one side and seeming to get caught in it for a moment until gravity took hold again and brought it back down to earth.

Chad walked slowly to the underside of the basket and picked up the ball, turning to face Wedu from across the three point line. "That ties it up again," he said, tossing the ball at him.

Wedu smiled. "How's your face?" he asked, motioning toward his own with a circular gesture. "If you want we could stop so you can get some gauze or something."

Sammy laughed, so did Fabian.

Wedu tossed Chad back the ball.

Chad wiped the blood from his face and looked at it. It almost covered the palm of his hand, all except for the ring finger. He smiled and slapped it against the ball, leaving his palm print there, the red almost invisible against the orange. "Let's do this," he said, tossing the ball to Jaycee.

Jaycee threw it at Theo hard but Theo caught it, the impact leaving his palms stinging red. Sammy was behind him again and reaching for the ball. He almost didn't need to feel it, he could tell from the stench. He turned and connected his elbow with the man's cheek and they both went into the chain link fence, sending the ball up into the air.

Payson, Arizona

Chad held the bottle of water high above his head and let the crystal-clear spring water rain down on him. It sparkled in the sun on its way down and seemed to fall in slow motion until it made impact, some of it splashing up into his eyes and hair and some of it going into his mouth. He didn't care which, but he drank down any that found its way into him ravenously.

It washed the blood from his upper lip and sent it streaming down his neck it diluted pink trails that stained the collar of his shirt.

"That was epic," he gasped. He passed the bottle to Jaycee, who took it quickly and brought it to his lips. "Did you see that last basket? I mean, Swish! Right in there. Didn't think it was ever going to come down."

Jaycee nodded as he drank, his adam's apple bobbing up and down his throat.

"And the guy," Theo laughed, pointing at Chad with tears running down his cheeks. "The guy with the bald head grabs you and he's like... like... *That's what we call Chinatown!*" he laughed again, burying his head in his hands. When he spoke it was in a much deeper voice, and he boxed his arms to demonstrate the size of the man. "What does that even mean? Oh, man."

Jaycee passed Theo the bottle, and Theo tossed the water from it full force into his face.

They were sitting on the curb outside William's Convenience with the sun on their backs. Cars went by a few feet in front of them and barely noticed that they were there, but they were. The heat coming off them could be felt by anyone that came within a few meters of them.

"Ten - six," Chad said, licking his salty lips as he watched the water bottle slosh back and forth in Theo's hand. "I cannot remember the last time I lost that bad... you guys must really suck."

Theo laughed.

Jaycee nudged him in the arm.

Chad nudged him back. After a moment the bottle came back to him and he took from it gratefully until it was gone.

Jaycee took the empty bottle and turned around, looking at the large metal trash can bolted to the wall of the store from over his shoulder. He tossed the bottle back over his head and it sailed through the air, almost got caught by a stray gust of wind, then finally landed against something soft and moist inside the depths of the garbage bag.

He turned around to the others, and they all started laughing.

CHAPTER 12

American Airlines, Flight 782

Lawrence Dyer was a drunk.

He'd had his first drink when he was seventeen. It had been a rum and coke made with that type of spiced rum that always made him shiver from head to toe, especially when he was taking a shot of it. He'd always been bad with the ladies and had known it... all through senior high the only time any girl had kissed him had been Nancy King, and that had only been once. And she'd been *fat*. But after only five Cuba Libre's he'd managed to get Daisy Stoller (the Homecoming Queen) into the sack at a party. He didn't remember how he'd done it or even the event itself, but he'd wasted no time in rolling over and repeating the event, hangover or no hangover.

After that he'd been with more than one Homecoming Queen, and always with the help of his good friend Jack. They'd been inseparable most of the way through college and even for the first few years of his career as a restaurant manager, but then he'd gotten married to Dolores.

And Dolores was *fat*.

He'd woken up next to her after a bad tear through all the bars on Smith Street. It had been the night of the annual Freshman pub crawl, and he'd hoped to slide into some sweet little ex-Homecoming Queen. But instead he'd gotten Dolores, and Dolores had gotten pregnant. Even before that, nobody would have ever confused her for a Queen - except, maybe, a drag queen.

They'd gotten married, and he'd been drunk out of his mind then too. He remembered the day well. He'd promised her that he'd stay off the Cuba Libre's and had for most of the evening, drinking tequila shooters instead - Dolores hadn't said anything about those. He'd had five before the ceremony (if you looked close in their wedding picture, you could see the straw of one of the glasses sticking up from behind the confessional) and another eight at the reception, and that's when he'd noticed Michelle.

Michelle was Dolores's cousin and one of the bridesmaids. She had still been dressed in the gaudy pink puff that Dolores had picked out for them all to wear. That was the secret of the bridesmaid dress, you know. They made all the other girls look ridiculous to distract from how hideous the bride might be. The dress had been strapless and held up with a wire frame that stuck out too far in front of Michelle's bosom. There was sparkling oil across her cleavage that caught the light from the disco ball, and he caught himself thinking about the jeans she'd been wearing the night before. They'd been tight, and had made her bottom look like an upside-down heart. She caught him leering at her once and shifted uncomfortably in that sea of fabric, sipping on her juice.

Michelle had never been Homecoming Queen either.

For one thing she wasn't yet old enough, but for another everyone else on her side of the family was just *fat*. He thought maybe that made her think she was fat, which is why she kept herself so thin. He thought maybe all girls should grow up thinking they're fat, just so they never forget to keep the fat off. She could have been Homecoming Queen if not for that, though.

He'd switched to Cuba Libre's after his thirteenth tequila shooter.

He'd fucked her an hour later in the coat room while everyone else was doing the chicken dance. He hadn't been able to see it for all that pink fluff, but he'd still found it. He recalled, sometimes in the dead of night, the way he'd bent down the wire frame of the dress to expose those perfect, sparkling breasts. They'd just been a handful each and the nipples were as pink as the dress and they'd always been pointing up, not like Dolores's. Dolores's were weighed down with *fat*.

Michelle had gotten pregnant too, and that was when Dolores had said it was time to give up the booze for good. She'd said that it had brought him nothing but trouble (she wouldn't have said so if she'd been in the coat room) and that it was time to give it up and be a man. By the time their son had turned one, she'd had him enrolled in a program.

And it had worked for a while.

He'd gone to meetings every Tuesday and every second Thursday. He'd collected chips and spoken and shared and scaled the steps until he was at the twelfth one and he'd felt good about himself doing it. He found that he didn't need the booze like he thought he would have. He could come home after a hard day's work and have some blueberry juice while watching the evening news with Dolores. He could play with Daniel and have fun and be at ease without ever being buzzed out of his mind.

But as it turned out, he'd been in the wrong program.

Because Cuba Libre's had never been his problem.

Three months ago he'd been at a company picnic with everyone from his department. Everyone had brought their families, and Dolores was watching Daniel at the bouncy castle while he ate sausage dogs and smiled through with teeth at the thinly-veiled vaguely-PC jokes that were being slung about at the expense at any visible minority not within earshot. There had been lots of girls there, but there had been only one like her.

She was the CEO's daughter, all of twenty-two with long brunette hair and the sort of pink-lipped smile that went from ear to ear. She had big brown eyes that seemed innocent enough but scanned the crowd between giggles as she sipped on her martini. He knew that scan, had done it himself enough times, and it lingered on him more than once. They'd become caught in each others's gaze only once, but it had felt like they'd held it forever.

He'd opened his mouth to speak but found it very dry. After three attempted conversations, he made his way to the open bar and ordered himself a Jack and Coke.

He had four while making his way from the bar to the barbeque, making sure that each time she did one of her martini-swilling scans of the room he was always within her field of vision. When he'd gone back to the bar the fifth time she'd joined him, and shared a Cuba Libre with him instead of her martini.

They'd found a spot in the handicapped washroom that was open enough for him to lay her on the floor. She seemed as though she'd known the way by heart. He'd taken off her panties and slung them over his shoulder, accidentally landing in the toilet and clogging it when the next person came in and flushed without looking. He'd fucked her with her black dress parting to either side of him as she pressed her palms against the towel dispenser for support, biting her lip so hard to stop from screaming that she broke the skin.

He'd driven home plastered out of his mind with his son singing nonsense songs in the back seat, and Dolores hadn't even noticed.

Since then he'd taken two Friday's off work and gone downtown, and both times he'd paid equal parts in cash for rum and for cheap motels.

Now he was on his way to Atlanta to visit his brother (who'd never married and only had interest in drinking whiskey). While he'd been waiting in the airport lounge he'd seen a sweet little blonde number with eyes like Anne Hathaway and had had a few Cuba Libre's with his pork sandwich. Now he was approaching twenty thousand feet, approaching his fifth Cuba Libre, and approaching out-and-out polluted. He hadn't spoken to the girl at the lounge, but there was a flight attendant walking back and forth and making sure that everyone was buckled in. She had a nice smile but she was *fat*, but by the time he finished that fifth Cuba Libre he didn't think he'd mind. She was walking back to the front of the plane right now to get some old biddy behind him a pillow, and as he watched her go a smile spread slowly over his sugar-coated lips.

"Not bad at all," he said, elbowing the man next to him gently and gesturing in her direction.

Victor turned and met the man's eye without emotion. He held the gaze until Lawrence became uncomfortable and cleared his throat, then turned back toward the front of the plane. Lawrence lifted the heavy tumbler glass they'd given him and said: "Cheers" before swallowing the last dollop.

He placed the glass back down on the little tray table that he'd folded down from the seat in front of him, letting both his palms rest upon it as though he were praying. After a moment he started to puff air out from his mouth in rapid rhythmic succession, then began to strum his fingers along the edge of the glass. The ring on his left hand made a steady clang every time it hit, moving the golden band up to the knuckle and then back down to its base with a clang.

Victor looked up once and watched the ring slide up and down again, then turned back to his magazine.

Lawrence leaned out into the hall to see if the flight attendant was on her way back yet. She was not. He'd already named her Nancy in his head. Nancy King. He'd ask her name and she'd tell him and he'd say he thought she looked like a Nancy. He'd known a girl once named Nancy. She was just gorgeous, you remind me of her. It would serve not only as an ice breaker and compliment, but a fine excuse to call her Nancy while he was sticking it to her in an Atlanta motel room and not have her kick him out of bed for it.

She was still behind the curtain, but he thought he saw her shoes sticking out from underneath it.

He turned back to Victor and leaned forward a bit to see the cover of the magazine he was reading.

"Rising through Recession: the top ten businesses on the grow in America," he read aloud, clucking his tongue against the roof of his mouth when he was done. He grinned stupidly at Victor again. "You in business?"

"I'm in a business," he replied, turning the page.

Lawrence snorted. "Yeah, I hear you there."

Victor continued reading.

"My restaurant's been on the outs a bit lately. Big guy upstairs doesn't have much time for me, but I say it can't all be the recession. I mean, there's not a recession everywhere, right? People think there is but there isn't. I think the companies in that little book are the ones that don't make up silly little excuses to explain away why it is they suck so bad."

Victor turned the page again. There was a large spread shot showing a high-rise building in Los Angeles and the blue sky behind it.

Lawrence leaned in closer and lowered his voice. "So you can't tell me you're on a business meeting and you're not planning on having a little fun. I've got one of those President's Club memberships. The Boss lets us use his whenever we're away, forgot to give it back last time... Could use a good wingman here in -"

Victor closed his magazine and laid it on his lap, then reached up and pressed the call button above their heads.

The curtain that the attendant had disappeared behind opened almost instantly and she came out smiling from ear to ear, carrying the pillow for the woman behind

Lawrence under one arm. She marched down to their row, her elbows bent at ninety-degree angles and swinging as though she were on parade. She handed the woman the pillow and bent down to smile at Victor, unintentionally exposing her cleavage to Lawrence at the same time. A small chain with a golden clam charm at the end dangled in front of his nose. "Yes sir, what can I do to help you?" she said, it her pleasant-but-rehearsed tone.

"Yes," Victor smiled. "Would you like to have sex with this man?"

Lawrence turned and stared at him wide-eyed, his face suddenly becoming pale.

"Excuse me?" the attendant said, both her smile and pleasant tone disappearing instantly.

"Well he's been drinking in excess trying to muster up enough nerve to engage you, and I thought I'd save us all some time. He's married with at least one child, but don't worry about that. He doesn't. The ring comes off so much it can barely stay on his finger."

She turned to Lawrence and looked him up and down. Though she tried to hide it with the same plastic smile she used on all her patrons, she still visibly sneered at him for a moment. When she stood back from him a pace she pulled up the front of her shirt to hide her breasts. After a moments pause she smiled, laughed, and met Lawrence's eye with a practised tone. "I don't drink anyway."

Victor turned from her to Lawrence, and a small smile perked at the corners of his lips as well. It was hard to tell, with all the scruff lining the sides of his face, but it was there.

"That's okay," he said. "He doesn't either. He's been

in a program... haven't you?"

Lawrence looked at Victor again. He tapped his finger against his upper lip but said nothing, just held the man's eye. After a moment he turned back to the attendant and smiled nervously, leaning forward onto his armrest. "I think I'd like to switch seats."

She nodded once and held out her arm. "Right this way sir."

Victor smiled and opened his magazine again, scanning to find where he'd left off before continuing.

When the attendant passed by again he stopped her. She smiled at him. After a moment's examination of her he smiled as well.

"Was there something else, sir?"

"A cold water, whenever you get a chance."

"Certainly," she beamed, then turned and walked back toward the curtained area.

He had his water within a minute.

He took a long sip, smiled, then read his article.

CHAPTER 13

Los Angeles, California

Leigh sank to the floor, paper cup pinched between her lips as she attempted to open the pill bottle in her hand without spilling her water. She was shaking with the effort to twist open the childproof cap. The label read Apoxasine-Prophylactic 250mg. She finally succeeded, flinging the cap across the floor. Still shaking, she poured two capsules into her palm and laid the bottle on the floor next to her. She took the cup of water in her other hand and quickly popped the pills into her mouth and took a swig of water. Almost immediately, her shaking slowed and then finally ceased. She let out the gasp of air she hadn't known she was keeping in.

She stayed on the floor for a moment with her eyes closed. She opened them slowly, bringing her gaze across the flesh of her hands. Her ashen complexion seemed to be inkier than normal. She flexed her fingers, trying to increase the flow of blood to the tips.

She stood slowly, leaning against the wall for support. She had made the mistake last time of standing immediately after taking the medication, a mistake that had resulted in her fainting. She had remained on the floor, unconscious for the better part of the afternoon that day, missing an important meeting she was supposed to have with Arthur. He had sent over his personal staff to collect her when she hadn't arrived, and it had resulted in another trip to the private clinic, more medication and more monitoring. She couldn't afford to miss work again today, no matter how sick or frightened she was.

Fully upright, she moved toward her bedroom closet. From it she drew a black Jackie O-type dress, high neck, clean lines. She paired it with a red jacket, high boots and red lipstick. Her look alone was often intimidating enough to get her what she wanted at her job. At the same time, her work style was so distinct from how she dressed when she was out and about that it also served as a disguise.

She was barely aware of her movement as she moved out of her room, dressed, to the bathroom. She combed her hair, sprayed a light mist of hair spray over it, and combed again. She was starting to feel – and look – sharper.

Leigh exhaled and adjusted her posture, smoothing her dress over her thighs as she did so. She coldly met her own gaze in the mirror, her ashen skin like porcelain. The way she hardened was shocking, even to her. Her daily routine turned her into another person.

Some days she hated the girl in the mirror.

Leigh ducked out of the apartment and headed for the elevator, a slim briefcase in hand. She walked at a brisk pace, heels clicking on the tiled floor. She reached the elevator quickly, her slim finger extending to the down button just as the doors opened. Her heart skipped a beat and she stepped back, anticipating the occupants to exit. Instead she was greeted by Arthur and two assistants.

"Leigh darling, the meeting has been moved to the jet this morning. Thought we'd pick you up," he said, extending a hand to her.

She delicately placed hers in his and entered the elevator, the doors sliding shut behind her. This, she reminded herself, was exactly why she put up a cool front everyday. Her life depended on it.

Atlanta, Georgia

Kelly was on her hands and knees in the loft.

Once again the humidity was almost unbearable. She took deep breaths through her mouth that seemed thick with moisture and heat, so much so that she never felt like she got any air at all.

She was naked again and Gavin was behind her. He was naked, too. That paper-white skin of his seemed to glow in the dark of the attic, his dark brown hair blending in with the darkened moist boards above. There was sweat holding it to his head like a cap and rolling down his face, dripping from his pointed chin onto his chest. When he'd taken off his shirt she'd seen that pattern of small, parallel scars that lined the ribs on his right side again, but hadn't said anything about it. Before she had really known what was happening he'd been inside, and now they were caught in the same back and forth rocking motion. Back and forth. Back, and forth. Both of them bending forward at the knees until she winced, then sliding back to a comfortable place before repeating the process again.

There was a splinter of wood sticking into her left palm, but she barely noticed it. Her teeth were clenched and she wanted to close her eyes, but the door to stairs was directly in front of her and she worried every time she shut them that someone would venture up.

She'd been in the living room talking to Quinn about if she'd thought about staying. She'd brought her out a bowl of porridge and they'd sat down across from each other on the couch comfortably. Charlotte had been sitting against the windowsill puffing on a cigarette and ignoring them both.

"I don't know," Quinn had sorted. "I could see it. It's definitely more fun than where I'm staying now."

"What about that guy? The guy you came with."

"Nick?" she'd laughed. "He's great, he really is... I mean really." She'd taken a sip of her juice. When she spoke again her tone had been more serious. "Actually, I asked him out."

"Didn't seem that way."

The smile left Quinn's face, and she seemed to fixate on a small blotch of ink on one of the couch cushions. "Well, you know how it is."

Gavin had come up behind Kelly then. He'd spoken for a minute about the party the night before, and then about the next few weeks, and then he leaned over and kissed her. One of his hands had laced its fingers around her own, while the other tilted her head up until their mouths touched. When the embrace ended he'd kept her by the hand and led her upstairs.

He'd kissed her against the wall, with the boards

against her back so soft she thought she'd go through as though they were cardboard. He'd taken off her shirt and let it fall into the stairwell. She could see the strap of it now, just inside her field of vision, dangling atop the first step.

He reached out and stroked the back of her head, letting her long golden hair travel smoothly through his fingers. It sent shivers down her spine that he could see in the candlelight, and he smiled.

She winced again, the smallest sound making its way from her throat.

"Shh," he said, his voice a hushed whisper as he ran his hand through her hair again. "It's okay, Princess."

Finally, she closed her eyes. It was the first words he'd spoken to her that day.

When he finished he let out a loud, mournful moan and clutched her by the hips, digging his thumbs in so hard that they left bruises. He fell onto her from the effort, their clammy flesh smacking together before her knees finally gave and they both toppled onto the floor side by side.

He smiled open-mouthed and happy as he gasped for air, laughing pleasantly to himself and playing with her hair.

She was turned away from him, her arms bent back under her head in leu of a pillow as she stared off into the darkness.

"Someday it will always be like this, you know," he said, staring up into the ceiling as though he could see the sky beyond it. "Nothing but pleasure and happiness and sensation. It can happen, I've seen it before... it felt like I lived that way for a long time. It's the way it was intended."

Kelly didn't say anything.

"There's a busyness to this country that I've never understood. Marx saw it, I think, and tried to change it... and look where it got him. Now people use Marxism as though its some sort of acceptable pejorative, but I don't think it is. I think that's something that's made up in our society. A term they've vilified to put down anyone who comes at them with social reform even though they freely admit that they need change to turn this around. History has never cared for social reform."

He turned toward her and smiled, his eyes travelling over her backside. Her hair fell across her shoulder blades as though it had been painted there, the thickness and uniformity of it amazing to him. He rolled over and placed an arm around her, kissing her tiny shoulder. His penis was limp and mushy against her back.

"Am I boring you?" he chuckled.

She turned her head so she could see him. "No..." she said, trailing off. She tried not to laugh. "It's just not... the kind of talk I'm used to... after."

"Sorry," he laughed, kissing his way down her arm tenderly. "Being with you gets me thinking. It makes me think."

Her mouth was small in the centre of her face, and she was just looking at him.

He turned back to her. "Being with you makes me think about the future."

She smiled, and he leaned in and kissed her again. His lips were salty with sweat but she found she didn't mind.

His hands were on her face suddenly, cupping it and stroking the trail of her cheekbones with his thumbs as he broke off the kiss and stared at her. *Into* her. "You are a princess," he said, his voice almost a whisper.

They kissed again. When he was done she rolled back over, and this time he stayed with her, their bodies clasped together like clammy spoons. He stroked her hair, watching how each strand was a slightly different shade from the last.

"Will you go to the store later and pick me up some oranges?" he asked after a few minutes, his lips tickling the supple skin on her back as he spoke.

"Sure," she replied, her tone high.

"And some nails, too. The long ones, what are the called? Annular nails. And paper, we're going to need lots of paper."

"What for?"

He kissed her shoulder again. "Thomas had the idea that we should build a shed out back. Maybe some bunks for when things get crowded, but mainly to store things."

"No, the paper."

He smiled. She couldn't see it, but she could feel his cheeks move against the base of her neck. "We're going to have to write it down."

CHAPTER 14

Atlanta, Georgia

"We hope you enjoyed your flight, and have a nice day," the flight attendant said, nodding politely to an old Indian woman as she walked by. The woman nodded back but did not smile. She was sweating profusely and clutching the handle of her carry-on so tight that her knuckles almost poked through the skin. Her pinky finger twitched every few steps, becoming straight and then snapping back into place again.

Victor squinted as the digit fell out of order again, then quickly snapped back. She didn't seem to be aware it was happening, and once as she'd entered the tarmac it had almost resulted in her dropping her bag. When she'd looked though, the finger had been perfectly in line with the others again.

"We hope you enjoyed your flight, and have a nice day," the flight attendant said again, smiling that pleasant but fake smile at the twenty-something boy that passed her. He had a tee-shirt on that said Yale, but he didn't look the type to have gone to Yale. Didn't look the type to have gone to anything post-secondary. Victor scanned the crowd and found a sweet young girl with well kept long hair that was eyeing the boy and smiling, though he hadn't noticed her yet.

He smiled, then stepped over the threshold separating the tunnel from the rest of the airport. He locked eyes with the flight attendant.

She did not speak, but there was a slight smile at the corners of her mouth and she nodded to him.

He chuckled a little, then nodded back as he stepped past her.

"Jesus, what did you do to piss her off?"

He turned around and found Tash standing behind him, her book bag slung over one shoulder. She looked at him from between her bangs, parted to one side and yet still falling into her face in thin little fingers. One even reached out and touched the tip of her nose. She smiled at him when their eyes met.

Nick sat behind her and stood up when Victor stepped closer. His eyes went all the way down Victor and then back up again until finally he smiled nervously.

"Absolutely nothing, I assure you," Victor smiled, stepping up until they were only a foot apart. "All I did was tell her the truth."

"Okay, sure," she laughed.

Victor leaned forward, then took a step back again. She took a small step forward to match, their eyes never unlocking. There was a moment when no one in the airport seemed to breathe, like all of the air had been sucked out of the room.

He raised his arms and stepped forward again and she

put out her hand to shake his. He stopped, stepped back again, then cleared his throat. She laughed, then stepped forward and put her arms around him.

"It's good to see you again," she smiled, her cheeks warm against the nape of his neck.

"You too," he whispered, squeezing her once and then letting her go.

She stepped back and he cleared his throat again, then turned to Nick and smiled. "You must be Nick," he said with confidence, extending his hand.

Nick took it and pumped it once. It felt enormous compared to his, as though he had the hands of a child. "Yes, sir," he said, his eyes bulging.

Victor laughed. "No need for that. Believe me, I'm the last person in the world you should be calling sir."

Nick nodded. "Yes, sir."

Victor smiled. He squinted, turning his head slightly. He was still clasping Nick's hand within his own, watching as the boy's eyes met his, then darted to one side quickly, searched the airport for something else to focus on, then came back to him again and started the process all over. His eyes were a pale metallic blue that meshed in with the cold walls of the airport and made them seem sunken.

"You're from Coral Beach, yes?"

"Yes si - - Yes."

"Hn," Victor hummed. He gave the boy one more pump with his arm and then let him go. He turned back to Tash and smiled. "Where did you park?"

Los Angeles, California

"I understand your prescription hasn't been working as well lately, Leigh?"

Leigh sat across from a middle-aged blonde woman with a notepad and pen. Arthur had flown Doctor Strachan in from a conference specifically for this visit, something Leigh was quite nervous about. Strachan was Arthur's personal physician and the top consultant for Shane's research team. The same research team that did a full workup each week in order to monitor and assess Leigh's condition. The same research team that only called Doctor Strachan if there were exceptional changes noted in their testing.

"I guess you could say that," Leigh said. "It's been a bit rough lately. My anxiety is definitely spiking, and I'm feeling tired more often."

"That's understandable given our test results. The latest dosage doesn't seem to be working as well as we hoped to stabilize your molecular structure. Apoxasine was initially intended to stabilize mothers while their unborn children were receiving in vitro genetic treatment, and while we've made some impressive strides these past months in modifying the treatment to suit your condition… it's just not the cure we were hoping for. We'll need you to continue to take the medication for now, but this really isn't going to be much help. It's just a bandage until we find a permanent fix."

Leigh felt the air leave her lungs. She glanced over at Arthur, who was sitting the next aisle over with pursed lips and hands folded together. "How much time do we have to slow this down?"

Doctor Strachan sighed. "Conservatively? Really only a few months. This is full blown. Whatever degradation is occurring in your molecular pattern, it's occurring far faster than we anticipated, and Apoxasine isn't buying us the time we expected it would. My advice would be to get your affairs in order in case we can't come up with a viable solution to this."

After the meeting, Leigh followed Arthur to the car almost blindly. She had known it was bad, but she figured it would be years before it got to a point where her own body would choke the air out of her. The realization left her hollow.

A man from the security team opened the door for them and Leigh slunk into the car. She lounged against the back seat, and as the door closed and the car moved forward, Arthur handed her a glass of whisky.

"Leigh, you know you've got the full support of the team behind you. We will figure this out in time. If you want, I'll let you take a leave for however long you like, just to de-stress and regroup. We'll find you a cure and then you can come back to work refreshed."

Leigh sipped at her drink and nodded, then took a deep breath and seemed to regain her composure. "For now, I just want things to stay normal. We'll tackle the founder's gala tonight, and revisit me taking a leave later."

Arthur raised his own glass in a toast. "Always a trooper, Leigh. I'll be glad to have you there."

Atlanta, Georgia

"King high takes it," Billy said, tapping the river twice and grinning. He had a toothpick clenched between his teeth that he flipped occasionally, letting the moist end dry until it felt sharp again and then switching.

He was sitting cross-legged on the floor across from Dennis, his back against the bare mattress he used for a bed. There was no blanket on it, just a pillow without a cover and a rumpled old sheet that had been thrown into one corner. Judy was on his right and Quinn was on his left, both girls sitting on their hips with their hair bathing one shoulder. Together they formed a circle, with the matted carpet between them understood as actually being the smooth felt of a poker table.

He pulled in the cigarettes they were using as chips, straightening them until they formed a nice little line in front of his crossed legs. They looked like pure white logs rolling down a river in unison. There was one unfiltered rollie in the middle that messed up the uniformity of the line and he looked at it, snarled, then glared at Dennis.

"What?" Dennis asked as he gathered up the cards. He shuffled them twice, then handed the pack over to Judy.

Billy did not respond. He shook his head and plucked the cigarette furthest from him out of the line with his thumb and forefinger and brought it to his lips, letting the toothpick fall onto the crotch of his pants when he did.

Quinn watched him as he lit the smoke, the way the blue flame of the torch shone on his face. He took two puffs, let the flame die, and then exhaled right in her face.

She didn't cough.

He smiled at her, then looked down at the stack of only four smokes she had next to her leg. "Good thing we're not playing strip," he grinned. "You'd be almost down to your socks."

She laughed. "I think the socks are the first to go."

"Not the way I play it."

Judy rolled her eyes and began to deal, starting with Billy and working her way around until they each had two cards. He hadn't taken his eyes off of Quinn the entire time the cards were being dealt, and now he picked them up (eyes still locked with hers). He glanced at them briefly, then laid them back onto the floor. He picked up one of his cigarettes and tossed it into the centre of the group.

Quinn put in two.

"I fold," Dennis grumbled, bringing his knees up to his chin and hugging into them. "Fucking bullshit cards."

"In," said Judy, putting in two of her own.

Billy puffed on his cigarette, still staring at Quinn through a soft haze of smoke. His gaze travelled down over her slender frame. She was wearing one of his tee shirts, a white one that never seemed to look clean with an impressionist fist coming up from the bottom and stopping just between her breasts. It was loose on her, only showing hints of her figure.

He looked down at his smokes and took the two normal ones and the rollie from his lineup and tossed them onto the carpet. "Raise two."

Quinn stared at them for a moment and let out a one-note laugh. They sat there like twigs, each one leaned against the other in no particular order with bits of nicotine sticking out of their tips. She turned from them to Billy and then back again, biting her lip.

"I fold," Judy frowned, slapping her cards down face-up. She's had a king of hearts and a two of clubs.

"Out of turn," Billy snarled, but did not take his eyes off Quinn.

"Fine then, when my turn comes around, pretend I folded then."

"It messes with the game."

"I don't see how."

"Then you're an idiot," he breathed. He watched as the exposed flesh of Quinn's neck rose and fell with every breath she took. It looked smooth and soft, and suddenly his mouth had filled with saliva.

She leaned in a little toward him, opening her mouth so that he could see the soft pink of her tongue. "I fold," she said slowly, then tossed her cards face down on the deck.

Billy scoffed, then laughed heartily as he pulled all the cigarettes he'd thrown away back in, along with the four Quinn and Judy had provided.

Dennis laughed.

She got up and brushed some dust off her calf, letting the two smokes that had been rested against her leg roll until they hit her in the foot.

"Where're you going?" he asked, craning his head to follow her up.

"Bathroom," she said, stepping over Dennis. "That allowed?"

He grinned at her. "Still gotta put in your blind."

She smiled over her shoulder at him as she left. He

couldn't see her mouth, but he could tell she was smiling from the way her cheeks pressed up against her eye.
"Then I guess it's a good thing we're not playing strip."

He smiled.

Quinn closed the bathroom cabinet, the mirror on its
front staring back at her with her own dark green eyes.
The soap she'd found was clenched in her right hand. It
was dried and cracked in the centre, with deep arid gouges that went all the way through it. Its edges were still
moist though, still soft and pliable from its last use.

In her other hand was a bottle of ibuprofen.

She popped the red cap off the bottle with her thumb
and spilled some long gray pills out into the soap dish.
Each one clinked and clacked as though they were made
of metal until they found their place and finally came to
rest. Sighing, she laid the open bottle on the opposite side
of the sink and stared at them.

The sink was a hodgepodge of different shades of
white, from the glimmering porcelain that was meant to
be to an eggshell right down to a grummy grayish-brown
of water stains. It was even more apparent with the pills
on it, their pure, solid colour a stark contrast to its spotted
mess. The tap was filthy too, with water spots and toothpaste stains in some places and gaping cancerous holes of
rust in others. There was one so large it looked like someone had given the faucet a tracheotomy.

She looked at herself again, her eyes bloodshot, taking a pill between her fingers and pushing it past her lips.
Then another. Then finally, a third. She scooped the rest

back into the bottle and then started the faucet. Despite the state of it, clean-looking, sparkling water spewed out, circled the drain, then was whisked back down the pipes. She watched it a moment to make sure it wouldn't suddenly change colour, then pulled her hair back and stuck her mouth under the stream.

She slurped back liquid until she was sure all three pills were gone, then stood back up.

Gavin stared at her from inside the mirror.

She yelped, jumped, and turned around quickly. He was shirtless and his belt was undone, and there were only inches between them even though the small of her back was pressed against the sink. She felt her heart slam inside her chest suddenly, and the headache that had been building in the neck and skull ever since she woke up suddenly became much, much worse.

He was staring at her, his narrow face devoid of emotion and his mouth tied up in a bow beneath his nose. She'd never noticed until now how pale he was. The flesh of his body was as white as cream paper, with only the barest of tone to it. It shone in the dim light of the bathroom, as though the only light in the room were coming from him. He was hairless and pure and white, even his nipple lacking pigment. The only flaw was a scar, a tiny, uneven x-shaped patch of pure white skin just to the right of his left breast.

She tried to back up but couldn't.

He leaned in slightly and his nostrils flared, then relaxed, and he smiled. "Sorry, I didn't mean to scare you."

He reached around her and she jumped again, shifting to give him a wide berth as he opened the cabinet and grabbed a fat, bulging tube of toothpaste.

She breathed a sigh of relief, though her heart still pounded. There was a tingling in her fingers and toes as though they'd gone to sleep. It got stronger and stronger until it was almost like needles poking their way into her pores.

"You didn't," she lied. "Just didn't get much sleep last night."

He watched her through the mirror as he started to brush his teeth, the foam bubbling out through his lips and dripping down into the sink in giant cottony clumps. She watched him, wanting to leave but unable to tear her eyes away from his. It wasn't like with Billy. Everything in her eyes tried to turn away and walk away, but she couldn't. Not until he broke contact first.

"I'm glad you're here, Quinn," he said, after spitting out a mouthful of paste. He stared at her again, focussing on her cheeks... the way they rounded out her face. There were faint traces of blood blisters far beneath the surface that gave her colour, and the more he looked at them the more they seemed to come out. Like a Magic Eye picture. "Your being here makes it right. It makes me think that everything's going to be just fine."

She was able to look away finally, but instead of turning she shifted her gaze from his reflection to her own. She seemed dwarfed by him, his head taking up almost all of the frame while her entire body seemed to squeeze into the narrow space that was left. If his head had been any larger, she might not have existed at all.

She looked at her cheeks and liked them, suddenly. She'd spent years trying to cover them up with foundation and blush, but now she saw them the way he did: each tiny red dot representing life itself, like stars all huddled together and awaiting their own Big Bang.

"What does that mean?" she asked finally, her voice so far away she barely heard it herself. She'd never spoken so softly in her life. She'd never felt the need to until now.

He smiled, then turned from her reflection to actually face her. He took her by the shoulders gently and stroked the edges of the fabric with his thumbs as he examined the shirt Billy had leant her. "The fist is for strength, rebellion," he said, his smile showing off his rounded teeth. "It suits you. You should never speak softly to me, Quinn. *That* does not suit you."

The tingle in her fingers was fading now, replaced by a warm feeling in her chest.

He smiled, then turned and picked up his toothbrush again.

She stepped out of the bathroom and started to walk away.

"Kelly needs a friend like you, Quinn," he said, not looking up to see if she was still there to listen.

She stopped, looking at him over her shoulder.

"Someone strong. Someone who won't let her let me walk all over her, if I try. She likes you, I think. Likes the way you act and think... so instead of hiding that strength behind a whisper, try spreading it around some. See what happens."

She squinted at him, then walked away. Her headache was gone, but she didn't think it had been the pills.

CHAPTER 15

Outside Payson, Arizona

Chad stepped out of the kitchen with a glass of orange juice in his hand. The hall was warm and there were large droplets of condensation on the outside of the glass that tumbled down over his knuckles, making stripes of moisture that glistened in the light from the hall. He'd gone in as soon as he'd gotten back from the city and had made a straight line for the fridge, but when he'd gotten there all of the Strawberry-Banana had been gone. He'd frowned, tapped his fingers against the fridge door for a moment, and had finally chosen orange juice. He drank a full glass, filled it again, then started pacing around the room and sipping on it.

The hall from the kitchen was long and on a slight curve, steep enough that you could never walk straight or see what was a few feet in front of you, but slight enough that he often thought that it was all in his mind. It made him feel drunk sometimes, like maybe Theo had made Screwdrivers in the Tropicana carton and not told anyone.

There were doors along the inward arch that lead back into the main rooms of the house as well as closets and a half bathroom or two, but for the most part there were at least two ways to enter and exit every room in the house. Once, just after he'd moved in, he'd gotten lost trying to find the stairs to his room. It was only by sheer luck that he'd found them.

He turned the corner and found Abby sitting on a petite couch with oak edges outside Victor's study. She was sitting cross-legged with a scrapbook in her lap, several pasted-in pictures and newspaper clippings staring back at her on a light pink background. A posy had been squat between the pages and had dried there, a brittle husk of what it had once been.

Her hair was down in front of her, tickling either side of her chest. She looked quiet and studious, calmly moving from one article to the next, her eyes darting quickly over the column. Her cheeks puffed out again and again, the air forming its own beat that only she could follow.

She looked beautiful.

He swallowed hard, a mouthful of juice almost going down the wrong way.

"Hey," he said shakily.

She looked up from the album at him, not shocked at all by his sudden appearance even though she hadn't known he was there. "Hey," she replied. "Did you have fun at your basketball game?"

"Yeah," he smiled. "We lost."

She scrunched up her nose at him and laughed. "That doesn't sound very fun."

"It was the way we did it."

She laughed again, then turned back to her book.

He watched her as she read, shifting from foot to foot. He held his glass in both his hands against the centre of his chest. The condensation from the glass and the sweat from his palms made the glass slip and slide so much that he thought he might drop it. After a moment he brought it to his lips and took another sip, although it seemed to do nothing to make his throat less dry.

He took a step forward. "What are you looking at?"

"Some pictures I found," she said, without looking up from them this time. "I think these are of Victor."

He stepped closer again until he was looking over her shoulder. The smell that came off of her was amazing, like lilies and virgin snow. He laid his drink down and leaned in as close as he dared, and suddenly his mouth wasn't dry at all anymore.

There was a picture of Victor standing in front of a large fighter jet. He was wearing a checkered red shirt and jeans and he was smiling so wide that she barely recognized him. His hair was pulled back in a ponytail and looked short, though it may well have been the same length it was now. His cheeks were high and scorched with sunburn.

The woman from Victor's other pictures was there again too. She had more visible freckles in this one and was dressed in a black tee and jeans that looked like they'd never had a crease in them. A leather jacket that couldn't possibly have been hers was slung over her right shoulder, and she was smiling sweetly into the camera.

"He looks so young," Chad said, reaching out and touching its edge.

Abby smiled at him. "I think he looks like you."

He turned to her. He hadn't realized how close they had gotten. Their cheeks were practically pressed against each other.

She smiled, then turned the picture over. "It was only printed two years ago."

"Can't be right. Must have been digital."

"Mm," she hummed, turning it back and looking at their faces again. "They're both happy. *Really* happy."

"I know. I almost didn't recognize him."

She snorted and poked him in the ribs. "Be nice. Seriously, they look like those pictures you see in newspapers... where the people work really hard to get something amazing done, and then the Mayor comes down for the grand opening and everyone's wearing these plastic smiles except them, because they're *really* happy about what's happening."

He turned from the picture to her again, the scent of her filling him.

She moved the picture aside. There was another behind it of just the jet. The word freedom had been stencilled across it in black calligraphy. She flipped back to the original, and saw that when Victor's head had been in the way, the only part of the word that had been visible had been *Free*.

"You know, I was actually coming in here to ask you something anyway," he said finally, watching as he saw the gears within her move. He loved watching her think. There was something incredible about it that he didn't think he would ever truly understand.

"Yeah? What's that?"

"I don't know. You seem pretty into this."

She turned to him and gave him an amused look, then shifted her posture so that she was facing him. "Better?"

He smiled. "No, I mean, if you weren't busy I was going to see if maybe you wanted to go out for dinner."

"Dinner?"

"Yeah. I'll pay."

Her eyebrows raised slightly, a smirk growing at one corner of her mouth.

"We just spend so much time as a group. I haven't really had a chance to sit down with you since Utah."

"We went on that laundry run together."

He laughed. "And while that was fun, I thought it might be nice to take you out. Wherever you want to go, whatever you want to get."

Her eyes lit up a little at that, her head tilting a little from side to side as she weighed the pros and cons.

The door behind her opened and Jaycee came in. He saw the two of them on the couch together and stopped in his tracks. "Sorry. Not interrupting anything, am I?"

"Ha," Abby said dryly, closing the scrapbook. "No."

Chad frowned.

"Actually, boy-o here was just talking about how he'd like some one-on-one time. Think he's still a little down in the dumps."

Chad looked from Abby to Jaycee and then back again. "No, really. It's not that."

"He seemed fine before," Jaycee said, stepping in and closing the door.

"Yeah, but apparently the group scene isn't his thing. I guess he didn't have many friends back in Utah."

"Can't say I blame him."

She smiled at him. "I was going to try and cheer him up, but did you want to go?"

Chad sighed, ran his hand through his hair, then turned to her and smiled. "You're not hungry?"

"Like you said, I've got this," she motioned back to the book. "Besides, three's a crowd."

He laughed at her, then turned back to Jaycee. "What do you think of Italian?"

Jaycee grinned. "Let me put on a better shirt."

"Dress nice, big guy. I'm paying." He turned back to Abby when he was in the doorway and smiled at her. "Some other time."

She scrunched her nose at him. "We'll see."

She watched them go, then opened the scrapbook again, shaking her head.

CHAPTER 16

Atlanta, Georgia

Victor sipped tea from his cup, holding its slender handle gently between his thumb and forefinger. Small droplets of the sweet liquid remained caught in the blonde scruff of his mustache and he tapped them away, lowering the teacup to its saucer and then lowering them both back to the table.

He turned the saucer on its side, examining the intricate pattern. There was a violet on either side, painted in serene hues with its three major bulbs in the centre and two others swirling around it like ions surrounding an atom, their pencil-thin stems marking the trail they followed. Bright green leaves came out from its peak and from its right side, glistening with dew drops that he had no idea how the painter had made look so real. There was a similar pattern inside the cup, but with only one bulb. Its colours were muted now for the liquid in it, but they still looked sweet and vibrant and alive, as though the tea really did have violet in it. He picked up the cup and brought it to his lips again, taking a small careful sip. He could almost taste it.

Tash came in from the bedroom with a plate of crackers and laid them down between their two saucers, rotating it until the two leaves pointed at their respective seats. He smiled at her as she sat down, unravelled her serviette and placed it on her lap. She spent a moment smoothing out its creases before she picked up her tea and took a sip.

She smiled herself, letting the gray wafts of steam bathe over her face. "Do you like it?" she asked, watching him from over the rim of her cup.

He nodded honestly. "It's wonderful. Orange pekoe?"

She nodded.

He took another sip. "There's something else though."

She smiled. Only the corners of it were visible over her cup. "Rose hips and lavendar. For tranquillity."

He bobbed his eyebrows, then took another sip and put the cup back down. It looked dainty and minuscule next to his massive hands, and he felt as though he might break it every time he picked it up by one of his gold-rimmed handles.

The top two buttons of his shirt were undone, and when he stretched back to see the room it opened to reveal more of his chest.

The tearoom was a thing of beauty. Her room was on the top floor of the house and had, previously, opened up to a flat roof that most people would have used for a garden or a place to lounge in the sun. Tash had built a greenhouse there. It was round, made of clear glass panes that went all the way around, separated only by the wooden frame that kept it all together. It came up to an open point at the top, which she'd covered in long, dry palm leaves. All around the base were violets and irises, their purples and greens smiling at him warmly. Sunlight glistened in and was trapped in the thick, moist air of the room and seemed to hang in the air forever. It was always summer here.

There was a short walkway separating her bedroom from the tearoom. She could see into it now from over his shoulder. Her queen bed was there, the curtains around it pulled open on all sides. It was made perfectly, its burgundy sheets and blankets tucked in on all sides and undisturbed.

He smiled. "I love what you've done here," he said finally. "It's amazing. It's like - -"

"A home?" she finished, smiling as she laid down her cup. She held it with both hands along the rim, ignoring the handle altogether.

He paused and looked at her. Her hair was damp with the humidity of the place, clinging to the soft curve of her scalp. "Heaven, I was going to say. But home will do."

She hummed happily.

He raised the cup again. "The China is beautiful."

"Thank you."

He squinted at her. "Nine eighty-seven?"

"Nine ninety-eight."

He turned over the saucer and found a golden oval there, with the words CHINA - 998 stamped in its centre. "Exquisite."

She smiled.

He took another sip, exposing the entirety of the violet within the cup from its brown liquid prison, then laid it down and leaned forward, surrounding it with his massive arms. "The kid seems nice," he said, motioning over his shoulder slightly. "Jumpy, maybe. He's not very sure of himself."

She grinned. "Is that a bad thing?"

"He's not sure of his place here. Of his place anywhere. *That's* a bad thing." He sighed, lowered his head, then looked back at her again. "I set out to inspire these people, Tasha. And I don't think I am."

"You're having a crisis."

"I'm living a crisis. I'm trying to stop it. And now we have this new fucker, this - -"

"Gavin."

"This *Gavin*, and they just follow him. And I find myself wondering what he would do about it."

She smiled. "I think you're over-thinking things."

He stopped, then nodded. "Maybe. Maybe we deal with this, get the girl back, and then maybe we can get a chance to rest... build some community here. Because before you know it, it'll be too late."

She nodded, taking a sip of her tea.

He lifted his glass, stopped, then looked over his shoulder again. "What can the kid do, anyway?"

"The kid has a name."

"I'm never going to bother learning it."

She rolled her eyes. "*Nick* has extrasensory ocular input."

He turned back to her, almost laughing. "X-Ray vision?"

"No," she said, dragging out the oh sound for effect. "I've done some brief examinations on him with the limited equipment that I have, and he seems to have more cones and rods in his eyes than he should. A lot more, and most of them look different than ours. I haven't been able to test it, but I think they wire back to a different part of the brain, too."

He raised his eyebrows, nodding respectfully. "To what end?"

"It's hard for even him to describe. I think he's had it since birth. But he can process visual information much faster than most people... probably faster than anything alive. He takes in everything, and it makes it seem as though his reflexes are faster... but they aren't."

"He just sees what's happening before we do, so he can react faster," he said softly, as though a light had gone on in his head.

"Yes. Exactly."

"What about the other, the girl. Iseult?"

"That name you remember, but you forget Nick?"

"It's unique."

Her eyes widened. "She can mediate blood flow. Control it, to a degree. I've seen her use it to heal people. She's smart, too. I think she could be a great surgeon someday."

"She's fifteen."

"I said someday."

"A fifteen year old does not have the capability of being smart."

She looked at him coldly for a moment, laying down her cup. "Noted."

He smiled at her. "I was kidding."

"No, you weren't."

He shrugged. "And the other... Quinn?"

Tash frowned, taking a sip of her tea.

"Tasha?"

"She's... we call it puppeteering. She can... animate the dead. Briefly."

Victor laid down his cup. When he spoke again his voice was deep and far away. "Excuse me?"

"It's like she can control the corpses for a time, make them talk or walk or do whatever she wants. But it doesn't last very long. They have to be fairly recently dead... no more than a few days."

"A few days?"

"A week at most."

"Nuh," he sighed, burying his head in his hands. He got up from the table and walked around, coming to one of the dew-covered windows. He stared out it, the grass beyond it becoming an undefinable mush through its distortion. He brought his finger up slowly, tracing a lower-case i in the condensation and then rubbing it out. He turned back to her suddenly, the damp ends of his hair whipping around him and spraying her. "How could you keep this from me? She's a level three."

"She's not, believe me. If you met her, you'd know."

He stared at her a moment, then let his posture relax. "You're not hiding anything."

"I never do. Not from you, anyway."

He sighed. "I would have preferred to have known."

She tilted her head at him, her lips pursing together. "And what about Abby Fisher?"

He looked at her from between the strands of his hair, then turned away again. "I don't know what you mean."

"You know exactly what I mean. Kinetic Disruption... but only when she's around someone as they die? I think I was owed a secret after that one. Tit for tat."

"How did you?"

"I have her file from PHI. Hunter brought it to me."

Victor grunted, deep in his throat.

"You should have brought her to me right away."

"She's over majority. That means she's one of mine."

"I could have been running tests. I should be figuring out how she's linked into all of - -"

Victor cut Tash off before she could finish the sentence. "Leave Abby out of this," he said, in a soft but authoritative voice.

Tash looked as though she were about to respond, then smiled softly and took another sip of her tea with both hands again. She motioned for him to sit back down and he turned back toward the window for a moment, then walked over and sat down. He picked up his tea and took a sip. It was starting to get cold now, but it was still good. It hummed in his mouth, tickling at his tongue on the way down.

"I'm sorry," he said finally.

"You don't need to be," she said. "Not ever."

He nodded. "The rest of my team you know about. Chad with the probability control, Theo the telepath."

"How's that going, by the way?"

"Good."

"And Maximus?"

Victor paused. "*Jaycee* is adjusting very well. He misses his girlfriend, I think, but other than that he's fine. Not much power there, but the others are taking to him. Nobody seems to be judging him."

"Nor should they."

"I know. But people do."

She nodded.

He looked around at the greenhouse again. The spot where he'd written on the wall was already invisible, covered in with vapour until it was the same pale shade of gray as everything else. He took a deep breath, the warm scent of violet going into him and draining the tension out of his shoulders. "You must come here all the time," he smiled, finishing his drink. "It's so relaxing."

She giggled and touched her nose to try and hide it.

"What?" he smiled.

"This is the first time I've entertained here."

He tilted his head, squinting at her.

"Come now, Victor," she smirked, raising her cup again. "The China, the flowers, the tea... I crave my elegance, but these aren't the things I love. These aren't the songs that sooth my savage beast."

He paused, tilting the empty teacup toward him. There was still a small drop travelling around its edge. He looked back to her.

She smiled, finishing off her own cup as well. "More?"

He stared into space for a moment, then nodded.

CHAPTER 17

Payson, Arizona

Jaycee laughed, so hard that warm soda almost came out of his nostrils. He brought his hand up to cover it, still chuckling in that dry half-silent way he always did, like he was choking rather than laughing.

"And then," Chad says, annunciating his words by bobbing his fork before him like a sword, "She says: You wouldn't have. It's a school."

Jaycee laughed again, lurching forward against the table with his eyes pressed closed and watering. "She didn't say that?"

"Hand to God," Chad chuckled, holding up his right hand for effect. He dug his fork down into his penne pasta and shovelled a large glob of it into his mouth. Out of the corner of his eye he saw a couple at the next table over staring at them. He turned to them and smiled, wiggling his fingers. They turned away quickly.

"Oh man, I wish I could have been there," Jaycee said, leaning back on his chair.

"Wasn't quite so funny at the time."

Jaycee raised an eyebrow at him.

"Okay it was, but I wasn't really in a position to laugh."

He laughed.

Chad took another helping of pasta and chicken into his mouth, the rich white sauce dripping off it back onto his plate. He pushed himself up off his chair to see over the desert menu between them and into Jaycee's side of the table. "You want another beer?"

Jaycee tilted his empty glass for a moment, licked his lips, then nodded. "Sure."

Chad nodded and motioned to the waitress.

She saw them from a few tables over and nodded.

He swallowed, then motioned to Jaycee. "What about you? You must have some stories."

"Oh yeah. Remember that time I got lynched? That was fun."

Chad laughed. "I'm serious. Guy doesn't grow up looking like you without learning to play the dozens."

Jaycee looked back at his glass for a moment, watching the way the light reflected off of it.

Chad's smile wilted slightly. "No offense."

He smiled. "None taken."

Chad watched him for a moment, then went back to his chicken penne.

Jaycee smiled and leaned in, resting his elbows on the table. "There was this one time during a pep rally..."

Washington, DC

The space between Kat's tenth and eleventh beers was

always a magical one.

She found it was just the right amount of alcohol, if she drank them quickly enough and had just the right amount of grease in her diet that day. It wasn't an exact science, and she was always working on perfecting it. Either way she was sipping on her eleventh beer now and her mind was afloat in brownish foamy liquid that made the back spasms and the memories and the hate wash away until all that was left was the warm fuzzy feeling that ebbed its way up from her toes and surrounded her like a blanket.

She walked dopily through her apartment, her shoulder hitting off one wall and then the other until finally making her way to the bathroom. She started to brush her teeth. The ceiling fan was overpowering here, making it impossible to hear anything else.

There was laughter in the other room.

It was light and bubbly, like someone lost in something truly hilarious without a care or thought in the world to anything else. The smile on the person's face was almost visible just from the sound of it. That kind of laugh could only come from lips turned up just so.

There was a clock on the wall of the bathroom that was broken, its hand twitching at the six after mark over and over again.

Kat put down her toothbrush and ventured out into the other room, the laughter getting louder and louder the closer she got.

When she reached the end of the hall there was nobody there.

Her reflection looked back at her in the dark of the television screen, a shadow-version of herself.

She went back into the bathroom and washed her hands, but no matter how much she did she could not get them clean.

New York City, Then

Victor pushed three chairs out of his way and let them fall to the floor with a loud cambering clang. They spread out in all directions as he pressed his face up against the window to Prewer Discount Travel, cupping his hands to protect against even the minimal light of the hallway. He growled, then kicked another chair aside and did the same a few feet down.

"Hey!" Tash yelled, her cheeks flushed and breathless as she jogged up beside him. She turned to the mess of chairs that now blocked the hallway. "That's nice. I'm sure that won't cause anyone any trouble."

"He's got to still be here," Victor grumbled, moving on to the newspaper office and peering inside.

Tash raised one thin eyebrow. "Why is that?"

"Because he's here!" Victor spat, turning toward her. He softened immediately. "He wouldn't want to wait. He never wants to wait. He'd have to get it done, right here and right now."

She paused, then opened her mouth to object... only to close it again. She nodded.

Victor turned back to the glass-mesh window of New York Transcon, peering into the darkness within for any sign of movement.

Tash let her gaze loll to one side, landing on a small white plate on the wall blinking orange at her. She furrowed her brow and stepped over to it, pulling out her cell phone as she did.

The letters on the panel were scrambled and meaningless. Frowning, she snapped a picture of the panel and brought it up on her screen, watching as the phone searched for something similar.

"Dammit," she huffed, letting it fall to her side.

"What?"

She held up the phone to him. The page was open to a schematic of the security panel from the manufacturer's web-site.

He took it and glanced down through, reaching the point she was talking about and frowning.

She nodded. "We made it bacon."

CHAPTER 18

Atlanta, Georgia

The house was large.

It was four floors high if one included the basement, and had once been a bed and breakfast back when this had been considered the good part of town. The white paint was peeling in many places, dried from the sun and ready to flake off like dandruff the moment it was touched by a human hand. The shutters and trim were a deep green like the needles of evergreens in the depth of winter. The same trim lined the veranda of concrete and hardwood that surrounded the first floor. It was surrounded by luscious green grass even though the rest of the street was devoid of it, stopping dead at the boundaries of the property as though it had hit an invisible wall.

Victor stood on the veranda and looked up at it, craning his neck to see, his hair billowing down over his back. It seemed to go up forever and cut into the clouds like a knife.

Tash watched him with her head slanted to one side. "Is something wrong?"

His eyebrows came together slightly, making a small but dark crease in his forehead. "I thought it would look different."

"How did you think it would look?"

"I don't know. Different."

"Right," she sighed, leaning across him and ringing the doorbell. They both waited for a moment, then she tried it again. "You'd think there was no one home."

"Its broken," Victor stated, staring at a long gash in the front of the house where the paint had been stripped away, revealing gray underneath.

She turned to him and frowned.

He stepped forward and twisted the doorknob, then opened the door and stepped inside. "It's not that kind of place anyway."

There was a crowd of at least twenty people in the living room, but they were all silent. All those that had been screaming drunkenly just a few nights before now stood around the couch in the centre of the room as though it were a coffin waiting to be closed. Some even had their hands clasped in front of them. They turned as one, as though they were puppets all controlled by one slender piece of string. Victor stopped when they did, moving over each set of eyes that had set upon him, so suddenly that Tash almost bumped into him.

Setting his jaw, he took another step forward until he was in the divide between the two halves of the house.

Quinn's eyes found Tash's, then fell away to a random spot along the floorboards. Tash frowned and then turned away.

Gavin was sitting on the couch. It had been turned

around to face the room and pressed back as far to the wall as it could be without endangering the space heater. The television had been pushed off to one side, screen in. He was laid back with his hands over either side of the couch with his shirt open, revealing a pasty white chest that was almost flawless except for a small vertical scar just under his adam's apple.

Kelly was at his side, all but curled up with him.

"It would appear we have a visitor," he smiled, his voice coming out as smooth as silk.

"Hope we're not intruding," Victor replied. He did not meet Gavin's gaze. He kept shifting it from one teen to the next.

"Not at all," Gavin said, flittering his palms in either direction. "We were just having a bit of a... a house meeting, I guess you'd call it."

There was a girl with brunette hair and freckles next to the couch that would not meet Victor's eye. She wore a small pendant on a gold chain around her neck that she was fiddling with even now, dancing the charm between her slender fingers and then rubbing it between her thumb and forefinger. One of her eyes had a coloured contact in it that made it look a bright and vibrant shade of violet. The other was her own natural brown. Victor stared at her for a long moment without saying anything, watching as the tiny piece of gold sparkling in the light from the window as it tumbled in and out of view.

Tash touched him on the arm, and his gaze shifted back onto Gavin without a word.

Gavin smiled. "Is there something I can do to help you?"

"We came for her," he said, cocking his head in Quinn's direction.

Quinn finally looked up. Her nose twitched a little and she looked straight at him, swallowing back hard when she did.

Gavin looked from Victor to Quinn and then back again. He looked as though he was trying not to laugh, even wiping a small bit of moisture from his lips as he did so. He shifted in his seat and got closer to Kelly, then turned back to Quinn and waved toward the door. "Well you heard him, girl. Get out."

Quinn looked at him and squinted.

"I said leave. I don't want you here anymore."

She smiled, then snorted and laughed. "Fuck you," she said, tossing a beer cap at him.

He laughed, turning back to Victor. "She can leave whenever she wants. She can also stay as long as she wants. So unless you're going to drag her out - -"

"I'm not," Victor said.

"She'll stay here as long as she pleases." He brought his arms down from atop the couch. One of them fell down across Kelly and hugged her in close enough that he could kiss her on top of her head. Victor turned to her. There was gooseflesh all along one of her arms even though all the people crowded together made the air hot and sticky with sweat. Her shirt was too small for her and exposed her midriff, as well as a series of small oval bruises in the meat of her hip. She was tracing lines on Gavin's torso with one finger, moving it in a series of small parallel lines over his ribs. But it wasn't idle, it seemed almost mechanical... somehow starting in the exact same spot time and time again despite the fact that the lines did not start in uniform places above each rib. There were dark spots beneath her fingernails that he could see through the chips in their polish that made her look like a leper.

Gavin took his arm out from around her and Victor watched her face fall, a glossy look coming over her eyes now that they were out of touch. He swallowed, then nodded, then turned back to watch Gavin lean forward.

"Come on," Tash said, touching Victor's arm again. "I think we've seen enough here."

"No, stay," Gavin said, motioning for the crowd to part. Two males in red shirts that had been standing next to each other separated to make room. One of them had been Thomas. "I always like hearing other opinions, makes me sure I'm not acting crazy. I love these guys, but they'd smile and nod no matter what bollocks I yammered out."

Victor took a step forward back into the house. Tash stayed where she was.

Gavin turned to Thomas and his smile disappeared. "Go fetch a chair for our guest."

Thomas nodded. "Sure," he said, but it was so quick and so low that it was almost inaudible. He returned a moment later carrying a red cushioned chair with large padded arms, balancing it on one foot as he walked to keep from dropping it. He set it down a few feet away from Gavin's couch, facing it.

Victor stepped forward again, putting his hand against the couch.

Gavin motioned toward the seat with his open palm.

Victor sat down. "If I'd known there was going to be a

debate, I'd have studied."

Gavin smiled. "Are you sure?"

Tash stood next to Victor and folded her arms. Her mouth was a small bow in the centre of her face, nearly invisible. She was staring at Quinn, who now met her eye without flinching. There was a boy with a red jacket on next to her, and she could smell the old leather from it, pungent and gross but nostalgic all at the same time. She chanced a glance in his direction. The man was tall and black. The coat had white arms and had a bright yellow C sewn into breast of one side. He smiled at her and she smiled back before turning back to Gavin.

The hairs on the back of Victor's neck stood on end and he turned to her. She shrugged and he rolled his eyes.

"We were talking about the war memorial they put up out by the library on King Street. Are you familiar with it?" Gavin said, smiling at their little interaction. Kelly was still touching his side, having moved in at an awkward angle just to stay in contact with him. As she touched him the hairs behind his ears separated and stood up.

"Not from around here."

Gavin smiled. "Oh, come on. I may be from across the pond but even I know a Georgia drawl when I hear one."

"Been away for a few years."

"Work?"

"A lot of it."

"That's a shame," Gavin said. He patted his leg and frowned, then turned toward Judy and made a circular motion with his hand. She produced a cigarette as though from thin air and handed it to him. He offered it first to Victor, sticking it out butt first. "Smoke?"

"No."

Gavin shrugged and then pursed the cig between his moist lips. He brought a lighter up to it and took a long drag as he ignited the tip, keeping the smoke in as long as he could before shooting it out in duel trails from each nostril. When he flicked the ashes he flicked them right onto the floor, embers and all. "A drink then? I'm sorry I neglected to offer one."

Victor shifted a little.

Gavin smiled.

"No thank you," Victor said, his voice a touch dryer than it had been a moment before.

Humming, Gavin took another drag of his smoke. "Like I was saying, a life spent working too much is a real shame. You should try and relax a little, my friend."

"Like you?"

He shrugged. "Wouldn't be much of a philosophy if I didn't follow it myself now, would it? I mean you know what they say Victor, nobody on their death bed wishes they'd spent more time at the office."

Victor tilted his head a little. So did Tash.

"We were talking about the memorial. It's this big copper thing they've got put up on a pedestal where there used to be a little fountain ducks could play in. On it there's this soldier all decked out in his combats and he's facing east, right to the point where the sun comes up over the trees in the morning. He's standing next to a cannon that's aimed out toward the trees and it is just massive," he laughed, holding his hands apart as wide as he could to illustrate. "Just this big, enormous phallic symbol that I cannot get over. I mean, I'm sure the artist who did it is very talented – the face of the guy looks like he's ready to bum a fag and start talking about the girl back home – but the whole thing is just wrong on so many levels."

Victor raised an eyebrow. "Not into war memorials?"

"Not as a rule, no. You?"

"I can find their place."

"Oh, so can I," he said quickly, raising up his hands in defence. "I mean, for me it's like a grave for all those poor blokes that got blown to bits overseas. Sometimes I'll visit one and I'll see some poor girl crying over one with a baby on her hip and I'll be glad that it's there... everyone needs a hat to hang their grief on, and it's hard to do it on a grave when you know there's no body in it."

Several of the gathered nodded solemnly. Quinn was one of them, finally turning away from Tash and becoming engrossed in what Gavin was saying.

"But it's just the symbology of it, for me, that's troublesome," Gavin continued. He relaxed a bit again now, his back against the couch.

"How so?" Victor asked. He had one eye on Quinn.

"Well, besides the giant penis that is the cannon, there's the soldier."

"What else are they going to put on a war memorial?" Tash smirked, snickering.

"No, not the soldier himself," he smiled. "What he's *wearing*. He's all decked out in his combats and his little matching hard hat. His... oh, what are they called?"

"Camouflage?" Kelly offered, beaming up at him.

"Camouflage," he nodded, snapping his fingers. He gave her a tiny kiss on the head as a reward. "He's ready for battle. They could have put him in anything they wanted. He could have been in dress uniform or in his greens or standing there with his helmet under one arm and a sad look in his eye... but no, they put him in camouflage with a big rifle in his hand and a giant cock coming out from between his legs ready to shoot out the sun if the fucking thing dares show its face."

Victor leaned back a little himself. "Not sure I follow."

"It's all a part of American culture. I tell you, it's not hard to tell you're from around here too, if you don't see it."

"Didn't say I was from around here."

"And by around here, I mean America. They've got you all so wired that this kind of thing is normal that you don't even see it for what it is. They put it right in front of you on a giant marble slab and you still can't see the forest for the trees. It's a military presence."

Victor tilted his head. "I don't think you know what that word means."

"Oh, I sure do. Thomas," he said, turning to look at the man in question. "Before you started coming here if you wanted to go somewhere to drink or get high, where would you go?"

Thomas thought about it a moment, then smiled. "The duck pond. Across from the library."

Gavin nodded. "Dennis, what about you?"

Dennis nodded. "For sure. I'd go there sometimes and old man McCreery would let me borrow some books from the stacks. I'd sit out on the fountain ledge and smoke pot and read, right out in the middle of the day."

"And Judy? Where did you used to take your daughter on warm days?"

Judy smiled. "To the fountain. She used to love to play with the ducks."

He nodded again. "And now it's gone. It was the symbol of innocence and beauty and, most of all, freedom. You could do what you wanted there. I'm sure the police came around sometimes, but never enough to be a bother. And I'm sure none of the people that came there would have said anything to you, Dennis, if you were just smoking a joint in the August sun and not bothering anyone."

Dennis nodded again.

Gavin took another puff of his cigarette. He was holding it between his thumb and forefinger close to his lips now, turning it into a joint. He took a long drag, a bleary look in his eyes. "I bet you'd never see soccer moms down there, would you? Or lefty war widows, God bless them." He panned the room, finding only vacant expressions that gave him his answer. "But you will now. Taking out the fountain and putting in the solider is social control. They put something in that would attract the type of people that, say, would give you funny looks if they saw you smoking a joint under a tree. Some might even call the cops, but even if they didn't, they'd turn up their noses at you and look at you sideways and make you feel uncomfortable until you'd just stop going there."

Dennis nodded. So did several others. Victor turned and watched them from over the chair's cushion, then came back to Gavin.

"And it's right next to the library and I bet they approved a nice little Starbucks-clone coffee shop that'd been trying to get in there for quite some time so that people like Mrs. W. I. D. Dow has a place to meet with her friends when they're going to talk about the way things are."

Tash frowned. "They did, actually."

Victor shot her a look.

"Let me tell you about the way things are, children," Gavin said, suddenly serious. He slapped his knee to punctuate the point, and although he was talking to everyone, he'd locked eyes on Victor. "This is just the first of it. There's so much social control that's just saturated into the way we run our day that you don't even see it anymore. Time was some people could, but slowly and surely we're all being brought in and made a part of the machine." He pointed at Victor. "Like you, you said you work?"

"As much as I can. Idle hands are the devil's plaything."

"That's an admirable way to look at it," he said, clicking his tongue. "Do you punch a clock?"

Victor paused, then shook his head.

"Ah, you see," Gavin laughed, excitedly shaking his finger. "I could tell you weren't one of them. You make your own hours, and that makes sense. But most people don't. We're a society run by time, and it all traces back to capitalism. To money."

Quinn laughed a little.

"It's true!" he exclaimed, turning to her. "Back when they ran their own fields, farmers wouldn't punch a clock. They wouldn't work for two-point-five hours then take a fifteen minute break before working another two-point-five. They worked until the job was done, and they took breaks when they needed to... if they needed a drink they drank, hungry they ate, shit they shat. Work started when it needed to start and ended when it needed to end, and they were some of the hardest working people on this planet. The salt of the earth."

"Still are," Victor interjected.

"Ah, but then society came in," Gavin said, waving a finger at him. "When the farms went under or got bought out and the men had to go work in factories, do you know what the hardest part was for most of them? Punching a clock. The idea of living life by this rigid, constrictive, nine-to-five timetable was just claustrophobic to them. It didn't make sense to them. Some of them had never been able to tell time, and now they had to be at work for a certain time and leave at a certain time and have their work done within that time and only eat a certain time. *Only eat a certain time*," he laughed. "I don't know about you, but the only *certain time* I eat is when I'm hungry."

Everyone nodded this time.

"It was so hard for most of them that many of them broke the clocks. Literally smashed their faces as a mark of rebellion. It happened all over America, and it wasn't an organized event... it was just the collective thought of a people. Society and its engineers had stressed them to that level. But where are they now?"

"Punching a clock," Victor said. There was a trace of a grin visible beneath his scruff.

"Punching a clock," Gavin said. He finished his smoke (which was down to the butt) and tossed it down against the floor, stomping his boot down on it for effect. "And society has won out ever since. Slowly but surely, every sense of faith and belief and individuality and community are stripped away and what are we left with? The desire for money, and the need to punch a sodding clock."

Victor smiled. He nodded, along with everyone else. Except Tash. "And we've all been programmed to think that to not do it like this would be the end of the world. And that anyone who doesn't think like this is our enemy."

"Exactly," Gavin said pointing at him. "Exactly. See, I knew you would get it. I knew the second I saw you come in here... you're a thinker. You... think. And nobody tells you how to. I knew you'd understand."

Victor turned and watched the heads as they nodded. He swallowed hard, his mouth very dry.

Tash saw his face finally, and a look of concern came over her. He'd lost the colour in his cheeks. They were almost the same shade as his beard.

"I understand," he said finally, his voice hoarse. "I see very clearly."

"Ah, but all that we see or seem is but a dream within a dream," Gavin said musically, holding out his hand in front of him. Kelly kissed him just below his nipple, leaving a small red lipstick mark. She was still running her hand in linear lines over his ribs. He laughed. "I'm just trying to have a discussion. Anyone can." He pointed into the crowd. "Yesterday Vanessa went on for a good thirty minutes about a character on her favourite soap. Said the writers treated him like Jesus. And that evening we watched an episode and, by God, if it wasn't true."

He smiled at Victor with that perfect row of teeth. "But it's just talk."

He slid his hand down Kelly's backside, gripping hard

when he arrived at her slender waist.

"Really?" Victor said, his tone low. "Because it actually sounds like you're selling religion."

Gavin smiled. "All religion, my friend, is simply evolved out of fraud, fear, greed, imagination and poetry."

"So that's a no?"

Gavin nodded once.

"Good. Because I bought me some Hindu yesterday. Not going to be buying any more for a while."

Gavin tilted his head, then licked his lips.

"I thought it was pretty funny."

Tash smirked.

"Well," Gavin sighed, leaning back on the chair again and exposing the nape of his neck. "I hope, at least, you're convinced we're not keeping Miss Quinn here against her will."

Victor squinted hard. He stood up and stepped out around the chair, then turned back around. "What happened to your neck?" he asked, motioning to the area just under his adam's apple on his own body.

Tash turned and shot him a look.

Kelly sat up for the first time since they'd come in. She looked at the spot where she'd been touching Gavin, then up to his neck, and then back again. She had a confused look on her face, and Victor watched her closely.

Gavin's smile faded, and he wiped his mouth and let his hands travel down over the scar on his neck. When he spoke again his voice was much lower. "Hunting accident."

"Hn. Knife or gun?"

"Knife."

"Animal?"

"Ptarmigan," Gavin said, rising up from the couch. When he stood he looked as though he might keep rising until he went all the way through the ceiling. Kelly moved away as though she knew what he had been about to do, otherwise she would have been flung from her seat.

Victor looked him in the eye, then looked down at his pale chest. It was devoid of all hair or even the stubble of it, and was as white as a corpse's. "What about the one here?" he asked, motioning with a small circle to his own central plexus. "Same accident?"

Gavin touched the smooth, flawless flesh there in the same circular motion. "Yes. There was quite a bit of blood."

Different members of the crowd exchanged perplexed glances, but said nothing.

Victor smiled. "Must have been a hell of a fight."

"Oh, it was. Do you hunt?"

"Only humans."

Gavin stopped, then stepped up closer to him until they were almost nose-to-nose. When he spoke again he whispered, his accent even thicker while he was doing so. "I think, at least, that your opinion of me has changed since you first stepped in here."

"Oh, yes," Victor agreed, nodding. He looked at the assembled masses, then at Kelly and Quinn, then met Gavin's eye. "I think you're a piece of dirt."

Gavin held his eye for a long moment, then smiled again and stepped back. "Think what you want. There's a famous anthropologist, Victor, who said once: dirt is simply matter out of place."

The colour drained from Victor's face and his mouth went dry.

"Her name was --"

"Mary Douglas," Victor finished. He turned and stepped toward the hallway and then out through the door.

Tash watched him go and sighed, letting her hands fall to her sides. She turned back to Quinn as though she wanted to say something, sighed again, and then left.

By the time she caught up to him he was already at the end of the driveway, where the grass ended and turned back into dusty gravel. "Well, that was useless," she huffed, running her fingers through her hair. "We learned he likes to quote Poe and Douglas. Who knew scholars were the new Pied Pipers?" Her hands were on her hips and she had her head turned back toward the house, which still looked massive even at a distance.

When Victor did not respond she turned back to him. "Hey, is everything okay?"

She walked around to his front. His fists were clenched so hard that his knuckles were white. He was breathing hard though his teeth and open mouth and sending tiny droplets of spittle out onto the dry ground. His eyes were set and did not change focus when she stepped in front of him, as though he were in some strange trace. His face was white, whiter than she'd ever seen it.

"What's wrong?"

He licked him lips, then turned to her. "Get my team here, now."

CHAPTER 19

Los Angeles, California

Everything sparkled. The chandelier overhead, the rings clicking against wine and champagne glasses, the jewels around women's necks and the glittering tie-clips on the department heads, CEO's and elite of L.A. Leigh wore dove-grey, a dress with a simple silhouette against the glitz and extravagance of the gala.

"So you see, that's the beauty of this exhibit," Arthur Shane said, swirling a glass of wine. "We've been working so diligently over the last eighteen years that it's time we show the public everything we've accomplished in the field. Even these, the prototypes and blueprints from our very first projects, while nothing near what we are working on now, are light years ahead of what society thinks is possible."

A woman near him smiled and leaned in closer. "I must admit Arthur, it's quite extraordinary to see what you've come up with. Most companies would be wary of showing off past experiments given how competitive the field is, but this is remarkable."

Leigh stood in the midst of a circle of Arthur's top clients as he showed them around the new exhibit. She had drank quite a bit already, trying to numb an ache that was growing in her joints, and felt as if she was floating between displays as they moved around. The conversation was boring to her. Every line to entice investors were ones she had heard, and delivered, before. Nonetheless, powerful investors were powerful allies, and with every added penny, more money was available to find a cure for her particular ailment. So she stayed quiet.

"Ah, Dean, it's been ages. How's life been treating you working with the competition?"

Another man had joined the group. He looked to be slightly older than Arthur, with more wrinkles creasing his otherwise handsome face and silver flecking his chestnut coif in a way that made him look distinguished. Arthur shook hands with him, grinning devilishly.

"You know me, Arthur. It's only as good as the progress we're making. I've got to say, things have been pretty exciting lately."

Arthur smiled, pulling Leigh in from the outskirts of the group. "Dean, I'd like you to meet Leigh Blackheart. She's a great asset to the company, bringing us in new resources and some stunning minds. Maybe she can convince you to re-join our little team. Leigh, this is my colleague, Dean Taft. He helped me get the company started back in the day. Absolutely one of the most brilliant geneticists I know."

Dean took Leigh's hand, smiling. "Pleased to meet you, Ms. Blackheart. Shall we find somewhere a little less noisy to chat?"

Leigh smiled. "Of course, sir. The pleasure is all mine."

Dean led her away from the mass of people, slipping out of the main hall into a more secluded wing of the museum. When they were out of earshot of the party guests, he began to talk.

"Arthur tells me you've been having a bit of a problem lately. Such a shame to hear that such a treasure as yourself might not be working much longer." Dean met Leigh's gaze coldly.

"I would expect a man of your expertise might be excited for the challenge I present, Mr. Taft. Can I count you among the friends I have trying to help me?"

"If I was such a friend, frankly, I'd have your predicament cured already. Arthur is getting soft. There is a price for my involvement, and he's forgetting that. He thinks your charms might persuade me to join the cause debt free. He is wrong."

Leigh bit her lip. "What price could I pay that he can't?"

Dean smiled. "I hear your curse is also a fairly useful talent. I left Shane because I had an offer too good to turn down. My price for leaving was surrendering some information my new company would rather I hadn't. You get it back for me, and you'll have your cure."

"What makes you so sure that you can trust me?" Leigh asked, the pleasant buzz having entirely worn off with the sobering proposition.

"Leigh, you're the type of girl who is willing to gamble quite a bit for life. I'd wager any price you have to pay for betraying Arthur is worth it in your eyes, and I'll have you know, I'm quite the gambler." Dean's smile struck her like ice as he said this.

"When you gamble, you win and you lose," Leigh said, pulling her hand back from his grasp.

"Given your odds, who seems like your winning team?"

Outside Payson, Arizona

Abby had let Theo drive the El Dorado to pickup Jaycee and Chad. Chad had called shotgun, and had subsequently fallen asleep in the front seat, and was now snoring loudly. It annoyed Abby to the point that she had begun mindlessly checking her watch to distract herself from the racket, and yet still hadn't noticed that the hands were stuck at five minutes to midnight.

She glanced at her phone, noticing several email notifications that had popped up recently. She flicked through them quickly, her eyebrows raising more and more with each one, when the phone began to ring.

"Hello?" she said, bringing the device to her ear.

Theo glanced back at her in the mirror, his eyes questioning. The only other person with Abby's current phone number was Victor, and he couldn't recall Victor ever calling one of them for anything. He resisted the urge to simply pluck the information on their conversation from her mind, and instead turned his attention back to the road.

"Yes, I saw them. What's happening?" Abby said, her brow furrowing. "I understand, but what exactly is so urgent about… Well, yes, I see your point. I'll let everyone know. We'll be there as soon as we can."

Jaycee's head popped up as Abby spoke, and he leaned forward to nudge Chad.

Chad's chin lolled, and he shook his head sleepily as he was prodded. There was a pool of drool on his chest. Jaycee poked him again, and Chad's head shot up and began to look around. When he caught sight of Jaycee, he leaned back to punch him, but Theo grabbed his hand and motioned back to where Abby was talking on the phone.

Chad's eyes lit up, and he turned full around in his seat to listen.

"Mhm, I'll make sure they're ready, no worries. We'll see you in a few hours, we've just got to run home first and pack. Talk to you soon."

Abby hit the end button on the call and looked up at the boys' expectant faces. "It looks like we're taking a trip."

Los Angeles, California

Leigh examined a glass display case carefully. Inside, a small figurine was perched on a pedestal, light hitting it from all directions. It was a 16th century Hungarian piece, but it didn't interest her. She was staring at the base of the figurine, noting a tripwire that would be set to activate if the object's weight was altered. She stepped back a step to take in the rest of the case when a noise startled her.

She turned, noticing a man standing behind her. He was wearing a security uniform with the museum's insignia embroidered onto the breast pocket. He smiled at her when their eyes met with a kind of sheepish, half-grin.

"Hello," she said, plastering on a smile and willing a

little bit of charm to creep into her features.

"Um, hello," he said, his voice crackling as if he had just hit puberty. He brought a hand up to his throat, his cheeks burning bright red.

Leigh supressed a giggle, forcing herself just to smile. "I'm a little lost," she said. She took a step toward him and tilted her head, showing off her slender neck. "I was with a tour and got separated."

The man raised an eyebrow and moved toward her. "Only tour that came through here today was a bunch of high school kids... and you don't look like one."

She swallowed, thinking up an excuse. "I'm a teacher," she replied, extending her hand forward. "My name is Leigh."

He took her hand and shook it gently. "You don't look old enough to be a teacher."

She smiled, looking down at the floor for a moment. Flattery was a pet peeve of hers, but she played on it.

"If I'd had a teacher like you in high school... well, I would've paid a little more attention in class, if you get my drift."

She forced a laugh, then took a look around. She had been sure this area was the last on security rounds, and the anxiety of finding anyone at all inside at this hour was bringing forth the familiar twisting feeling in her gut that she tried to fight. Some primeval part of her screamed to transform and kill him, to destroy evidence of her being there. "I'm sorry, are you closed?" she asked, her anxiety creeping into her voice.

He smiled warmly. "Yes, ma'am. We've been closed for about an hour now. You must have gotten very lost." They started to walk together toward the exit, and he placed his arm on her shoulder casually.

"Mmm," she smiled, taking a quick glance at his arm on her shoulder. "Yes. I was examining this exhibit and must have gotten lost in thought." Her voice wandered as she motioned toward the new exhibit. "One of my... students was interested in it. Do you know when it opens?"

"Oh, a few days time," he smiled. "All of the displays are ready. I've gotten a good look at it while on night patrols... it's pretty impressive." He turned toward her and grinned, one eyebrow raised skyward. "Don't suppose you'd like the nickel tour?"

Leigh smiled coyly at him, taking a step toward the entrance to the exhibit. "I'd be... delighted," she said, doing her best to seem interested in him.

She noticed he adjusted his belt as the both of them started toward the exhibit. He held up the yellow tape that blocked it off to let her pass under.

The room was large and seemed to go on forever, each table a display full of dancing lights and dazzling effects. Some were more simplistic than others, with computer terminals running three-dimensional schematics. One had a virtual reality helmet attached, presumably so that the wearer could see something too large to have fit onto a display. It was less 'done up' than it had been the night of the gala, but still just as impressive.

She scanned the room, and her smile faded until her face was almost expressionless. She caught sight of the security cameras and breathed a sigh of relief. No red lights blinked to indicate they were on. Leigh continued to scan the room, eyes finally coming to rest on one a computer terminal set into a dos prompt, waiting a command line. She smiled a little, almost forgetting the guard behind her as she stepped toward it.

Behind her, the watchmen looked around at the display. He had clearly never been in here before, despite his previous statements. "That's weird," he grunted, taking a step toward the north wall. "The air conditioner's off."

Leigh's head spun around as he spoke. Without a thought she flew toward him as he stepped toward the grate on the wall with his hand outstretched.

He looked down as she reached him. She was soundless, and it was only when she was already on him that she realized she wasn't breathing, or even walking.

It was only when he noticed something on the floor and bent to examine it that she realized what had happened. She recoiled, pulling back quickly, but it was not quick enough.

The watchman's eyes followed the black tar she had become down the hall.

He looked up, his face turning as white as Leigh's had been. She had almost completely reformed when he caught sight of her, the last bits of liquid slithering up to form her feet. She smiled at him, but the pain she was in twisted it into a snear, revealing black gums.

The guard quickly reached for his service revolver. Leigh didn't give it a second thought. She had gambled. These were the cards she was dealt, and she could either stay in the game or go belly up.

His yells of terror echoed throughout the halls even after he lost consciousness.

CHAPTER 20

Payson, Arizona

The airport terminal in Payson was one large flat room that looked small on the outside but stretched on forever on the inside. Though there were only six hangers it was often busy and crowded, always filled with people coming and going from one plane to the next. The seating area was very small as most travellers were only there for thirty minutes at a time. Payson Airport was a popular stopover point, allowing planes to refuel and patrons to switch carriers before taking off again.

Security was just in front of the hanger and was only separated from it by a long glass wall. Chad, Abby and Theo were sitting in the waiting area next to a *Sweet Tarts* pastry café and watching as a large man in baggy pants cupped his hands over Jaycee's midsection on the other side of the glass.

Chad glowered at the sight and folded his arms in front of his chest. "That is bullshit."

"It was a random spot check," Abby said, still watching Jaycee.

"There was absolutely nothing random about that."

On the other side of the glass, Jaycee leaned forward and spread his legs as the security officer reached for his metal detector.

Theo stared at the officer until he was in perfect focus, then closed his eyes.

The officer's name was Lee Coolidge, and as Theo focussed on him through the dark of his eyelids he saw the man as a large billboard behind Jaycee. On the billboard, shimmering in the bright lights all around it, was the scene from the movie Lee had just seen the night before. It was the one where Samuel L. Jackson killed the two boys that assaulted his daughter, and in the scene Matthew McConaughey was giving his closing statement to the jury.

He opened his eyes. "It was random."

Chad looked at him and turned up his nose.

Abby slapped her hands onto her knees and got up. "Our flight should be boarding soon. I'm getting a coffee. Anyone else need anything?"

Theo shook his head.

"Pepsi," Chad nodded, still watching Jaycee anxiously.

Theo rolled his eyes, then turned his attention to the television screen bolted to the ceiling a few feet away. It was turned to a twenty-four hour news and weather channel that spouted the same stories over and over again every five minutes and seemed to be what all airports turned their stations to, as it was the only thing on television guaranteed not to offend.

There was a picture on the tv he recognized. He'd seen it many times before, and he leaned forward onto his knees to see it. It was the Los Angeles Science Center, a tall building that was topped with a sloped point that made it look futuristic and impressive. The front-facing wall was made almost entirely of green glass that shimmered and caught the sunlight well.

There was an Asian woman on the screen in front of the Science Center. It looked as though she was actually there, rather than in front of a green screen. "This is Miranda Tilby keeping you live from the Los Angeles Science Center; where the city was stunned hours ago when a local security guard reported the death of his partner in the newly completed technology exhibit donated by Shane Industries."

Theo squinted and stood up.

"Few details have been released, however we can confirm for you that our sources within the coroner's office are examining this incident as a death by drowning, despite no water being found at the scene. Police are investigating every angle in this brutal crime, and we will keep you updated with more details as they are made available."

His eyes went wide and he turned to look at Abby, who was still ordering at the *Sweet Tarts* counter. Chad was watching as Jaycee put his shirt back on and joked with Lee the security officer, his cheeks hot and flushed.

"I'm going to go check on our flight," Theo said, stepping back a pace.

"Sure," Chad said, waving him off nonchalantly.

Theo turned and made three steps toward their gate before turning on a dime and marching down the terminal to Gate 4: direct flight to Los Angeles.

There line was just forming for the flight, and at the

front of it a blonde woman with a big smile that threatened to escape the sides of her mouth. He got in line and waited to be served and focussed in on her, the space behind her becoming a giant billboard that displayed all the thoughts she was thinking at that particular moment. Right now the album cover to Taylor Swift's single *Love Story*, and the song blared over the speakers of her mind until Theo's ears were ringing. Despite the noise he stayed tuned in.

When he got up to her he took out his ID and held it out to her. Her thumb brushed against his on the underside of the card and suddenly the song got louder, and there were more thoughts underneath. She thought he was cute, and for a moment the song was pushed to the back of her mind and he was looking into his own eyes on the billboard.

"There's a ticket waiting for me," he said, smiling at her boyishly.

"Okay," she nodded, then looked at a sheet of paper under her desk. "Under what name?"

The screen changed, and he could see the sheet perfectly.

Cory Frank
Leslie Nicholson
Jennifer Bruce
Michael Stevens

"Michael Stevens," he said, smiling.

"Okay," she smiled, handing him his ticket. She took out a highlighter and circled his seat number. "That's where you'll be sitting."

"Thank you," he grinned, then stepped past her into the gate. He looked at the ticket again and allowed himself a smile, then turned back and saw that, while *Love Song* was still playing, the image on the screen was now a still shot of his grinning face.

The ticket was first class.

Abby stepped back to her seat and handed Chad his Pepsi. Jaycee was next to him, lounging across three seats. She handed him an iced coffee, which he took gladly. "Where's Theo?"

Chad turned around. "He's right --" He stopped, realizing that there was no one standing in the direction he was pointing in. He looked around the terminal, found nothing, then let out an aggravated sigh. "Fuck."

Behind Abby's head, the news story about the Science Center started to play again.

"Few details have been released, however we can confirm for you that our sources within the coroner's office are examining this incident as a death by drowning, despite no water being found at the scene. Police are investigating every angle in this brutal crime, and we will keep you updated with more details as they are made available."

Abby turned around slowly and looked at the screen, refusing to blink.

Had Theo been there to see it, her billboard would have consisted entirely of one four-letter word in capital letters and bright, red paint.

CHAPTER 21

Atlanta, Georgia

There was a row of slot machines in the terminal.

Chad had only ever seen that once before, when he'd had a stopover in Vegas while coming home from a vacation with his family. He'd sat there looking over his shoulder for his father or for airport security and emptied the change from his pocket into it, coming up with bars every time and leaving with a ticket for almost ten times what he'd walked in with. He'd thought he was the luckiest man alive.

Until he realized he had no way to cash it.

Looking at it, he realized that that ticket was still home somewhere in an old shoebox under his bed along with the only comic book he'd ever owned, Amazing Spider-Man #378, and a few baseball cards with battered edges. He wondered if Karen would find it.

As he watched, the lights on the top and sides of the bandit closest to him spun and sparkled, chiming steadily along with the music that sung out the happy tune of B, C, D, B. That little four-note pattern was the key to all happiness, he'd discovered. B, C, D, B, over and over again. When you won it made it go faster, and it really sounded musical.

Chad stared at it with his bag over one shoulder as Abby and Jaycee came up behind him. Abby's hair was a mess from sleeping in the airplane even during the short flight. Planes had always put her to sleep, she'd said before taking off, and had ever since she was a little girl. She'd slept between he and Jaycee with her head tilted just slightly toward him. He'd noticed rather quickly that he could see down her shirt but didn't look, turning in that direction only to right her head when it looked like she might wake up with a stiff neck and to laugh when a small line of drool managed to make its way from her open mouth.

Victor stepped up to them, unnoticed by Chad until he stepped between him and the VLTs, snapping him out of the trance the machines had him in and bringing him back to reality. He smiled.

Victor looked at each of them, then back at Chad. "Where's Theo?"

Chad frowned. He turned back to Abby, who tilted her head in a kind of shrug that somehow didn't involve her shoulders at all.

"He took off," she said finally, fidgeting with the bag that was weighing down her shoulder. It was light brown with little dark brown flowers all over it.

"What?" Victor said, his arms falling forward slightly. He took his cell phone out of his pocket and texted something before snapping it shut again.

"He ditched us in the airport," Chad added pointedly. "We couldn't find him. You know what he's like, if he didn't want to be found --"

"That little fucker," Victor said under his breath.

Abby's eyes shot up.

He turned and looked out across the terminal at the sea of people coming and going, their faces smudging together like one giant blur of flesh. He couldn't find any one detail to latch onto, not even for an instant. He sucked his bottom lip in until even the wiry hairs of his scruff were in his mouth, then let them all go and reached out for Abby's bag.

She handed it to him tentatively.

He nodded to her and only to her, and the four of them started toward the exit.

Chad paused and watched the slot machines again. There were two children playing near it, running around it for a moment as though it were a slide on a playground, laughing and giggling. One was stark white and the other was mulatto, and he guessed that the woman sitting a few metres away engrossed in the latest edition of Reader's Digest was their mother.

The bells and lights of the slot machine jangled out B, C, D, B over and over again.

The children played and laughed happily, blissfully unaware of what made them so.

Atlanta, Georgia

Victor stepped out to his car with Abby's bag over his shoulder, pressing the button on his key ring twice to unlock it.

It was long a burnt orange, the finish on it catching the sunlight even in the motorcade. The headlights were large and round, sticking out from the face of the car like two all-seeing eyes. The glass on it was perfectly clean, reflecting Victor's image back at him even as he opened the backdoor and tossed Abby's bag in.

Chad stopped dead in his tracks five feet from the car and just stared at it. Abby and Jaycee kept walking. Abby took the front seat.

"Something wrong?" Victor asked, leaning on the roof of the car.

"It's the El Dorado," he said, pointing to it as though no one else could see it.

"It's *an* El Dorado," Victor smirked.

"You've got more than one?"

"Two for one sale," he said, climbing into the driver's seat and shutting the door behind him.

Chad followed him, getting in the back with Jaycee.

"Never feel at home without it."

Abby laughed.

Atlanta, Georgia

Kelly held the small sack of oranges close to her bosom, their cool flesh wet and leathery against her own. She'd juggled them all the way from the corner store. She hadn't gone all the way up to the market for just one grocery item, although she'd wanted to. The sun was warm and the day was nice, and she would have enjoyed the walk. And the oranges were better at the market, and cheaper. The more she thought of reasons she should have gone, the worse she felt about the clammy bundle in her arms.

There were twelve in all. One was bruised and showing signs of rot.

Eight cardboard boxes of nails were displayed end-to-end on the shelf before her. None of them were labelled and they all looked the same.

She reached out and picked one up cautiously between her thumb and forefinger. It was long with a flat head and several treads underneath it. It didn't look like something that would have been called an annular nail, but then, she thought, what did?

She put the nail back and several others moved up to meet it. One even jumped out of the box, its tip catching the tip of her nails and holding on. It startled her so fiercely that she dropped them and let out a small, impish yelp.

"Can I help you?" an older man called from the front of the store. He was balding and plump and wore a large green apron out in front of him that reminded her of a character from a children's program she's watched as a child, though for the life of her she couldn't remember which one.

She smiled at him. "I think so. I need a certain type of nail."

He smiled back at her, coming out from around the counter and walking over. She felt a shiver travel down her spine so fierce that she almost dropped her fruit, and suddenly his smile didn't seem quite so warm. It seemed cold. Behind the counter he'd been concerned with her needs, and now it seemed he was concerned with his own. It was his eyes that had changed. She'd seen that same change before but only now recognized it, and the realization made her shrivel into herself. When she spoke again her voice was soft like a mouse, in a way she hadn't felt in years. "I need annular nails."

He tilted his head and gave her an odd look, then stepped past her to one of the boxes on the far right. He took the whole box off the shelf and displayed it to her, holding it close to his body at waist height.

The nails were small and had spirals going from the bottom to the top. They looked like screws with the heads of nails, like some sort of mythological nail. The screw with the head of a nail. A lion with the head of a bird.

She swallowed, then nodded. "I'll take the box," she said, forcing herself to smile.

He nodded, then brought them up behind the cash register.

After she'd paid for them she carried them out by the holes on either side of the box, careful not to touch any of the sharp annular metal inside.

CHAPTER 22

Atlanta, Georgia

The El Dorado pulled up to Tash's house via a long dirt road that was so narrow tree limbs scraped against the windows on either side, making long squealing noises that cut through Abby's skull and made her teeth clench. Her hair was pulled back in a ponytail again and when she ran her nails through it they scraped painfully along her scalp and cut deep gouges in the thin flesh there.

The house was large. Larger than the one outside Payson. It seemed to be more elegantly built, if in a hodgepodge manner. There was a large middle section as well as an east wing and a west wing, each of which had uniquely different designs. The west wing was redbrick and mortar with a high tower on the end and intricate latticework up one side where vines grew, turning orange now with fall. The east wing looked far more elegant, with clay designs in original mouldings under each windowsill that sprouted vacant flowerbeds beneath.

There was a gazebo on the roof that was walled to look like a greenhouse. Abby stared at it for some time when she got out of the car, until Chad and Jaycee were already at the door. She stepped quickly to meet them, and arrived on the stoop just as Tash was opening the door.

Tash smiled brightly, extending her arms but moving to embrace no one, then stepped aside to let them in. "It's nice to finally meet all of you," she said in a overtly-cheery fashion.

Chad and Jaycee entered first, then Victor. Abby stopped just before the door. There was a small brass plaque just below the doorbell. Engraved on it was "A little learning is a dangerous thing; Drink deep, or taste not the Persian spring."

She eyed it for a moment, then followed Victor and closed the door behind her.

"We're going to be having dinner in just a few minutes," Tash said to them all, clasping her hands together at her abdomen like the host of a restaurant. "I hope everybody likes steak. Iseult and Nick have been out at the grill all afternoon."

Jaycee's eyes went up. He poked Chad lightly with his elbow.

"You're not serious," Chad chuckled under his breath. "After last night?"

Jaycee shrugged.

Abby stared at the bookcase adjacent to the front porch. It was short but wide, running almost the entire width of the wall until the staircase. There was an identical one on the other side of it. They were full of texts, some of them the old hardcover books with no words on their spine and some of them newer softcovers with colourful pictures and quotes along them. Several in a row made a picture that clearly wasn't complete yet of a babbling brook and a small child reading beside it wearing a straw hat and overalls. She eyed each of these carefully. Some were literary classics, some were anthropological texts, but many were on genetics and forensic science. She recognized one on blood spatter analysis, having read the majority of it for a thesis paper.

Chad and Jaycee started into a sunlit room that was yellow and bright and inviting, their forms becoming shadowed silhouettes as they stepped into the light.

Victor started to join them, but Abby took him by the arm and spun him around. When he locked eyes with her he stepped back a pace, a quizzical look coming over him.

"So it was just b.s. then, what you said?"

Victor smiled a little, tilting his head to one side. He wasn't really looking at her anymore, as much as he was looking at the null space just above her nose. It was an old sales trick and she knew it. "I'm not sure I follow you."

"It would be ridiculous to use a school like Port Haven did... that is what you said, right? That they were just *asking* for trouble?" she turned toward the bookcase and then back to him, her eyes full of spite. "You going to try and tell me this isn't a school?"

Victor nodded once. "Things aren't always quite so black and white."

She squinted her eyes at that.

He put his hand on her back and gently lead her into the dining room. Chad and Jaycee had already sat down, and Iseult was coming in from outside with a steaming plate of meat that smelled like barbeque sauce and on-ions.

Nick was standing outside on the porch. The back wall of the dining room was a large window divided into eight different sections and creating a dome-like structure. He watched them through the glass as though they couldn't see them, moving from one face to the next with one hand on his hip and one hand on his spatula. He was wearing a green apron of the sort that handymen often wore, with rings in the front for hammers and pouches for nails.

He met everyone's eyes and then finally settled on Victor's. He paused there for a moment, the both of them lingering on the other until Nick finally turned his head and let out a cough from deep within his throat, rendered silent by the thick panes of glass. It was like watching a silent movie reel. Victor watched this for another moment, then nodded happily as Iseult held out the steaming plate of steaks. He dug his fork into the one on the top - a t-bone - and eased it onto his plate.

Nick came in just as he was hoisting his apron over his head and took his seat across from Tash.

"Everything looks good," Abby said, smiling warmly at Iseult.

"Isn't quite the reception I was expecting," Chad remarked, already taking a large scoop out of the soft pillowy innards of his baked potato. "Last time Victor took us on a road trip the first stop was a town in the middle of butt-fuck nowhere where this idiot was about to get lynched," he bobbed his head in Jaycee's direction. "No offense."

Jaycee shrugged as though he hadn't even considered it capable of offending.

"This situation's a little more delicate," Victor said, cupping his hands in front of his face. Steam was rising up from the meat on his plate and bathing his chin and neck in condensation. "I thought we'd try a different approach."

Chad swayed his head from side to side, then took a bite of his steak.

Victor watched them for another moment, letting the steam billow up and around him, turning his hair a curling gray.

Tash watched him with her fork in her mouth, then slowly lowered it to her plate and cleared her throat. She stared at him for a full minute as he watched the others eat. "Victor..."

"Yeah," he nodded, frowning so that dimples formed at either side of his mouth. "Yeah, I know."

Jaycee eyed him suspiciously. "You look like my Uncle Rory when he told us he had cancer."

"Oh," Abby cooed. "I'm so sorry."

"It's okay I just made him up," he shrugged. "Still, he looks bad."

Victor nodded, and finally his gaze fell back to Chad. "Do you remember when I told you the world was going to hell?"

Chad paused, tilted his head, then nodded.

"Well yesterday I met one of the people leading the way."

They all stopped eating. Iseult had a heaping spoonful of mashed potato and butter on her fork that was dripping back onto her plate.

"Gavin?" Nick asked sceptically, thinking back to his

memory of the man with the beer in one hand and Kelly on the other, his face so pale that he looked like the slightest bit of sun would incinerate him.

Victor nodded. "I think he's controlling those kids."

Chad turned to Abby with some alarm and then back to Victor. "What, you mean like some kind of mind control?"

"No. The regular way."

Chad leaned back against his seat.

"They're fractured and disenfranchised youth with little to lose. They don't identify with the society around them and that's what he's attacking. Right now he's just using rhetoric and wordplay, and he's very good at that. But he won't settle for that for too much longer."

"How could you possibly know that?"

Victor was silent for a long moment. He moved his tongue around his mouth slowly, as though he were trying to get something out his teeth. "I did the math."

Nick scrunched up his face. "I don't buy it. I mean, I've no doubt this guy is a douchebag... but you're talking about him like he can influence people into doing something they wouldn't normally. I haven't known Quinn for very long, but I don't think she's like that. I don't think she would be lead anywhere."

"Live in the world for a while," Jaycee drawled, leaning forward so that he could meet Nick's eye. "You'll see it happens everywhere."

"Mob mentality is a powerful thing," Abby said.

"I've seen it before," Victor murmured.

Abby shot him a calculating look.

"Any reason we aren't just calling the police?" Chad

asked, scooping the last of the potato out of its skin and plopping it into his mouth. "I mean, that is what one would do in this situation... right?"

"Hasn't done anything wrong, yet. People have a right to free assembly. Even if he has broken a law, we'd still have to prove it."

"So what's the play?"

Victor frowned, twisting his neck to one side until a bubble of calcium within it popped. "Right now the play is to get Quinn out of there before things really hit the fan, which I'd lay odds will be soon."

Nick shifted uncomfortably in his chair.

Jaycee turned to look at him, then turned back to the group. "And that's it? There's no other interest here? This is just like with me, we get her out of trouble and hope that she comes back here with open arms?"

Victor was silent again, his eyes gazing off into the nothingness between Jaycee and Chad's chairs, eventually coming to focus on the dark spaces between the boards of the patio.

"Victor?" Chad asked, raising one eyebrow.

"Hn?"

"Jaycee asked you a question. *Is there* any other angle here?"

Victor turned to Tash for a moment, then back to Chad. "No. No, of course not."

Atlanta, Georgia

Kelly opened the front door, careful not to drop the oranges as she did so. They wobbled and weebled around the red mesh bag they were in until she brought her knee up to stop them. She forced the door the rest of the way open with a small kick and an even smaller huff. The door-knob hit the wall hard and left a small indent there as her hair fell in front of her eyes in two disjointed strands.

Gavin stood at the bottom of the stairs. He was wearing a thin black tee-shirt, the contrast between the milky white of his flesh and the pitch black of the fabric making him stand out from a background that was already out of focus in the low light of the hallway. His hair had been let down and parted in the middle to form two brackets that came down on either side of his eyes.

There were four others standing around them, each looking at him intently, though his eyes seemed to be trained solely on Thomas. He was gripping Thomas's shoulder hard, kneading the doughy clumps of flesh be-tween his fingers while he pointed at him with his other hand, their faces only inches apart.

At first it looked like they were fighting, but the other three were calm so Kelly said nothing.

"Words have no power to impress the mind," Gavin said, his voice a hushed whisper, "Without the exquisite horror of their reality." He spun from Thomas then, meet-ing each of their eyes individually: first Mitchell, then Ja-son, then Charlotte and Dennis. Each one of them nodded when he got to them, and at the last one he smiled. He turned that smile back to Mitchell. "Do you know what Stockholm Syndrome is? It's this thing that happens to people in captivity where they start to sympathize with their captors, and I think it's happening to us here. Ev-ery minute of every day we get brainwashed by society into telling us what to eat what to buy how to dress. We all have to have the newest phone or the most expensive sneaker. And we've been told by society that we're all beautiful, lovely people who will find someone to love us someday but we aren't and some of us won't. It's all just propaganda. We use that word like it's something that went out of style after the Cold War but look at us now. Every day stopping to look both ways and to always tip out waitresses and," he stopped, noticing Kelly standing in the doorway for the first time, "and to kiss the girls," he finished, stepping past the others to kiss Kelly on the lips.

She fidgeted, then stepped back a pace. "I got everything you were looking for."

"Ah!" he smiled, as though just noticing that her arms were full of stock. He took the box of nails from her and laid them down on the floor, then took the oranges and tore a hole in one side of the bag that held them.

"Hey," she laughed, "What are you doing?"

He gripped two oranges at once, tossing one to Mitchell and then another to Thomas. He held out the bag and the other three took an orange each as well. He took one himself, then let the bag fall to the floor beside him. Two more oranges toppled out, rolling lopsided over the floor toward the dining room.

Thomas had already dug his thumbnail into the skin when Gavin held up his fruit as if he were toasting them. "Reality is not all bread and wine, my friends," he said, examining the way the light reflected off of the orange's dented, porous surface. "Sometimes reality is sweet and bitter and acidic all at the same time." He brought the orange into his mouth, peel and all, and took a large bite. His teeth sunk past the skin and juice squirted out, bubbling down his lips and over his chin. He ripped it away, chewed for a moment, then swallowed.

Jason chuckled and shook his head, then continued to peel his orange.

Thomas looked down at the half-moon shaped cut in his own, liquid seeping out of it slowly, then brought it to his mouth and took a bite.

Gavin smiled. "Never forget this. Never forget that there are ways of doing things beyond what you have been taught. The world is a big place, gentlemen, and nobody can tell us what corner of it we have to sit in."

He bent in and kissed Kelly again, wrapping his hand around her waist and drawing her close. His face was sticky with citrus and his lips were dry. He broke off the kiss after a moment then took her by the hand and began to lead her up the stairs. "Bring the paper," he said as she followed him without a word.

She looked back at Charlotte before she disappeared around the corner.

Dennis turned back toward the others, a smirk travelling far up one side of his face. He turned to the front door, which was still open and letting in cool October air. He smiled and stepped outside, the other four following him.

CHAPTER 23

Atlanta, Georgia

The statue had been of Private Jack Turner.

He'd gone overseas while his face was still plump with baby fat and his eyes still lit up when people spoke about America. He'd managed a few years out of it, but every time he made it back home between tours his face looked more and more haggard, to the point that on his last visit his mother hadn't been able to tell the difference between he and his father, who was thirty years his senior.

Those lines, some of them formed from worry and some from rendered flesh, had been brought out when his likeness had been carved and welded into smooth copper and erected across the street from McCreery's Bookstore, where a small duck pond had been before his death at the hands of enemy fire. His mother had taken him to that duck pond as a small boy to feed the ducks white bread bought by the loaf at the deli, back when you were allowed to feed ducks white bread. Before we cared so much about the welfare of ducks that we studied the nutritional value of the bread we were feeding them, and so little about our young men that we sent them away by sea and by air, any way we could get them there. Turner's service record was displayed proudly on the base, also carved in copper. It told of his three commendations and his (posthumous) medal of honour.

It did not tell about the one time he'd gotten jittery during a peacekeeping mission and accidentally opened fire on an elderly couple trying to get home before curfew. It also left out that he used to go to that same duck pond every Sunday night with his friend Jimmy and his girlfriend Pearl to get stoned under an old elm tree, feeding the ducks rye bread. It also didn't say that Jack lost his virginity on the steps of that fountain at one o'clock in the morning one night while he was fifteen. Jimmy had been grounded and he and Pearl had gone alone.

When Jimmy thought that he'd gotten his girlfriend pregnant, he'd put a bullet through the back of his own head in his father's bedroom, just five blocks away.

Jack's greenish-brown, pupil-less eyes stared out toward the leafless trees that reached up into the moonlight like fingers scraping at the navy tapestry of the night.

Thomas jumped up onto the pedestal next to Jack and hung his arm around him, swinging around his neck and laughing wildly. In his other hand he had a bottle of strawberry wine and he smashed it across Jack's copper face, sending glass and alcohol showering down against the walkway behind. He laughed again, then pulled himself in and kissed the stature full on the mouth.

Underneath, Charlotte laughed with the same throaty cackle she'd had since puberty and clapped her hands in front of her face.

"Ha, nyah," Thomas hummed, spitting out a small pellet of green glass. His upper lip had a thin gash going through it that made it look cleft, and small tendrils of blood spilled from it and down his chin like spider legs.

Dennis came around the corner laughing. His mouth was open even when there was no sound coming out, almost as though someone were turning his volume up and down. When he wasn't laughing his lips continued to move as it they were, an insidious pantomime of real laughter.

Thomas laughed as Jason and Mitchell circled around to their side of the statue. Still leaning from Jack Turner's neck as though he were a girl that had come down to the docks, he turned and eyed the long cannon next to him. "It really is a giant penis, isn't it?" he snickered, lifting one leg and mounting it so that the barrel came from between his legs. "Hey Charlotte, wanna come up for a ride now?"

Charlotte laughed, bending over and spitting the whole time.

"You wish," Jason murmured.

"No, no way," Thomas laughed, still bleeding from the face. He unzipped his pants. "There was a pond here once, and I say there's going to be again!" He pissed up into the air and it came down in a steady yellow arc, splashing down on the concrete below right between Dennis and Charlotte, both of whom had to step back a pace to avoid getting splashed.

"What the fuck, man?" Dennis yelled.

Charlotte just laughed some more, looking up at Thomas whenever she could open her eyes.

Jason smiled as Thomas shook and put himself away. There was a hastily-rolled joint between his lips that had been sogged with his own sweat while it had rested on his ear and now smelled like a hybrid of dogfood a body odour. He sucked back on it nonetheless, letting the blue-tinted smoke rise up from its tip into his eyes despite how it irritated them.

He turned around and eyed McCreery's Bookstore. There weren't as many books in the display window as he remembered. One that was there was a paperback copy of *Heaven's Harlots* with a sketch of a young girl on the cover that looked like she would have been bearing her breasts if not for the fact that the end of the cover cut her off. It was surrounded by three books by Stephen King and one by Thomas Harris. There was a crack in the glass that looked like it had started in the bottom right months ago but had stretched all the way up so that it almost reached the top lefthand corner of the window.

The coffee shop next door, christened *Laringo's*, had a similar large window in the front with its name stencilled across it in cursive letters. The paint inside and out was done in drab browns and earthtones, and even from here Jason could see some of the wiry little chairs within and that big glass counter with overpriced deli sandwiches in it.

There were large rocks arranged along the walkway's edge. He reached over and picked one up, feeling the weight of it in his hand.

Charlotte climbed up onto the cannon and kissed Thomas on the lips.

Mitchell took a hacksaw out of his duffle-bag.

CHAPTER 24

Atlanta, Georgia

Nick stared out into the open darkness that surrounded Tash's house. Victor's El Dorado was still parked in the same spot, nuzzled in the shadow of the east-wing's eave on one side and an old elm tree on the other. Between the two a thin strip of moonlight slipped past, creating a glimmering bright line over the car's roof and cutting it in two. He found his eye focussing on it for what seemed like an eternity, then turned away from it back to his room.

The walls were sparse, especially for a boy his age. There were no posters or pictures on the walls. His bed was in the corner next to him and only had a single purple blanket on it. There had been more, but they'd been kicked off and shoved under the bed during his first night and never been thought of again. There was an oakwood bookcase near the foot of the bed with no books in it. A night table of the same style was next to him, a battered hardcover Reader's Digest collection unread under his lamp.

There was a book bag on his bed that looked squatted

and pregnant, the bottom portion plump while the top half crumpled onto itself limply. He would have thought that he would have had enough earthy possessions to have at least filled a single knapsack, but the shrivelled foreskin of it on his bed proved otherwise. As it turned out, the only things that had tied him to this place in time had been three tee shirts (one of which had so many holes in it anyone else would have said it was unwearable) two pairs of jeans, four pairs of underwear and two pairs of socks. The rest, as his mother would have said, was a wash.

He eyed the Reader's Digest book for a moment. It was a woodsy brown with a Pegasus embossed into the bottom right corner in gold, almost invisible except under direct light. He considered taking it with him for a moment, then thought of the long bookshelf downstairs and the empty spot he'd created in it between volumes twenty-eight and thirty when he'd removed this one and decided against it. Instead he picked it up and placed it reverently in the centre of his pillow, the weight depressing it in the same way his head would have.

His mouth twitched and he eyed his bedroom door, then turned back toward the window.

It took two hearty pulls to open it, the bottom pane sliding up until it was level with the first. Cold fall air erupted forth, soundless and secretive as it turned his room into an ice box. The shiver of it brought gooseflesh to his skin and he recalled, briefly, his date with Quinn just a few nights before. Hadn't it been warm then? He couldn't remember.

Pausing only briefly, he hoisted one leg out of the window and rested it on the eave below. He stayed like that for a moment, straddling both realities, before finally bringing his other leg around and allowing himself to drop.

The eave was steep and slippery, a full fall frost nipping at its edges. He found himself picking up speed as he scaled down it, unable to stop himself as the incline brought him closer and closer to the edge. When he reached the rain gutter he pushed off and his body felt weightless for an instant before gravity finally took hold and dragged him back down to earth.

He landed on the grassy island ten feet from the El Dorado, without ever having escaped the shadow of the eave.

He turned back toward the house quickly, finding a light on three rooms over from his. Chad and Victor were in it, Victor sitting with his back to the window. Chad was facing it, but from several feet back, and he did not seem to register Nick's movement.

He continued to watch for a moment, then turned and ran down the driveway.

"Where do you think you're going?" came a voice from the darkness.

Nick turned, so fast that his feet slipped on the dewy grass and he fell, landing on his ass. His eyes scanned the darkness, seeing everything and yet finding nothing. Finally the elm tree he'd been watching seemed to grow eyes, each of them a deep urine yellow. The branches twitched in the breeze and Jaycee became visible, the moonlight accenting his taut, hairless frame. He was leaning against the trunk of the elm with his arms folded across his chest and one leg propped up against it.

Nick frowned bitterly and rose to his feet. "Not sure that's any of your business."

Jaycee stepped out of the tree's shadow, the moonlight now bathing him fully. His sallow face was wrought with lines that looked like wrinkles at first but were not. He wasn't old enough to have them. They were places where the muscles beneath had malformed, sometimes on their own and sometimes to accommodate the exaggerated arc of his skull. His eyes were like triangular slits as they scanned over the boy standing before him with evening dew soaked into the seat of his pants. "If you're thinking about running, I wouldn't recommend it. Believe me, I doesn't work out in the end."

Nick's lip curled slightly. "I'd have to agree with that. And seeing as running is what got me this far to begin with, I don't think a little more will hurt."

He turned his back to Jaycee and stomped his way a few feet down the path.

"It's a girl, isn't it?"

Nick stopped in his tracks.

Jaycee's arms relaxed and he closed the distance between the both of them casually, like a man out for a stroll in the park.

Nick spun around and locked eyes with him. "So what're you, some kind of mind-reader?"

"No. I'm unbearably handsome. You couldn't tell?"

Nick laughed and loosened a little.

"I've got a girl back home. I'd do anything for her, and did. But it didn't always work out the best. I'm not saying it right. I'm not eloquent. I'm just saying there's other ways to solve these things than just storming off and being the brave knight. You have to think. Am I making any sense?"

"Not really," Nick shrugged. "And you can't stop me."

Jaycee glowered. "Kid, who ever said anything about stopping you?"

They talked for several more minutes, and then the both of them turned and started down the driveway together. Within moments they had both been eaten by the shadows of the trees and became invisible

Chad watched from over Victor's shoulder as the last remnants of moonlight disappeared from Jaycee's back.

"They're gone," he said, finally flicking his eyes from the window back to Victor. "You sure this was a good idea?"

Victor stared at him for a moment, but said nothing.

CHAPTER 25

New York City, Then

"In here!" Tash yelled, rushing to the security guard's side so quickly that she scraped her knees along the hard floor of The Pasta Palace. *She grabbed him by the shoulder and pulled him onto his back. He flopped over and cracked his elbow against the tile hard, but did not even wince to register it.*

Victor came up behind her, sweat drenching the underside of his shirt. "Is he?"

"I think so," she replied, pressing two fingers against his carotid artery. "Yes."

"Jesus," he sighed, stepping forward until he could see the man and Tash at the same time.

His face was bruised and blistered, with great welts over his eyes and a milky vomit in both corners of his mouth.

Victor's eyes went wide. "Jesus."

Tash nodded, checking for the man's pulse one last time. She saw his baton sticking out of his belt and slid it out, palming the grip in her hand and feeling its weight.

"I never would have thought Jona could have done this."

"Men will surprise you," Tash whispered, then rose to her

feet and spun around in one quick motion, bringing the baton up and around in a smooth arc. It connected with Jona's temple but he did not move, the baton making a loud whack that vibrated down its shaft and made her feel as though her hand was going to break. "Fuck!" she snapped, backing off a step and clutching her hand.

Jona stared down at them, the white flecks in his grayish skin getting caught in the moonlight from the stairwell and making him glow. He stood over seven feet tall and glowered down at them as if from atop a mountain, his powerful arms hanging at his sides as though he were carrying lead weights. He stared at them with blank eyes, the whites so bright that they almost glowed and the rest so black that they were like holes they could have fallen into.

"Jona," Victor breathed, staring at him wide-eyed.

Jona tilted his head toward him and smiled. "Hello, Prophet."

CHAPTER 26

Atlanta, Georgia

The house was quiet that night. There were no lights on and it sat askew in its patch of lush greenery like a tomb, the moonlight accenting its edges but making the interior of it almost indistinguishable.

Jaycee and Nick stepped up to it, Nick adjusting the straps of his book bag. There was a large splotch of sweat on his back where the bag had rested roughly the shape of Russia.

"This is the place?" Jaycee asked, sticking out his chin in the direction of the house.

Nick nodded.

"Hnn."

"What?"

"Nothing. Just... not what I expected."

"I told you it was a house. What did you expect? A Chevy with a fridge in the back?"

Jaycee shrugged. "I don't know. Thought it'd be more run down, I guess."

Nick shook his head, then stepped around to see the

side of the building. He looked up to the sole window that led into Gavin's loft, near the peak of the roof. The window was dark, without even a candle flickering behind its down curtains. "I don't think anyone's awake. I think we're --" He stopped in mid-sentence, his gaze lolling to the right.

"What is it?" Jaycee asked, his voice concerned as he stepped to see what Nick was seeing.

Thirty feet from the base of the house and almost directly from the base of Gavin's window, there was a shed peeking its way up from the grass.

It wasn't large, only about ten feet by five with white wooden panels on all four sides. It was high, almost ten full feet on one side but sloping down on the other so that the ceiling was lopsided.

It sat with its back wall flush with the edge of the lawn, and the ground around it was undisturbed. It had no windows and only one door that faced the house like a sentry keeping watch.

It reminded Jaycee of his home, back in Idaho.

"That wasn't there before," Nick said quietly.

Jaycee shot him a perturbed look. "You mean you didn't notice it before."

"No, I mean it wasn't there." He took a step forward.

Jaycee put a heavy hand on his shoulder.

He stopped, then nodded.

"So what's the play?"

Nick turned to him and his mind went blank. He hadn't thought very much about that. In the house getting out and getting here to Kelly and Quinn had seemed of the utmost importance. But now that he was here, there were flies in the ointment of his plan. He'd brought his clothes, but was he staying? Surely not. He didn't want to be here anymore now than when he'd been dragged here, days previous. He wanted to get the girl and get out. Girls. Get the girls and get out. But he had a sense that that wasn't going to be as simple as it ought to have been. So he'd come prepared, as he'd always been taught to do.

"Let's just get in there," he said finally. "Let's find the girls and... and I don't know. But they're not safe."

"*We're* not safe," Jaycee corrected. "But fine."

The both of them walked up the rickety, creeking steps that led up to the doorway. They paused at the door, each uncertain on how to proceed, until Jaycee finally reached out and opened it. They both stepped inside.

The entire house was dark, with only a pale blue light caressing the walls to separate them from the rest of the nothingness around them.

There was a man asleep on the couch where Gavin had been lecturing, his feet dangling off the edge. His boots were strewn haphazardly across the floor beneath them and looked as though they'd fallen there at some point during the night. On the coffee table next to him was a bottle of wine with a few spare drops still settled at the bottom. There were thirteen glasses on the table with it, one of which was on its side with a long crack running down through it.

The stairs in front of them were pitch black, like a gaping square hole in time that would swallow them up if they went near it.

Nick stood in the middle of it all, the space where all four paths converged, and felt as though he couldn't breathe.

Jaycee stood next to him, as silent as a statue. They remained there for several long moments, until finally he straightened up. "Are we done now?"

Nick closed his eyes, then nodded. "Yeah."

"Good," he said. "Now let's get out of here before --"

There was a sound in the kitchen.

Jaycee stopped and closed his eyes. The both of them turned toward it.

At first there was nothing, just more long gray hallway with a rectangular black void against the far wall. But as they stared into it, movement started to occur. Something shimmering in the low light and fumbled from side to side, then moved up and finally back down again. There was an audible ping of glass striking against something unyielding. Fabrics rustling against tile and nails scraping against wood.

Jaycee bent down slightly, his powerful hands curling into fists.

Nick shot him a glance and shook his head.

The figure in the darkness stood finally and started to come into view. The light from outside refracted off the vaguely hourglass shape of her body and, for a moment, Nick thought that perhaps it was Kelly having ventured back down into the kitchen where they'd first met.

The figure raised her bottle to her lips again, took the last bit of liquid from it, then let it fall to the ground at her feet. She was heedless of whether or not it broke, and it did not. She stepped forward again, and now Nick could see the boxy frame of her shoulders and the pale, almost paper-white complexion of her skin. Her hair was red a fiery, cropped close and sticking off from her at wild angles.

Charlotte hummed happily as she stepped toward them, all but falling into Nick's arms with a thin smile that spread from ear to ear. "Nnnnnnay, you," she said, her face so close to his that he could taste the whiskey on her breath, "Didn' think you'd be back any time soon."

Jaycee smirked at them as Nick tried to back up but found it impossible to do so.

"An I see you've brought a friend," she said, eyeing Jaycee up and down. "I think me and you could have us a little fun I think." She leaned back her head and laughed, her mouth open so wide when she did that the ridges going down her mouth were clearly visible. One of her hands came up and then stroked all the way down one of Jaycee's arms, her nails making tiny white trails in it.

"Nick..."

"Yes, Charlotte, definitely," Nick said, nodding and producing a fake smile. "I've brought a friend just for you and for whatever you want."

Jaycee glared at him.

"Yum," said hummed.

"Yes, yum," Nick continued. "Tasty, nummy goodness. But right now I need to know where Kelly is. And Quinn. I need you to tell me where Kelly and Quinn are."

She sniffed. "Quinn? Quinn's up with Billy again tonight. Think they're upstairs. Kelly's..." she made a dismissive -pfft- sound with her lips, blowing air up onto her face and displacing some of her hair with it. "You know where Kelly is."

She laughed again, louder this time, tipping her head

back so far that nick had to hold her to keep her from smashing her head.

"Stop her!" Jaycee spat.

"Gee, thanks," Nick growled, shooting him an annoyed look. "I never would have thought of that."

A light came on somewhere upstairs, only faint traces of it finding its way to them. But it was more than enough to get their attention.

"Fuck," Nick huffed, still holding Charlotte around her slender waist.

"If you say so," she chuckled playfully.

Nick rolled his eyes and debated dropping her.

There was noise upstairs. The steady, uneven pattern of many different footsteps.

"We're boned," Jaycee said. "We have to get out of here."

Nick didn't say anything, still trying to get Charlotte to her feet.

Kelly appeared in the stairwell, the soft glow from the light reflecting off the wall creating a halo around her. She stopped when she saw the three of them and made no face, just watched the scene as though it was some obscure modern art that she didn't quite understand. The boy, the belly-dancer, and the devil. It was like something Da Vinci would have painted had Da Vinci been alive in the eighties and quite stoned at all times.

After a moment the halo disappeared and there was only darkness behind her. An instant later the lights were all on, revealing Gavin standing behind her with his hand on the switch.

The harsh, all-encompassing light did little to shed

any explanation on the situation.

Gavin placed a hand on Kelly's shoulder. Her own hands came together and Nick watched them as they met, a small shiver running down his spine.

Charlotte bent back again, her body forming a letter K with Nick's, meeting only at the pelvis. Jaycee stood between them.

"Well," Gavin smiled, hugging into Kelly from behind, "This is interesting, isn't it?"

Charlotte smiled, picking herself up and slinging her arms around Nick. "I found a boy at the bottom of my whiskey bottle," she said, laughing to herself. "Like the prize in the Cracker Jack box."

"You sure did," he smiled, turning to Nick. "I thought I might see you again."

Nick took a step back from Charlotte and she finally let him go, albeit reluctantly. He stood straight and addressed them both, though he was looking only at Kelly. "I couldn't stay away."

Kelly smiled.

Gavin lost his, turning to Jaycee instead. "And who is this?"

"My name is Jean-Claude Maximus," he said, straightening his posture as he did.

"Jean-Claude. French, isn't it? I adored France."

Jaycee narrowed his eyes, his nostrils flaring.

Gavin's smile returned. He turned and kissed Kelly on the cheek. "Kelly, would you be a dear and fetch our new friends some tea?"

Jaycee and Nick looked at each other, then at Gavin.

"Well it's a little early for alcohol. Unless it's still late for you both, at which point --"

"Tea's fine," Nick said, again looking at Kelly. She stepped away from Gavin and walked down the stairs, stopping when she was next to him. Her face seemed bathed with diffuse blue light even though all the bulbs were on. She separated her hands finally and extended one to Nick. "Nice to see you again," she said.

Nick looked down at the extended hand, his eye flicking and fluttering as though in the middle of REM sleep. After a moment he coughed, then took her hand and shook it gently.

"Any type of tea in particular?"

The hairs of his arm stood on end as she took her slender hand away. "Anything's fine."

Their eyes locked for a moment and she turned to Jaycee, extending the hand again. He took it and gave it one gentle pump before letting it go again. "And you?" she asked, her mouth making a small crimson letter O when she spoke.

"Earl Gray?" he asked.

She nodded. "Lemon?"

"Please."

She nodded politely and made her way into the kitchen, turning on the light there and disappearing out of the view of the door.

Nick and Jaycee both continued to keep their eyes on the doorframe, even after she was out of sight.

"Nnnmmmore guests," Charlotte said, sitting on the floor against the wall now. "Gonna have to make some room."

"Yes," Gavin hummed happily, drawing both their attention away from Kelly again. "We're going to have to do something about that."

Atlanta, Georgia

Abby was sound asleep the second her head hit the pillow.

She had always slept best in a strange bed. There was something about the cool down of sheets that weren't regularly slept in and rooms that weren't regularly heated that made her skin sit, and her only regret in those situations was that she couldn't be awake longer to enjoy her sleep... but she realized there were definite problem with that dynamic.

She remembered her first night in Port Haven. The sheets had been tucked so tight that she hadn't dared to displace them, instead squirming in between them from the top like trying to fit between two stuck-together pieces of paper. She'd snuggled into those cold feathered pillows and been out before she could even turn off the light. The same had been true when she'd moved to Arizona, the first night she'd spent in the room Victor had prepared for her. There'd been potpourri of lilacs in a glass jar on the night stand that had made everything seem fresh and wonderful.

Here, although the room was sparse, there was a cool freshness to the air that made her want to curl up in the bed and sleep until her body wouldn't let her anymore. For the first time in almost a month, she was smiling in her sleep.

Her door opened, shining light across her eyes. She

opened them blearily, immediately aware of a figure standing in the pool of light that was her bedroom door.

She squinted, rising slowly as her eyes adjusted and Chad came fully into view. There was something wrong with his face. He wasn't crying or puffy-eyed or pouting, but he still looked upset somehow. She turned and saw that the digital clock next to her read 5:47, but didn't say anything about it to him.

He took two steps in, then let out a small sigh. "Can I stay in here for a while?" he asked, his voice weak and faraway.

Still squinting, she nodded.

He nodded his thanks and closed the door behind him, then laid down on the oval mat in the middle of her room. After a moment she handed him a pillow and he took it carefully, doubling it over and shoving his arm behind it for support.

Within minutes they were both asleep again.

CHAPTER 27

Atlanta, Georgia

The sun glinted over the trees and entered Victor's study, imprinting the fingers of naked branches onto the wall as they swayed aimlessly in the stark fall breeze.

The walls were pale yellow. Victor sat behind a large oak desk with his back to the window, feeling the heat of the sun's rays on his back radiating upward. The desk was filled with papers but was not cluttered, every sheet arranged into neatly formed little piles of varying heights. The organizational system made little sense to anyone but him, but worked well.

A space had been cleared in the middle of the desk large enough that he could hunch over it with his elbows far apart, as he often did when working late. He was scribbling into a suede notebook that was small enough to fit into his back pocket, held closed by a black elastic band.

The rest of the room was small. There was less than a meter between his back on the window. Beside it in the opposite corner was a small bookshelf with a television propped precariously on it tuned to the local channel, the sound down so low that it was barely audible even to him. It was an old set with a VCR attached.

His hair dangled in front of him on either side of his face as he wrote. Some of it was in his mouth.

The notebook was half filled but there were more like it. Halfway down the current page he was working on he'd written Nick's name in a clear, thin hand that made his normally illegible script look even worse by comparison. The N covered four full ruled lines, and each of the other lower case letters took up three. He drew a circle around the name and tapped his pen against it over and over again, making a series of small half-moon inked dents against the page.

He let out a puff of air and blinked twice. It was only then that he noticed that Tash was standing in the doorway.

"How could you?"

Victor watched her for a moment as though expecting her to do something, then leaned back on his chair. "What are we talking about?"

"Nick's gone. He left during the night."

"Hn."

"Jaycee too."

"Hnn."

"Don't pretend like you didn't know anything about it. I've known you too long."

Victor said nothing. He folded his arms in front of his chest.

"You can be a real son of a bitch, you know that?"

"I didn't plan this, if that's what you're thinking."

"But you knew. Somehow or another you knew that

this was going to happen. This or something like it."

Victor stared again.

Tash shook her head. "God damn it, Victor. This isn't the right way and you know this isn't the right way and you know that."

Victor's mouth twitched downward. He took a small cup of tea off his desk and drank the last sip out of it, then turned his swivel chair toward the window. The El Dorado shone the sun's light up at him blindingly.

Tash stiffened. "You're going to get them killed. Again. With Hunter at least it was his lifestyle."

Victor leaned in a pressed the volume up button on the television. The number rose and he hunched over in his chair closer to the small screen. There was a store window on the screen, most of it broken out. All that was left attached to its frame was a large stylized letter *L*.

"We're going back there today. We've got the get them out of there, now. I don't care what it --" She stopped and looked at the screen. The crawl across the bottom of the screen read *Laringo's* Café in big block letters on blue ribbon. The camera had panned back to show the entire storefront window. It had been beaten in and the table and chairs inside had been broken and slung about. Some that had been bolted to the wall had been pulled forth then smashed through the glass display case by the counter.

Riding the frame of the window was the butt of a large copper cannon.

Tash tilted her head to one side.

The feed changed to a different image now. It was Private Jack Turner's copper head. It had been sawed off just below the chin and placed on the marble pedestal between his legs. Lipstick had been added to his lips and blush to his face. The camera panned back to show that the area surrounding the Private had been adorned with a flock of tiny rubber ducks, each of them placed strategically. One was sitting atop the Private's neck replacing his head.

"What in the world?" Tash said, leaning down next to Victor to get closer to the screen.

"This is it," Victor said, his hands clasped in front of his chin.

CHAPTER 28

Atlanta, Georgia

Private Jack Turner's copper head had been sawed off just below the chin and placed on the marble pedestal between his legs. Lipstick had been added to his lips and blush to his face. The camera panned back to show that the area surrounding the Private had been adorned in a flock of tiny rubber ducks, each of them placed strategically. One was sitting atop the Private's neck replacing his head.

The crowd surrounding the television roared tremendously, several clapped their hands. Billy Oates slapped Thomas on the back so hard that he almost spilled his beer. Thomas smiled, the whiskers that had been growing for the last day moving slightly as he did, then took another large gulp from the can. It was early, but they were light beer. Or lite beer, as it stated on the can.

Several more beer cans were cracked open and many high-fives and low-fives were exchanged, as well as one or two high-tens. Dennis and Mitchell hugged each other in that we're-not-really-going-to-hug-we're-just-going-to-pat-each-other's-backs-and-mash-our-chests-together sort of way.

Jaycee watched from the archway. His shirt was tied around his waist and his arms were folded against his chest, much in the way that they had been when he discovered Nick late the night before. He leaned against the wall and watched the news report for a moment before scanning his eyes over the crowd.

Gavin was on the couch in the middle of it all, facing the television. His arm was around Kelly.

Quinn watched the impromptu party from the other side of the room. Her eyes flitted to Jaycee once or twice, but mostly stayed on the barrage of beer foam and comradery happening all around her. Her cheeks were green and her face stony and emotionless, until someone handed her a beer. It had already been opened for her. She smiled and took a sip.

Nick watched the back of Kelly's head, alternating between her and Quinn every few seconds. After a moment of this he backed up a pace until he was level with Jaycee. "What am I watching here?"

"You've been here before. Don't know why you're asking me questions."

Gavin smiled, taking his arm out from around Kelly. Chuckling, he rose to his feet slowly and walked the short distance to the television, laying his hand on top of it. "Ducks," he said, as more shots of the rubber ducks appeared on the screen. "That's quite good. Quite the message there, I doubt even the dumbest of soccer moms will be able to miss that." He smiled, scanning the crowd and stopping at Thomas. "You?"

Thomas nodded.

Gavin made his way to each of the others and asked the same question.

Jason, Dennis and Mitchell all smiled and nodded, raising their drinks.

"Me too," Charlotte said from the corner, a new orange cooler in her hand.

"Yes," he nodded, turning again to the screen. "This will upset them. This will have them all on edge. It doesn't take much, you know, to show people that their lives aren't what they thought they were. Even the most dutiful and composed man can be broken when even the slightest thing doesn't go his way. His door freezes shut one winters morning and he can't get out of his house. His cellular phone stops working. A neighbour's house gets broken into. Any break in the routine will make a man feel on edge and tight in the chest." The image on the screen went back to a wide shot of *Laringo's* Café. "But it's what they need to break from the doldrum of their lives." He pushed the television over onto the floor with such force that the screen shattered and the power cord snapped out of the back of it, sending errant blue sparks from the loose wire. Everyone stopped and jumped back a pace. Kelly had to move her feet back quickly to stop her toes from getting smashed, her eyes bulging wide.

Nick took a step forward, but Jaycee put a hand on his shoulder.

"Are you out of your minds?!" Gavin screamed, his head lurching forward at them and the veins on his neck popping out all at once. He was glared at the five responsible with bloodshot eyes. "You think this is the way to reach them, this - this - vandalism?" He stopped, his face becoming flush with sweat. For a moment he looked even whiter than usual. When he spoke again his voice was almost a whisper. "I ask for the saints of Brixton and Broadwater and I get the looters. The pillagers. The *Americans*." He turned at met each of their eyes. "Get out to the shed."

Thomas and the others nodded solemnly, then hung their heads and turned to walk out to the shed.

As they passed by, Jaycee tried to meet each of their gazes and failed.

Gavin slumped back into the couch, noticing finally that Kelly had curled her feet up under herself.   "I'm sorry," he said, leaning in and kissing her on the cheek. "But you can't educate the world by acting like fools."

She nodded hurriedly.

Nick turned to face Jaycee head on. Jaycee nodded reluctantly.

Atlanta, Georgia

"This is the beginning of it," Victor said, turning his computer monitor toward Tash, Chad, Iseult and Abby. It had a screen shot of the Jack Turner Memorial on it, one taken before it had been vandalized and not long after it had been originally erected. There were still bits of ribbon tied to the trees around it from where it had been presented on its opening day. "I'm positive."

Chad squinted at the screen with his arms crossed. "I don't get it," he said after a moment.

"He was talking about this statue when we went to

try and get Quinn back," Tash explained. "He made a big deal out of it being this form of social control, getting rid of a drug haunt and putting in something that attracted the 'right type' of people again."

Chad turned back to the picture. "I don't buy it."

"That's because it's bull shit," Abby countered, leaning forward a little. "You could attach that kind of message to anything. Office towers replacing trees as the highest points on the horizon signifies God being replaced by corporate America blah blah blah."

Iseult looked at her and smiled.

"You're both right," Victor nodded, "But that has little to do with the point. It's not the message behind what he's saying, it's where he's steering these kids that's got me worried."

"Juvenile Hall?"

Victor shook his head. "Social reform."

Chad rolled his eyes. "Well, we can't have that."

"Social reform in and of itself isn't a bad thing, but it is a destructive thing. There's been very little social reform, ever, that hasn't been wrought with bloodshed and horror and murder. We can talk about MLK and Malcolm X and Jesus Christ until the cows come home, but at the end of the day we all know it's true."

Tash nodded.

"The problem is, Gavin doesn't have social reform in mind. He's talking about social reform and social injustice, but there's no coherency to it... there's no message at the end. He's not blaming a specific race or gender or political sect, he's just blaming the world for being the way it is. He's making them angry at everything and nothing all at once, making them raging and directionless."

"To what end?" Chad asked, finally looking interested.

Victor met his eye. "To give them a direction."

The four of them were quiet for a long moment.

"He has an endgame in mind," he continued. "I don't know what it is yet, but I can bet you that it's not good."

"Why's that?" Iseult asked, finally speaking up.

Abby turned to her. "How many cults you know that have happy endings?"

Chad turned to her at once. "Cults? I'm sorry, we're talking about a cult?" he turned to Victor, who nodded once. "Oh, fuck that man. My dad always said, you can't fight fanatics."

Abby raised an eyebrow. "Did your dad ever really say that?"

"No, but it doesn't make it any less true. I grew up in *Salt Lake City*. Believe me, you don't want to mess with religious nuts."

"They aren't religious," Victor corrected. "They aren't *anything*, not yet anyway." He stepped away from the screen toward them. "Here's what we do know. They trust him, all of them. I imagine he came to live there just like any other drifter would. He didn't come there and start cultivating the masses, he started out as one of the masses. He befriended them, played all sides, was everybody's buddy, until finally they all looked to him. He decided if they were going drinking, what movie they'd turn on, where the furniture should go... everything. Every group has a defacto leader, whether they know it or not, and he became that guy - but it was never by accident. Don't kid yourselves. And once he was in that position he started to separate himself. He wasn't one of the guys anymore, he was above them. Initiate new people coming in, make them feel like brothers and sisters. He has a separate room to himself, likely higher up than the rest. Possibly an attic. And it's all by design."

"How could you possibly know all this?" Abby asked.

Victor looked at her.

"Math, right. Sorry. Forget I asked."

Victor nodded. "He still pretends he's one of them, but he's not now. They don't sit around and chat over beer anymore, he lectures them. He doesn't date among them, he takes one of them as his own. His property. He might have even had more than one of them, but I doubt it. One thing I'm very sure of, though: he's confident. Even when Tash and I were there, he was confident. Which tells me that he's done this before. Has it down to a science, as a point of fact."

Tash narrowed her eyes, thinking back to Gavin talking amongst the teens and nodding. "But to what end? I mean, the end can't really be social reform or even a large-scale riot. If it was and he was as practised as you claim he is, we'd already know about it. We would have recognized him."

"So it has to be something lower key."

Tash thought for a moment. "It depends on him. Gavin, the leader. Sometimes it's a highly-complex larceny scheme... get the kids to follow you, then get them to give you their money. Or steal money for you. Or whatever. Other times it's about sex, and that kind of game never really ends, it just gets worse and worse. Only way to stop that is to take out the leader."

"Not even then," Victor said.

"I'm guessing you don't think this is about money. And if it was about sex it would be open-ended, and you seem sure that it has a definite end in sight... so I'm guessing you're thinking this is the third type then."

Abby, Chad and Iseult all turned to look at Tash. "What's the third type?" Chad asked.

Tash was quiet for a moment. She chanced a glance at Victor, who shook his head. She frowned, then turned to them. "In the third type, the end goal is murder."

Victor sighed, stepping back a pace.

Chad looked as though he'd been hit in the gut with something. "But... you said there were, like, thirty of them."

Tash nodded.

"Oh, God," he urged a little, then turned back to Victor. "Is this what we're doing here? Did you know about this?" He tried to stand, but Abby caught his hand.

Victor shook his head. "I thought he was another person like one of you. Someone who might be able to help."

"And is he?" It was Abby this time. She was more accustomed to death than Chad was, but even so the news hit her hard. She didn't think she'd ever truly get used to hearing things like that, or at least she hoped she wouldn't.

"I think so. He's got a scar that I don't think anyone else sees. And I think other people see different scars."

"That's some power," Chad droned. "Better watch out

when he starts using that one."

"I don't think that's his power, but it's definitely enough to point me in that direction."

Abby let out a long huff of air and ran her fingers through her hair. After a moment she looked up at the computer, which still had the picture of Jack Turner on it. She slapped her hands against her knees, got up, and made her way over to the keyboard.

"What're you doing?" Victor asked, raising an eyebrow at her.

She opened a new tab in the browser window that Victor had open and brought up a search engine. "We've got to find out more on him. About what he does."

Victor smiled. "I've tried that already. A last name would be helpful, because all I get from searching "Gavin cult" are underground movie and film references."

"How about, "Gavin Halloween"?" Tash offered. "The time of year may not be a coincidence."

"Tried that too," he frowned. "Got nothing but kids named Gavin dressed up like pumpkins and Transformers."

Abby smiled. "I don't think that *I* could do better searching for it," she said, turning toward Chad. All the others's eyes followed.

Chad sat up straight. "Oh, you have got to be kidding me."

Abby backed away from the keyboard, sliding it in his direction.

Chad sighed, then stepped forward. "This has got to be one of the most hair-brained things I have ever heard in my life," he said, even as he typed the words Gavin Halloween into the search bar.

It spat out over five million results in less than a second, the top ones being a digital golf game, a video of a boy named Gavin in his Halloween costume, and a social media page inviting people to a birthday party in Tennessee.

"See?" he said, stepping back from the keyboard. "Nothing."

All five of them were quiet. After a full minute had passed, Tash stood up and walked over as though she were going to type something into the keyboard, then hesitated, turning to Chad instead. "Type in: Gavin, Mary Douglas quotes," she said softly.

Victor perked his ears.

Chad huffed, then typed into the search bar again. They chicklet keys clattered under his fingertips as they flew across it, then pressed enter dramatically. The hourglass spun for a moment, then a new page populated. Once again there were far too many results, this time close to three million. The first was an article on the *Bride of Frankenstein.*

Victor frowned. "I think we're thinking about this wrong."

"I don't really know how you thought it would work anyway. Did you think the search engine would give different results just because I'm the one using it?"

Victor stroked the scruff under his nose for a moment. "Keep at it."

"Keep at what? We're not doing anything."

"Uh-Huh. And keep at it." He stepped out into the kitchen with Tash to get some tea.

Atlanta, Georgia

Chad sat with his eyes too close to the computer screen. His fingers typed the words **Hallowed Barker** into the search bar and then hovered over the enter key, then he paused and backed up the word **Barker** and replaced it with the word **Robert**. He sighed and pressed enter, then leaned back on the chair and waited for the screen to load.

Abby was sitting on the couch again. Iseult was laying on it with her feet across Abby's lap.

Chad scanned down through the first few links displayed in blue, hovered over one to get a view of the page it lead to, then went back up to the search bar and deleted the whole thing.

Victor walked back into the room with a steaming cup of coffee and placed it down next to him.

Chad eyed it for a moment, then turned back to him. "Cinnamon?"

"Irish Cream."

Chad nodded and took the cup, drinking it heartily.

"How's it coming?"

"It's not coming at all. It's gibberish. I am literally typing in gibberish. I am typing in things that make no sense and hoping it to help us more than things that would make sense."

"Any commonalities?"

Chad sighed and ran his fingers through his hair. "Blog posts, news articles, and porn. There is nothing I have typed in that hasn't come up with porn."

Victor raised an eyebrow at him.

"What?"

"Nothing. Anything to the news articles?"

"No. There's nothing to any of it. It's gibberish."

Victor scanned down through the page that Chad just had, looking only at the titles of the articles. "Type something else."

Chad frowned, then typed in **Mango Slave Meter** and hit enter.

Another host of articles came up, the first of which a long list of internet memes.

The second was a blog post, titled *Minimum Slave Labour*. Underneath the url were three lines from the article. It read: "All dirt is simply matter out of place" and was followed by an ellipses before starting the article proper, which started out as a scathing deriding of minimum wage rates in some states. The sentence shown seemed to focus in on Massachusetts, where the minimum wage for tipped employees was apparently only $2.63 an hour.

"That's it," Victor said softly, staring at the blue linked headline.

Tash's head perked up and she walked in from the kitchen.

"I've been finding blogs from sites like this the whole time," Chad said as he clicked on the link. There was a banner with books on it all across the top of the page. The title of the blog came up as TheNewGoodWord, with the quote from Mary Douglas showing up underneath it. The article then started proper. To the left of the article, just like in a newspaper op/ed piece, the photo of the author showed up.

He was young with a clean-shaven, thin face. His pointed chin was sticking out toward the camera as if engaging the reader, also daring them the way a school-yard bully would. His hair was dark brown and hung in curls, coming down on either side of his face and getting tangled in his eyes. His lips were thin, and although he wasn't smiling, one seemed to be lingering behind them and waiting to come out.

"That's him," Tash said, glowering at the picture. There was an anger in her eyes that Iseult had never seen before. "That's the guy."

"The posts are from years ago," Chad said, flicking down through the dates. "And there are a lot. They start in May and go right up to... October. At least one a week, sometimes as many as three a day."

"Any way to check and see where they're from?" Victor asked.

Abby pointed to the profile button in the top right hand corner.

"They think they were written from Philadelphia," Chad read.

"Think?"

"They can't be sure. It's based off IP, which can be faked. But it's usually fairly accurate."

Victor leaned in and took the mouse from Chad, then started to scroll down through the articles. "They stop around Halloween," he breathed, opening a new browser window. "Start a new search."

"For what?"

"Murder, Philadelphia, and October of that year."

Chad nodded, typing quickly. An instant after he

pressed enter a new bunch of results appeared, but only the first one was important. Chad said nothing and clicked on the link.

It had been a townhouse then, a quiet one room dwelling with a large basement that nobody on the street had ever really suspected of anything. The neighbours had been so trusting that they'd smelled the telltale odour of decay for a full three days before alerting the police. When the police had arrived, they found fourteen teenagers dead in that large basement, some of them shot but most of them killed with a knife wound to the neck. There were pale blue curtains up to divide the open space into rooms for each person, and they were all spattered and weighed down with blood. There had been a girl upstairs in the living room, separate from the others. Another had been found in an upstairs bedroom, strangled to death.

Abby swallowed hard.

Victor got closer and Chad moved aside without a word. Victor switched back to the blog post window quickly, scrolling down through the text.

"What are you doing?" Abby asked, her face a pale green. "We found it."

"We found part of it," Victor corrected, finding a large paragraph and highlighting it. "He's been playing this game for quite a while... at least four years, if the dates on the blog are to be believed."

He opened a new browser window and pasted the text he'd copied into the search bar. The hourglass spun for a moment, then came up with just over a dozen hits. The first one was TheNewGoodWord blog again, its link changed to purple. The second was a different address altogether, dated a year later. He clicked the link. A similar blog site came up, this one with a panoramic shot of the ocean as its banner, overlayed with the same Mary Douglas quote.

The profile identified it as being from California.

"There are more," Victor said, rising to his feet and grabbing his jacket off the back of the chair. He looked at Chad and Abby sternly. "Find them."

"Where are you going?" Tash asked, stepping after him.

Victor paused at the door and fixed his collar, frowning as he met her eye. "I'm going to go get Nick."

CHAPTER 29

Atlanta, Georgia

The shed loomed at the end of the property like a ghost house. Made up of old boards and panels, it already looked old and abandoned even though it had only been built the night before. Long talons of moss crept their way from the corners of the siding and stretched upward in bending, weaving patterns, trying desperately to reach the sun. An earwig scuttled across the door and then disappeared from view somewhere behind its hinge.

An eerie green glow escaped from the bottom of the door, creeping its way across the grass until finally fading into nothingness halfway to the house. Gavin's feet were bathed in it now as he walked the distance between the house and the shed, stepping casually but with his gaze never leaving the door. When he finally reached it he turned and looked back at the house for a moment, then stepped inside without a word and shut it behind him.

Nick, Jaycee and Quinn watched from the large greenhouse window in the kitchen. Quinn was eating one of the apples while Jaycee sipped on one of Charlotte's coolers.

"Are they still in there?" Quinn asked, without turning to either of them. She was referring to the five responsible for the memorial prank: Thomas, Jason, Dennis, Mitchell and Charlotte herself.

"That's the first time the doors opened since they went in," Jaycee said in a grim, factual tone. "And there's no other way out that I can see."

Nick stared at it, the soft green glow from under the doorframe haunting him. "Must be cramped."

Jaycee frowned at him, showing off his misaligned teeth, then hopped off the counter and stepped up next to Quinn. "You're sure that wasn't there yesterday?"

Quinn shook her head.

"Quinn?"

"No - I mean, yes. I'm sure," she paused, getting reabsorbed back into that pale green glow. "It wasn't there." Jaycee let out a long sigh through his nostrils. The air went straight instead of down, puffing against Quinn's hair. "I don't know what I'm doing here."

Jaycee paused and turned toward her. Her head was up to about his chest, and when he looked at her he saw her for what she really was. Not the spoiled, bratty flake but another lost soul just trying to find a place in a world where it seemed as though all the niches had already been filled. "None of us do," he said calmly, smiling at her. "I think that's part of the point."

She turned back to him and smiled. She even laughed a little.

Nick frowned and shook his head, getting closer to the window.

There was no movement from the shed, just that same

steady stream of light and the faint hint of shadows moving across it.

"Fuck this," he said, slamming his hands down against the counter and turning toward the stairs.

"Nick," Jaycee called after him. But he was already gone.

Nick bound up the stairs two at a time. When he got to the top he raced down the hall as fast as he could. Most of the doors were shut. Megan was lying on her bed next to Billy Oates, who seemed to register who Nick was but felt no need to do anything about it. At the end of the hall was the second stairwell. It was dark, an oily black square on the otherwise white walls. Nick ran through the doorway, almost slipping on the damp floorboards and starting up the second set of stairs. They seemed to go up forever, swaying this way and that under his weight as he ran, as though he were climbing into some high belltower on a rope bridge instead of the third floor of a home.

The walls were wet with condensation. They seemed to breathe, the light from the top flickering and making them expand and contract. A heater hidden in the darkness hissed every few seconds, adding to the illusion. There was no door at the top of the stairs, and when he reached it he found himself immediately immersed in Gavin's loft.

Kelly had been lying on the mattress wearing her boxers and a thin white tee-shirt. She turned around quickly when she heard someone coming up the stairs, her expression changing from shocked to pleasant to shocked again all in the span of a second. "What are you doing here?" she hissed, getting up and stepping toward him.

"You can't be up here!"

"I had to come and see you," he said quickly, breathing hard. "While he was away."

"What?" she asked, her voice straining again. "What are you talking about?"

He grabbed her by the arms and a tingling sensation went up his hands, making his fingers numb. The skin above where he grabbed seemed discoloured and he let her go again, realizing that there was a large vertical bruise across one of her arms. He swallowed hard. "You've got to get out of here."

She laughed at him, shaking her head wildly. "You're crazy," she said finally, taking a step back from him, "You are absolutely bonkers, do you know that? I don't even know you!"

He opened his mouth to say something and his mouth went dry. He closed it again.

She stepped back over to the mattress, regaining some of her composure. "You might want to get back downstairs. If he sees you up here Christ only knows what he'll do."

Nick's eyes looked sad for a moment, and he nodded. He turned to walk away, then back again. "I don't know me either," he said finally. His voice was small and weak.

"What?"

"I don't know me either. I feel like I've been lost for I don't know how long now, and that nothing makes sense. Less than nothing. And I've been trying to make sense of it all here. I moved here a while back with Tash and Iseult and Quinn and everything seemed like it was going to start making sense but it didn't. And I was out on this date with Quinn --"

Kelly raised an eyebrow.

Nick frowned. "Nothing felt real. Nothing felt right. It was like I was going through my life with oven-mitts on. I couldn't feel anything right. I was starting to think there was something wrong with me."

Kelly smirked a little, her face full of bright oranges and deep, deep shadows in the firelight. "And you're going to try and tell me that meeting me changed all that, right?" she snorted. "That we were meant to be together, and that you could tell right away. I hate to break it to you, but if you think like that then you should spend a little more time in the real world for a while."

"I wasn't going to say that," he said, taking a step toward her again and this time she did not back away. "I don't know what this is. I don't know what's going on... all I know is, for the first time in years, it feels like the gloves are off. The oven-mitts. When I'm around you it's like I can feel... something. Anything."

She watched him for a moment. The candle light from behind her burned in his eyes almost too perfectly, like they were the glassy eyes of a doll. She felt something flutter up in her chest as though it were alive and her throat went dry, a thin layer of sweat across her face making her glow. She swallowed. "I don't know what you're talking about."

He let out a small, one-note laugh. "Maybe," he breathed. "I don't need you to feel the same way about me. I don't need you to feel anything at all about me. In the end, this has absolutely nothing to *do* with me."

She titled her head at him quizzically.

"This is about you. You are the only thing I've ever encountered that could make me feel whole about... about anything. And I can't stand the thought of something bad happening to you. Of you not being out there."

"Nothing bad is going to happen to me."

"Really?" he asked, touching her arm where is was bruised again.

She yanked away from him, and they were both quiet for a moment.

"Well than just answer me this," he said, steeling himself for the answer. "Are you happy here?"

She opened her mouth to retort immediately, but no sound came up. The question whirled and swirled in her head over and over again, and the more times she tried to come up with an answer, the more upset she got. Her lower lip started to tremble, so she closed it.

"That's what I thought," he said, taking her by the hand. "Now come on, we're got to --"

He turned around and saw Gavin standing in the doorway. His hair was matted down with sweat that was soaked into his shirt in giant oval circles under his arms and neck. His mouth was open and he was breathing through it, each one of his evenly spaced teeth visible. There was a scar that ran across his lip and went right down to the bottom of his chin, the flesh there white and bumpy as though it had been peeled back and reopened multiple times before it had finally healed properly.

"What are you doing up here?" he yelled, grabbing Nick by the shoulders and squeezing hard.

"Gavin, no!" Kelly yelled, her voice high and pleading, "It's not what you think. He wasn't doing anything!"

Nick's face wrenched in pain as Gavin's fingers poked into his shoulders. He felt like his head was about to sink down into his body as his feet tried to find their footing and failed to do so.

"Answer me!" Gavin yelled, so loud that his voice shook. His cheeks were red and purple with heat. Kelly had never seen him this angry.

Nick's face was turning red. He was trying to answer but couldn't, his tongue a swollen lump inside his mouth.

"Stop it, Gavin!" Kelly screamed again, pushing on Gavin's arm, "You're hurting him!"

Gavin threw Nick to one side and let him go, letting him slam into the unfinished boards of the wall. Something in Nick's shoulder found a nail sticking out in the boards and tore, threatening to do much worse before it came out an split-second later and he fell to the floor in a pile. He took in a long, deep, gasping breath, his body desperate for oxygen. His lungs felt like they were on fire.

Gavin spun around and faced Kelly, their faces only millimetres apart. His rage bore deep gouges in his face and when he spoke he spat at her. "What were you doing with him?"

"Nothing!" she screamed honestly, motioning toward him and then back to Gavin. "Nothing, I swear!"

"Don't lie to me, Princess! Don't you ever fucking cheat me!"

"I'm not! I'm not!" she cried, the tears that were threatening to come when Nick had spoken to her now falling. "He just came up here and he was talking crazy but he was just talking, honest! It was nothing! It wasn't even a big deal!"

Gavin stopped, his nostrils flaring. He turned back to Nick, still struggling to breathe on the floor, his hair whipping around him as he did. He jutted a finger out towards him, stabbing with it. "If I ever catch you up here again, a place to stay will be the least of your worries," he spat. "I'll beat you till you can't remember your own name."

Nick snorted, then laughed a little, raising his head. "S'funny," he slurred, smiling a little out of one corner of his mouth. "I thought you only beat on little girls?"

Snarling, Gavin pulled back and punched Nick in the jaw. His head whipped around and connected with the beams of the wall again. He fell to the floor.

A soft, tinkling sound made its way across the floor boards toward the stairs. Gavin twitched, leaning his head in that direction and bending over to see what it was. At first he saw nothing, then the firelight glinted off something small and circular on the floor. He raised an eyebrow, then turned back to Nick.

He grabbed him by the collar and pulled him inside the light.

"No!" Nick yelled, fighting his grip fruitlessly. Gavin grabbed him by the chin with one hand and forced him to face him. Nick held his eyes shut and yelled, "Jaycee! *Maximus*! Quinn! Help!" Gavin brought his other hand up and rested his thumb and forefinger on either of Nick's eyelids as Kelly cringed, then pried them open.

The force of Gavin's hit had been strong enough that it knocked the contacts out of Nick's eyes, revealing their true appearance.

Nick stared back at Gavin with an eye that was pure white, without any iris or hint of a pupil at all. The eyes twitched this way and that, the motion almost imperceivable except for the movement of the veins in either corner.

"Well well," Gavin hissed, smiling wickedly. "What do we have here?"

CHAPTER 30

Atlanta, Georgia

Jaycee stepped out into the main hallway slowly, the stairs coming into view from around the corner an ominous predator that had not spotted him yet. He swallowed back hard, feeling his throat ache for moisture as he waited for the stairs to produce something. For them to spit a person down their winding, uneven conveyer belt.

He turned back to Quinn, still standing in the light of the kitchen's bay window. She shrugged. The shed was still behind her, nestled just over her left shoulder. It seemed to leer at them through the window, an eyeless face with a crooked maw for a door. Jaycee had half expected to turn around and find that the shed had disappeared as quickly as it had appeared. It had came out of thin air and he wouldn't have been at all surprised to see it vanish in the same fashion, with Gavin standing there next to it like David Copperfield, his hands swirling and extravagant and feminine.

There hadn't been a sound from upstairs since Nick's footsteps had faded, and now Jaycee's feet curled against the carpet and his fingers tapped nervously against his leg. He stared at the place where the eighth stair up disappeared behind the corner.

There was a knock at the front door, only feet from where he stood, and he jumped back. Feeling his heart in his neck, he turned back to Quinn. She made a sweeping motion toward the door, turning back over her shoulder and looking at the shed again. It seemed like it had gotten closer to her, although when she looked she saw that the back of the shed was still flush with the grass. It was like the entire property had shrunk. As though the grass were the edge of the universe that had been expanding ever outward ever since the Big Bang and now was slowly retreating back toward its centre and taking the shed with it.

Jaycee let out a long breath of air, then opened the door.

Victor stood on the porch. Hair hung in front of his eyes, hiding all but their whites, and he looked to be glowering at Jaycee. "Where's Nick?" he said, his mouth barely moving. His bottom row of teeth were visible, with tiny peaks of his gums sticking out like the sharp peaks on a polygraph test.

Jaycee turned to look over his shoulder again, then stepped outside and gently shut the door behind him. "He just went upstairs. You shouldn't be here."

Victor stepped back from the door and into the light of the veranda, frowning visibly. "You need to get him and get out, quickly. Quinn too, if you can."

"He's just a kid and he's confused, but I think there's something out back you should be-"

"Gavin's a murderer."

Jaycee stopped, his tongue swelling up in his mouth and becoming unmovable for a moment. He stared at Victor with large, unblinking eyes and when he spoke again it was a whisper. "He's a what?"

"We've confirmed sixteen deaths so far, with a high probability of more. *Lots* more."

Jaycee stared at him.

"I've got Chad and Abby working on the details. If we get enough we'll go to the police, but right now it's all circumstantial blog crap. The facts add up though. I need you to get Nick and get out, I don't care if you have to drag him."

"I won't leave him," he said finally, finding his voice.

Victor eyed him for a long moment, then nodded slowly. He reached into his pocket and pulled out a small redand-black cell phone. He turned it on with a flush button at the top and typed something quickly, his fingers huge compared to the tiny buttons of the keypad. He stared at the screen for a moment, smiled, and then extended the phone in his open palm to Jaycee.

Jaycee squinted, then reached out and took it. "Thanks."

"It's a loaner," Victor corrected. "Text Tash if you need anything, or if anything odd happens at all. She'll make sure I get it."

Jaycee nodded.

Victor took several paces down the steps, then turned at the foot of it and looked back again. "Don't believe anything he says. Anything. But don't disbelieve it either. Treat every word like a piece of a puzzle. They're out of order, but they all fit somewhere."

He turned and looked as though he were going to leave again, then turned back one last time. "Have you seen his scar?"

Jaycee raised an eyebrow. "What?"

"The scar I was talking about. Have you seen it?"

Jaycee thought back to Gavin on the stairs, when he'd come up behind Kelly and put his arms around her. After a moment he shook his head. "No. I haven't seen it yet."

Victor nodded. "Keep an eye out for it."

Jaycee nodded, then turned and headed back into the house as Victor got back into his car and drove off.

Upstairs in his loft, Gavin watched from his window as the car pulled away from the grass and back out along the dirt road.

Atlanta, Georgia

Chad's fingers pinched his face. He stared at the screen as he tapped the down arrow over and over again, the preview screen that covered the right side of the screen changing with each stroke. Each one was a different article or web page, some of them going back years. They'd found six so far but were sure there were more, and each one of them had one thing in common - they all ended in late October.

Abby set down a mug from Metal Planet next to him, steam rising up from it and dissipating in the light from the screen.

He eyed it for a moment, then the mug next to it. It was still half full of coffee and he was sure she'd only just brought it a moment ago. The mug had Mickey Mouse's face plastered across it. He took a sip from it, realized that it had gone bitterly cold, then set it aside and took a gulp from the Metal Planet mug, his eyes wandering back to the screen.

Abby watched as the images raced by, resting her cheek against the heel of her hand. She curled her feet back up underneath her, reclaiming the same position she'd had before, the couch cushions yielding to her weight.

There was an image of a car wreck on the screen briefly, then a school photo of a young boy of about thirteen. He had freckles and gaps between the boy's teeth that made him look even younger than he was, but there was a helpful caption in dark font underneath it, just in case anyone was confused.

When he clicked the down arrow again there was a large black-and-white picture on the screen. It was a concrete room lined with bodies, each one of them covered up by a sheet. There was a man crouched over one dressed in dark, holding something under the sheet he had held up. It was hard for them to tell at first what they were looking at. The first sentence of the accompanying article read: **twenty found dead in Scranton.**

Chad paused, frowned, and then wrote something on the notepad he had nestled between the keyboard and the screen. He read on down through the article for a moment, then pressed the down arrow again.

"How does that work?" Abby asked finally, her head still rested on her shoulder.

Chad turned to look at her briefly. The screen bathed her skin in a soft blue light. He smiled, then turned back and pressed to down arrow. "Not sure it does, really," he admitted, shrugging.

"The luck thing I mean."

"I know."

"If you really were a... what did Victor call it?"

"Probability alterer."

"Yeah, if you really were, wouldn't you have found what you're looking for by now?"

Chad frowned. "He says that luck is subjective. Or some such new-age nonsense like that."

Abby paused, then nodded.

Chad flicked through several more screens.

"Who did you vote for in the last election?"

He laughed, then turned back toward her again. "What?"

"Who did you vote for?"

"Why?"

"I want to know if they won."

Chad rolled his eyes and turned back to the screen again. He took his cup and took another long drink from it, smacking his lips together when he was done. "This is good."

"Thank you."

"What'd you do to it?"

"Hmm? Oh. Eggshells and orange peels with the grounds up in the top."

He paused, looked at the cup, then shrugged and took another sip.

She watched him go through a few more screens. "You don't miss her right now, do you?"

He was quiet for a moment. Even when he did speak,

he did not turn away from the screen. "No. Times like this I'm glad she's not here."

Her mouth warbled. "There don't have to *be* times like this, you know."

He stopped and leaned back on his chair for the first time in an hour. He picked up his coffee again and stared intently on the image on the screen.

Abby sat up to see it better. When he saw her moving he tilted the screen toward her a little to help.

The image on the screen was a bust of a young woman with short blonde hair styled close around her head. Her face seemed sallow and tired, as though she'd lost the will to feel anything, and Chad thought that if her cheeks had been any more translucent he could have poked his finger right through them as though they were tissue paper. Her mouth was drawn up in a scowl and her eyes were slanted and drawn together as she glared at something beyond the camera's view, her face bathed in a warm orange glow.

The caption below the picture read London, England.

Chad sipped his coffee, not caring that the hot liquid seared his upper lip.

Abby read down through the first paragraph of the article and then glanced back up at the picture, the woman's steely blue eyes sparkling in the firelight. "What are we looking at?" she asked, taking the mouse and scrolling down some more.

Chad opened his mouth to answer, then stopped himself.

Washington, DC

There were ghosts on the streets of Washington.

Halloween was not a day in the city but a week-long affair, with each sub-group of the city claiming its own "night" with which to celebrate, many of them overlapping. Wednesday had been Pride Night, and there were still streamers and bits of pink feathers tattering the streets from end to end as Kat walked through it all.

She was holding a six-pack of beer by the plastic handle. It was cutting into her flesh but she found that she didn't care. Couldn't even feel it, for that matter. She'd finished an entire case already and hadn't experienced the effects of the tenth-to-eleventh drink this time, so she'd decided to brave the chill and see if seventeen was her magical number tonight.

She hadn't gone to work today. She'd woken up at noon and decided against it. They'd called three times. The first two times she hadn't answered. The third time she'd picked up and told Patrick, the assistant manager, that some of his more humiliating appendages were small even by British standards and hung up the phone before opening another beer.

She doubted she'd be going in again tomorrow.

There were three twenty-something girls on a stoop dressed as Sailor Scouts. They looked at her when she walked by and giggled. She smiled back curtly and continued on her way.

It was cold. Colder than it had any right to be in Washington this time of day, this time of year. Her nose was shivering; she could feel it twitch every time she took a deep breath.

A young boy dressed with a white sheet over his head looked up at her and smiled. He had a sparkler in his hand and almost his entire face was visible, courtesy of overprotective parents going a bit scissor happy on the eye-holes in the sheet.

None of them had candy, which was a shame, because she could have used some.

Behind her, a man in a dark cloak appeared out of a nearby alleyway. There was a hood over his pale white complexion that shadowed most of his face from sight.

She saw his reflection is a store window and tensed. She slowed down and eventually stopped, allowing him to step in front of her. He passed her and turned to look at her as he did, his eyes red with coloured contacts and his mouth clacking with fake fangs. He smiled at her, then continued down the street.

She exhaled, realizing for the first time that she had even held her breath to begin with.

Kat looked down at her hands and found that they were bleeding. She'd clenched them so tight that her nails had made four tiny semi-circles in the palm of each and now blood pushed its way to the surface of them.

Kat curled her lip at it and kept walking.

She opened her thirteenth beer before getting back to her flat.

CHAPTER 31

Atlanta, Georgia

When Kelly Saunders was five years old, she had had to get her tonsils and her adenoids out. She'd suffered through twelve horrible, aching throat infections during that year alone, during some of the worst of which she'd been unable to eat anything or drink anything except water for days at a time. She'd lost almost five pounds that year, and she had never been an especially plump child to begin with.

During her night in the hospital her father had stayed with her, and when she went to sleep he had been reading in the lounge chair next to her bed. When she had woken up hours later he had been gone, and the lights were out in the hospital. She'd gotten scared and left after waiting for someone to find her, wandering the dark halls as nurses and orderlies travelled blindly from room the room without seeing her.

At some point she'd made it to radiology. All the doors had had symbols on them like three-fingered black handprints on yellow backgrounds. In the dark they looked like dark eyes, looking at her wherever she went.

The first person to see her had been an old man with a large nose and crooked, smelly teeth. He'd sat behind a desk that was three times her size and stretched out over it, swinging his head down close to her and howling like an owl "Who who who are you?" She'd screamed and she'd run, ducking inside another room with the black eyes on it with no door knob.

It was dark inside, and things felt cold and metallic beneath her feet. She felt a draft coming from everywhere, all the winds of the world seeping in to converge upon her at their apex and woosh up from beneath her, tickling her under her hospital gown.

She struck her head on something sharp and stuck out her hand to grab it, slicing her palm as well.

The lights came on in the room suddenly, with a loud smack like thunder and a soft, faded electric hum. The room was large, at least twice the size of her room back home, and was the same sort of shiny silver as the nickels her uncle used to pull out from behind her ear. There was a table in the middle of the room next to her that was the same colour. It was reflecting her eyes back at her now in its glossy surface, the red of her blood distorting the mirror image and making the lines skew and rearrange.

Hanging overhead was a long mechanical arm with dozens of joints and wires coming off of it, some of which were sky blue and went all the way up to a ceiling she couldn't even see. At the end of the arm was a white square eye without any pupil or symbol or anything on it. It stared at her for a long moment after the lights came on and she stared back, transfixed by its unearthly presence.

It flashed at her, a bright light coming from somewhere behind the eye and blinding her. She screamed and stumbled backward, slipping on the slick floor and falling onto her tailbone. It flashed at her again and she started to cry, the room around her illuminating into bright hues and deep shadows with each blast from the eye. It flashed three more times before its pace quickened, becoming a strobe, blinking at her so quickly that it sent her into a seizure. She threw her head back without trying to, the base of her skull slamming against the floor hard enough to rattle her teeth. Her body shook and she tried to close her eyes but couldn't, and she started to cry hot tears that streamed down her face. She'd stayed that way until her father found her. He'd pulled her from the room by her arms and the shaking had stopped. He'd pointed his finger in her face and yelled, and his breath had smelled like whiskey and cigarettes.

Now she was wandering the second floor of Gavin's house. She had started out looking for Charlotte or Thomas, but now wandered the halls looking for anyone to talk to. Although she found many people (there was never any shortage of people in the house) she could not find anyone that she wanted to have a conversation with. They all looked fine at first, but as she got closer to them a doubt swelled up in the middle of her chest. The closer she got the bigger it became, like a balloon, eventually getting so big that it seemed to block off her throat and she had to get away in order to breathe.

She stepped into Billy's room and found it empty. There were dirty clothes all over the floor and, without knowing why, she started to pick them up and pile them in her arms to bring down to the laundry room. She had an armful of three shirts, a pair of jeans, and two pairs of underwear when tears found their way to her cheeks. They pitted down onto the underwear and turned their gray colour black with moisture. She tried to laugh and deny that she even was crying, but the more she tried the worse it got until she was the same sobbing, uncontrollable mess she had been at five. She dropped Billy's clothes to the floor and then let herself fall down right beside it, choking sobs finding her throat like boney fingers and refusing to let go.

She stayed there for some time, the smell of sweat and urine from Billy's clothes her only company.

The door opened and Quinn stepped in. She didn't say anything or come near Kelly at first, uncomfortable for one of the first times since she'd hit puberty. Though her mouth was dry and her hands seemed to be fused together beneath her breasts, she managed to croak out: " 'No', what?"

Kelly sniffed, wiping her tears away with the heel of her hand and looking up at Quinn. "What do you mean?"

"You were saying no," she replied softly. "You kept saying it."

"Did I?" Kelly said, smiling. Her chin crumpled as the smile distorted and more tears came, followed by a new cacophony of sobs.

Wincing, Quinn sat down next to her and put an arm on her back. Kelly jerked away once, then Quinn laid her hand there again. The second time it was not refused.

"I'm sorry," Kelly said, laughing and crying at once.

"I'm not usually like this. God, I can't stop."

"It's okay," Quinn said quietly, looking over her shoulder to see if anyone was watching from the door. There was nobody there. "Is something wrong?"

"No, I just... Nick was saying some things to me and I just... I don't know what's wrong."

Quinn stiffened.

"He was just asking me these questions and they were, they were so *stupid*. I mean they were. They were *stupid*. But now I can't get them out of my head and nothing makes sense anymore. I feel like throwing up and I think maybe I did throw up in Judy's room and I just have no idea what's happening anymore."

Quinn put her hand under Kelly's chin and tilted it up until they were looking at each other. "Kelly, everything's going to be alright, okay? We've got friends outside and... well... no matter what happens, they're going to get us through this. I think."

Kelly started to cry again.

Quinn made her head stay in place. "Kelly, I have something important to ask you. Where is Nick now?"

Kelly sobbed again, then buried herself in Quinn's shoulder.

After a moment she started to moan the word 'no' again, chanting it slowly in a heart-breakingly low tone. Quinn didn't even think she was aware that she was doing it. Once she'd repeated it a dozen times, a new phrase perked through the drone: "It's all my fault..."

CHAPTER 32

Atlanta, Georgia

When Victor entered the house Tash was waiting for him by the staircase. She had been in the midst of placing a copy of *War* with battered red edges back on the shelf. Startled, she put the book back on the shelf in the wrong place, wedged between two volumes of *National Geographic*.

As the door slammed shut Chad came around the corner into the foyer. Wordlessly, he handed Victor a sheaf of papers, the leaves still hot and the ink still wet.

Victor looked from Chad to the pages and then back again as he took off his coat. His gaze shifted to Tash, who seemed to be perfectly comfortable with his extended gaze, meeting his eye with patience and silence.

"Where's Abby?" he said, closing the closet door.

Chad opened his mouth as though he'd been ready to say something else, then stopped himself.

"She's upstairs," Tash said quietly. "Getting ready."

Victor raised an eyebrow. Chad held out the papers to him and he took them. The first page was nothing but text, a printout of the article Chad had found. Victor scanned down through it quickly, his eyes flipping back and forth. "This wasn't the only one you found."

Chad shook his head. "This was the only one that was different."

Victor stuck out his lower lip and continued to read. He'd gotten three paragraphs in before stopping and flipping to the next page. It was the printout of the picture Chad had found. Victor turned from the picture to Chad, holding it up. "A survivor?"

"The *only* survivor," Chad corrected. "Gavin met her ten years ago in England. It's the earliest date we could find on him. She and a friend managed to get out of the blaze, but the other girl died under suspicious circumstances in hospital shortly before she would have been released."

Victor turned back to the picture. Kat Smith looked past him with steely blue eyes, her bottle blonde hair coming out pure platinum white on the printed page and fading into the busy city background behind her. She scowled out at him from the page. It was the kind of scowl you could recognize anger in. "You found her," he said.

"She's in Washington now," Chad nodded, even as Abby came down from atop the stairs. She had a knapsack in her hand.

Victor turned from her to Chad, then to Tash. She shrugged at him with one shoulder. "You think you're going to bring this girl back into things and go after him, don't you?"

Abby stopped on the last stair and stared at him, her arms caught in mid air on either side of her as though someone had taken a photograph of her while she plummeted into a pool. Victor turned and walked into the kitchen and she followed him, followed by Chad and Tash.

"We have to go after him," Abby said forcefully to Victor's back, even as he made his way to the fridge and fished out a tall glass of orange juice. "He's a murderer. Jaycee and Nick are there right now."

"And Quinn," Chad reminded.

"And Quinn," Abby said, "Whoever she is."

Victor drank half of the tall glass in one motion, then wiped his arm in his sleeve and met her eye. "I understand your anger. I do. But going after him won't solve anything. Not like this."

Her cheeks flushed.

Chad shook his head. "You fuck head."

"Whoa," Tash said, stepping forward.

Chad ignored her. "All that talk about making the world better, and you're content to just sit there on the side lines. How is that going to help? And how do you have all the answers?"

"I most certainly do not," Victor snapped, laying his glass down on the counter. "I don't know what to do and I don't know what's going to happen. But I know damn well what not to do and what could happen if we run in there with guns blazing and take the guy out in a house filled with drunks and teens and God only knows what else." He let out a long, hot breath through both nostrils. It seemed to drain him. When he spoke again his voice was distant. "The last thing we need is to turn them from *followers* into *believers*."

It took Chad and Abby off guard, and the both of them

softened.

Victor finished his drink. Tash stepped forward and took the glass to the sink. He looked at Chad and then Abby and then Chad again, as if waiting for something, then reached deep into his back pocket and pulled out a credit card. He held it out to Abby, but Chad snatched it instead.

"You two are going to Washington," he said, relenting. It was not an order nor was it a question.

"You're okay with that?" Chad asked, squinting.

Victor nodded. "We'll need all the help we can get if this thing really does hit the fan. We've got people on the inside now, Jaycee's working his magic."

"What can he do?"

"More than you think. I think. Anyway, get to going. Money's no object."

"First class it is."

Victor leered at him.

Abby snatched the card back from him.

"I'll let you know if something goes sideways. Just get her here," Victor said, as the two of them turned to leave. "She might have some clue on how to stop him without turning this into a bloodbath on both sides."

Chad nodded, as he and Abby spun and made their way to the door.

For some reason, they found themselves running.

CHAPTER 33

Atlanta, Georgia

The moon was high in the sky, and Gavin sat on the table in the middle of the living room again. His hand was clasped tightly over his mouth, his thumb and forefinger pinching either side of his nose so that his breath came in short, whistling gasps from between his fingers.

His followers surrounded him, packed tightly into the room until there was standing room only. The archway formed an invisible line in the sand that everyone had pushed and clamoured to get on the right side of. If you were in the room you were "in," if you were out you were "out." And nobody wanted to be out.

Kelly sat on the couch next to Quinn, her hands wedged tight between her legs. There was a bruise behind her ear that looked to most like the shadow her hair made, but Quinn saw the blue and purple tinge along its edges and recognized it for what it was.

Jaycee sat on the window ledge with his arms folded in front of him, squinting at Gavin and then back to Kelly and Quinn.

"There is always resistance," Gavin said finally, his eyes closed.

Jaycee's gaze snapped back to him.

Gavin straightened, letting his hand fall from his face and dangle loosely between his legs. He swallowed hard and cleared his throat. "For every time there has been change, there has been someone willing to stand up and say that things shouldn't change. That things are fine the way they are. That we don't have the right."

He stopped and looked at those amassed. Several nodded. Many stiffened, as though waiting for something more. He sniffed. "Things are not fine. This country - this world - is crumbling around us, and it has happened before. Decades ago the people of this country stood up and said as one that they would not be oppressed, and they were heard. It was at that point, right then, that the youth of a generation could have stopped all the corruption and the villainy once and for all. They could have changed the world, but they settled for a consumerist heaven instead."

Jaycee leaned forward. So did several people sitting across from him along the wall.

Gavin smiled weakly. "And those is power made sure that it could never happen the same way again. Not here, not anywhere. They changed history, as is always the way. Those who win get to write the history of the event."

Several people nodded.

"Do you know who the greatest activists were during the Vietnam War? The soldiers. The biggest change in the tide of the war didn't come from the hippies and the yuppies dancing about on street corners with their signs and their chicken-feet symbols, it was the soldiers actively protesting the War from behind enemy lines. From in-country.

"Some refused to fight, but even more kept to their guns and waited. Because men of valour can only be pushed so far. And when they were ordered to advance on a village or a group of civilians, they would turn their guns on their platoon commanders. Or they would frag them. Do you know what fragging is?"

Several shook their heads.

"If a commander got too out of hand, the platoon would decide as a group to take care of them. There would be warnings. There might be a grenade pin left on their bunk at night, or even a smoke bomb laid underneath it... but if these warnings were not headed, the next grenade would be real. A fragmentation grenade would be thrown into his bunk, and then they wouldn't have to follow his orders anymore.

"But now we don't hear about things like that. We don't remember. When we think about anti-war protests we think of the marches and the sit-ins back home, not the men in a foreign land that had enemies on all sides and still decided to fight for what was right instead of what they were told to fight for. And what did they get for it?"

"They got spat upon," Jaycee said in a low voice.

"No!" Gavin shouted, standing and pointing a finger at him. "That was the trick. That was the con. That was the hinge that the entire scheme depended on and we bought it, hook line and sinker. We did. Each and every one of us! Because the story goes that that soldier was coming home and there were picketers and hippies protesting and they spat on him and called him a baby-killer. Does that make any sense? The hippies wanted the soldiers to come home, so why would they be protesting the soldier's arrival? They were never anti-soldier, they were anti-war. They were on the same side. The whole story doesn't make sense.

"Because the most effective protests were the ones done by the soldiers after they returned from active duty. They staged mock-terrorist attacks on towns and large, dramatic demonstrations and more than anything they returned home with real, first-hand and indisputable rhetoric about what was going on over there. The soldiers weren't spat on by the protestors, the soldiers *were* the protestors. And that was something that couldn't be allowed. So the Veteran was split into two characters: the soldier and the hippie. And if you believe what they tell you they hated each other. And once that lie was ingrained deep enough into the public consciousness, the truths of the solider revolt didn't make sense anymore. None of it made sense anyway. And when the entirety of society believes a lie as the only undeniable truth, than it's the truth that gets tossed out the window. And now we can't protest anymore, because we don't want to do to this generation of soldiers what we did to them. Even though we didn't do anything to them.

"It's a culture of lies. Of deceit. And it has been going on since the beginning of time immortal. Throughout history there are changes in what is knowledge and what is history, but every few hundred years there's a jump. A discontinuity in the way in which knowledge is accepted and presented and in which stories are told. This seems sudden but is always gradual. Enough people had to stop thinking the way they were told and to collectively start to think a different way. To say that this was not right. To start a new regime in discourse and knowledge."

"And that's you I suppose?" Jaycee said, turning toward Gavin fully and letting his arms fall to his sides.

Gavin shook his head. "No. You don't get it. It's never just one. That's what has stopped this society from rejuvenating itself when everything in history says it should have long ago. We focus on the accomplishments and greatness of the one, not of society as a whole. When the current regime falls and the new one takes over, one will likely rise to the front of the pack. And they will make the changes that the current leaders cannot. And do you know what will happen then?"

"There'll be peace and good will for all?"

"Nothing will happen then. The whole process will start itself over again. Because society cannot exist without those that seek to overthrow it. Without those seeking a different sedimentation of knowledge and of power."

Jaycee was taken aback, his head bobbing a little while Gavin spoke.

Gavin sat again, lowering his voice to the calm tone it had been when he had started. "And so, there has always been resistance. There *will* always be resistance. It's in the nature of what is happening, of the social change. It doesn't mean we need to hate our enemies or even dislike them. What it does mean is that they can't be allowed to stop us. The change is overdue, and nothing can get in its way."

Most of the group nodded. Despite herself, Quinn discovered that she had nodded too.

"There's a new resistance now. A new threat to the change," he looked at Jaycee again, then back to the crowd. "They're protecting their world and their society. They're protecting the old ways of doing things and they should be commended for that. But what the government was to the soldiers, they are to us. What the slave-masters were to the blacks, they are to us. And what the Romans were to Christ himself, they are to us. As good and as pure and as well-intentioned as they may be, they cannot be allowed to continue and they cannot be allowed to succeed. Because beyond anything else, beyond their capacity for good and their ability to help, they have the *infinite* capacity for harm."

The crowd nodded as one. Jaycee stood to watch it, all the heads moving like a human wave in an auditorium. His eyes grew wide as he saw the looks on their faces, resolute and determined. He'd seen it before in his church back home. That look of peace and certainty that overtook a person's features when they were sure. When they believed. When everything had fallen into place and they knew what they had to do.

It sent a shiver through him.

Gavin stepped forward and took Kelly by her chin, tilting her head up to him. "You are my Princess," he said with great gravitas, pushing back her hair and revealing the bruise behind her ear. "I have searched for you through all the people and the years and the countries. I stand here and I peer into your face, wonderful and fearful and doubtful, and I dream the dreams that no mortal has ever dared to dream before. And I think, this time, it will be different from the others." He leaned down and kissed her once on her lip. "This time the change is really at hand."

He took her by the hand and stood her up. Without another word the both of them walked through the crowd, the people parting for them and then moving to fill in the gap behind them. The two of them went up the stairs and out of sight, walking with the slow deliberateness of royalty. Once they were gone the crowd dispersed, each of them heading off to their own corners of the house.

Jaycee stepped over to Quinn. "What the fuck was that about?"

Quinn frowned. "I have no idea."

He let out a deep sigh, then took Victor's phone out of his pocket and flipped it open. He stared at the screen for a moment, the blue light from it reflecting in his eyes and turning them a bright shade of green. After a moment his nails clacked at the keys several times, then he shut the phone again. "Help is on the way, but we can't count on it. And even if we could we couldn't count on it soon." He looked about restlessly, finally looking out past the hall and the kitchen to the shed beyond it. It stood like a tower framed by the arches of the house all around it in layers, like a Salvador Dali painting.

"Does she have any idea where Nick is?" he asked, still staring out into the night.

Quinn shook her head.

He twitched. "I really think it's time you left and went back to Tash's."

"I got him into this."

"That's absolutely true. And I really think it's time you left and went back to Tash's."

She shook her head again.

"Then get upstairs. Find somewhere to rest, but don't get too comfortable. There's no place here that's truly safe."

She got up and headed for the stairwell where Kelly and Gavin had disappeared. When she reached it she turned to face him. "How do you know all this stuff, anyway?"

"You pick up a thing or two being a target your whole life," he said under his breath.

She nodded, then headed up the stairs.

Jaycee stood alone in the room for a long moment, staring out past the hall and the kitchen and out into the yard beyond. The lights were off and it was dark, yet somehow he could see everything. The moon was bright and full and comforting, but that wasn't where the light was coming from. Not all of it. There was a green glow that bathed the kitchen and the hall and even Jaycee himself with its radiance, but try as he might he could not see its source. It was as though it came from everywhere and nowhere all at the same time; that sickly green warmth that was somehow as warm as his mother's touch and as cold as his grave.

Without being aware of it at first, he took a step toward it. Then another. And slowly the archway faded into his peripheral vision and the hall was surrounding him. The doorway to the kitchen seemed to be growing, while the shed beyond it strangely seemed the same size no matter how many steps he took. It was like trying to chase the moon itself, watching it travel along the horizon with you but never really catching it. Never really coming close.

The kitchen was cold and blue and full of shadows that started from nowhere and bled into everything, the only haven from the dark the island in its centre. Its smooth surface was aglow with the light from outside, shimmering up as though it was producing it. He stood there next to it for a moment and let his hand pass through the beam, the light passing through the gaps between each finger as though it were solid. It almost felt solid, thick with dust and heat and anticipation. He turned to the bay window, now fully aware of the shed. The house melted into the background shadows and it was all he could see, the glowing green light coming from around the creases in its planks.

He stepped out through the back door and felt the cool fall grass on his feet. It was covered in dew and there were nightcrawlers in it. He could see them squirming and wriggling about. It brought him back to reality, the cool touch on his feet like a splash of cold water on his face.

He crept up upon the shed slowly, as though he was afraid it was going to see him.

He had seen it in the light and knew that it was no bigger than his own shack back in Idaho. That he had in fact seen some outhouses larger in his day. But now the shadows of the boards and the nails mixed and intermingled with the night around it and it seemed to go on forever. The only thing that remained stagnant was the glowing green rectangle. It stood there like a door in the middle of space. Like some passage that, if opened, would take him down to hell. As he got closer, he saw that the light from the doorframe was thick with dust as well, like the air in the kitchen had been. There was a stench on the air that he couldn't articulate, like mouldy oranges and vomit. And now that he was directly in front of it, he could hear the hum.

It was low, so much so that he didn't register it at first. Like the mechanical whirr of machinery heard through many layers of concrete. He felt it more than heard it, in the back of his mouth, right down at the base of his molars. They vibrated and screamed out in pain in tune with the dull hum, until finally his brain tuned it out and he had to struggle to hear it again. It was like white noise but worse, and he could feel it forming into a headache at the base of his skull even now. It was black noise.

"Nick?" he whispered, placing one palm on the door. It was warm despite the fact that the air around it was cool. He pulled his hand away at first, then cautiously replaced it. He turned around to see if anyone was there, then spoke again, louder. "Nick? Nick, if you're there say something."

There was no response but the hum, and the stench of putrid citrus.

He picked up the lock and held it in the palm of his hand, feeling its weight. He pulled hard on it. Nothing happened. He tugged three more times and nothing happened, before finally stepping back and forcing his shoulder forward into the door. It seemed to bend, but nothing changed. He did it again. And again. On the fourth time one of the boards let out a long, screaming crack, but when he stopped to see where it was he could find no evidence of it. The green light wasn't shimmering out of anywhere new. Now his shoulder hurt, rubbed raw from the coarse grain of the wood. There were red scratches down it that looked like an artist's crosshatching with red ink. He frowned, then placed his hand back on the door again. "If you're in there, stay strong. I'm going to figure out a way out of this."

He turned back toward the house and started walking, digging the phone out of his pocket as he did. He texted

still no nick :(

then opened the back door and stepped back into the kitchen. The light from the island was still emanating upward, casting eerie shadows that looked like the reflection of water upon the ceiling.

"What were you doing?"

Jaycee turned around quickly.

Kelly was standing next to the fridge with a bottle of cranberry-apple soda in her hand. It was dangling between her fingers by her hip, and the white moonlight got caught in the red liquid and turned her hips a bright crimson.

He glared at her for a long moment, glancing out at the hall to make sure they were alone. "Same as you, I suppose."

She held the soda out to him. When he didn't take it she shrugged and popped the stopper before taking a long drink.

Her eyes were red and puffy. She had arranged her hair to cover the bruise on her neck again. He stared at it for a long time. In the low light of the kitchen it looked like a bullet hole in her neck that went on and on forever, like a black hole.

She stopped drinking and met his gaze. "Do you

mind?"

"Yes," he said simply, curling his lip in disgust.

She shook her head. "I don't know what you're on about, but you'd better not let Gavin or the others catch you out by the shed. He doesn't want anyone going out there, do you understand that?"

"I understand that if I knew someone who treated a dog half as bad as he treats you I'd take them out back and tattoo them," he said, his drawl apparent for the first time since they'd met.

The bluntness stopped her short and she took a moment to recover, taking the time to fix her hair and hide the black mark again. "You don't know what you're talking about."

"Actually I do. I know exactly what I'm talking about. I know what it's like to be loved by someone you think is so much better than you. Because all that shit he was talking about society? It's all true. We need a change, and one of the first ones is that we need to stop putting one person up on a pedestal. But just because we need that doesn't mean we'll do it. It doesn't even mean we'll want to. And where I come from the person my whole town put up on a pedestal was *her*. And she loved *me*. And that made me feel great. It made me feel worthy, no matter what anybody said. No matter what my parents had said. And I was willing to do anything, to go along with anything, to hold onto that feeling as long as I could. It was like a drug."

She didn't meet his eye for a long moment. When she did there was spite in her gaze, but also the beginnings of tears. "Well if you know so much, why're you trying to stop me?"

"Because my drug was like strawberry wine. Yours is heroin. And it's going to kill you."

She snorted, then took another swig of her drink.

"You think being with him makes you special. Like you wanted to be in that spotlight with him so bad. Trick is, you were the only one shining it on him. He doesn't make you special. You make him special. Try shining it on yourself."

"I'm not that special."

"No?"

"No."

Jaycee smirked. "I don't know much, but I'm guessing your cell phone rarely dies. So you've got one up on me already."

She squinted at him and tilted her head to one side.

He laughed and took a step toward her, holding out his hand. "I'll actually take a sip of that now, if you don't mind."

She finished her sip and then handed him the bottle, base first.

He grabbed her wrist instead and pulled her forward, pinning her between himself and the island. With his other hand he pushed the hair back from her neck and exposed it fully, then let her go and stepped back a pace from her.

"You can't love someone and do that to them," he said. He downed the last of the soda and then laid the bottle down on the counter. "It just doesn't work that way."

He walked out of the kitchen and went upstairs to find Quinn.

Kelly stayed against the island for quite some time.

When she finally felt safe enough to move she went to the bathroom and pulled back her hair, examining the large black oval that Gavin had left there. It was tender to her touch, and after only a moment she began to cry again.

CHAPTER 34

Washington, DC

Chad and Abby stood in front of the tall apartment on Cambridge Road, just twenty minutes from the White House and the Lincoln Memorial. It was what his mother had used to call a "jellybean house," tall and thin and sandwiched between four others, sharing walls and each its own unique colour. The one they stood in front of was white, its only distinguishing feature that it had no distinguishing features.

"Do you think this is the place?" Abby asked, stepping up behind him so that they stood shoulder-to-shoulder.

He shrugged. "I don't think anything. Do you have any idea how many Kat or Kathleen Smith's there are in Washington?"

"I'd venture a lot."

"I'd venture hundreds."

"But you picked this one first. That's why we got you to pick."

He nodded, his hair bobbing slightly. "I don't think this is going to work."

"I don't know. It didn't take much for me to uproot."

"We're not saving her from a dull life. We've saving her from her disguise."

Abby paused, looking the whitewashed house up and down again, then nodded.

Chad let out a long breath and then the two of them walked up the steps to the front door at once. He knocked hard.

Several tense moments passed, and then the door opened. A short woman with pixie-cut platinum blonde hair stood in front of them, holding the door with an arm that was tensed and ready to slam it shut again. "If the next words out of your mouth are 'have you heard the good word,' I'll have several choice words for you."

Her accent had dulled, but still noticeably British. When she spoke she barely moved her lips at all.

"Are you Kat?" Chad asked.

She nodded.

"Kat *Smith*?" Abby qualified, taking a step forward.

She nodded again. "I'd like it if you got to the point. I've already filled out my census and my visa is good for another two years."

Chad shook his head. "We'd like to talk to you about a man named Gavin."

Kat's arm twitched, and for a second he thought she was going to slam the door in their faces. "Is this some kind of sick joke? I moved half way around the world to get away from you vultures."

"Should have gone the other way," Abby smirked. "Less nosy people in Asia, I hear."

This time the door did swing shut. Chad reached out

and stopped it, laying his palm flat against the window pane and bracing the bottom of the door with his foot.

"I'm calling the police!" Kat yelled, though she made no effort to get her phone.

"You do that," Chad said. "But we need to know what you know about him."

"What I know about him? I know he's delusional. That he's crazy. That he took everything from me for no other reason than I was walking down the wrong street on Halloween and now I'm here and I just want to be rid of it. Of him."

"We need more than that," Abby said finally, leaning into the door. "You're the only one who has walked away from him alive."

Kat finally stopped trying to close the door. It opened and hit the wall behind it, and she took a pace back from the frame. Neither Chad nor Abby tried to enter. She sighed, and Chad could smell the alcohol on her breath now. "He tried to make me his princess," she said, staring at some random spot on her floor. She sneered. "When I was a little girl I'd dreamed of finding out I was a princess one day. I dressed as one for Halloween when I was little. Do you know what that's like? To wish for something all your life and then turn around and have someone pervert it?"

"Yes," Abby said.

Chad looked at her for a moment, then turned back to Kat.

"It's like I wished him into being."

"You didn't."

"Like I made him out of nothing and then he killed my

friend." She placed her hand back on the door and started to close it, though she did it slowly this time. She wasn't slamming it in their faces again. "I'm sorry. I don't know what you want or why you're here, but I can't help you."

"Please," Abby plead, stepping forward. "If we're right, you might be the only one who knows how to stop him."

Kat stopped closing the door. She squinted out at them, staring into Abby's eyes and then Chad's, then opened the door. "What did you say?"

"We have to stop him, or more people are going to die. We need to know what was different about you and what you did."

"Gavin's... alive?"

Chad looked at Abby quizzically for a moment, then nodded.

Kat stared at them for a long moment.

"Who are you and what do you want with us?" Kat asked from her place next to Ashby. They were both laying on a satin bed in the centre of a large, square room. There were bodies, ten bodies in the room with them, each one on their own chair and each one completely bloodless.

"My name isn't rightly pronounced by the slithering muscles in your mouths," the man smirked, looking down at them hungrily. He gestured down to his own chest. "But this one used to be called Gavin."

He locked eyes with Kat and held it for a long moment until she squirmed uncomfortably.

"You, Miss Smith, will soon be transformed into my princess."

"Now now, sweetness, there's no use in trying to fight it. One way or another, come midnight, the rest of your life will belong to me. One way or another, you will be a part of my darkness."

∞

"Up!" Ashby shrieked, Kat already bolting up the stairs ahead of her. She reached the door at the top first, prying it open and pushing Kat inside. She felt her world come out from beneath her as something grabbed her by the ankle and yanked hard. Her head slammed against the floor as she started down the stairs, the door slamming shut behind her.

Kat was alone in the tiny attic. She turned and stared at the door for a long moment, its metal frame mocking her silently. All thoughts were erased from her mind but one: save Ashby, whatever the cost may be. She ran her fingers through her hair and she looked around. Furniture, paintings, chests and dust. She would have to look harder for a weapon. She knelt down next to a small wooden box and opened it.

The contents of the box were dusty and old. There were medical supplies that she didn't think had been in use at any point in the last century. Small glass vials that still contained liquid but were also crusted over and foggy. She huffed long and loud, picking up the shelf by either side and tossing it aside, its contents breaking over the floor.

The level below it wasn't as dusty. It contained small darts and several needles that appeared to have blood on their ends which she decided to avoid... and two guns, sitting there amongst the rest. They seemed out of place, like two elephants on a subway. She picked them up and checked their slides, breathing a sigh of relief when she found that they were loaded.

She closed her eyes and counted to ten to compose herself, then headed for the door, careful to avoid the broken glass.

Pressing her ear to the door, she strained to hear the sounds of her pursuers. Two separate breathing patterns.

Her next decision would haunt her for years to come.

The room was filled with more of the masked men, all surrounding a large rack in the middle of the room. It was plywood and tilted up for all to see, someone in the back tightening its gears every few moments to make the ropes binding its occupant in place grew tighter and tighter.

Strapped onto the rack was Ashby, the ropes burning into her wrists and ankles.

"'That we are true lovers run into strange capers: but as all is mortal in love in nature so is all in nature in love mortal in folly,'" he stated, turning to face Kat, an ugly smirk playing across his lips. "Shakespeare's As You Like It. And we are true lovers, you and I. You can feel it. I know you can."

She twisted, letting it rip out and raced over to where the guns remained. Without thinking, she shot the rest of the cult followers dead, cursing herself for missing three shots, and for *regretting missing the shots. Then she turned to Gavin.*

"You don't want to shoot me, Kat. It's not too late to finish the ritual," he murmured, almost fearfully.

"Bloody Hell! You are crazy, understand? Crazy!" Kat yelled, finally snapping. "You killed the only real friend I've ever had and you just expect me to comply?" she screamed, motioning to that which she had not yet acknowledged, Ashby's still form. Kat was in tears now.

She aimed and fired.

The bullet hit Gavin in the stomach and he curled into himself, folding into a ball.

She ran to Ashby. She was still clinging to life. Kat felt her heart soar at the discovery. "I'm gonna get you out of here," she murmured into Ashby's hair as she picked her up and cradled her gently in her arms.

She left the room ignoring Gavin's pleas for help.

Kat blinked, still holding the door as though she were going to slam in it Chad and Abby's faces.

"Alright," she said, and her voice had a harder, harsher tone to it. "Alright, I'll come with you."

Los Angeles, California

Theo sat in the pressroom of the Los Angeles Channel 5 News Station, his guest pass dangling from a lanyard around his neck. He was sitting in the middle of a couch made for three with his arms and legs stretched out in such a way that no one else dared to sit down.

There was a paper cup with water in it dangling from

his loose fingers.

His eyes were closed and his mouth was open, and as he faced the newsroom it was like watching a thousand screens all at once, each of them blaring their own broadcast with their own slants and biases and each with the person thinking it as the anchor.

"Police are still looking for Audrey Marshall, the nine year old that went missing nine days ago from Hillview Grove --"

"- say that large amounts of the greenhouse gas may be able to be used for something other than -"

"- new virus that experts say is undetectable by conventional virus scanners."

One by one each billboard fell away, ignored by him and switching off to mute before turning to black completely. As he narrowed his search further and further the existing screens got louder and louder, until he could barely hear the real world around him.

"-The individual who has been terrorizing the business community has been trapped. With Cooperation from Arthur Shane the second, owner of Shane Incorporated."

Theo stopped, focussing in on the man reading over the copy for air.

"The police made this building into a trap for the creature that we now know calls itself Black Heart. As it is, Black Heart has sealed itself inside of Shane headquarters, with thirty-one hostages consisting of both Shane employees and customers using the firm downstairs."

Theo opened his eyes and sprang to his feet.

CHAPTER 35

Atlanta, Georgia

The back stoop was warm for October, and Richie felt it on his skin. He closed his eyes and smiled, letting the sun's rays fall down upon his face even as a chilly breeze softly caressed its way through his hair.

Gavin stood below him on the grass with one foot propped up on the stair. He was leaning on his knee and held a vodka cooler gingerly in his hand, flipping the neck of the bottle between his fingers and letting small drips of alcohol splash out of the bottle and onto the ground. He smiled. "It's a wonderful day, isn't it?"

Richie beamed and opened his eyes. "Yes."

Gavin took a sip of his drink. "I heard what you were saying the other day, by the way. About how people around here can be - - what was the term you used?"

"Close-minded."

"*Yes*," Gavin said, pointing the mouth of his bottle at Richie. "That was the one. I've noticed it, too. Noticed it a lot since I came here, and a whole lot more over the last few days. People just don't like new ideas."

"It scares them, sometimes. Change is slower down here... they still use racial slurs in everyday speech that anyone else in the country would have to look up to see what it meant."

"It's a Bible Belt thing," Gavin nodded. "There isn't a lot of cosmopolitanism going on around here. In fact, more and more I'm seeing a kind of metropolitan provincialism... like people aren't aware of the worth of things that go on outside the borders of their cities."

Richie shook his head. "I really hate this place."

Gavin turned to him and gave him a warm smile. "Don't say that. Places can change. People can change. I know it doesn't seem like it now, but think about what this place would have been like two hundred years ago, or even twenty years ago. Then think of it now! And twenty years, that's nothing! Even two-hundred years... just a drop in the bucket. It's all a matter of fighting each battle as it comes, all the while keeping your eye on the bigger picture."

Richie nodded. "The bigger picture."

"The bigger picture."

He stepped down off the stoop to be level with Gavin, even though he could not be. He was at least half a foot taller than him. When he came down he saw the scar that connected Gavin's earlobe to his jaw. He tried not to look at it, averting his eyes to the wasted dirt land that surrounded their property. "One battle at a time. Like those resisters that - -"

"Don't bother about that," Gavin snorted, waving the idea away. He held up his finger and then finished his beer, laying the empty bottle on the bottom stairs of the stoop. "Everything there is taken care of."

"But you said - -"

"A lapse in judgement. We all have them."

Richie nodded.

Gavin put a hand on his shoulder, and the both of them started walking toward the shed. "Speaking of which, I've got something I've been meaning to show you."

Atlanta, Georgia

Jaycee watched from the kitchen window as Gavin and Richie disappeared into the shed. The green glow that was usually almost invisible during the day shone brightly for a moment, almost as though it was a conscious effort on the part of the shed to not let him see inside. He frowned, then turned around and marched back out into the living room.

Billy was sitting on the couch with his feet up on the coffee table. He was reading from a battered copy of *Sports Illustrated* that looked too thin to contain all the pages that it should, and was folded completely around. He was holding the book close to his face and straining his eyes so that he could still read it.

Quinn was sitting against the window with Kirby. She was wearing someone else's shirt, but he wasn't sure whose. Shane and Patrick were on the floor next to her, as well as three girls that Jaycee didn't recognize and hadn't seen before. He felt as though the youth in this house were like ants; that no matter how many were accounted for there were always more willing to crawl out of the woodwork.

Judy was coming down the stairs behind him.

"This'll have to do," he mumbled, then stepped into the centre of the room. "Listen up, because I've got to make this quick. I'm in no mood to get into a verbal debate with Bella Lugosi back there."

Dennis rolled his eyes and started to get up.

Jaycee held up one finger to him. "Just wait a second. I swear I'm not even going to try and attack him or his rhetoric."

"Because you can't," Judy said, cocking her head arrogantly as she entered the room from behind Jaycee. Her arms were crossed.

"Because I can't," he nodded. "Absolutely right. Nobody can. It's just that sort of right-sounding speechifying that nobody can argue with. But that's not the point. But here's the rub: no matter how right he is, no matter how correct he is, you're all still puppets. You're all still being used."

"Fuck you," Billy snarled.

"I don't care that he's good at what he does. And neither should you. At the end of the day, I don't think any of you really care about what he says. I think that's just a convenient excuse to allow you to be sanctimonious as you sit there and let yourselves be lead. Because at the end of the day, puppets don't care."

"I'm not a puppet."

Judy nodded, along with several others. One or two more heard the commotion and were filtering into the living room.

"You're a *puppet*. And you don't even need me to tell you that you are. Because the puppet doesn't care who the person pulling the strings is. Doesn't matter if it's Jim Henson making a great movie or some kid in his backyard making a shoebox show. At the end of the day the only people who don't give a crap are the puppets."

Several people looked down.

"But here's the plot twist," he smiled, his voice softening. "You can prove me wrong and you can make all this go away, and you don't have to turn away from Gavin or anything he says or anything. All you have to do is not be here, in this house, for one night. Tonight."

Kirby and several others squinted. "Why would we do that?"

"Why wouldn't you do that?"

"We believe in him. We believe what he's saying. He's never given us any reason to doubt him."

"Didn't say he did. But if I told you I believe that *my* faith makes me bulletproof, what would you say to me?"

"I'd say prove it," Billy laughed.

"Exactly. But proving it would mean me taking a bullet, and I'm not willing to do that because the risk to my body isn't worth it. If I'm wrong I'm happy enough being alive and ignorant. But what if I told you that I believe my saviour is a rat with green eyes that lives in that fridge?" He pointed out toward the kitchen.

"I'd say prove it."

"And I would. I would go out to the fridge and open it. If there's a rat with green eyes there then I've proven myself right. If not I've proven myself wrong and I need to find a new thing to model my life around. But the risk of looking was so minimal that it was worth putting my faith to the test. And faith isn't worth anything unless you test it."

Billy frowned.

Quinn's eyes lit up. So did Kirby's. And few others seemed to perk up as well.

"Here's the thing, you can't know what will happen. I don't know what will happen. I don't even know what's happening now. But you have this one chance to prove that you aren't what the world thinks you are. That you aren't just some puppet. And because you can't know what's going to happen, the only thing you can control is what you do to prepare for that uncertainty.

"Think of what will happen if you don't act. If I'm right, you're all going to die. If I'm wrong, everything continues as normal. You can spend the rest of your life drinking it up like you're in a college without the class. And if you do act, and I'm right, it would save your lives. But what if I'm wrong and you act? What would happen?"

There was silence. They all looked at each other.

"Exactly. Nothing. Gavin has said that you can come and go as you please. You'll have wasted a few hours of your time. That's it. So in my mind it doesn't matter who's right and who's wrong. What it comes down to is which action has a worse consequence. It comes down to thinking in rows, rather than in columns."

One or two nodded. Billy frowned and went back to his magazine.

Jaycee turned and walked back out toward the kitchen. He took out his phone and starting to text as he walked.

Quinn got up and followed him.

CHAPTER 36

Los Angeles, California

Leigh clenched her teeth as she stared through the Venetian blinds at the crowd gathered around the Shane building. The people on the street all blended together at this distance, their movements seen only as ripples in the human wave that surrounded them.

Sweat was tumbling down her forehead in great grey clumps. She turned away from the window wringing both her hands through her hair and squeezing. Water dribbled from between her fingers and pitted onto the floor.

"Fuck," she cursed, pacing the tight area between the window and the wall again and again, shutting her eyes stiffly and waiting for the answer to come to her. When she opened them again, they were all looking at her.

Thirteen Shane employees with sweat and tears pouring out onto their three-piece suits, all of them with their eyes fixated on her, watching her every twitch and motion. They ranged in age and sex and race, and they all knelt with their hands behind their heads and their eyes following her as though some hypnotist had commanded them to.

One man in second row was particularly attentive. He kept looking her up and down and sneering, as if to say: *I could take her*. He wouldn't try though, but he was judging her for doing this, she could tell.

-MEEEEEP!-

The phone started to ring again for the fourth time in as many minutes. The sound sent a shock down the wooden desk that she could feel in her toes. She did not turn to look at it, but felt a brief release from the intense glares of everyone in the room as they all did, if only for an instant.

-MEEEEEP!-

She reached over to the receiver without looking and picked it up, then slammed it back down against its cradle.

The crowd jumped, almost in unison.

She leaned against the desk for support and took several deep breaths while staring at the floor. There was a telephone jack with nothing plugged into it that caught her eye for no particular reason, only that it was in her immediate field of vision and did not have eyes with which to stare back at her. Her cheeks puffed out as she exhaled deep, heavy breaths, and more sweat drenched its way down her face onto her neck.

The man in the second row gave her the elevator again, letting out a small puff of air.

Her head shot up as soon as she heard it and locked eyes with him. It was the first time she'd actually made direct eye contact with either of them since taking the room, and she was relieved to find it empowering. He shied away almost immediately, now the only person in the room that *wasn't* looking directly at her.

"You," she said, motioning him toward her with two fingers. "Get up."

He turned to the woman next to him, as if to say *Get up*.

"No, you," she repeated, pointing at him directly this time.

Swallowing hard, he got to his feet. He still hunched, as if the lowered elevation somehow hid him amongst those around him.

"Come here."

He closed his eyes and stepped over the first row of hostages. When he was in front of them all, she could see that he was an average height, with a cheap navy suit and a haircut that belonged in an eighties rock band. His face was boney and thin, but the rest of him looked like he'd missed a few too many runs on the treadmill. Still, he had the look of someone who at least *thought* they were in decent shape.

-MEEEEEP!-

She picked up the phone and quickly brought it to her ear. "I want out of here, okay? That's all I want. You get me out of here, you get these idiots. Every three minutes I'm still in here, I kill one of - -"

The lights went out, making the small office area seem too large to comprehend. Darkness had a way of distorting perception like that, making even the closest wall seem like it could be miles and miles away.

She grabbed the man next to her around the neck and dug her nails in, her eyes darting aimlessly around the room, waiting desperately to adjust to the light. Slowly the shapes of the men and women before her came back into view from the light of the window and her mouth curled back downward into a scowl.

"You think that's fucking funny, do you?" she yelled into the phone, her eyes ballooning out of her face. "You've got two minutes before I off Mr. Roboto here, so you'd better wise the fuck right up, you fuck!"

She slammed down the receiver again, this time so hard that the phone snapped itself in two.

"Please..." the man gasped, his hands wanting to come up and pry her fingers from him but not doing so all the same. "Please, don't do this."

"Shove it," she snarled, giving him a little shake as she turned back toward the window. She pried the blinds open again, staring at the ever-growing crowd of police cars and pedestrians that were gathering around the building. None of them seemed to be moving about as she expected. None of them appeared to be clearing a path for her car or helicopter or pedal bike or what-the-fuck-ever. She let go of the blinds again and turned back toward the hostages, holding the man between them like a shield. She let out a long sigh, then wrapped her free hand around him until it rested on his abdomen. If someone had looked in and not known what was going on, they might have thought the two were spooning.

Her touch was light, like the sharp edge of a blade pulled just enough to tug at the ripples in your skin. Her hands were warm and damp, soaking through his shirt after only a moment and making it stick to his stomach like a thick layer of sweat.

He turned his head down despite his better judgement, her nails scratching at his neck, and watched her hand as it lay against his gut. Her palm was clammy and damp, making the ashen flesh come alive with sparks of moisture. A muscle near the base of her thumb twitched, making the rest of the appendage shudder its echo along in time.

Her heart slammed against her chest like a battering ram, each vein reverberating as waves of blood crashed through them. The sweat that drenched her hand started to gain a dark tinge to it and squeeze its way through her pores. At first the darkness was minuscule compared to the salty pools around it, like thousands of tiny blackheads. The heads swirled and wove about in their own tiny currents, growing and spreading until the liquid that covered her hand was blackened and writhing.

Her fingernails were sweating, too. As impossible as it was, beads of black had formed on each nail as deep as shoe polish dripping down from one finger to the next and becoming more the consistency of wax than sweat. Fingerprints became shrivelled and loose as though they'd been immersed in water, their lans and grooves changing into something unrecognizable from what they had been moments before.

The muscle and bone of her hand began to melt and shift in a way no human hand could, caving in on itself and losing its shape while somehow retaining its mass, flowing down and then circling back to bear like water circulating through a fountain.

She was melting.

When the pooling flesh touched against the man again,

it was like a puddle of water had been poured slowly into the conclave of his chest, then left to warm in the summer sun. It stayed there for almost a full minute, defying gravity without a ripple or wave, before suddenly becoming sharp.

The liquid somehow pierced his sternum, sending bursts of pain into the massive cluster of nerves it found there.

Leigh started to cry, but forced herself to hold it back.

The man screamed, all the air expelling itself from his lungs in one massive, mournful burst.

She sighed, then took a quick gulp of air as she found herself finally capable of doing so again.

She slid her hand back out of him whole and solid, all five fingers wriggling and consistent. The only sign that the event had even taken place was the splash of crimson that covered her hand in a swirling, unnatural pattern. It had almost stained her, as though when she'd reformed it had mixed with the blood as well, creating a tattoo on her flesh.

With a sickeningly moist sound, like a knife slicing through ripe grapefruit, she removed her nails from his neck. He crumpled onto himself as he fell to the floor, like a puppet whose strings had been cut.

Her face was expressionless, yet exhausted. Sweat clung to every spare piece of skin, especially along her upper lip. Her cheeks now appeared chubby as her jaw went slack, every haggard breath shaking them violently.

"Guh," she said finally, taking a step over the body toward the crowd and getting it out of her sight. She stumbled once, her legs made of rubber.

She slowly forced her body and mind back to composure as she stared at the people in front of her.

"You see that?" she said brazenly. "You see what just happened?"

-MEEEEEP!-

The phone across the room sprang to life again. She turned only slightly toward it before slashing a long nail through the air, pointing at a forty-something blonde woman in the back row. "You, get that! Tell them what I just did! Tell them that I want out of here, free and clear, or I do it to this guy!"

-MEEEEEP!-

She swirled toward the front row, her torso turning so fast that it seemed to be independent from her hips, connected only in the loosest possible sense of the word. She grabbed the first man she found there. He was trembling and soaked with tears and urine. She forced him to his feet.

Immediately they were at eye-level, and she could see his cheap navy suit and a haircut that belonged in an eighties metal hair band. His face was boney and thin, but the rest of him was flabby and out of shape.

It was the man she'd killed a moment ago.

Despite the already pale nature of her flesh, she managed to become even whiter. Loosening her grip on the quivering man, she turned her eyes back to the crowd. She moved her eyes over her hostages slowly and carefully, counting each one. Her lips moved slightly as she mouthed each number, taking care to make sure her eyes weren't playing tricks on her. Then she counted again, finding that no matter how many times she did, there were still thirteen. More than that, they all stared forward in absolute, unwavering fear... but for the first time in nearly an hour, it wasn't directed at her. She turned slowly, chewing on the inside of her cheek as she came around a full one hundred and eighty degrees.

There was a man hunched over the spot where the body should have been, but wasn't. He wasn't the eighties hair-band man, but someone much different and much younger. Though the simple act of standing seemed to take tremendous strength, his will seemed too strong for him to fall. His eyes bore holes into hers, unblinking and unwavering, hidden only slightly by the damp bangs that fell in front of them. His jaw was set and clenched, cheeks shaking with each deep breath he took. One arm was wrapped around his mid-section, holding in his innards as blood gushed out onto his arm along with bile and shit from his ruptured intestines. The smell was magnificently putrid.

The free hand hung by his side lazily, swaying back and forth as though it was a disconnected pendulum; useless, but somehow ready to strike as well.

At the end of each finger a thin hook of bone poked through.

It took Leigh a moment to register that they were claws.

The blood that was still coming from his mid-section was no longer red but a deep, shadowed black that rivalled her own.

He took one long breath. The veins in his eyes bulged a deep coal black.

She leapt quickly, the transition from shock to offense so sudden and clean that even she was surprised by it. Her motion though the air was so fluid that when it changed direction it was jarring, like watching water move about freely of its own accord, independent of gravity. He dodged to the left, letting the screaming wave connect to his arm. What looked like liquid sliced and dug down to the bone, rending the flesh there into long, rectangular ribbons.

He screamed as blood gushed outward and upward, splashing to the floor as his body tried desperately to heal, still in the midst of recovering from the wound to his chest. The sensation was uncanny, like when rain ripped around you so fast that it felt like it was stinging and slicing at your flesh, only this time it was.

"Damn it!" he hissed, spinning and backing up to get away from her, almost slamming his back into the people knelt there. He turned to them angrily. "What're you waiting for, an invitation? Get the fuck out of here!"

The hostages got to their feet. One or two stayed frozen where they were for a moment before the jarring of bodies toward the doors knocked them back to reality. They were screaming now, maybe because they finally felt safe enough to scream.

Leigh raked her nails across the man's face as he turned back to her, her fingers almost talons in their own right. All surprise had eroded from her face and she stared at him with a cool poise, her lips drawn up in a small black bow. He brought his hand up to his face, screaming as he felt her pass though his cheek and into his teeth. When he brought his hands up to his face she slashed at his stomach again and he doubled over in pain.

"Stop!" he yelled, swinging wild and digging his claws into her shoulder.

She screamed so loud that it seemed like it was coming from everywhere. It was like gargling, thousands of bubbles popping at once until finally the flesh his claws were in gained the same tar-like consistency her hand had a few minutes before and the slipped through his grasp.

She backed, breathing hard.

He did the same.

The hostages were gone now.

"What the hell are you?" he asked between laboured breaths. The words came out slurred, the sound distorted by the gash that had punctured his cheek.

She huffed through her nose, then looked him up and down and nodded toward his talons. She opened her mouth to speak, closed it, took several more breaths, then tried again. "You're one to talk."

He did not respond, watching as her skin seemed to literally crawl. Her eyes seemed to swirl about like whirlpools.

She lunged forward again, slamming both hands against his shoulders and forcing him to the ground. She pinned him down and dug her knees into his sides. Somehow they became so sharp that they broke his skin. There was a hiss from inside him as something, got punctured.

The man ground his teeth together and fought back the urge to scream.

She turned her head slightly, looking down at him with a mixture of puzzlement and curiosity, her mouth becoming a tiny sphere in the centre of her face. Something was wrong, although she could not quite but her finger on what. It felt like there was water boiling deep inside her stomach. She opened her mouth and black vomit sprayed from her as though someone had turned on a hose. It drenched down over him just as he was taking in a lungful of air.

She let out an unearthly noise, her neck straining and stretching forward as more and more of her mass spewed down his throat and suffocated him. Still, she held him tight, her fingers like vice grips.

His claws came up like lightning and slashed at her wrists.

She tumbled backward, screaming that gurglingly sick scream again as she cradled both her arms in front of her, staring down at them as if she were coddling a child.

He got to his feet vomiting up the vomit she'd poured into him. When most of it was gone he looked up again, watching her as she still touched her disjointed flesh tenderly. It bled, the colour a spectacular crimson red.

He almost smiled, but found the gash in his cheek prevented it. "Had to turn solid to hold me down, huh?" he said, squatting down and withdrawing the talons from his other hand.

She tried to respond but couldn't, everything coming out like a haggard growl.

He crouched down then leapt at her from all fours, connecting with her mid-section and forcing her back into a line of chairs. She splashed against them, travelling up in a wide arc and falling all around him as he passed through her, slamming into the chairs himself. One caught him in the eye, and for a moment all he could see was pristine, white light.

"Rahg!" he bellowed, rising to his feet and spinning to face her.

The room was empty.

He stood completely still, only his pupils moving from side to side over the room as he stood ankle deep in the blood.

The room was silent at first, then a bubbling sound started to come up again, as if from nowhere. It was her scream, rising and emanating through the room.

"What the sweet holy fuck," he whispered, bringing the claws of his right hand to the wrist of his left and pushing until there was blood.

Suddenly his feet were taken out from under him and he slammed his head back against the hardwood floor. The puddle he'd been standing in came out from under him like a rug, arching upward and becoming a massive wave that hovered above him, ready to crash down. Her scream rose to deafening levels as he looked up at the wave in horror. He took a deep breath.

"Amateur," Leigh said from behind him.

He turned around and she brought her talons across his eyes. He fell into the chairs with his back arching against the metal frame at an odd angle, then crashed to the floor. She waited for a moment for him to get back up.

He did not.

The anger fell from her face and became concern. Her hands started to shake and sweat once again dotted its way across her brow.

She turned toward the exit.

Theo was standing in there glowering at her, his eyes slit and expression seething.

CHAPTER 37

Atlanta, Georgia

When Kelly came down the stairs, Billy and Kirby were talking in the corner of the living room with Megan, Steven and Banner. They turned and looked over their shoulders at her. She stared back at them for a moment with her eyebrows arched, then turned and started toward the kitchen.

Out the window of the would-be dining room, she could see Gavin sitting alone out on the front step. She didn't think she had ever seen him do it before, and for some reason the sight of him sitting with the sun caressing his hair and his shoulders made her smile. The sides of her mouth hurt with the motion, and the grin disappeared quickly.

Changing course, she walked back into the hall and stepped outside.

The air was warm for late October. If it hadn't been for the breeze she might even have described it as hot.

There was a case of beer next to him on the veranda, with three of the empty bottles lying about upright and on their sides in a disjointed cluster near his hip. A fourth bottle was in his hand and was half empty. He had peeled the label from it and was now staring at the paper and goo left over as though waiting for it to do something, turning the bottle slowly in his palm.

"Penny for your thoughts," she said, stepping up beside him. She did not sit down, not without being invited.

He smirked. "Too many for a penny."

"A dollar then?"

He shook his head.

"Name your price."

"Nothing less than a million for these puppies. They're worth it."

"I've no doubt," she laughed. She leaned against the post.

He turned a smiled at her, at the way the sun kissed her flesh. Slowly, his smile faded away until it was a shadowy, hard grimace. "Are you the real one?" he asked, although it wasn't clear if it was rhetorical or not.

"What do you mean?"

"I've known a lot of women, Kelly. A lot of women."

"I don't need to hear about --"

"And every last one of them I thought was the one. The one that could save me from this... cycle," he began to mumble off, then came back. "I was never the type to just dine and dash. To fuck around. I thought each and every one of them was the real deal, and I was wrong about them all. None of them worked in the end. So I just need to know: are you the real, honest-to-be-true one? Or am I just going to be left with that hollow nothing again?"

She paused, swallowing hard. "I am. I guess I am. I don't know."

"You're my princess?" he smirked.

She laughed. "Sure, Charming. I'm your princess. Whatever you want me to be. How many have you had anyway?"

His smiled faded, his eyes becoming dark with shadow. With one motion he stood and threw the bottle down between his feet, sending alcohol and broken glass spiralling in all directions.

"Jesus!" she jumped. Her hair stood out on end.

"That's not what you're supposed to say!" he screamed, his cheeks red. He jutted a finger out at her, almost poking her in the chest with it. "It's not right. It's... scripted, somewhere. I don't know what it is, but I know damn well what it isn't!"

Kelly stepped back a pace toward the door, staring at him. "I - - I don't know what I said."

"Not what you said, what you didn't say," he said under his breath, running his fingers through his hair. He stepped off the veranda and out onto the grass once more, feeling it between his bare feet. "We that are true lovers run into strange capers: but as all is mortal in love in nature so is all in nature in love mortal in folly."

"What?" she squinted.

"Nothing," he sighed, not turning around to look at her. "Just go back inside."

She stayed where she was for a moment, watching him as he stood barefoot on his lawn. Then she backed away a pace and finally turned around and stepped into the house.

She went to the fridge again and got herself a drink.

Atlanta, Georgia

Victor sipped on his tea, then brushed a little of it from his moustache. He laid the cup back onto its saucer and picked up his cell phone, scrolling through his last few messages from Jaycee and Abby again. A worried look passed over his face. He selected Jaycee's name and typed

Text every thirty.

and watched as the spinning hourglass animation displayed over and over again before bringing him back to the phone's home screen. He waited a moment to see if a return message would appear. When it did not he laid the phone back on the edge of the table.

Tash sat across from him, holding her cup in both hands with her elbows resting lazily on the table. "You're worried about them."

He shot her an annoyed look. "You must be empathic."

She smiled, ignoring his sarcasm. "You've got the same look on your face that he always would when you were out. Pensive. Anxious. Unsure."

"It was different," he said, his voice almost a whisper. "I was trained. I knew how to handle myself."

"So do they," Tash shrugged. "The girl more so than anyone. Port Haven's not just a finishing school you know."

He winced.

"You feel like you could be doing more."

"I feel like I should have just called the police."

"I've tried that."

"I feel like I should have just marched in there and did what needed to be done."

"*You've* tried that. It didn't work out so well in the past."

He looked down at his tea. "Guess it boils down to if you think in columns or if you think in rows," he frowned. He finished the tea then stood up. "It's about risk over reward."

"But are you thinking about the risks in the long term or the short term? If you go in there and you fight Gavin and you make things right, what happens tomorrow? Or the next day? Or two years from now?"

Victor got a faraway look in his eye for a moment, then turned to Tash. He stared at her for a long moment. "You're nervous," he said finally.

"For you, yes. Very."

His phone buzzed and he picked it up quickly and flipped it open.

"Jaycee?"

He shook his head. "Abby. They'll be landing soon."

Tash raised an eyebrow at him, then watched him put on his coat.

Atlanta, Georgia

Kelly had been kneeling on Gavin's bed, facing the collection of items and paper in front of it. Two of the candles that lit it had gone out, and the few that were left were dwindling. The light was a dark orange and made things barely visible, the paper that she'd gotten for him almost impossible to read. He'd written on almost all of it. Some was in a swooping, cursive hand while other pages were scrawled in a quick, slanted text. It ranged from unreadable to unidentifiable.

He came up behind her and placed his hand on her waist, sliding it around until he was holding her. His arms felt like knives pressing into her flesh with their flat edges – not cutting yet, but threatening to with even the slightest movement in either direction. His lips on her neck felt cold and sickening, and she felt her shoulder arching and rolling to try and get him off instinctively.

"I apologize, Princess," he said, slurring his s's until he sounded like an anthromorphisized snake. He squeezed her closer.

She closed her eyes, her voice devoid of all expression. Her mouth was a small thing in the centre of her face.

"Can I ask you something?" she said, even as he pulled her closer. He wasn't wearing his shirt. She could feel the heat of his skin all against her back even through her own.

"Of course," he said, his lips on her ear. "You can ask me anything."

Where is Nick? she thought. She opened her mouth to ask it twice, but both times she shut it again. His arms drew her tighter, and she felt as though she couldn't breathe. His hands were on her and she couldn't move.

"Princess?"

She bit her quivering lip and fought back tears for what felt like the umpteenth time. "Nothing," she said finally. "I just needed to know if I could."

He laid her back onto the mattress and pushed the covers aside. The gust they created blew the rest of the candles out and she was grateful, for although she could not bear to close her eyes she could not bear to see either. She wished for blindness and for deafness and to not be able to feel his touch as his slithery body found its way around her arms and her waist and her neck, pulling tight until she couldn't move or breathe or even scream. She tried to scream. In her mind she was screaming loud enough to shatter the windows and crack the floor boards.

He was on her and inside her and around her. He was in all of her senses at once, pushing and pulling and uncomfortable. She shut each of them down one by one, pretending not to see then pretending not to hear then pretending not to feel. But she couldn't pretend not to care.

The more she turned them off the more her mind made up their own, shooting endorphins and chemicals through her mind until she became convinced she *could* see.

"Nobody that left home at your age ever amounted to nothing or nobody," her father had said with that gruff Bible Belt drawl. He turned his fork back toward his dinner, taking a big shovelful of chicken and cabbage and pushing it into his mouth. "You'll never find anything to make you feel as good and as warm as this house and this town and this family. I hope you're hearing me."

When she felt as though she couldn't keep the scream inside anymore it was done. She let out a long, wet sigh then rolled over and closed her eyes.

Gavin sat next to her for a long moment, his ass resting on the bed and his feet planted firmly against the floor. He struck a match and relit several of the candles, then arranged the scattered paper into several small (and random) piles. He turned back to her then, her pale body aglow in the candlelight.

"Princess?" he asked, reaching out and touching her shoulder gently.

She did not move or stir. Her breathing was slow and constant.

He stared at her for a long moment, his hand lingering on her flesh. He looked thoughtful, then licked his lips. "Kelly?"

Still, she did not stir.

He frowned, then got up and put his clothes on and walked down the stairs.

As soon as she heard him step on the last stair her eyes opened and she got up.

CHAPTER 38

Atlanta, Georgia

Jaycee sat in the stairwell and wrung his hands, feeling the callouses of each palm meet each other. Kirby was standing across from him with a far off look in his eye, nodding politely.

"There's too much here that doesn't make sense," Jaycee said again, meeting the older man's eye. "You must see it. The kids don't, but you must."

Kirby though for a moment, then nodded solemnly.

"There's a question then of what are we --"

He stopped suddenly. Gavin stepped into the stairwell from behind him and he moved out of the way, casting his eyes down toward the baseboard. Gavin did not say a word, barely even acknowledging that Jaycee was even there. Judy was with him, stepping along one or two paces behind him.

When he reached the bottom of the stairs he smiled politely and made a "ladies first" type of motion toward the main hall. She smiled, nodded, then made her way out toward the kitchen with Gavin in tow.

They exited the house through the back door and made their way across the lawn toward the shed.

Jaycee stared at them as they went, even after Kirby resumed the conversation.

Atlanta, Georgia

Gavin made his way to the door of the shed and stopped in front of it. He looked it up and down and smiled, then reached into his pocket and began to fish for his keys.

"It's really amazing what the boys managed to do almost overnight," Judy mused, standing a few feet back. She wasn't wearing shoes and the wet grass covered her feet and made her feel cool all over. Even though she liked it she shivered, rubbing her hands over her arms to keep warm.

He smirked as he giggled the key into the lock. "The ingenuity of the people in this country has never ceased to amaze me. I've seen men build far more in far less time, and it's always incredible."

The lock made a sharp snapping sound and the bolt came loose from its base. He slid it out from its place on the door and stepped back from it, again making the same dramatic sweeping gesture, bowing toward Judy.

She giggled, then opened the door and stepped inside.

Nick tried to scream, but it was muffled by the torn strip of fabric in his mouth.

Judy gasped, and it seemed like there was no air in the tiny shed.

Nick's hands and feet were bound behind him, all four limbs clasped tightly beside the small of his back. Chains sprung out from the same place and attached to the walls at seemingly random intervals, like the tentacles of some clichéd 90's horror villain come to life.

His eyes were pupil-less and bulged, and when she saw it a horrible tightness formed in her chest. It looked as though he had been blinded.

He let out another muffled yelp, straining against his chains and lurching in her direction.

There were electrical lamps hanging from the ceiling, the type that miners used. The metal cages that surrounded them were rusted and cracked.

Bodies lined the wall behind him, and she recognized them instantly. Even if she had not, it was the stench that made it seem like there was no air in the room. Dennis stared out at her, his head resting awkwardly against the gravel floor. His eyes were calloused and cloudy, the blue tint gone and bleeding into the black iris, making it all one homogenous milky tinge. His hair was ruffled and matted with his own blood.

Thomas lay on top of him. His mouth hung open and was gray around the lips. They looked like they had been caught in some carnal embrace. Jason and Mitchell were on top of him, and Charlotte on top of them. Her shirt was missing, and there were long gashes across her neck. Her face was frozen in a look of perpetual horror. Richie was at the top of the pile, and was fresh enough that blood was still seeping down from his wounds and through Charlotte's jeans.

Nick screamed again.

Judy turned around and Gavin punched her in the face. She fell backward into Nick, forcing him back onto the pile of bodies. Her weight stretched his chains to their limit, the strain on his arms and legs making him cry out in muffled, anguished pain.

She opened her eyes and looked at him. There was blood gushing out of her nose in several long tendrils that overlapped her mouth and continued down her chin. It looked like a red-legged spider trying to escape from her nostrils. His eyes bulged and he nodded his head toward the exit, never once breaking her gaze. She realized that he wasn't blind, but had no time to do anything with the information.

Gavin grabbed her by the hair and pulled her off of him, kicking the door shut behind him.

Nick screamed and yelled something angrily at Gavin, once again fighting against his bonds.

Gavin grabbed Judy by the face and pushed her against the wall of the shed, puckering her lips out in the fishy sort of way that grandparents seemed fond of doing to their grandchildren. He smiled that same wide, closed-mouth smile he had on his face whenever he was really into one of his lectures. The smile of being right, and being whole, and being recognized for it.

She opened her mouth to scream but no sound came out.

He flung her on her back with ease, kneeling and attaching chains at her ankles. She tried to twist her body and reach them before he could snap the clasps shut, but she was too slow. All the action resulted in was her scratching at her legs as Gavin hoisted the chain along a pulley, sending her upside-down and into the air. She whimpered fearfully as he came toward her then.

She struggled, but could do little in the position. He stood directly in front of her, then knelt to be eye-level with her, a look of pity in his eyes. He easily held both her arms with one hand, keeping her in place as she heard the sound of metal moving over the floor toward her. He brought his free hand to her cheek, stroking it as if to calm her. She saw a glint out of the corner of her eye, and her heart jumped in her chest. He brought the knife across her throat quickly, with no hesitation. She had a panicked look for a moment, as if she wanted to speak but couldn't, then her body relaxed.

The blood poured from her throat into the basin below her, and all Nick could do was sob against his gag.

Gavin took her by the back of her head again. "I'd love to be able to use you," he said to Nick from over Judy's shoulder. "With those eyes I imagine you'd add something interesting to the mix. Some new flavour, if you will. But they're something you're not. They have something you never will." He licked Judy's blood from his lips and smiled. "Conviction."

CHAPTER 39

Atlanta, Georgia

"This is fucking madness," Jaycee frowned as he typed into his phone. He was standing on the front porch with six of Gavin's followers and Quinn.

"What are you doing?" she asked. Her face was flushed and warm.

"Telling Victor that we're getting out of here with the people that agreed to leave. I'll come back after and try to find Nick."

Her posture straightened. "I'm not leaving without Kelly."

Jaycee stopped typing and let his hands fall by his sides. "You have got to be kidding me. That is probably the last person we'd be able to get to come. You might as well say you're not going period."

"You're wrong. I think she'll come. We have to find her."

"I think you're underestimating the Stockholm effect," he muttered, sending his text.

The comment got several unhappy glares from the

crowd.

"It was a joke, okay? I'm stressed."

Quinn huffed and pushed past him, forcing her way back into the house.

"Quinn!" he called out after her, slamming his palms against the doorframe. "*Quinn!*"

She ran up the stairs and started down the main hallway toward the second stairwell. A man named Roy lay against the wall about half way down. The position looked so uncomfortable that she thought he was dead for a moment until she saw his chest moving up and down. There was white powder smeared across the underside of each of his nostrils. His hair was falling out in matted clumps.

Kelly came down the steps and she stopped. Both girls stared at each other for a long moment.

"Do you know where Nick is?" they both asked, almost in unison.

They walked toward each other and embraced.

"No," Kelly answered finally, holding Quinn tight. "I don't know where he is. It's all my fault."

"No, it's mine. It really, really is mine."

"He was trying to tell me something, I think. It didn't make sense at first but now I think it does and --"

"We need to find him."

Kelly nodded and the both of them turned back toward the stairwell.

Gavin stood at the top of it, his eyes red with rage.

CHAPTER 40

Atlanta, Georgia

Victor stood at the edge of the terminal, watching as lines upon lines of travellers made their way past him to the luggage carousel. He watched each of them pass but kept his gaze trained on the large clear doors at the top of the staircase, waiting to see a head of blonde or auburn hair pop out of the crowd and make its way down.

His phone chimed once and he dug it out of his pocket:

getting out with anyone that will come with. no nick.

"Fuck," he hissed, even as he typed his reply:

Good.

When he looked up from his phone Chad had almost reached him, carrying Kat's bag over one shoulder. Abby was behind him and Kat trailed in the back.

"What took you?" he snapped, looking Chad up and down.

"Yeah, turns out it was a plane, not a teleporter," Chad drawled. He turned to the girls. "Victor, this is Kat Smith. Kat this is --"

"We have absolutely no time," Victor said, cutting him off. "If we're going to do something we have to do it now."

Abby straitened. Her hands turned into fists so tight her knuckles cracked.

Victor cocked his head toward Kat. "Are you in?"

Kat's eyes flashed in a way they hadn't in a very long time. "Very."

"Good," he turned around without another word and started toward the parking lot.

The three of them followed.

Atlanta, Georgia

"No!" Kelly screamed as Gavin threw her to the floor of the shed. The side of her head slammed against the gravel and made several long red streaks by her temple, prying the hair around her ear out by its roots.

Nick screamed again as Gavin stood in the doorway again, his silhouette darkened by the setting sun behind him.

Kelly scrambled to her feet and tried to force her way past him. He grabbed her by the wrists and kept her away from him, only the furthest of her kicks able to reach his shins. He twisted her and slammed her against the wall where he'd pinned Judy only minutes before, then pushed her to the floor again.

"You were supposed to be the one," he snarled. He spit at her. It landed just below her left breast. "You were supposed to be my princess."

She coughed so hard that her lungs felt like they were

on fire.

He threw her to her knees and turned, slamming the door as he went. There was a definitive click as the lock turned against the other side.

The lights were on, their bulbs bathing the room in their harsh green glow.

She turned and saw Nick and the pile of bodies behind him, Judy's fresh corpse resting daintily across the top. "Oh my God!" she gasped, rushing forward. Her eyes welled up as she reached him and she wrapped her arms around him, squeezing him as tightly as she dared. "I'm sorry," she said, sniffing back hard, "I'm so, so sorry." She pulled back and held his face in her hands, her fingers gliding gently over a large gash along the side of his head that almost matched her own. "Oh, God..." she moaned, biting her lip. Her fingers found their way to the piece of shirt that gagged him. She forced her nails between the cloth and his cheeks and pushed it down around his neck.

He gasped and coughed, able to breathe without getting the unrelenting stench of death and rot for the first time in hours. He spat a large glob of mucus and blood out onto the ground, then turned his head back up to face her.

"I'm so sorry," she said again, holding his head in her hands (careful not to press on his gash). "I'm so sorry."

"It's alright," he said gruffly, his mouth dry and filled with cotton. "It is."

She held his head and pushed her own forward, their open mouths meeting.

For the briefest of moments the chaos of the world

around them fell away and crumbled below them, becoming nothing but dust and ashes. The hairs on the back of his neck stood on end and he closed his eyes, the smell of her hair overpowering everything else until she was all he could sense. Her lips moved and his moved with them, as though they knew what they were doing all on their own.

When she ended the kiss tears had found their way to her cheeks again and she hugged into him once more, burying her head into his shoulder. She held him like that for a full minute, then kissed him on his exposed shoulder and pulled back, sniffing hard. "We've got to get you out of these chains," she said, her voice wet.

He nodded and pulled against them.

New York City, Then

Tash slammed into the table of The Pasta Palace, *feeling something in her back jolt and cringe as she did so. The table beneath her bent up onto its hinges under her weight and snapped, buckling between her and the wall before coming down on top of her. She screamed and cursed, forcing herself back up onto her knees and then vomiting from the effort.*

Jona smiled his jackal smile as he watched her, holding the nightstick she'd purloined in his hand and clasping it tightly. It looked like a child's toy in his massive paws, something insignificant and useless.

Victor brought his fists back and slammed them into Jona's chest twice, so hard that the albino actually stumbled back a pace. He looked surprised for a moment, then gleeful.

"That one wasn't bad, Prophet," he sneered, then backhand-

ed Victor so hard that he went through the glass window of the restaurant and out into the moonlit hallway.

Victor coughed, the blood that came up looking black in the bluish light of the moon. He spat twice and tried to get up. His brain screamed at his limbs to move and act, but they refused to do so. He stayed there on his hands and knees in the sea of shattered glass, feeling the warm trickle of urine spread down the leg of his jeans.

Jona stepped through the doorway of The Pasta Palace, having to duck in order to do so. "This is just sad, you know," he said, stepping forward until Victor was at his feet. "After all this time, I thought the end would be more... spectacular." He grabbed Victor by the scruff of his shirt and pulled him up, the collar bringing up hard against his adam's apple and choking him. His feet kicked and fought to find their footing, but didn't. "You know? I thought it would be... better. I thought I would get to outsmart you. To prove how much better I was at this game than you. But this... race, and now the violence. It's not the way I would have picked."

He grabbed Victor by the neck.

"But it's strangely exhilarating."

Victor croaked, his lips and cheeks turning a deep blue and his eyes bulging.

Jona smiled. "I asked you once what you thought of me. You said I was inept at fieldwork. A poser, I believe you said. Let me ask, Prophet, has your opinion of me changed?"

Gagging, Victor nodded.

"Oh?" he slackened his grip. "Let's hear it then."

"I think... you're a piece of dirt."

Jona slammed him against the wall of Trombly Real Estate, cracking the brick and the mortar behind it and making a long

gash along the back of Victor' head. His smile had gone now, replaced with a long frown that made his face stretch down. "Dirt
is simply matter out of place," he whispered softly. "Soon my
place will become apparent, Prophet. And when that day comes,
it's you who'll be 'the dirt.'"

A fork jabbed into his shoulder. He dropped Victor and
turned around.

Tash stood in the glass-less window of the restaurant, holding three forks between the fingers of each of her hands. There
was a trail of blood bisecting her face from an open gash in her
forehead, and her eyes burned like bright flames against the shade
all around. "Dirt might be matter out of place," she said, breathing hard. "But shit is shit no matter where you shove it."

He chuckled, then turned back to her. "Really? Forks?
That's what this has come down to?"

"Not exactly," she glared, dropping the cutlery and bringing her gun out from behind her. She fired twice, each shot landing in the wall on either side of Jona. He ducked, covering his
ears with his massive hands.

Growling, he picked up one of the chairs Victor had gathered
and threw it at her, knocking her down off her perch. She landed
on her stomach, several shards of glass poking at her. She spun
around onto her back and Jona was on top of her, pinning her
shoulders to the floor with each of his massive thumbs.

"Change is a constant," he said, even as she writhed under
the pressure on her joints. "It it the one thing that all societies
have to endure. Call it trade or diffusion or rebellion... I don't
much care what you label it. But the truth is: it's here. It is
upon us. And after tonight, nothing can stop its wheels from
turning."

"You talk far too much," Tash spat, firing her gun twice

more.

The bullets collected with the fluorescent lights above, bringing the entire apparatus down. Jona leapt back out of the way and Tash scrambled to her feet, reaching the wall and flicking all of the switches on.

Light and electricity pulsed through the glass tubes and shone bright, until the corner of the fixture connected with the floor and they shattered, erupting in a flash of brightness and brilliance and singed oxygen.

When Jona opened his eyes again, Tash and Victor were gone.

Atlanta, Georgia

The speedometer on the El Dorado arched up over ninety as Victor slid between two cars and then back into the right lane again, hanging a sharp right and pressing on the gas even harder. The engine revved and roared, straining against itself as its mechanical scream grew louder and louder, without pausing or plateauing.

"Jesus!" Abby cursed as they pulled out around a semi-truck into oncoming traffic, passing it before zipping back into the correct lane. "What the fuck is the matter with you?"

Victor did not respond. He glared forward and gripped the steering wheel, so tight that his knuckles turned white.

CHAPTER 41

Atlanta, Georgia

Gavin pulled the knot tight around Quinn's wrist, watching as the flesh around it was pinched and turned white. He moved about his task without emotion, his face devoid of anything as he stared blankly ahead, more at the wall behind her than at her.

Lamar was binding her feet to the opposite end of the long board. It was a piece of two-by-four that had been left over after the completion of the shed, and he'd painted it the reddish-brown of the clay dunes back home. The colour reminded him of the scent of his mother's bread, and the way it felt in his mouth when it was fresh from the oven.

Banner and Clive went about their tasks heartily, pulling their ropes so tight that they drew blood. Lamar watched them, unable to truly process what he was seeing or what he was doing. He let his hands slow until they weren't even moving anymore, his knot going limp around Quinn's ankle.

When he looked up again Gavin was standing over

him.

"Is something wrong?"

Lamar stared at him for a moment. "... No."

"You have doubts?"

"No!"

"That's normal, Lamar. I have doubts, too."

He paused for a long moment. He turned from Gavin to Quinn. Her eyes were open but she didn't say anything. She just hung her head and stared at the floor that hovered beneath her, blood oozing from a welt on the side of her mouth.

He turned back to Gavin. "You do?"

"Of course. Everyone does sometimes. But you and I know that this is the only way. That we have to show them that we won't live by their rules anymore, not ever again."

Slowly Lamar nodded, then squat down and went back to binding Quinn's leg.

Talan stood in the back of the room with his arms folded.

Gavin took Quinn by the chin and forced her to look at him. He stared at her with cold, blank eyes until she curled her lip and twisted to try and get away.

"Yes, you'll do fine."

Atlanta, Georgia

Victor pumped the accelerator as the El Dorado sped through a red light. Two cars stopped so fast they spun, slamming into each other side-on.

Kat cursed loudly, turning around in her seat to see

the cars as they shrunk into the distance.

"Fuck!" Chad screamed, leaning forward into the front seat. "Are you trying to get us killed?"

"Won't happen," Victor drawled under his breath.

"Why the fuck not?"

"You're in the car."

Chad threw up his hands as the El Dorado topped one-twenty.

Atlanta, Georgia

"Nnn-Guh!" Kelly strained as she pulled Nick's chains against their bracings. Despite the urge to shut her eyes she kept them open and trained on the screws and bolts that kept the chain anchored, waiting to see if they would bend or pull.

They did not.

Nick took a breath for the first time in a full minute, gasping for air that stung at his lungs and burned his nostrils. His chest ached with it and his cheeks were red with blood blisters. His eyes, normally an even white, were tattered with veins. "It's okay," he said, his arm nearly out of its socket. "I can go again."

She braced a foot against the wall on either side of him and pulled on the chain again, her face turning a bright purple.

"Come on," he said.

She slipped and fell back, slamming the back of her head against the wall and tumbling to the floor behind him.

"Kelly! Kelly, are you okay? Kelly!"

She groaned and opened her eyes. The right side of her face was covered in the clear, soapy fluid that coated the floor behind Nick. At first when she opened her eyes all she could see was light, but after a moment shapes started to appear.

Judy was staring at her, her almond eyes open and milky.

She gasped and scrambled to her feet, getting up so fast she slipped and fell back onto her tailbone.

There were arms sticking out at odd angles: bending and twisting in ways that live nerves wouldn't have allowed when they were alive. Judy's chest was obscured by Jeremy's arm and that by Dennis's foot, like they had all died playing some horrific game of Twister.

Underneath the crook of Dennis's leg was a long sliver of metal with a ring on one end and four tumblers on the other.

"Jesus Christ," she said, pulling herself forward again. She could hear her grandmother's voice in the back of her head even now, chiding her for taking the Lord's name in vain. The sound echoed in her ears as she strained, her fingertips barely touching the ring of the key.

"What is it?" Nick yelled, straining to look over his shoulder. "What's happening?"

"It's the key!" she gasped, trying not the let her face touch the bodies as she reached in further.

Nick turned more, his chains rattling.

She pushed forward, spreading her middle finger as far as she could until she felt the calcium in the joints and phalanges threaten to pop. She held her breath again and closed her eyes, forcing herself forward until her head poked into a chilly mush that was Jason's midsection. She let out the breath and a low groan, then forced herself forward again.

Jason's weight shifted as she did this, bringing Judy down off the top of the pile and on top of her.

Atlanta, Georgia

Gavin stood up from his place on the floor and stared at Quinn. The spite was gone from her now for the first time since she'd moved here, and he thought that maybe, for once, he was seeing the *real* Quinn Emberly.

Atlanta, Georgia

Kelly strained under Judy's weight as her hand patted at the floor surrounding the key, trying to find it again and again. Judy stared at her with gaping open eyes, the colour of them seeming to change again and again every time Kelly opened her own and saw them. They were like swirling pools of swamp water, marbles that had been left in the sun for too long, stained by its rays.

She choked back a sob and ignored Nick's pleas of encouragement, focusing on nothing but the key and the place where she had last seen it.

Though her grandmother's voice was still ringing in her ears, a new one had overpowered it now.

"You'll never find anything to make you feel as good and as warm as this house and this town and this family. I hope you're hearing me."

Her hand connected with brass and she gripped it,

pulling herself out from under Judy's weight as soon as she was sure she had a grip. She gasped, her hair matted to her face with sweat and blood and whatever bile was on the floor.

Her hands shaking, she made her way to Nick's chains.

CHAPTER 42

New York City, Then

Tash elbowed the front window of the car open unlocked it, its alarm piercing the night air like a blade. She opened the back door and lay Victor down inside. He slumped down hard despite her efforts to be gentle, his head knocking against the opposite door.

There was blood coming out of his mouth, and even more coming out of a long gash across his ribs.

She tucked his feet back and closed the door, casting a cautious glance back toward McElheny Square. She could hear sirens in the distance, and see the large hole that Victor had put in the front door.

Cursing, she got in the front seat and ducked down beneath the steering wheel. She jabbed one of her picks into the crack between the wheel case and the dashboard and pried it loose until the entire case fell aside and revealed the jumble of wires that connected to the starting motor.

She kicked the case out into the parking lot.

Fidgeting and sticking her tongue out one corner of her mouth, she pulled out the two red wires and pushed them to-

gether. The radio blared some nineties rock.

She reached up and hit the button to stop it, then pulled a brown wire free and connected the two together.

The car roared to life.

She sat up and slammed the car into drive, then sped away out of the parking lot with the alarm still blaring.

Atlanta, Georgia

Gavin buried his blade deep into Quinn's side, sliding between the bottom two ribs on her left side.

She took a breath through her mouth and kept her eyes fixated on his. He stared at her the way she'd always wanted a man to, his attention fully on her and taking in her every twitch and sound and movement, emotionless and expressionless and just caught in the moment of who she was and what she was doing.

A warmth spread over her, emanating from her side and then tickling its way down her legs and into her feet. It was like slipping into a warm bath.

Lamar winced, watching as Quinn's blood pushed its way out from around the knife and soaked into her shirt. He took a step back from it, the wall against his shoulder blades bringing him back to reality.

Gavin withdrew the knife from where it had been held erect in Quinn's flesh. He let out a deep breath, then turned around and stabbed Lamar through the neck.

Banner and Clive yelled, both of them rising to their feet. They were both down again a moment later, Banner with a hole through his temple and Clive with one in his chest. He turned his blade on Talan, who had been moving toward him but now stopped with his hands raised.

"I have dreamed dreams no mortal ever dared to dream before," Gavin said, pulling Talan close and bringing the knife across Talan's throat.

Gavin tucked the blade back into his pants and kneeled down over Talan, laying his palm flat against his head for a moment. When he brought it back it was covered in hot, sticky blood. He pressed it against his shirt and let it soak in to the fabric over his heart. He repeated this with Clive, Banner and Lamar until his hands were soaked and stained with red, then drew an eye on the palm of each hand with the finger of the other.

He turned back to Quinn and grabbed her face, covering it with sticky handprints. His thumbs rode the edges of her mouth and he kissed her, quickly and forcibly.

There was a loud bang downstairs, followed by a crash.

Gavin turned from Quinn while still clutching her head in his grip, a rueful snarl spreading across his face. He let her go, then took his gun back out of his waistband and marched out the door.

Quinn's head went limp.

CHAPTER 43

Atlanta, Georgia

Victor looked down at the remains of Gavin's front door where it lay in the centre of the hall. It was propped up on its left side by its knob, creaking and crackling under its own weight as it tried despite itself to lie flat.

"Jesus," Chad huffed, stepping in from behind Victor. "Knock much?"

Abby and Kat came in as well, stepping over door until there was one of them on either side of it.

"Spread out," Victor said, his mouth barely moving. "We don't know how many there are."

Kat and Abby both nodded. Kat stepped into the living room while Abby started down the hall into the kitchen.

Chad stepped forward until he was parallel with Victor. "So what's the plan here?"

Victor stared forward.

"I assume you're not going to buy him off."

"Men like Gavin can't be bought."

"Right. And the police aren't here, so I can only assume we're in a Helm's Deep-type situation."

Victor stared forward.

"Helm's Deep was the --"

"I understood the reference."

Chad paused, then nodded. "Well as you recall, that didn't turn out so good for the invaders."

There was a sound behind them and they both turned to see Jaycee coming up onto the porch, breathless.

"Doing the right thing means doing it even when you know you're going to lose," Victor said, almost to himself. He nodded toward Jaycee. "What's the news?"

"I got about a dozen of them to go. They're in the city, hanging out at a little bistro on Third. I gave them all the cash I had, it should keep them occupied for a few hours."

Victor nodded. "It's not much, but it'll cut down on his forces. Or at least on his casualties."

"If they had left they wouldn't have been casualties," came Gavin's voice, and all three men turned to face him on the stairwell. His was standing casually, with one leg on the top stair and the other two steps below it. He looked as though he were posing for a graduation photo. A gun was cradled in his hand and his finger was on the trigger, resting comfortably against his thigh. His blade glinted on his hip.

Victor turned to face him, several feet below him yet staring him down all the same.

"Only the believers have to die."

Jaycee's eyes went wide for a moment, then narrowed again until they were tiny, yellowed slits. "Where's Nick?"

Gavin smirked. "You still don't get it, do you? It's over.

I don't care anymore. Live, die. Win, lose. It's all just... idiotic. It's mortal, and it's stupid and I've no time for it."

"I'm sure we can help you with that," Victor said under his breath.

"I'm really not interested." He turned and looked all around the house, as though the three men weren't even there. "This place had such potential. I came here and thought: maybe. Maybe this will be the last one I need."

Victor's face slackened a little. "What did you do?"

Gavin reached out and touched the wall, feeling its cold flatness against the palm of his hand.

It was only then that Victor noticed the blood on them. He took a step forward.

Gavin raised his gun. "Don't be an idiot. I might have lost, but it doesn't mean that anything changes. The ladder is still out there, and just like Everest, it must be climbed. Just its being there begs us to climb it."

Five of Gavin's followers made their way in from the hallway.

Chad clenched and then unclenched his fingers, shifting his weight onto his other foot.

Gavin turned to him and looked him up and down. He smiled. "Is this really what you've brought for me? Children?"

"That's a bit of the pot calling the kettle black," Victor said.

"So you admit then, that we are both... black."

Victor said nothing.

"And this is why I'm going to leave. This is why you couldn't possibly have won. Because you will not admit what you --"

He stopped, stammering for the first time since Victor had met him.

Kat Smith walked into the hallway from the living room.

CHAPTER 44

Atlanta, Georgia

Nick and Kelly made it up the stairs to the loft, the dank and mouldy air clawing at Nick's lungs each time he took a deep breath. He coughed hard time and again, making it hard for Kelly to help him up.

The shrine was gone, only a few candles left scattered along the floor.

The bodies of Lamar, Banner, Clive and Talan lay there, almost forming a human compass. Above them and pinned to the sloping wall was Quinn, tied to her giant wooden x and bleeding madly from her side. The knife wound at her side was gaping.

"Oh my God," Nick gasped, suddenly able to stand on his own again as he rushed over to her. "Oh my God! Quinn! Quinn, are you there?"

Quinn raised her head lazily. No colour was left in her face and her eyes were unfocused. She opened her mouth to try and speak, but couldn't.

Nick pried at the rope that was binding her feet desperately. "We're going to get you out of here. It's going to be okay."

Kelly started on the other foot, untying it quickly and then moving on to her wrist.

Quinn slumped forward and Nick caught her, moving so fast that Kelly could barely have seen him.

"Quinn!" he yelled, pushing her hair back out of her face. It was wet with sweat and stuck there stubbornly. "Say something, Quinn. Say anything! You can't just... *do* this! You're too stubborn for this, you're too --"

Quinn sniffled, a painful smile tickling the edges of her lips before agony overcame her again. "Jokes on you," she croaked as Kelly loosened the last of her restraints. "I was faking, you dumb shit."

He squinted at her and shook his head.

"The tough girl act... hate to break it to you."

He smiled, but his eyes were tearing up. "I kind of suspected."

Kelly stood over them, watching as more and more blood soaked into Quinn's clothes.

"Did it work at least?"

Nick bit his lip, then nodded. "Yeah... Uh-Huh. It sure did."

She stared at him for a moment. "You're a really shitty liar."

Her head lolled a moment, then came back up to meet his.

"Quinn!" he yelled, forcing her up. "Quinn, stay with me. I need you to stay with me." He propped her up on against his shoulder and Kelly came around to the other side of her and did the same. The both of them started toward the stairs with her. "We're getting you help."

"No..." Quinn winced. She said it twice more as they went down the stairs, then again as they entered the hallway. "No, I can end this."

"You sure can. Can't she, Kelly?"

Kelly nodded. "I think so."

"Yeah. But right now, we need to get you to a hospital."

"No," she said again, pushing against his face. All her weight was on Kelly then for a moment, and the both of them fell to the ground. "I can end this!"

"Quinn, for God's sake!" Nick yelled. "I need you to--"

He stopped in mid sentence.

Quinn's eyes were glowing a bright white. "Let's show these fuckers why this is my town."

New York City, Then

Tash pushed down on the gas just as the light turned red, swerving the car out into oncoming traffic and then pulling it back again. She switched lanes and pulled out around the semi she'd been behind for almost a minute and zipped around it before darting back again.

The alarm still blared.

She turned around and saw Victor. He was on his side now, and there was a long sticky pool of blood coming from his mouth.

She waited a second to see if his chest moved, then turned back to the road.

It hadn't.

CHAPTER 45

Atlanta, Georgia

Gavin and Kat stared at each other for a moment, neither of them speaking or moving. Each of Kat's breaths were louder than the last, her nostrils flaring and flaming until she felt as though she'd been running on steam all her life and the no one had ever told her. She looked at him and it all came back: the years of solitude, the drinking, the anger.

She stared at him. His face was covered in scars – burns that ranged in intensity from reddening to completely disfiguring, all up the left side of his face. Part of his top-left eyelid had melted and joined with its bottom half, and there were patches of dead and charred skin all through his cheeks, like cancerous looking freckles. His neck was red and blotchy, and his hair was thin and looked to be coming out in clumps on his bad side.

She saw him, and more than that, so did everyone else.

Jaycee winced when he saw the burns, but Chad and Victor did not move. Gavin's followers stopped and stared at him.

"No!" he screamed, waving his gun toward her but not firing. He tried to cover his face with his other arm but it was a futile attempt; the worst burns were still visible. "No! You're a liar!"

He stepped down off the stairs and leveled his gun at her. Kat held her ground, an old defiance surging within her from where it had been buried for so long.

Victor finally stepped forward, drawing back his massive fist.

Chad held out his hands, closed his eyes, and hoped.

The glass windows of the house all came in at once, the shards raining down everywhere. Judy and Dennis burst in though them, crawling over the glass and ignoring it even as it sliced at their palms and feet and faces, each one of them making their way toward Gavin. Thomas crawled through the door behind Jaycee on his stomach, pulling himself forward with arms that seemed too long and rubbery to be real. His mouth hung open garishly and he was missing teeth. Mitchell and Charlotte were behind, with Jason in the lawn beyond them, stumbling forward and dragging his intestines behind him.

Richie burst through the living room window, his eyes glassy and white. The flesh on his fists was ripped but no blood came from them.

Gavin turned the gun away from Kat and back to the horde of dead bodies that was making its way toward him, lumbering and falling like puppets on poorly made strings.

Chad opened his eyes and watched, horrified. "Did I do that?"

"I've got doubts," Jaycee mumbled.

Victor stepped back, fists still at the ready. "It's Quinn."

"No..." Gavin whispered, taking a step back onto the stairs. "This is not the way the ladder should go!"

Atlanta, Georgia

Blood trickled from Quinn's nose and ears, her chest convulsing. Her cheeks were turning blue and her eyes remained that hauntingly soulless glowing white. She ground her teeth together so hard that they hurt Nick's ears, a series of tiny whimpers coming from her the only sign that she was in any pain at all.

Her fingers danced about, as though she was playing some invisible keyboard sitting across her lap.

Her head lay on Nick's lap and he stroked her hair.

They heard the crash downstairs, and then the screams.

"That's enough, Quinn," Nick whispered, bringing his lips down close to her ear. "You have to stop it now."

Kelly said nothing, clutching Quinn's hand and stroking it.

Quinn shook her head slowly, though it might have been a tremor.

Her back arched, and her eyes began to glow even brighter.

CHAPTER 46

Atlanta, Georgia

Dennis drew back and slammed his fist into one of Gavin's followers, with such force that his ring and pinky fingers dislocated. They hung by their joints like swinging vines and he pulled them back again, forcing the broken appendage into Megan's jaw.

Gavin stepped back a pace again, almost tripping. His gun fell from his hands as an army of his dead came through the walls of his home, breaking the filthy windows and letting in the cool night air of the real world in for the first time in months.

"Don't just stand there," Victor said, motioning toward the crowd.

Chad nodded. He stepped forward and drove a fist hard into Patrick's abdomen. Patrick doubled over, the blow sending him to the floor.

Jaycee leapt back like a cat, avoiding the scuffle as Mitchell and Jason made their way past him. His head nearly touched the ceiling and he seemed to hang there weightless for a moment, like a ballet dancer, before coming back down to earth and landing soundlessly on all fours. He shot himself forward, the muscles in his calves rippling with force, and crashed into Roy's midsection, sending both men toppling to the floor.

Frank jumped on Victor's back and began to pound on his shoulders furiously with his tiny curled fists. Victor gritted his teeth and threw his weight back, pushing him off. His hair whipped back around with the sharpness of a blade as he turned and glared at the teen, his eyes becoming tiny black beads in the centre of his head.

Frank looked as though he was about to step forward and attack again, but didn't.

"You've never been very sure of yourself," Victor said, low enough that only they could hear.

Frank opened his mouth to object, then closed it again. His hand was raised to come down and strike but hung there impotently in midair.

"It's because, in your heart of hearts, you've always known that you're a failure." He turned from him and grabbed Billy by the scruff of his neck and slammed him into the adjacent wall. When Billy turned to face him he punched him in the face so hard that his cheek made a horrible wet crack that echoed through the hall above all the other commotion.

Frank stood spellbound for a moment, staring into the null space where Victor had been.

A moment later Charlotte slammed into him and took a bite out of his left ear.

Kat circled along the edge of the battle, never once taking her eyes off of Gavin.

"No..." Gavin whispered, looking from one of them to

the other. They moved so fast that he couldn't tell them apart anymore; Chad's hair looking as though maybe it was Victor's and Jaycee's hairless head lost in the dog pile of followers and former followers. He stepped back again, finally finding his footing and turning back up the stairs. He stumbled for three paces, then started to run.

He jumped the stairs two at a time, knocking down the frame that encapsulated the Robert Frost poem as he went. He tripped once on someone's coat, cursed, then threw it aside and continued up the stairs. He made it to the top, the long empty hallway seemed as though it went on for miles. He gasped, then stared to run.

Abby shot out of the first open doorway and tackled him, slamming him into the opposite door.

"Monster!" she screamed, pulling back her small fist and striking him hard across the chin with it, and then again. Her teeth clenched and spit flew from her, and she felt something inside the hinge of her jaw crack. Blood rushed to her head and she felt the warmth of it fill her. She struck him again, then again, until blood spurted out of his nose. "Murderer!"

He pushed back her shoulder and kicked her in the stomach, hearing a satisfying wet sound as his foot connected with her abdomen. The air left her, and for a moment it was like there wasn't any left in the world. She coughed then pushed forward again, grabbing at his face and pulling on it.

He yelled, then pushed her back and punched her across the face.

She spun into the wall, struck it, and then hit the floor.

"Bitch," he spat, then continued down the hall.

He rounded the corner and saw Nick, Kelly and Quinn sitting on the floor half way down.

It took them a moment to register his presence; the scars on his face making him appear as a melted wax sculpture of his former self.

Nick stood and stared at Gavin from across the hall with blank eyes and clenched fists. He stepped forward over Kelly and Quinn, standing between Gavin and the two girls.

Gavin snarled, shaking his head over and over. "It was you... things were going fine, and then there was you."

Nick didn't say anything.

"If there's one last bit of joy I can take from this, you are it."

Gavin ran forward and drew up his arms, then swung them down and connected them with Nick's shoulders.

"No!" Kelly screamed, her face illuminating in blue.

Nick bent down, then came back up and punched Gavin in the cheek. It had come so quickly that it was like a movie with frames cut out, and even though the boy was lanky and lean it knocked Gavin back a pace.

Nick glared. "Mass times *acceleration*, dipshit."

Gavin stared at him, seemingly stunned.

"Guess you aren't so knowledgeable after all."

Gavin roared, pushing forward and tackling Nick to the ground.

Atlanta, Georgia

Roy's hair came out in great fluffy clumps as Jaycee

gripped at it, trying to find something to latch onto as the addict pushed and fought and swung his arms wildly. Jaycee pulled back his fist, the knuckles on them dry and crackling from the Atlanta heat, and pushed forward into Roy's face.

The hair came loose, the sweat from it making it stick between his fingers.

He got up and backed up a pace until he was back with Victor and Chad in the centre of the room. When he felt their backs against his he allowed himself a moment, bending over and leaning against his knees as he gasped for air. "Didn't think there would be so many."

"Always seems like more when they're beating down the doors," Victor said, clearing his throat.

Chad nodded; sweat dribbling down his neck and pooling in a large stain around his collar.

The corpses that Quinn had summoned had stopped moving, each of them standing on unsure feet, wobbling back and forth with blank, dead expressions.

Jaycee squinted, turning to examine each of them. He was ashamed that he did not recognize some of them, even though he'd known some of them only a few hours and some of them not at all. All the same, they were helping him fight, even beyond their last breaths. He thought he should at least have known their names.

Charlotte stood in front of him, swaying in the warm breeze that came out of the broken window. Her face was a grey-green and broken blood vessels were becoming evident under her skin, giving her the look of someone who'd gotten very sick after eating some bad crab. She still looked alive in everything but her eyes, and Jaycee couldn't help but remember how she'd looked just a few days ago, hanging around Nick's neck with a liquor bottle dangling between her fingers and her lipstick smeared across her face. He'd made many assumptions of her in those few minutes, some of which he was ashamed of now, but the one description he thought she wouldn't have minded hearing was that she was *lively*.

Now her ears and nose had turned dark brown and had a thick mucus membrane over them.

Suddenly, from somewhere deep inside, he felt pity.

Charlotte reached out and racked her nails across Jaycee's chest, leaving four long red marks there that stung like fire and iodine had been poured into them.

"What the fuck?" he screamed, backing up into Chad and knocking them both over.

Dennis lunged toward Victor as all of the dead began to converge upon them. His finger was still dangling from his hand limply, and looked as though it were ready to fall off.

Judy turned and started attacking the wall, clawing at it until the plaster peeled back and termites began to spew out of the hole. She clawed so hard that she ripped the nails from their roots, but kept going anyway. There was a long cackling sound from her as she tried to scream with a swallowed tongue.

"What's happening?" Chad asked, scrambling to his feet.

Victor stepped to one side of Dennis and pushed him to the floor. "Quinn must be losing control of them."

"Christ, I --" he stopped and looked around, stepping away from a struggling Richie as he did. "Where's Kat?"

Victor turned, noticing now for the first time that Kat was gone as well.

He cursed.

New York City, Then

Tash burst through the doors of New York Mercy with Victor hanging off one of her shoulders. He weighed much more than she did, despite his compact size. She could barely walk, both of her fingers laced together around his waist as she dragged him into the emergency room, leaving a long trail of blood on the floor behind them.

"Get a stretcher!" a nurse screamed, pressing a button behind the counter and then rushing out from around her wicket.

Tash finally let go with one final grunt of pain, and Victor slammed into the hospital floor.

"What happened here?" the nurse asked, even as more doctors and nurses came from around the corner.

Tash gasped for air, then stood up straight and silent.

"What happened?"

Tash turned, her glare locking with the nurse. "Fix him."

Atlanta, Georgia

Gavin wrapped his long, snaky fingers around Nick's neck and squeezed, applying pressure slowly and steadily, staring into his pupil-less eyes the whole time.

"Are you looking at me? I hope you are," he whispered, letting blood drip down from his nose onto Nick's upper lip. "It's been a long time since I looked someone in the eye when it happened, but I think you're worth it."

Nick gasped for air and got none, his throat going dry. He wanted to cough, the itch of choking almost as much agony as the fingers crushing into his thorax. His eyes saw everything, every second and millisecond of what was happening, as though it were happening in slow motion. He reached out and grabbed at Gavin's face, but it was as though his fingers had no energy.

"You know there were times, when I was fucking her, that this was really all I wanted... this is almost better than winning. Because if I'd won... *really* won... you wouldn't even know that I beat you. But now at least, you get to know that I killed you."

"Stop it!" Kelly screamed, pounding her fists into his shoulder. "You're killing him!"

He turned and snarled at her, letting go of Nick and grabbing her wrist in mid-strike.

Nick gasped and coughed and gasped again, his lungs burning as they filled with air.

Abby turned the corner, still clutching her face. "Jesus." She rushed to Quinn, whose head had slumped over at an awkward angle with nobody there to support it, craning her neck painfully. She propped Quinn up and looked her over; the gash in her ribs was mottled looking. There wasn't blood coming out of it now. "Don't do this," she said, forcing Quinn's eyes open. "Don't."

Gavin stood and gripped Kelly's wrist until she thought it would break, then drew back and struck her across the face. She stumbled, only his grip keeping her up.

She turned back to him, trails of blood trickling down from her nose and over her chin. Once again she was bathed in blue and the sneer melted from Gavin's face.

"Don't ever touch me again!" she screamed as electricity arched from her fingertips and slammed into Gavin's face and chest, sending him back into the wall behind him. The surge made his grip on her wrist tighten until he couldn't let go, jolting and spasming and singeing him to the point where small tendrils of smoke drifted up from his face. She finally pushed him off of her and the arc stopped, electric blue sparks and trails still travelling from one finger to the next. She looked down at her hands, then at Nick.

She smiled.

"Bitch," Gavin coughed dryly, struggling to his feet. "The three of you. You're all fucking bitches."

"Don't do this," Abby whispered, trying to keep Quinn's gaze fixated on her. "Stop fighting it and you'll be fine."

Quinn smirked. "One more for the road."

She let out her breath, and didn't take another.

Her hand fell limply to her side, and the glow in her eyes finally faded until there was less there than a normal person's.

"What a pity," Gavin said, his voice like sandpaper. "One less little whore for me."

Abby glared up at him.

Her eyes were glowing bright orange.

He stopped in his tracks and tilted his head at her.

She tried to speak, her teeth appearing black against the bright orange fire emanating from inside her throat. The first word was muffled, but the second was quite clear: "... You."

Her head shot back and a wave of flame and heat erupting from her and spread out, so quick that it knocked Gavin back off his feet. The paint peeled and the boards blasted fire, sending smouldering flames up from the screws and the nails that held them together until everything was burning and melting and soot. Kelly and Nick blew back, Kelly slamming into the wall and Nick sliding along the floor and pushing up the flaming, smouldering carpet before he even had a chance to get up. The air around them was so dry that it sucked the air straight from their lungs. It felt like being inside a furnace, and for the briefest of moments everything was being pushed toward and away from Abby at the same time.

Abby fell forward onto the floor and gasped, getting a lungful of flame as she did. She pulled back from it.

Everything was on fire: the ceiling, the walls, and the floor. It was like a circle of flame that some biker would have to make his way through while jumping over ten jeeps and drinking a fifth of vodka standing of his head, and seemed just as impossible to navigate.

Nick rose to his feet slowly, still blue and the hair on the top of his head completely burned off. Kelly rose up as well, her body bisecting the flames around her. She screamed, beating them off and rolling out of their path.

"We've got to get out of here!" Abby yelled, barely able to be heard above the fire.

Nick nodded and helped Kelly to her feet. The three of them started back down the hall.

Abby paused and turned back the way they'd come. "Where the hell is Gavin?"

The other two turned. Quinn's body had been engulfed in flames, but there was no one there.

CHAPTER 47

New York City, Then

Jona crouched alongside his truck with his head pushed up against the grill, hacking as more bile and spit drained from him nose and mouth out into the gravel below. Stomach acid burned the lining of his throat and his nostrils and he cursed twice before sticking his finger down his throat again.

More vomit came up, including a dubious-looking red blob he could not identify.

He sniffed back hard, then laughed again. He threw his head up and looked at the stars, the harvest moon big and bright and taking up the whole night sky.

He bent over and shoved his finger down his throat one last time. This time the page came up, ripped and torn at the edges and covered in slime, but still perfectly intact.

He spread it out onto the hood of his car and stared at it, his eyes running over it and searching.

His blood still smeared the right margin of the page, but the words were gone.

The page was blank, as though it had never been used.

CHAPTER 48

Atlanta, Georgia

Fire spread along the ceiling of the first floor suddenly, arching out from all the cracks and gaps where the walls didn't quite meet them.

Judy and Dennis fell flat, Dennis slumping into Jaycee's arms like his prom date had after one too many tequila shooters. He let Dennis fall to the floor and stepped back a pace, his hands in the air.

They looked up as the fire spread, mesmerized at first before the danger set in.

"What in the world?" Chad asked, clicking his tongue against the roof of his mouth.

"Abby," Victor replied.

Chad turned to him, his eyes wide.

Above Victor, the beam dividing the hall and the living room came loose.

"Look out!" Chad screamed, diving forward. He knocked Victor out of the way just as the flaming beam came down, crashing into the alcohol-stained carpet and setting it ablaze as well.

"Lucky," Victor said, raising an eyebrow.

Chad grimaced, then got to his feet. The beam blocked them from the hall.

Jaycee stood on the other side, an anxious look coming over him.

"It's okay," Victor said, holding out his hand. "We'll use the window. We need to get out of here!"

"Couldn't agree more," Abby said, waddling down the stairs between Nick and Kelly. "Now even, would be great."

"Quinn?"

"Gone."

"Gavin?"

"Flew."

Another section of wall came down across the couch that Gavin had sat on giving his lectures.

"Can we do this another time?" Chad barked, heading toward the window.

"Yes."

All of them headed for the exit. Jaycee reached out to help Nick, then stopped cold and turned around. "Where's Kat?"

They all stopped and turned back toward the hallway. The fire had spread all throughout the walls, bubbling up black billowing smoke as it torched the paint.

Jaycee let go of Nick's arm and started toward the stairs, bounding up them three at a time.

Victor watched him go, and let out a curse under his breath.

Atlanta, Georgia

The loft was filled with smoke trying to escape from wherever it could, finding holes in the boards that even the light and the rain didn't know were there. It made the room black with soot and dust and tiny fluttering pieces of plastic that stank of oil and burnt hair.

Gavin rummaged around in it blindly; barely able to find the bed he'd laid on so many nights over the past few months. He tossed a small urn aside, spilling its charred contents out onto the floor. Doubted candles were scattered until there was nothing in front of him but the bare corner where the sloped wall met the tattered, mouldy floor.

"Where are you?" he demanded, running his palms along the boards as though expecting them to do something. He coughed as the plastic soot filled his throat. He coughed until he saw spots and he worried that maybe he wouldn't be able to take another real breath. He still searched, running his fingers along the corner and ignoring the way the rusty nails pulled and ripped at the grooves of his flesh.

"I'm right here," came a hard voice from behind him, so low that he didn't even recognize it as human at first. He spun around, unable to focus on anything in the darkness.

Kat shot him in the shoulder.

Blood erupted out his back and he slammed into the wall, knocking his head against the ceiling and then tumbling to the floor in a tattered heap. He winced and writhed, trying to move into a position that didn't scream out in pain at him and unable to do so.

Kat stepped forward until she could see him clearly, the smoke from her gun joining the smoke that billowed all around her. Her face was cold, her mouth a small thing in the centre of her face. She opened it to speak, then closed it again.

Jaycee came to the bottom of the stairs and saw the back of her platinum-blonde head sticking out amidst the swirling darkness. He bound up the stairs toward it.

Blood came in tiny spurts from the hole in Gavin's shoulder, each squirt making his face whiter and whiter until he looked like a ghost bleeding in the darkness. He coughed again, then screamed as the muscles in his arm pinched and spasmed along with it. When he was done he laughed a little, laying with his back against the wall and staring up at Kat. "Maybe it did work this time, Princess."

Kat raised the gun until the barrel was nothing but a hole in space to him and pulled back the hammer.

Jaycee stepped up behind her slowly. "You don't... have to do this."

Gavin smirked, ignoring Jaycee. "Aren't you going to tell me all about your friend? Miss What's-Her-Name? How you're doing this for her? Or for you? Or for all the people that came between then and now?"

"No," Kat said, and emptied the rest of the clip into Gavin's face.

Jaycee screamed, jumping back a pace.

Kat let the gun drop to the floor. It slammed flat on its side without bouncing at all. She turned and stared at

Jaycee, her eyes deep, sallow sockets inside her head.

Fire spread up through the stairs, bathing them both in light again until the soot and the fumes were almost non-existent. She looked warm in the glow of the fire, but nothing could bring light to those eyes, so dark that the pupils seemed like caves. They were welled with tears but she didn't cry, in fact seemed incapable of it.

He looked past her to Gavin, lying still on the floor with his mouth open and his face one bloody, gnarled scar of blood and raw skin, glimmering in the orange glow of the fire like some perverse opaque Jack-O-Lantern. His eyes, or what were left of them, were black and shadowed with blood and death and suffering.

The flames leapt up again. He grabbed Kat by the hand, and the both of them pushed through the window on the far side of the loft.

The fire followed them, searching for more air.

EPILOGUE

Atlanta, Georgia

"Ow," Victor frowned as Tash pressed the bandage smooth against his bare chest. She shot him an amused look, then rolled her eyes. "What was that for?"

"Ow, he says."

"It hurt."

Again, she gave him the look that told him she was holding back laughter. "The things I've seen you go through, and this is what you're complaining about?"

"It's different when the adrenaline gets pumping."

She nodded, then stood and slid his tea closer to him on the table. "Drink it. It's got herbs in it."

He nodded, slipping his finger into the tiny handle of the cup. It was almost like a ring, and he could feel the tip of his digit tingling as the blood to it slowed.

She walked over to the first aid kit on the counter and started to put her gauze away, rolling it over her finger.

He took a long sip, brushed the edge of his moustache, then laid it back down. "I'm sorry about Quinn."

She stopped and turned back to him. Her face was still

and warm. She looked drawn out, as though someone had attached hooks to either side of her chin and was slowly attaching weights to them. "So am I."

He nodded.

"I did this to stop burying people I knew."

"Wars have casualties."

"I'm not fighting a war, I'm teaching children."

He got up and stepped up behind her, looking down at the yard far below. After a moment of the two of them standing like boards, straight and parallel, he wrapped his massive arms around her and pulled her into a hug. She closed her eyes, and for the first time in days, smiled.

He kept his eyes trained on the yard below, watching as Nick, Kelly and Jaycee tossed a football back and forth. "If only the enemy cared about that distinction."

Nick lobbed the ball high and Jaycee jumped to catch it, hitting his shoulder to the ground with all his weight behind it and laughing.

Atlanta, Georgia

Abby sat at the edge of the table playing solitaire, her cards laid out in eight small piles in front of her. This was the one card game that stuck with her. She frowned, scanning the cards from one side to the other every time she flipped a new one off the top of the deck.

Jack of spades on seven of hearts.

Two of clubs on seven of clubs.

Six of hearts on queen of clubs.

Eight of spades on queen of diamonds.

The hearts weren't hearts though, they were tiny stylized apples. Victor had brought them back from a hotel and casino in Las Vegas. There was even a sticker on them certifying that they'd been used in a real game of poker on the strip, along with the signature of the dealer who'd used them.

Chad watched her from the side of the table, his hands clasped together in front of him. He wiped his mouth and then pulled out his cell phone, typed a text, and then waited for it to go through as the little animation of a mailbox on the screen spun about. When it was gone he put it away again.

Jack of apples on two of diamonds.

Nine of diamonds on two of spades.

Four of spades on two of clubs.

She pushed a stand of hair away from her face, forcing it to join the rest of her ponytail. There was still a glisten of sweat across her forehead from her morning jog.

Ace of diamonds on four of spades.

Four of apples on four of clubs.

Ace of spades on four of apples.

Chad reached into his pocket and pulled out a battered old pull-away ticket, announcing a top prize of five hundred dollars across its back in red numbers, with a yellow explosion behind it. He flicked it back and forth against the knuckles of the opposite hand over and over again, making the same wet smacking sound her cards made as the flipped them off the deck.

Flip.

Flip.

Flip.

He stopped, holding the ticket between the thumb

and forefinger of either hand. He took a deep breath, then ripped it down its centre.

She looked up at him but did not register what he was doing, instead just turning back to her game.

Eight of clubs on jack of spades.

He tossed the bisected ticket down on the chair between them and laced his fingers back together. He watched her for a long moment, that same strand of hair falling in front of her face only to be pushed back again.

"I'd like to take you to dinner tonight," he said.

She stopped herself from dealing the next card, turning her head up and meeting his gaze for the first time since they sat down.

Atlanta, Georgia

Victor sat at his desk, scribbling into a small notebook. It was leather, and looked as though it could have fit into his breast pocket if he'd wanted it to. The ink bled onto the page and made the letters blur together until it seemed as though they were just a series of scrawls and loops along each line. He paused and looked them over every few sentences, nodding each time as though satisfied with the way it had turned out.

Kat watched him from the door, leaning against its archway. She'd been standing there for six full minutes, watching him write and waiting for him to notice or show interest in her presence. Finally she raised her torn knuckles and rapped three times on the doorframe. "Knock knock."

His face did not change. He set his bookmark and

closed the book, sliding it to one side away from her. He leaned back on his chair and folded his fingers together at his lap.

She waited for him to say something. He did not.

"I was impressed with you," she said finally, turning to make sure that nobody was outside the hall to hear her say it. "With the crew you've put together out here. They're green, and they're lucky... but they're good."

"Thank you."

She nodded, coming into the room fully. "They work well together. They work off each other well. That's a rare thing."

He stared at her, but didn't say anything.

"I think if you'd had a team like this in operation ten years ago... well, maybe I wouldn't be who I am today. Maybe Ashby wouldn't be dead. Maybe Gavin wouldn't have gotten in ten years of practice before someone finally put a stop to him."

He tilted his head, then nodded.

"But you took too long to act. If you'd done something when this all started, you'd have had a lot less blood on your hands."

"I disagree. I think if I'd done something at the beginning there would have been more blood. And over a longer time."

"You wouldn't have lost one of your own."

"Do you always gauge casualties based on their proximity to you?"

"You don't?"

There was a long silence between them, in which the air was thick and hot. Their stares never left one another.

"I think I should be on your team," she said finally, standing a little straighter. "I think I can do some good."

He watched her again, without moving or changing his expression. "'The lines between us and who we fight are important, but they are not straight. They ebb and flow, and we can never focus on them... but we should never forget they're there.'"

She smirked. "A quote?"

"Yes."

"From whom?"

He glared at her.

"I think you need someone who objects to you. Someone who will stand up and tell you you're wrong when you're wrong, because you will be wrong sometimes. *Everyone* is wrong sometimes, and when that happens with things as delicate as they are... you won't just lose one of the balls you're juggling, you'll lose them all."

He stared at her for another moment, then pulled himself back toward his desk and picked up his notebook again. "No."

"No?"

"No. You think you know better, but you can't see into the future. You can't know what might have happened, how things might have turned out if you'd dealt with Gavin a different way. You killed a man content to burn to death in his own house, not because he would have posed a continued threat or to save another human life; you did it because you wanted to."

She stiffened. "Yes."

He locked eyes with her. "I will not tolerate murderers on my team or in my presence."

She opened her mouth and then shut it again. She nodded, licking her teeth. "Does that policy go both ways?"

"Get out," he said without even looking at her, scribbling something down in his notebook.

She nodded, then turned and left.

New York City, Then

Victor opened his eyes.

There was a steady beep somewhere to his left that he recognized as the rhythm of a heart monitor. There was a tube behind each of his ears that met in front of his nose and pumped oxygen into each nostril, and his head felt like it was floating somewhere above the third cloud to the right.

Tash was sitting on the chair next to him, her legs crossed at the calf. She was reading from a large hardcover edition of Imajica.

"How is that?" he said, moving up into a sitting position. "I've been meaning to read it."

She dropped the book and wrapped her arms around him, burying the back of her head into the crook of his neck. She held him so tight that he thought it would have hurt, but it didn't.

He frowned. "Morphine?"

She nodded, letting him go and sitting on the edge of the bed. "Yes. Quite a bit of it."

"Morphine means it was bad," he reasoned, squinting as though it were hard to follow even the most rudimentary train of thought. He turned to her and met her watery gaze. "Was it bad?"

She nodded. "You had a concussion and brain swelling. Your ribs were pretty broken up and they think you're going to have some slipped disk problems, once you can get up and around."

He sighed, then nodded. "Any major organs?"

She shook her head.

"How long was I out?"

"Four days. The swelling has gone down but it's not gone... they were thinking they'd have to drill."

He shot her a look. "You wouldn't have let them."

"I'm not next of kin."

A tired look came over him then, and he held out his arms for another hug. She embraced him fully, squeezing him until he felt it even through the drugs.

"I'm sorry," she said.

"I don't think I've ever seen you cry before."

She pulled back and tilted her head ruefully. "I'm not cry-ing."

"I know. Makes me wish I'd stayed out a few more days."

She laughed, and then there was quiet between them for sev-eral long minutes.

"He got the page then?" he said finally, staring at a dark spot in his sheets.

She nodded.

He frowned, then let out a long sigh.

"I'm sorry."

"It wasn't your fault."

"There was nothing you could have done."

"It wasn't my fault, either."

She squinted at him.

He stayed there, staring at the spot in the sheets for a long time. "What would have happened if I'd died that night?"

She wet her lips. "You didn't."

"But if I had... you would have carried on? Kept up the mission?"

She nodded.

"And if something had happened to you, heaven forbid, I would have kept going. It wouldn't have been easy, but I would have kept going."

"I know you would have --"

He held up a hand to stop her, then turned and met her gaze. "But Tasha... what if we'd both died?"

She opened her mouth to respond, then closed it again.

He stared at the sheet again, squinting his eyes. His pupils moved back and forth, as though he were reading something that only he could see. "I don't think we can do this alone anymore," he whispered, defeated, laying back on the bed.

She nodded.

He met her eyes. "And I don't think we can do it together anymore."

She paused and swallowed hard. "I'm sorry?"

"Everything we know, everything he taught us... it's too much to lose. If we're together and another day like today happens, then that's it. It's all over. We're done. And I don't think we'll ever get this lucky again."

Tash gritted her teeth together, then nodded once. "You should get some sleep," she said, sitting back down without looking at him. "I'd like to try and finish my book."

He watched her for a moment, then turned back onto his side and shut his eyes. He did not sleep, and several minutes later he thought he heard the slow sound of Tasha crying.

But he knew, deep down, that that was impossible.

Albuquerque, New Mexico

Gavin knelt on the floor in the dark room. There were candles all around him, but none of them were lit.

He was sobbing steadily, the tears staining his still-open wounds.

His shirt was still marked with blood and stank of rot, decay, and smoke. It wafted off him in waves, filling the room the second he had stepped into it.

"I'm sorry..." he said, cupping his hands and then pressing them onto the floor. "I tried, I swear I did. I tried my best."

There was no answer from the darkness.

Shivering, he lit one of the candles. There was a cloth hanging in front of him with runes printed all the way down it, some disappearing off the edge of the fabric.

"Please, let me know what I may do, in penance."

The shrine moved and turned, the light finally bathing Jona's face in its ethereal glow.

He held out a revolver.

"Shoot yourself."

ENGEN TIMELINE

With over twenty novels spread over three different series by many different authors, the Engen Universe of titles is growing every day and into genres we couldn't have imagined! From the original ten book *Black Womb* thriller series, its crime novel sequel series *Xander Drew*, our flagship adventure title *Infinity*, or single-novels like *Jacobi Street* or *light|dark*, there's something in the Engen Universe for everyone with more books by more authors on the way soon!

...But how do the events relate to one another, chronologically? While some astute readers have guessed at the potential timeline (some accurately, some not), we're going to finally set the question of the Engen Timeline to rest.

Turn the page for an up-to-date guide of the ever-widening world of Engen, featuring the works of Ellen Curtis, Andrea Hackett, Ali House, Sarah Thompson, Jay Paulin, and Matthew LeDrew!

In the 10 Years Prior Black September

"Reptilia" by Matthew LeDrew
published in *light | dark*.
Danger descends on a small secluded town in the
form of a deadly virus with fantastic and terrible
side-effects. Can a small group of doctors escape
alive?

Compendium by Ellen Curtis
Three short stories forming the basis for the
Engen Universe's ties to suspense, genetic
engeneering, and the supernatural. Features the
stories "The Tourniquet Revival," "Falling into
Fire" and "At Midnight, the Dawn."

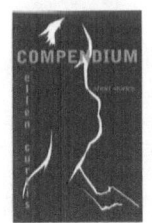

"The Theogony" by Matthew LeDrew
published in *light | dark*.
A tale of young Theo Flaherty of the *Infinity* series
and his time admitted against his will to the Black
Springs hospital, where he learns to paint, and
seeks out his father.

Black September

"Revving Engen" by Matthew LeDrew
published in *light | dark*.
A direct lead-in to both *Infinity* and *Black Womb*,
Tasha travels to Coral Beach, Maine on a hot tip
about a recently discovered young man with
incredible abilities.

Infinity by Ellen Curtis & Matthew LeDrew
Faced with a destiny he's uncertain of, the
enigmatic Victor must bring together four unique
people with very special abilities... or face the
tasks ahead alone. Guaranteed to excite!

Black Womb by Matthew LeDrew
Fifteen years ago, something happened in Coral Beach, Maine that resulted in the present death of a seventeen-year-old boy. Now four high-school students must try to solve the mystery... before the killer picks them off.

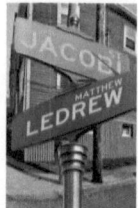

Jacobi Street by Matthew LeDrew
When a mysterious painting shows up at an art gallery he works at, Bob must work with Eddie and Sloan to track down its sinister origins and convince the people living on Jacobi Street of them, before its too late!

Transformations in Pain by Matthew LeDrew
When two girls are assaulted and one is hospitalized, the residents of Coral Beach must put their shared tragedies behind them and stop the man responsible, as well as unlock the secrets behind the true nature of the Womb...

Year One: October

Smoke and Mirrors by Matthew LeDrew
The approaching trial of Genblade brings closure to the people of Coral Beach, until people start showing up dead in the same manner they did when he was at large.

"Scarlett" by Andrea Hackett
published in *light|dark*.
Introducing Scarlett, the slightly damaged hunter on a mission to save others from the monsters from her past.

"The Inevitable" by Ali House
published in *The Lightbulb Forest*
A young woman must contend with the
emergence of a frightening new power alongside
the emotional high of a first date.

The Tourniquet Reprisal by Curtis & LeDrew
A man lives in Atlanta, Georgia that people
don't talk about, but everyone knows he's there.
He arrived a year ago and turned a gaggle
of uneducated youth into something new,
something to fear.

Roulette by Matthew LeDrew
As the teen suicide rate in Coral Beach starts to
climb astronomically fast, Xander travels to Los
Angeles to fight his most terrifying adversary
yet... and learns that the only thing worse than
looking for release... is finding it.

Year One: November

Exodus of Angels by Curtis & LeDrew
Victor's enigmatic past is illuminated when
Jaycee accompanies him to visit a new friend
in the paliative care ward of the Black Springs
hospital, where Theo also happens to be
searching for a cure for Leigh.

Ghosts of the Past by Matthew LeDrew
Coral Beach faces its most awesome threat when
one of Engen's past mistakes is unleashed upon
the unsuspecting populous. Friends and enemies
unite to fight a common enemy... but will even
that be enough?

Touch Your Nose by Matthew LeDrew
Simon Monk must infiltrate the San Fransico branch of Shane Industries, a massive company with deep ties to the Engen Universe. Where do his true loyalties lie? And can he get out without causing harm?

Ignorance is Bliss by Matthew LeDrew
After being set through the ringer one too many times, Xander decides that his life with Julie needs a little more attention… which is bad news because a new villain has come to town with his sights set on Adam Genblade.

"Gristle While You Work" by Jay Paulin published in *light | dark*.
A short story centering around the rise of a new, and possibly cannibalistic, serial killer in the Engen Universe.

Becoming by Matthew LeDrew
For months Xander Drew has been doing his level best to keep the streets of Coral Beach clean, which means it's time for the forces of darkness to strike back… all at once.

Inner Child by Matthew LeDrew
Julie is hospitalized with life-threatening wounds to both body and soul. But the real threat comes from the hospital walls themselves, as a demonic presence makes itself known to Xander and his friends.

End of Year One

Gang War by Matthew LeDrew
The Tees, a homicidal gang of evil men, has finally been taken down by Xander Drew. But his victory is short lived, as retired Tees are mysteriously killed. With a town of suspects, anyone can be the culprit... including one of their own.

Chains by Matthew LeDrew
Sociopath Derek Smith has been freed from prison and is praying on the weak; and none are weaker than August Styles: a pregnant girl with Down Syndrome who has run away from home.

"Omega" by Ellen Curtis
published in *light|dark*.
A sinister division of Engen begins a series of experiments on pregnant women in a fashion eerily similar to those that created the original Black Womb project.

The Long Road by Matthew LeDrew
Xander meets the American people — and realizes that the world is harsh and wicked, but can also be soft and gentle, even loving. Xander Drew comes of age on the road, and sets his new direction.

Year Two

Cinders by Matthew LeDrew
Detective Horton enters a violent and dangerous world he didn't know existed beneath the veneer of order and structure that he has based his entire deductive method around.

Sinister Intent by Matthew LeDrew
One of the killers Detective Horton could not catch has resurfaced: a serial killer who flaunts his sinister intent in front of the Los Angeles Police Department, making it so that no one is safe.

Faith by Matthew LeDrew
Xander's mysterious and troublesome past returns to haunt him on the streets of Los Angeles; a place where even more people can get caught in the crossfire of the games of death and deceit that makes up his life.

Flickers in the Night by Matthew LeDrew
Lisa Rowdan is hunted by her haunting -- and powerful -- ex-boyfriend Ryan through a lonely city street. Can she escape him?
One of over twenty great sprine-tingling short stories!

Family Values by Matthew LeDrew
Xander and his new friends Crowley, Lisa, and Tim investigate a series of kidnappings and murders that stretch back decades, all of which have the same similar twist: victims being found after years of being missing.

The Future

Fate's Shadow by Matthew LeDrew
When one of Xander's old cases comes up for trial, Megan Greene returns with it. The former friends are led into conflict regarding her client's innocence. However, they put their difference aside when they both become targets of the vigilante known as Shiro Gilbert.

The Future

"Remers" by Sarah Thompson published in *light | dark*.
In the not-too-distant future of the Engen Universe, young athletes are the targets of a scouting program to create the next stage of super soldier with cybernetic enhancements.

THE XANDER DREW SERIES

Prologue: The Long Road (May 2014)

COMING SOON FROM ENGEN BOOKS:

FIRST AID

When Xander takes his feud with mob boss Stephen Fields to the streets, his attracts the attention of the *Infinity* team of Tash, Nick, Kelly, and Iseult. Before the arrive, he'll have pushed the mob boss into an all out gang war, the likes of which the city will never recover from.

The early years of **Xander Drew** as he struggles with the evils of his small rural hometown of Coral Beach, Maine. Cursed with the heart of the Womb and the gift of seeing the world around him for what it really is, Xander must learn the hard lessons about the nature of humanity to traverse the minefield of criminals, gangs, and abusers that stand between him and ultimate happiness -- but most of all that **sometimes it takes a monster, to catch a monster.**

"THE WRITING OF ITS GENERATION- - VISUAL, TO-THE-POINT AND IN-THE-MOMENT."

- The Northeast Avalon Times

The Coral Beach Casefiles series by Matthew LeDrew:

For more information, please visit

www.engenbooks.com

about the authors

Ellen Curtis is a writer and web tv personality born and raised in St. Johns, Newfoundland; whose aptitude for the written word began at a young age, when she began writing short stories, poetry, lyrics and novellas.

She was 'discovered' at a Sci-Fi on the Rock writing panel in 2008, and her first collection of stories, *Compendium*, was published just over a year later in October 2009.

Since then she has risen to become one of Engen's lead authors, working on high-profile projects such as the *Infinity* series of adventure novels, as well as continuing her own endeavours.

In her spare time she enjoys reading, art, music and spending time near the ocean.

Matthew LeDrew studied Journalism at College of the North Atlantic in Stephenville, Newfoundland and has worked with Transcontinental Publishing, as well as the student-youth magazine *The Troubador*.

He has written over fifteen other novels for Engen Books: the ten book *Coral Beach Casefiles* series, *Infinity*, *Exodus of Angels*, *Jacobi Street*, *Touch Your Nose*, and *The Long Road*.

He lives in St. Johns, Newfoundland.